WHERE THE AIR IS CLEAR

TRANSLATED BY SAM HILEMAN

WHERE THE AIR IS CLEAR

A NOVEL BY **CARLOS FUENTES**

FARRAR, STRAUS AND GIROUX · NEW YORK

PART ONE

My name is Ixca Cienfuegos. I was born and I live in Mexico City. Which is not so grave: in Mexico City there is never tragedy but only outrage. Outraged, the blood that stings through me like maguey thorns. Outraged, the unchecked paralysis that stains and clots every dawn. Also outraged, my eternal mortal leap toward tomorrow. The game, action, faith, day after day and not just those days of triumph or defeat; and looking down, I see hidden pores and know that they have held me against the valley's deepest floor. Spirit of Anáhuac, who does not crush grapes but hearts; who drinks no earthly balm . . . your wine is the jelly of your own courage; who does not trap for the flayed pelt of happiness . . . you stalk only yourself, through wet black depths where stone warps and there are jade eyes. Kneeling, crowned with a wreath of cactus, flagellated by your own—by our—hand, your dance adangle from a feather plume and a busfender. Dead in flowery war, a bar scrap, at the hour of truth, the only timely hour. Poet without compassion, artist of agony, courteous bum who shoots craps with my inarticulate prayer and loses it: condemn me, me always more than others, of my outrage, my downfall never to be known to anyone else, who topples me before unpitying gods and exhorts me on to meetings between my selves only; O face of my destruction, countenance of dry earth and gold blood, tough face of bragging music and mud brown! war in void, yellow guts of bullies! . . . But my head sobs and cannot stop its search for comfort, for a homeland, a clitoris, the sweetness of another skeleton, a soothing canticle that sings mockery of all caged beasts. Life among turned backs, from fear to turn its back. Broken body of hungering stumps blind to the attackers, vocation to a freedom which escapes in the net of crossroads: and with the remnant wetting our little brushes, we sit beside the road and play with paints. . . . Dead at birth, you burned your ships that other men could use your decay to build an age; living in death, you disinterred the word which would have tied our tongues in brotherhood. You bided in the last sun. Then the final conquest steeped through your sponge body, now merely physical, titled, bemedaled. Over the racket of nickelodeons and motorcars, from the sludge where gaudy reptiles crawled, I hear your drumroll. Snakes, those historic creatures, drowse in your urns. In your eyes shine the dog-pack suns of the high tropics and in your body, a halo of feathers. Don't break, my brother. Don't yield. Sharpen your knives, deny everything, feeling no pity, without parleying, without even looking. Let go your migrant nostalgia and all your loose ends and every day begin again from birth. And at last recover the flame again in the guitar-strumming moment of basketed and invisible illusion when it will seem that all your memories are clear and you are ablaze. Recover it alone, for none of your heroes will return to help you. You have come to spread with me, though you don't know me, our tableland of jeweled death. Here we live, you and I. In these streets our smells pass and mingle, sweat and chili, new brick and underground gas, our taut vagabond bodies, but never our eyes. Never have we knelt side by side, you and I, to take of the same Host. Joined in licentiousness, created together, we die each for himself, isolated. Here we fall, and what are we going to do about it? But cling to me, brother. If only to see if someday our fingers touch. Fall with me on our moon-scar city, city scratched by sewers, crystal city of vapor and alkali frost, city witness to all we forget, city of carnivorous walls, city of motionless pain, city of immense brevities, city of fixed sun, ashing city of slow fire, city to its neck in water, city of merry lethargy, city of twisted stinks, city rigid between air and worms, city ancient in light, old city cradled among birds of omen, city new upon sculptured dust, city in the true image of gigantic

4

heaven, city of dark varnish and cut stone, city beneath glistening mud, city of entrails and tendons, city of the violated outrage, city of resigned market plazas, city of anxious failures, city tempested by domes, city woven by amnesias, bitch city, hungry city, sumptuous villa, leper city. Incandescent prickly pear. Eagle without wings. Here we bide. And what are we going to do about it? Where the air is clear.

GLADYS GARCIA

"Morning!"

The floor-sweeper goosed her and Gladys breathed cold morning. She glanced a last time into the gray cabaret mirror: glasses soggy with butts, Chupamirto yawning over the bongo drum. Yellow light inside translucent palms went out, resorting bark opacity. A cat ran street puddles; its eyes, last night's brooches. Gladys took her shoes off, rested, puckered her little mouth, gold-sashed teeth, lit her last, new-every-fifteen-minutes cigarette. Guerrero Street was not flooded now, she could put her shoes back on. Bikes were beginning to hiss without shadows along Bucareli; already a few streetcars. The avenue was a cornucopia of refuse: wadded derelict dailies, garbage from Chinese cafés, dead dogs, an old crone poking a boot with a stick, sleeping street children stirring in their nests of magazines and newspapers. Dawn had the palest funeral glow. From the statue of the Little Horse to Colonia los Doctores, the street, was one long dragged asphalt coffin, and only a resurrection could give it life and feeling. Would it live, under the light of the sun? From the watching place of Charles IV and his court of insane neons

LOTUSLIKE　　WE MIX FOUR-FIFTHS OF YOUR
HIGHBALL　　　GOODRICH
OF YOUR HIGHBALL　　　FOUR-FIFTHS

And Gladys could talk about only one-fifth of the city cocktail, most of day was unknown to her: the afternoon rain-hour paper hats of vendors, their stipendiary bellies, the powdery aged air that roils munching convolutions through the modern ruins of

5

an enormous village. She walked on, alone, small dumpling body wrapped in violet velvet shine, strung on two toothpicks stuck into platform shoes; yawning, scraping her gold teeth, face bovine, eyes cheerless. What a bore to be walking down Bucareli all by herself at six-fifteen in the morning! She dah-dah-dah-ed the litany taught night after night by the Bali-Hai's fat pianist.

Woman, woman divine, that was what Beto sang to me, he sure hooked me quick with that line about being a hack and we'd go for a vacation in his cab: what a line, what a man! Hop in the cab, old girl, girl I'm going to pump, he said: "You alone, pug-nose?"

"I'm with you. May I sit down?"

Chupamirto knew him and dedicated mambos to him over the mike. I'm the cabby, why sure, why not, the hack.

"Sort of juicy, aren't you, pug-nose," noooose, as his hand made her cream flow.

"Take it easy, iceman. Don't get too hot."

"And whose fault is it if . . ."

"Ai, I'm so sorry."

Why sure, why not, the hack and a sweet-talking line like nobody else, joking the way I like, with his thick canary-yellow sweater.

"So some little grade-school pimp got you started, pug-nose?"

"Grade school? You're kidding!"

"We all get started. Including myself. A goon they called the Indian got me into plenty of trouble. I was soft in those days. I hadn't wised up, and he twisted my ear until he talked me into knocking off a *cuate*, a twin, a buddy. They sent me up for two years, pug-nose. But you ought to see the Indian now. I looked him up and what I did to him was no joke. Well, now I stay loose. You got to, hacking. They try to beat you down, they tell you go screw your mother, me they tell to go screw my mother. You can't win."

And now that he was telling her, he had stopped joking.

"If it wasn't for broads and dancing, kid, I'd be a rich man by now. But I just got to dance. Every day I got to, it's a vice,

6

it's a monkey, smooth, tah-tah-tatta-taaah, any step you want. That's how I am, pug-nose."

That's how we all are. But she never sat with him again. Dark men like blondes, a blonde snapped him away, Beto. And now a bony old runt with bad breath sought her out, every Friday night, pretending to be a big wheel in government. No one else was giving her money. He drank like a whale and would tighten his belt and yell: Race of Indians! whore race of Indians! And afterward the big lie that he came Fridays because his wife believed he had to work late, balancing the books for the week.

"Do you like the Bali-Hai's show?"

"Love it, my dear, and you too. . . ."

"Then why don't you come more often? Why just Fridays? Of course, if you have something else to do . . . ."

"Haven't I told you I have the old woman fooled about Fridays? Look, someday, my dear. . . ."

Here Gladys had come to birth, in the empty palaces of the tableland, the great flat-snouted and suffocating city, the city forever spreading like a creeping blot. Once some grocerymen with a car wanted to take her to Cuernavaca, but the car broke down on Tlápan. She knew neither sea nor mountains, mustard bloom, the meeting of sun and horizon, ripeness of medlar trees, nor any simple loveliness. What a pretty lake the sea must be. She was moored to smoke and concrete, to the gathering up of garbage lost diamonds. Eyes shut, always shut. Subdued, at last, she reached Doctores. She lit the pious candle: You are rich and we are poor. You have everything and we have nothing. So maybe you are not after all the Mother of Sorrows? the turtle has no waist . . . and went to bed. What did she have to show for it? Drink counters, chips, fallen on the table without echo. Ten pesos. She was not making much these days, customers were tighter. How old? I'm thirty. And screwed out? Ask Beto. For the first time it occurred to her to wonder what she would do when she could no longer make her living at the Bali-Hai. How would she get along? Tomorrow I'm going to a store and see what they pay salesclerks. She would have to make a good impression: LiLiana's fox. If not, then she would use her own rabbit. What'd I do with that perfume they gave me in front of the movie? Mascara until it dripped. Nothing's worse than a gringa, pale as flour. . . . Counters, chips *la cucha racha no pué caminá*, huddled against the cold wall in candlelight, feeling that her legs were going and her belly swelling, swelling huge . . . may your virginal cloak always cover our children, protect them, hold them yours forever, O heavenly Treasury of the Sacred Heart of Jesus, our children. . . .

Out of the women's clothing store, onto the avenue. Rain swirled at her, jumbled by gray walls. City rain, contaminated with stenches, that never reaches soil. Mineral rain springing at heads submissively bent beneath the livid drum-head sky, bowed heads wet with rain and oil, lackeys to Mexican heaven waiting in hopeless silence against walls, like condemned prisoners, for the fusilade which still does not come, bone and grease bodies compacted before the rain and dissolving in vapors of asphalt and gasoline, mummies for one minute, together, together beneath the rain. Flaking signs, yawn of cobblestones, city like a crippled cloud, timeless stinks of armpits and crotches, oil-sizzled tortillas and green fruit, the softest murmur of wheels, dripping music. Without agreeing to, the sky opened, which neither walls nor Mexicans asked it to. Rain fought dust, wind and faces struggled, pasted against the soggy walls, draggling mustaches, glazed eyes, sloshing feet, slovenly, unhealthy flesh plagued by boils and cataracts, sleeping flesh-niches and eternal idols, on their knees against walls, sieved by loneliness, and scratching at what gnaws inside the refuse heaps. So they wait. So you wait: there, near the damp beginning; rain falls on your lurking, there are coughs and little phlegms; and will you embrace, alone, together, together under the rain, one great embrace when the black firmament commands? She wiped a drip off her nose. Her mascara was running like ink. Her rabbit smelled. She waited, clasping her hands.

So I'm crazy, eh? Just you watch. That's what you get for fooling with big shots. Well, fuck them! What time? Six. It opens at nine. And raining buckets.

"Now you'll be scrubbed, little sugar doll . . ." from a passing, braking bike. Night was opening, her night, night reserved for her by angels and emptiness. She walked along Juárez and the city smelled of cooking gas. Where were the other kind, her kind, the kind she liked? Wasn't there anywhere a door to a warm room where she could find them, her people? . . .

My father trapped birds. He would leave the house early in the morning to set his traps while mother sat with spiked coffee and we got the cages ready. Beside the Nonoalco bridge. They named me Gaudencia and Guadencia, I was born one twenty-second of January. The tin walls and the tin roof were hot in summer, our blood steamed. In one cot, father and mother and the baby, and we, I and my brothers, in the other. I didn't notice, I never knew who it was. But the tin was hot and we were hot, we were just kids, I was thirteen. That's how you start. To this day I've never gone back to see them.

In front of the Hotel del Prado she stumbled into a cluster of tall men and bejeweled blonde women who were smoking with holders. Even if they looked like gringos, they were speaking Spanish. . . .

"Hurry up, Pichi, we're taking a cab."

"Coming, *chéri*. Just let me fix my veil."

"We'll see you at Bobó's, Norma. Don't be late. For orgies, British punctuality."

"Aside from the fact that when the good-byes start, Bobó's fountain changes from champagne to rum."

"*Ciao*, sweet."

"Too-toot."

They looked like gods who had risen like statues, there on the sidewalk amid the wrinkles and troubles of lesser beings: And what beings! she herself, low as the lowest, sister to peddlers of cheap tourist junk, vendors of lottery tickets, newspaper boys, beggars and hacks, river of oil-stained undershirts, shawls, corduroy pants, broken sandals plodding the great street, wearing tracks in it. But at the second trinket stall, between one filled with fake alligator handbags and another where sugared peanuts were sold, she invested two pesos in an aluminum cigarette holder.

9

While his hand dutifully continued its attention to Pichi's right breast, Junior prattled like a tourist guide. "You'll see what terrific parties Bobó gives! The poet Manuel Zamacona will be there . . ." Each jolt pushed him harder against her, and in the rainy darkness, the cab missed few holes. Pichi turned her head to the left to see her watch. ". . . the existentialist philosopher Estévez. Prince Vampa, Bobó's volunteer uncle. That international society broad, Charlotte García. Hundreds of aristocrats, painters, queers. All of Mexico City. Bobó has trick lights, he changes the color to suit the decorum, and he isn't scandalized if a couple lock themselves in his bedroom for half an hour. Oh, they know how to live it up! My papá's fantastic: Every time I come home from Bobó's, he makes a long face, like this, and begins to roar through his cornflakes, 'degenerates, dipsomaniacs, fairies!' Poor Papá. The weakness of the self-made man, eh? Meanwhile, of course, he goes on giving me my allowance."

Pichi nuzzled her little poodle-cut under Junior's chin.

"But it's so fabulous, Junior, to meet such enormous intellectuals! The cream of the cream, as they say. . . . You know, you aren't the only one who had a hard time getting to be independent. You wouldn't believe what a struggle it was for me, and if I hadn't taken that psychology course, God only knows what complexes I'd . . . Mmmmmm! Such sweet lotion you use. . . ."

The taxi stopped in front of an apartment building. Mosaic balconies, huge glass torso. From open penthouse windows floated ice chimes.

"Look now," Junior said to the driver. "Go to Monte Arrat, three thousand ninety-four, and pick a lady up. She'll be waiting."

"Sorry, Mac," said the driver affectedly, mincingly. He rubbed the red scar on his forehead. "Not today. If I could, I'd be glad to."

"What do you mean, not today? Since when, not today?" Already preparing himself for his entrance into Bobó's drawing room, Junior was tugging his sleeves down to show his silk cuffs.

10

"Nope, really, any day but today. Barrilaco is too far."

Junior thumbed his lighter, held it near the driver's placard. "The honorable Don Juan Morales? Plates Thirty-seven thousand two hundred forty-two. I'll be talking with the owner of your fleet."

Juan Morales smiled.

"Good luck . . ."

And he pulled away, holding back sneering with the horn. He rubbed his scar and began to whistle.

"Snotty," grumbled Junior as they moved to the elevator. "Every day snottier. Well. . . . And now, a little kiss, eh, like this. . . . Hey! don't tell me you don't . . ."

"Later, Junior, you'll muss my veil. Go on, tell me, who else?"

"Well, of the aging set, Pimpinela and the Golden Girl. Pierrot's the most, you know . . . he says that she's the Terrible Girl of Excellent Family. Then . . . let's see, Cienfuegos, and be careful there. I'll keep him away from you."

A lacquered door opened on air heavy with tobacco: conquering fume, layer of coquettish scents, ear-lobe fragrances. Into it Pichi and Junior ran, crying, "Bobó! Bobó!"

He danced toward them. "Darlings! Enter and apprehend Eternal Verity! Yonder strolls a beggar with tray and victuals! *Voici*, O Rimbaud! *le temps des assassins*," and hopped away, waistcoat a florid proclamation of bonhommie, shushing his guests. For the entertainer, a declaimer of verse (from the Caribbean circuit, naturally), had taken her place on a low platform near the stairs, and there was observing the floor very hard and suspiciously. At length, silence. With great stretching fingers and a dramatic jerk of her shoulders she closed the bodice of her neo-Hellenic gown, turned her eyes to the clear sky:

"Oh, soul-spheres over my homeland,
Dove stars cricket-breasted
Those whom night has wrested
From Rubén Darío's moan-land . . ."

Bobó's guests took her as bass chord and went on making their own melodies. Youths and old women formed court around

11

Manuel Zamacona. Two girls wearing glasses were in a corner, being lectured by Estévez. Delicate, discreet, balancing a huge snifter of lovely cognac, Pierrot Caseaux spoke softly. In the circle around Prince Vampa, Charlotte García brandished her pince-nez over the heads of the masses and Gus's head, too, and bitched about the absence of photographers. Silvia and Roberto Régules, having put on their favorite fixed smiles, sat coldly on the sofa, waiting for a slow train which anyhow they preferred not to catch. The Argentine humanist Dardo Moratto was at the bookcase, sniffing its few volumes. From far away spheres the declaiming voice accompanied them, from precisely the distance which a good bar pianist keeps below the murmur of his clientele. Pichi and Junior, first sniffing and saying *hmmmm,* moved to get drinks. Bobó rushed up to them again. "The best is still to come! Wait until Lally and the bongo drummers get here!"

Ixca Cienfuegos came through the door and waited, lighting a cigarette, twisting his face first and last keep loose and let it carry you, don't ask questions, don't see faces, float on noise and shadow, on blur. Now he changes the lights: yellow, a happy change. Bobó ought to put in an X-ray. What's missing? Mirrors, to repeat the blurs to infinity. Glitter and shoulders and backs, so many armpits so many times shaved, conscience in their breasts, the reflex wisdom of how to inhale smoke. Just float, on flesh and scent, stink that can't be escaped but yes, can be made elegant. Faces: but later. For now, just be carried, forgetting yourself, the secret of contentment. But that's to forget them. too. Don't let them get away so lightly . . . squash them . . .

Scarlet, brown, cobalt-blue walls lost behind photo reproductions: Chagall, Boccioni, Miró, and one original, blue buffaloes on a liver-stained field, by Juan Soriano. Along the floor, at the droop of the loop in their cyclical process of coming to be, were ranged idols . . . a dwarf Coatlicue's open wound. Cane and vine spouted against the enormous window. Pale-blue provincial tiles decorated the wall behind the bar, and among them was an *Esquire* cutout of a gringa, naked in her nylon and telephoning with the rapturous look of a girl being sweetly and expertly pawed.

Manuel Zamacona, lying back on a sofa, ran his fingers

12

through his shock of hair. His profile was Greek plus two large puffy cheeks; a plume of smoke issued from his lips, spiraling upward with an altar slowness. Youthful scribblers invited to make Bobó's crazy potpourri crazier, painted old culture vamps who had once let themselves be led astray by Ezra Pound held his acolytes' eyes fixed precisely on the silhouette of his angles which Zamacona considered most becoming.

"Now, exactly what the poet cannot escape today is the duty to call bread and wine something else. This obviously presupposes a clear understanding of what bread and wine are. Then the poet may take off, fly to the center of things, dominate them, end his slavery to them . . ."

"But above all, the poet," said an astigmatic youth, "is he who names things."

"Yes. But he doesn't precede his christenings with the UP or AP symbols. Or, granting that the level of understanding on which poetry has existed historically is a little lofty, simply because of this poetry today must root into the living epoch: is that what you believe? Be capped with 'intelligibility,' and with the passing of the epoch, pass too?"

"Ah! That's sensitive!"

"Survive, I say, Señor Zamacona, endure . . . ."

"Yes, whichever is more convenient. All of you talk about Yankee imperialism. I ask whether by cheapening our words, which is to say, our imagination, we don't aid it. And whether on the other hand when we try to raise our words and imagination to the highest expressiveness—surviving, enduring, if you care—whether we don't become now and again, not only better men, but better Mexicans. . . ."

"The struggle against imperialism has to be direct, it has to reach the people. . . ."

"Yes. I don't at all depreciate our poor people, you know. But, in honesty, which of these lines do you think reaches our people more clearly. . . . 'I come back to you, solitude, empty water, water of my too-dead dreams,' or, 'Mighty Father Stalin, workers' bulwark'? Moreover, keep things straight. Anti-imperialism be welcomed, my friend, but let the battle be fought on the battleground, not by scribbling socialistic couplets. What are you really after? The downfall of imperialism? Or only the feeling that you're an honorable young chap allied with the virtuous?"

The astigmatic youth leaped up, swirling ashes on the painted faces of the aging muses.

"Decadent, sold-out artists! How much does Washington pay you?"

Serenely Manuel Zamacona exhaled smoke. "It seems even to be a comedian requires a certain honesty and imagination," he observed.

Federico Robles touched a button and the electric voice of his secretary replied, "Yes, *Señor?*" He bent his head and put his mouth near the microphone. His thumb stroked his silk tie.

"Call the Limited together for ten Saturday morning, and be on time. Business: transfer of Librado Ibarra's interest. If Ibarra calls again, put him on. That's all."

"Yes, *Señor.*"

The machine clicked, and he got up from his leather chair. He stood at the window, before his ghostly reflection. Pale he had become, like General Díaz, until he almost looked distinguished. His fingers touched pleats that were designed to hide his paunch. With sensual pleasure he looked at his manicured nails. The machine clicked again. "Señor Ibarra is on the phone, sir."

"All right, put him on." He closed his eyes. Librado Ibarra. Librado Ibarra. A portrait in one line: three thousand pesos and a partner in the Limited. Ratty suit, eternal stink of cheap cooking, and small swollen bulbous eyes. Balding, his thin hair combed and gummed to hide it.

"Well, Ibarra, how are you? How's the leg coming along? You don't say. No, I was out of the office, didn't they tell you? Well, what can I do for you?" Foot crushed by a machine: the machine clanked on, began to clatter, to chew the foreign matter that had come into it: flesh of an old man who had become only what is ground between bolts and cogs. . . . "Yes, naturally. I was sorry not to get to the hospital, but you know that besides our little Limited, I've other companies that are more . . . No, I received no message from you. I know . . . Well, what can be done about

14

it?" A partner, by right of three thousand pesos, one of twenty-three associates, old man in stinking suits, but an old man useful to watch the workers, see that they didn't goldbrick. . . . "Eh, Ibarra? An accident at work? What are you talking about? Eh? What sort of a man do you think you're talking to?" . . . Responsibility, Limited. R. L. . . . "Oh, no, my friend, wrong from beginning to end. You were presenting your services to the company as an associate, not an employee. Eat your damn work accidents, eat them, I say. . . . Don't be so innocent, Ibarra. You think any serious banking house would be doing business with us if I weren't backing the Limited? Get along with you. . . ." Three thousand pesos: all his savings, the same old song: all my savings and now I'm crippled and . . .

Robles's fist slammed down on the glass tabletop, opening a green vein across the glass. "A meeting to compromise? Look, blockhead, you're not an employee, you're an associate. You begin to understand? Don't talk about any meeting to compromise anything. Get off it, eh? You know what a blacklist is? Eh? All right. . . . You *what?* Saturday, Saturday morning. I'll try to get your motion passed unanimously, eh? Then you can take your little investment out. . . ." For it takes work to get any business moving, large or small, people don't know. A crushed foot, three thousand pesos were not going to, he wouldn't let them . . . damn country, everything against you. And if you begin to give way in the little matters, then . . .

"Good-bye, Ibarra. Get well, eh?"

He hung up. Now the letter for the corporation: My dear friend: I am sure you know that it is predicted that of all new businesses organized this year, more than 50 per cent will be of corporate structure? Doesn't it seem significant to you . . .

Robles touched a button.

Bobó's furniture: what could be said about it? It demanded and invited Lower Empire Posture . . . the elegant flop: low small tables with small wagons full of blue glass grapes, low chairs, low everything. A little glass bookcase and Indian filing within it, Malraux on beauty (uncut), the complete works of

Mickey Spillane, and Rimbaud's *Illuminations*, while *The Songs of Maldoror* and two Peruvian ash trays stood on a wooden lectern. Each stair step had its cactus. Each guest had his drink: Pierre Caseaux was still balancing his enormous lissome cognac, and in front of him Pichi and Junior were bouncing laughter back and forth rhythmically, compelling the excellent *bon vivant* to take notice of them.

"Pichi, Pierre has just come back from England."

"From Savile Row, darlings. There is no other country which exists only on one street. This last trip, however, I made a happy discovery. The culinary austerity has had a positive affect on the other, the traditional austerity. You know? Now they begin to enjoy life, vis-à-viscera. Junior! Who is this lovely creature on your arm?"

Roberto Régules smiled, and observed the profile of his wife. The flesh under her chin had begun to soften and sag. When they had married, he had imagined that he would never see, nor feel himself so disturbed by, any sign of age in her. Passion. Love. Companionship. So it had been programmed. Roberto Régules smiled. "Go on, Silvia, why don't you go on and go to him? Why are you waiting? They all know, don't they? What sort of absurd appearances are you trying to keep up?"

Silvia did not move a muscle. Her eyes went on smiling, approving, from far away, "Be quiet," she said. "If it weren't for the children . . ."

Bernardito Supratous and Amadeo Tortosa took seats on the sofa beside Manuel Zamacona, forcing him, with an expression of irritation, to sit up straight. He passed his hand across his forehead. "We must go back to the attitude of the epoch-makers, Pascal, Goethe, and feel reverent before life, say with Keats, I am convinced I create only because of the desire and happiness of achieving beauty . . . even when every morning, I burn the work of the night before. Can't we have Quevedos today, men who exercise the simple, healthy, whole-man profession of creator?"

Tortosa coughed and spread his arms. "But my dear Manuel! You miss all the meaning of social flow. You live too much in the

16

past, you sigh for fallen ideals. Obviously, and unfortunately, one has to theorize before acting. But theory means vision, and in the last instance it must be action. You have to share the pain of the impoverished, the demanding anguish of solidarity. . . ."

"Of course we have to fight against this monstrous world! We can't go on, a conventional culture, cowed by the *bourgeoisie*. Culture has become decorative, with interchangeable parts. We have to make it over from the beginning, tirelessly, with reverence! We have to labor until all men feel themselves Leonardos! And that's the poet's mission, profound and sacred communication. And another word for it is love."

Supratous *dixit*. "*Ciertamente, l'amour est une réalité dans le domaine de l'imagination*."

Face glowing, mouth proud, Juan Morales swung open the doors into the cellar restaurant.

"Inside, old woman! Hop, squirts!"

Rosa fingered the bodice of her cotton dress. The children ran toward a vacant table. Juan strolled forward full of contentment. He twisted the ends of his stiff mustache. A waiter bowed.

"This way, *señores*. Here."

Pepe and Juanito put their chins on the table and began to read the greasy menu. Rosa fingered her bodice. Juan sat and put a toothpick to his mouth.

"They ought to be in bed," said Rosa. "They have to go to school tomorrow, and . . ."

"Today is special, old girl. Let's see, boys. What'll it be?"

Juan Morales scratched the red scar across his forehead. Twenty years hacking at night is no joke. I can tell you, *mano*, so can this scar I got. How many drunks, in twenty years? How many sons of bitches. To Azcapotzalco, buddy, to Buenos Sires, at three or four in the morning, and then all of a sudden, one of them clobbers you from behind. Or you have to get out and haul him out and it ends up with broken ribs. For twenty pesos a night. Well, that's over now.

"Well, have you decided?"

17

"Look, Papá. Those kids over there are eating cake. That's what we want."

"Juan."

"Shhhh, woman. Today is special."

And those who take the cab only to take you, not to a street but a sandbagging. That's how they jumped me and they almost did for me, Rosita. What if I hadn't been wide awake that night? Didn't my father used to tell me: Juan, you were born to play the fool, to fuck yourself and carry others' burdens. Don't forget to lie when you have to. Do what you want to do. You don't have to answer to any man except yourself, and no one remembers us long. That was at home in the country, the little quiet country. Here in the capital, you had to keep on your toes. If you don't, *mano*, you've had it.

"*All right*, waiter. A roast chicken, well browned, for the whole family. Some of those little cakes with strawberries, with cream. And tell the *mariachis* to come play for us."

Poor Rosa, always alone. I wasn't even with her when the children were born. Always ready with my coffee at seven in the evening, with hot water for me to shave at seven in the morning. But the sheets were always cold, always frozen, when I went to bed in the morning, as if instead of her, only night and frost had slept there. As if she didn't have her body and her blood and her belly full of my children. I never used to see them. Well, now I will. Things are going to be different.

"What shall they play for us, Rosa?"

"Let the children . . ."

"*Juan Charrasqueado, Juan Charrasqueado!*"

The cellar had faint smells of roasted corn, just-warmed tortillas, grease, fresh rain. Juan rubbed his stomach. He looked around: tables with flowered tablecloths, cane chairs, brown-skinned men, wearing serge and olive gabardine, talking about bullfighting and whores, women with curl-crinkled black hair just come out of the movies, artificial eyelashes, violet lips. And which of them wasn't looking at Juan Morales? At Juan Morales and his family?

"*De aquellos campos no quedaba ni una flor,*" sang the

18

mariachis. "Not a single flower was left in that desolate country-side."

"Juan, we can't . . ."

"Why can't we? This is what I've always wanted. A bottle of wine, a gold-label bottle of wine. . . ."

And what if I hadn't taken that gringo today, what if I hadn't been at the stand when the hotel telephoned. What if the gringo hadn't asked me to go watch the races with him and hadn't given me forty pesos in bets. . . .

"Look, *mano,* you've won, go to the window and collect."

"What do you mean, I've won? What happened? How?"

"Beginner's luck, *mano.* You like it, eh?"

"For once in my life I've got money! *Salud,* old woman."

". . . *pistola en mano se le echaron de la montón . . .*" sang the *mariachis.*

Rosa spread her big mestizo smile and sucked strawberry juice from her fingers.

Eight hundred pesos. Beginners luck, *mano,* but don't come back or they'll take you for your shirt. Who was going back? He was going to change to dayshift, he was going to go to bed at eleven at night and get up at six in the morning, like the rest of the world. Now he had eight hundred pesos. He would begin again, to hear the *mariachis,* to make Rosa's bed warm. . . .

Rodrigo Pola walked out of the elevator with his head bent and his eyebrows already arching. His gabardine suit—"Charcoal. The latest in London."—stood out among the darker tones of the other male guests. He approached the group around Manuel.

"*L'amour est une réalité dans le domaine de l'imagination . . .*"

Ixca Cienfuegos rested both hands against the wall, then thought better of it and began to suck a black cocktail olive. Supratous: *L'amour est une réalité.* . . . Remarks of that sort, impenetrable silence otherwise, had won him fame as an oracle. Reader exclusively of biographies, vicarious life, the elaborate product of his own pedestal. One quotation to show he was acquainted with the *Life of Talleyrand,* another to let his genius peep out through rays of Machiavelli, Napoleon, Shaw, Wilde,

Walter Lippmann. So he pranced along: vision, courage, conceptual brilliance, reduced to the circularity of his admiring group. And López Wilson, astigmatic revolutionist come to spy upon his enemy's terrain, to piss on that frivolous earth and be eyewitness to the dying of capitalism while at the same time enjoying its death-orgies. Yes: they were all here, all of them. From the provincial poet too conscious that he was for the first time being instructed in worldly dissipation, to the *à la mode* couple, professionally groomed, for whom the world is an empire-glass for their charms and good humors; to the potato-faced novelist heaving inside with God knows what entrails of moldered earth, a volcano spewing talent through stone opacity and in his one-note voice telling of towns and haciendas, village priests and politicians, country maidens whose lives had withered in virtuous spinsterhood. There he was, there he strutted, unpublished, but an author, elated over the twentieth printing of his first twenty fragments of a page. What difference does it make? He's our boy, isn't he? He's our buddy, we get a kick out of him. And that's what counts, friend, in Mexico that's all that counts!

Yes, they were all here. Including the bureaucratic Mexican intellectual, heir to all the horse sense and most of the horse shit in the world, and proud of his heritage; the poetic socialists whose Dada is Marx, the peep-and-tell scribbler whose Sunday-Supplement column juggles reputations with careful clumsiness, keeping some high, making others fall.

And, before them, those of the other army: the niched, secure crowd, the great scorners (and will it never be understood by the Mexican intellectual that to them, the society whirl, he is merely an object of contempt and scorn). The young woman who has announced her intention to become a great international whore; thus far she has managed to include two picture actors, a boxer, a wide-lay test in Hollywood, three seasons on the Riviera, a millionaire. There, too, stands a great family's last sprig, last of the true gentlemen in his own opinion, and by the same judge, irresistible, born to glow in drawing rooms behind his ivory cigarette-scepter, born to seduce those women who have a certain desire for variety, to frighten just plain virgins. And all the little Mexican girls . . . blonde, elegant, sheathed in black and sure they were giving international tone to the saddest unhappiest flea-bitten land in the world. And their husbands, soaring lawyers, zooming industrialists, come to Bobó's, sure that here they were entering the pastures of authentic kicks, the paradise at the end of Hustle Road.

And still others: those bewitched by greatness. Obscure young men, sons of grade-school teachers and minor civil servants, all shining with their common glitter of breeding pasted on with spit: check vests, duck-tail haircuts. And still others the flotsam of destitute sirs, counts, and marquis, war-leveled; their mistress of ceremony, Charlotte García.

And Bobó, desperately trying to weave them all together, in a buzz of carelessness and merriment, into a "set." Into The Set.

And, finally, those who mattered, who could be hurt. Rodrigo Pola, snapping back after every repulse to slap the hand that repulsed him; Manuel Zamacona, who would reach for and never touch the holy of holies, never quite really understand . . . and Norma . . . and Federico. Who would have the bravery and the patience to keep remembering.

A distant murmur of relevant virtues:

> "Because I feel I do not feel
> When my blood informs me now
> That apart from you there is nothing alive,
> The Reaper comes and I know
> That in return there is departure . . ."

The group around Manuel mumbled, murmured, and assented. Tortosa whirled his vanes: "I believe that I have established understanding with the masses. Don't look at me that way. You don't have to be a cook to judge a sandwich. Now you see me at Bobó's party, sitting and drinking, but you'll never see me give up my concern for the impoverished, not for one minute. Yes. . . . We would do well to ask ourselves, what right do we have to have books, to read T. S. Eliot of a Sunday morning, to make every meal a feast, to sit at Bobó's, exchanging pretty

21

words, when in our own land we have before us the tragedy of wetbacks and of starvation in the valley of Mezquital?"

"I don't care to recall my more pedantic readings," Zamacona interrupted, "but I daresay you, too, hold your breath when you're on a bus beside a beggar."

Pola raised a finger. "Do we have to be either the ass in the street or, on the other hand, a *homme révolté . . .*"

"Aim before you fire, my friend," growled Zamacona. "Camus, who is French enough . . ."

"*Perdón,*" said Bernardito, sensing his golden opportunity. "*C'est pas français parce que c'est idiot.*"

And finding himself riddled by looks of horror, he shrugged in a way that indicated no one understood his allusions, while Rodrigo Pola, raising his voice said, "I love poetry . . ."

"But does poetry love you?" inquired a quiet voice at his shoulder. It was Ixca Cienfuegos.

"Is that Cienfuegos?"

"That, dear Prince, is him. He himself. The one and only. Like God, he's everywhere, but no one ever sees him. In and out of government offices, society drawing rooms, friend of magnates. He's said to be the brain behind a great banker. He's said to be a gigolo and a marijuana addict. He comes, he goes . . . in brief, another clown in the unharmonious circus in which we live."

Gus delicately settled his red corduroy jacket: "Harmony! Harmony! *Princeps meus,* the Greeks understood that harmony is everything. In harmony, all opposites are resolved, and if one puts harmony before habit, one may go to bed with anyone one cares to. And not, as these cream puffs insist, only with leathery stinking women. Men never smell bad."

Prince Vampa agreed from his pillar of smoke. Charlotte García, who had just joined them, smiled into the splash of her martini: "Taste is all relative, say what you please. You know what courage it takes for me to come *chez* Bobó's. Things with Lally haven't been going well at all. But when she comes, I'm going to tell her the truth: that she's perverse, that she has hurt me deeply, and that I adore her. Ah, last of the Vampas! I'm so tired, so bored." Charlotte stroked her throat, like a snake charmer. "I've a longing to break up someone's married bliss. Bobó has made an enormous booboo inviting all these useless young literati. Look at them! What a lack of security, of true sans-façon. We live in a miniature Africa! *Joie de vivre* and all that are very well, but a cocktail party is a cocktail party and ought to have practical consequences. Bobó still doesn't understand that today's new rich will be tomorrow's aristocrats, just as today's aristocrats were yesterday's new rich."

"And day-before-yesterday's aristocrats?" asked Prince Vampa, injured.

"Ah, my dear," replied Charlotte, pinching the nobleman's pale cheek, "that's the only time that isn't important. In Mexico they're today's petty bureaucrats. Except, of course, those who, like you, are too busy to work. . . . But look who's just come! The great beauty of yesterday! See, little crow's-feet beginning . . . la, la!"

Natasha, wrapped to her ears in green velvet, heavily powdered, her kiss-me-quick curls crowned by a little shimmy-era gold turban, entered with the serenity of the woman who had been Queen of the *Fasto* at San Fermín since 1935, and the monarch of Mexico City's international set. Several young writers rose immediately, instinctively, from the softest divan. Natasha accepted the empty divan, sat, and waited. . . .

Ixca Cienfuegos smiled. Always the same rites, careful dress and self-restraint, readiness for the excuses, the confidences, the tactile stage. Little devils we will be. There's Pola, on his fifth daiquiri, thinking, "I am better than they are, I give myself the luxury of being bored by them." Keep an eye on him. And now the hungry fish begins to nibble the bait, there goes the first, Silvia rising in chase of Pierrot. . . . Ixca smiled.

Taking advantage of the dimmer light, she slipped near Pedro Caseaux. Her hands nervously touched her hairnet, glinting with small diamonds. "Pierrot . . . one little moment?"

Caseaux pulled his ear. "Another one more little moment, darling? Our friendship has lived only by little moments. I don't much care for that, you know. Look at Régules. He's as angry as a Nibelung. Preserve me from these domestic scenes. Adieu."

Natasha smiled from the divan. She had guessed the technique. She could have saved Silvia the trouble. Poor Pierre. His hair was going.

Norma Larragoiti de Robles entered just as Bobó changed the lights from blue to green. Her jewels glowed the brighter for it, the *coup-de-soleil* in her hair, her golden earrings, her violet eyelids. Rodrigo Pola quickly moved toward her. And hidden behind a tumbler of Scotch, Caseaux whispered, "Pichi, our dear Junior needs attention, a cup of coffee. Help me carry him to the bedroom. Soft now, easy. . . ."

Junior, in a garrulous falsetto, was shouting at everyone near the bar, "Ooooh, what sur-reeeealism, Oooooh, what Heideggerrrr . . . ." He shifted to Calypso, with exaggerated gestures, "Lemme go, Emeldah dahling. You're biting mah fingah . . ."

"How disagreeable," Pichi commented. "Why do you suppose he lost control of himself so? Adler, you know, believes . . ."

Junior was stretched on the bed and passed into eclipse.

"Good, now he can't hurt himself. Let's watch him sleep. Poor Junior. There is a snobbery based on the discovery that no Santa Claus exists. How can a malicious little girl like you——"

"Why do you say that, Señor Caseaux? Junior taught me that——"

"Señor Caseaux, Señor Caseaux! Call me Pierrot, as everyone else does."

"But manners don't prevent——"

"Heat." Pierrot took Pichi by the hips and slowly kissed her throat.

"Mmmmmmmm."

"My princess, may we suppose that you're a virgin?"

"Pierrot! It's all right to play, but . . . but first one has to get ready intellectually, and then . . . mmmmmmm! and then make life . . ." Pichi's voice became faint and dilute, like a dropping drip of filtrate.

"Mens sana in corpore insano."

"And if someone comes in? Pierrot, Pierrot, my veil! My buttons!"

"I locked the door." Pierrot felt for the lamp cord and pulled it.

"Pierrot, and with Junior here?"

24

"He'll think he's still at the party. Come, my lovely."

"Ah! Pierrot, Pierrot!"

"Madono, ma maîtresse . . . et cetera, et cetera . . . au fond de ma détresse . . ."

"Mmmmmmm."

Natasha passed her veined hands over her hard white cheek-bones. Beneath the high velvet throat, her own throat was palpitating. She had the sensation of touching the strings of a spongy cello. She had watched them go up to the bedroom, Pierrot and that little girl who was so like the Natasha of an earlier time, and she had imagined everything. She recalled Pierrot in 1935, gilded with European capitals, the Bryonic seducer of all womankind. She could not restrain an audible groan. Wrapped in velvet, with a brilliant face, she rose and left a party drowning in its shrill shadows.

A light tinkle of glasses over the murmur of voices: the Bar Montenegro. Scents of cushiony carpeting, make-up and gin, the décor golden. A telephone came and went in the hands of a waiter, breaking dates, making excuses, arranging Cook's tours. Cuquis was in her element. She wriggled her shoulders to let her stole slip to the back of her chair.

"And where are you living now, Gloria?"

"In Chile, dear. Life there, you know, is as it was here in Don Porfirio's time. A very exclusive set . . . and what a set! They receive, magnificently, in the Hípico, the Unión, at Viña del Mar, cold champagne, *des choses flambées,* you know. . . . And not for a long time has there been an invasion of these used-car dealers from Tennessee. Look around."

Gloria pursed her lips before her hand mirror and began to powder her nose carefully.

"Sure, sure. . . . They're gay and colorful, but look here, I don't get the impression that they're an active, businesslike people . . ."

"Being a diplomat's wife isn't all partying, though," Gloria went on. "Someone said that there are four professions which can never be abandoned. Diplomat, newspaperman, clown, and whore. And you, pretty pampered sweet?"

Cuquis shook her small curly head, showed her teeth. "Little old Mexico City never changes, you know. . . ."

"*Oooh, the most beautiful old ruins you can imagine: quite a trip, and cheap, too . . .*"

"*. . . girls go on having their first babies five months after they marry . . . pressure cookers.*"

"And romance?"

"All right, I'll tell you. I met a real dream. If I had to sell body and soul to get that gentleman, dear, I'd do it without a thought. There ought to be a classified column for bodies and souls, shouldn't there?"

A group of North Americans wearing straw hats entered, shouting, "*Viva México!*" Gloria shuddered ostentatiously. The tourists' guide, dark, short, wore a too-large dun-colored jacket.

"Listen, there's going to be a charity ball at the home of Robles, the banker. Don't miss it, Gloria. As it's a subscription ball and I'm going with my dreamboat, it's my great chance to see the house without speaking to the host. You'll see why I want to get rid of that little end of nothing I call husband. Exchange him for a prince of men. He took me to his hacienda, you know, and to Acapulco. Romance under the palms! He even offered to take precautions. Can you imagine?"

"*. . . happy birthday to you, happy birthday dear Larry, happy . . .*"

"Finish your drink, pet. They're expecting us at Bobó's."

Cuquis wriggled her shoulders. "In your eye."

By a strong effort Rosenda got to her feet. Immediately, knees melting inside the wide yellowing gown, she had to grab the bed. Her eyes stared into a piece of mirror tacked to the wall; an onion-skin old face stared back. She went to the cupboard, felt at the familiar spot, found the sour aging photographs, and returned to the bed with them and sat. The first was a girl with curls a little absurd for her age, leaning against a photo studio's Greek column with a hand on her hip and her body in the curve of the letter *S*; across it was the signature *Rosenda Zubarán, 1910.* Across the second was written *Rosenda Z. de Pola,* a woman seated but somehow in the same posture, the same tilt of head, holding a delicate and wide-eyed baby. Then the portrait of a hard-faced soldier with glistening hair and a soldier's smile, plumed helmet on his stiff arm, Rosenda began to tremble, the veins of her neck danced without rhythm, she became short of breath and let the photographs drop to the floor while her eyes closed and she thought about a platter heaped with milk candy and candied fruit, a home shut up like a scissors case, an immense endless wall where she ran with whirling eyes and which, at a moment of terror when her flesh rose, flowered with little clouds of brilliant dust, every bullet a sun which lit its own setting and was about to star-flash spangled corneas of an old woman who now, collapsing, let spittle drip down on her breast.

A rib of smoke hung vertical in the drawing room. Bobó had sat on a stair step, alone with his glass, to gaze his fill at his production; merriment, happiness, a hit. Sweet bedlam flowed around his blue ears. Bobó *ex machina*. A hit, a hit! And now the Countess Aspacúccoli had just arrived!

The Countess steered straight to Vampa, Gus, and Charlotte, and without preamble growled in her Montenegro accent, "Dearly beloveds, I've nothing at home except Rice Krispies. Head me toward food."

The young women wearing glasses were still in their corner, nervously agreeing with Estévez. "Now the Mexican is that entity, anonymous, unjointed, which adjusts itself to its situation with at most curiosity or fear. A Dasein, on the contrary, has taken cognizance of man's finitude, that man is a gathering of potentialities, the last of which is death . . . which is always observed at third-hand, never experienced in his own skin. For how can Dasein be projected into death?"

The young women wearing spectacles made their sweaters bounce with sweaty happiness. They were deeply moved.

"He is a being who exists for death; a relationship between pure being and nothingness . . . an Argentine. Excuse me . . .I cannot philosophize abstractly enough. . . ."

Dardo Moratto poked with his doughy manicured fingers. "Go on, Estévez, go on. It's quite interesting, interesting, indeed, to see the beginnings of things. You're working well here, you're doing things. Introduce me to your young ladies. But . . . where are you going?"

"To the bathroom," spat Estévez.

"Ah! Well, *señoritas,* I suppose you are acquainted with the story of the invention of the water closet?" The young women wearing glasses giggled and admitted their ignorance. Moratto tightened his necktie, touched the corners of his wide piqué collar. "*Ché,* what an abyss in your culture! Sir John Wooton, Elizabethan courtier, Latinist, translator of Vergil. Who was beloved; nevertheless, he was plotted against at court. Elizabeth imprisoned him in one of those miserable cold old castles. How could he avail himself of the precious moments of clarity which occur when defecating, and go on with his translation of the *Aeneid,* if he had to dash across a frosty garden to an outhouse?" Moratto gestured elaborately, spilling his glass. "Oh, excuse me, *Señora!* Have I stained your dress?"

"It's nothing." Norma Robles turned back to Rodrigo and said, "Almost thirteen years, Roderico *mío.* But the advantage of living in Mexico City is that no one ever looks for anyone, and as there are no changes of season, time passes without being noticed. So why do you notice it?"

"Thirteen years, Norma."

"And?"

"Is your husband coming?"

"My what?" She chewed an olive and spread her eyes. And laughing as never before, as though to herself, she said, "Roderico *mío.* . . . At least——"

"Norma . . ." Rodrigo wanted to take her warm jeweled hand.

"Ah, be quiet. You still think we're in that garden of our long-gone adolescence." She drowned laughter in her drink. "In you I shall shipwreck, stormy gin!"

He had never seen her so beautiful. Double veils hung from a pin of light. She was someone else.

"You've become quite aggressive, Rodrigo. Time has changed you for the better."

28

"That depends on your viewpoint." He held his hand out with the palm up.

"No, no, no, don't begin one of those interminable labor lectures. In the first place, you'll bore me. In the second, you're wrong. Only the rich know the abyss which separates us from the poor, and the poor never find out unless some renegade landowner tells them, so we're safe. But comes the revolution, *tu,* and the first to be shot are the renegades and the useless intellectuals. *Ja!*"

Rodrigo looked at the match flame between his fingers and said nothing.

Dardo Moratto's voice wound on sinuously. "So Sir John invented the john, and translated Virgil while shitting. The great work could be finished! Imagine, to this very day the English have never dedicated a monument to the memory of Sir John, Latinist, courtier, and translator of Virgil!"

"Ah, Rodrigo, don't tell me you've become only one of those characters who must always be laughed at. Tch-tch. Here! A daiquiri for the *Señor!*"

The servant, Fidelio, almost spilled his tray. Almost eleven. Almost eleven, and Gabriel is coming, and me here . . . I got to go . . .

"Watch where you're going!" Bobó hissed at him. "What's wrong with you today?"

Norma took the drinks and wove her arms like drowsy snakes. "Ah, how pleasant it is to have a fat financial wizard for a husband. Very strict as to conscience, but his conscience strict only about his responsibilities! If he didn't look me up once a week, I'd think he had gone off with another woman. Jealousy is the side of love I don't care for. I'd be lost, bewitched, most tragic, Rodrigo. I'd miss all the parties where I meet old friends I thought were lost forever. And you, little man, what are you doing these days?"

"Nothing special. I write a little . . ."

Norma's gloved hands clapped silently. "Good, good, literature is an accessory just as important as handbags and brandy."

"Norma . . . I don't know . . . I go on loving you."

"Bravo! How original! The infection spreads! Who do you think you are, eh?" And she turned to the window, singing, "Ai, what a draft! Bobó, what will you take to close that window? What if we should give our poets sore throats?"

> "Oh, you who do not falter,
> Who have something, I don't know what,
> Give me back those times when
> By not sinning, you sinned. . . ."

"Good, and now? You want to pretend that we're back in that noisy little garden, playing footsy? Wouldn't it be better to hold hands in Movieland? That's how you always were, you know, and you'll go on just the same; when you're ninety, you'll be sneaking behind a door to kiss old women in an old folks' home. But that's all, eh? That's all you'll ever do with a woman. All right! We'll be seeing each other."

She turned her back to him and began to wave, for Pimpinela de Ovando had just entered, tall, with an aquiline nose, her metallic eyes burning with coldness. Ixca Cienfuegos smiled. Norma and Pimpinela, embracing. Give me cash and I'll give you class. Give me class and I'll give you cash.

"Will you see your husband tomorrow?" Pimpinela asked, spreading a collective smile around the party.

"*Hélas, oui,*" Norma exclaimed. She was not conscious that she was imitating Pimpinela's air.

"Don't forget to remind him about my three hundred shares, dear. Three hundred. You promised, remember?"

"I don't know, Pimpinela. I never . . ."

Pimpinela widened her smile. "Ah, before we're off on something else, my aunt wants you to have dinner with her. Next Thursday."

Norma could not keep her eyes from shining.

"Doña Lorenza Ortíz de Ovando?"

The stink of vomit, sleep, heavy breathed air lifted the second the bus braked. "*May*-ee-co!" the driver roared. Bird cages were taken down from the windows, passengers stirred awake, chickens moved in their crates, cheap valises and secondhand shoes

30

shuffled. Gabriel tried to clean the window to see to comb his hair; he cocked his baseball cap and took down his leather jacket. Mexico City! Now to run, spend a few pesos for a taxi, and get home quick. With his hand pressed against his wallet, Gabriel pushed to the exit. A group of whores were crossing Netzahualcóyotl Plaza with their knees wrapped and their heels muddy.

"Now, Mac, or don't bother to see me again!"

"With me you'll stop suffering, daddy."

"You name it, I'm for it."

"I'll pay with dollars!"

"Sure, sure, what you'll pay with is the big joke."

Gabriel set off, walking along the street, smelling the pungent odors of brown bodies, looking at his new reflection, crew-cut, prosperous, in the show windows of shoe stores. The city towered over him, crowded down on him as if there were no sky. He came back from California's open fields to breathe tomato skins. "Taxi!" Straight streets, cluttered with trash, and now low peeling houses. He amused himself reading the signs over bar doors, over the doors of funeral parlors clustered along Transito, white store fronts, and outside, on display, always a white-enameled child's coffin. He could smell the dead stiff blood of a child behind every door; in his own home four had died, too young, before they had done anything, neither work nor fuck, nor anything important in life.

Gabriel snapped his fingers with impatience. A wad of dollars in his pocket, shining presents, so they could all live better. It was his first year, and he had brought back everything he could carry, legal or contraband, risking bullets and drowning when he crossed the Rio. Well, it was that or push an ice-cream cart along the streets of Mexico City. And he had said so to Tuno, when they were together at harvest time in Texas, "So what if they don't let you in their crappy restaurants? You able to get in the Ambassador in Mexico City? Besides, the only thing here is to get money." Gabriel rapped the wooden door of 28-B. "Hey, I'm back!"

His yellow-toothed mother, his father's always drowsy face, his big sister who was beginning to be good-looking, the two little boys in overalls and holey shirts: "Gabriel, Gabriel, you're bigger, you're grown up!"

"This has got everything for all of you, so let's go, open it!" The room lit by candles, prints of virgins and saints over the iron cot. "For you, Pepa, because you're getting fat, this is what the gringo girls use to squeeze themselves in. Very fine."

"Ah, Gabriel, how strange," his mother repeated over and over. "And a baseball cap just like mine for you, old man. The Cleveland Indians, that's where Beto Avila socks his home runs. And old woman, just look. So you won't have to work so hard."

"And what kind of damn thing is this, my son?"

"I'll show you. Where's Fidelio?"

"He's working, Gabriel, in a house in the Lomas. But explain this machine to me."

"Look, you put the glass vase on top of the white machine and you fill it with beans or fruit or whatever you want to grind up, and it grinds it up for you."

"Let's see it. Go ahead."

"No, Mamá, you got to plug it into the lights first."

"But we don't have electricity, child."

"God damn. That's right. Well, just use it as a vase, that's all you can do. Hey, I'm starving! Where're my tortillas?" He would not change Mexican cooking for anything, but next year once again he would take off northward, to the land where there was work and money, and electricity.

Rodrigo Pola downed his seventh daiquiri and looked around the room and discovered it full of well-being and distinction, shining words that floated among smoke wreathes. His blood tapped out a shining word: success. Each letter glittered apart and alone: s-u-c-c-e-s-s. He grabbed another daiquiri. He would work a charm with that magic word. His inflamed, groggy eyes wanted to turn inward so that he could talk with himself, and with his eyes addressing the inside of his skull, he observed that this was not merely the obvious way to change nothing into something, but in truth it was a way to change something into nothing, to waste it. He threw his glass on the carpet and went to Bobó. "Got to keep this moving. I shall now perform."

"Shhh, shhhh!" finger to damp lips, Bobó ran among them, gathering a circle, stood in the middle of it and trumpet-cupped his hands: "Tah-rah-rah!"

Guests left their sofas and cushions and crowded around Rodrigo, the comedian. He did not see their faces, he took off blindly; his act was a parody of Fitzpatrick's travel talk, it had always been a great success, years ago among his prep-school friends, and just a while ago at a saloon. "Now we have arrived at Mexico City's Little Venice, the floating gardens of Chuchemirco. Ho! Did you catch that little blonde drifting by in her lovely flowery canoe? Pretty girl, may we join you?"

They began to move back to their seats, to form groups again, to light cigarettes.

Pola went on, "And here we have that famous musician, poet, and lunatic, who is going to tell us how he composes!" He screwed up his face, sucked in his cheeks to begin his imitation of Agustín Lara. And then he did see the few faces that were still watching him: bored, as if watching rain come, blowing smoke out, aware of him only vaguely. Just one smile, and that a smile he would have paid not to see, Norma's. Pimpinela murmured to her and they moved away. With his face twisted and his cheeks hollow, Rodrigo felt his knees collapse. No one was left now. Bobó and his servants began to goose Rodrigo, trying to stir him into action. Alone in the middle of the room, he stared at the floor and sang as in a dream . . ."*Santa, Santa mía* . . ."

Entered Paco Delquinto, drunk: touseled and balding and graying, a check shirt and yellow shoes, Bohemian by nature, painter, newspaper-writer, perennially finishing twentieth in the bicycle race to Bajío, and with him a girl wearing a fixed stare, bobby socks, and an existentialist pony tail. Bobó flew down from his stair-step Belvedere. "*Avanti*, Delquinto! The only man in Mexico who knows how to make make-believe of famous Mexico's dying sparkle. . . ."

"Literature, virtue, bribery, eternal spring," Delquinto cried with a grotesque face.

"Illustrious government, state, religion," Bobó sang on rapturously.

"And to hell with the oil thieves," the Countess tried to finish through a mouthful of caviar.

Juliette, with pressed lips, observed them disgustedly.

"Down with community!" Delquinto shouted. "Anyone who wants to write about us will have to find a new way to make fire! We're already the ash of ashes, the breakdown of words, the twentieth blank carbon copy! The Mexican creator, rich, original: Naaaa . . . everyone glued to his little job, like a fungus, developing tics instead of vices, talking about the Mexican this, the Paraguayan that. . . . Artists of the world, unite, we have nothing to lose but your talent! Oh, Barbara, *quelle connerie la guerre*. . . . *Dulce Filis,* what the hell are you thinking about?"

Juliette arched an eyebrow and continued her indignant silence. Her white bobby socks, on such a night, were perfect: for a second Bernardito Supratous believed that he had met his life's companion.

The Countess, back in her cluster, accepted more caviar and soda crackers: "Evaristo is making almost nothing . . . six hundred pesos a month. Only these parties keep me from starving. But one day . . ."

"Inviting Delquinto, what taste!" Gus hissed.

"I move we have a cocktail party Saturday, *chez moi,*" said Charlotte. Prince Vampa gave her a look which implied that Saturday evenings were fit only for the family baths of petty bourgeois, so she changed immediately. "Well, Tuesday. Gus, you check the airlines to see if any celebrities will be here from New York or Los Angeles. You, Prince, lend me your family crest for the invitations. To work! We can start making telephone calls right now and break this tedium. Can you imagine that I didn't let myself cry today, so I would look pretty *here?*"

Juliette sat on the floor with blank eyes while Delquinto swayed off to mix a couple of submarines. Supratous timidly sprang at her: "Ah, *que vous êtes jeune, et que vous êtes femme——*"

"You give me a pain in the ass," said Juliette.

Cautiously the aging painter roped one of the girls wearing spectacles. "I see that you are chained by the conventionalism of a bourgeois family. It's not just that so great a talent should be lost, smothered by vulgarity . . . you were born for art . . . come to see me, my dear, here is my card. . . ."

Estévez was whispering into Tortosa's ear, "And why is the Mexican unhappy?"

Manuel Zamacona had decided to save, to save, and seizing Bobó by the shoulders: "How can we keep it from sinking, a country where instead of poetry, men read ads that proclaim the need to use anti-sweat cream on pain of losing your sweetheart, to gargle with chlorophyll on pain of being unpopular? Paradox, metaphor, imagination, to what a chasm you lead!"

The provincial novelist was telling the Countess, who was now chewing potato chips, that, "Beyond Apatitlán there's a desert plain, and then you climb to San Tanoredo de los Reyes. There the clouds are low, the people are sad. The earth offers nothing . . . dunes and desolation. But a little farther it descends, you begin to feel the heat, you are near Chimalpapán, where there is grass again and the Government is starting to build a dam. Where the Atolotes live, a gang of outlaws who hide on the other side of the border and cross it to carry off the prettiest women. I remember once . . ."

López Wilson meanwhile, was invoking dialectic for the exclusive benefit of an incredulous Prince Vampa.

Lally, Bobó's mistress, arrived with five bongo drummers.

It is night now (blind Hortensia Chacón said without words) and I would like to be able to know it by something except its breathing. It is what I need least, and therefore what I would most like to have again, not every night but only one special hour of darkness. She passed her hands over the wrinkled sheets of her bed and with her fingertips tried to feel the depression, deep, a little damp, where Federico Robles had lain. And so for several minutes, compacted hours, thinking that only weariness told her when to go to sleep, when to wake and, more important than either, when to expect him. She smelled the evening, motor exhausts, as she had smelled children when they were led out of their school across the street and heard their sounds, seeming babble which in Hortensia's ears was shaped into precise words. And the scent of the children's street-bought transparent sugar candy, the sappy smell, soap and plums, of the vegetable store on the ground floor. She put her nose to the sheets and tried to find Federico's body. With one finger she traced him: eyes, mouth, neck, stomach, arms, legs; then she lay on that white shadow and embraced it, and said, always without speaking: I wait for you, because you demand that of me and I have always wanted it. And it isn't because of the darkness. My darkness lies on my anxiety and my waiting, but with you all my body stops feeling hurt and exposed in darkness, as naked in darkness as at the beginning. . . .

A home in Colonia Navarte, decorated with bullfight paintings by Ruano Llopis. A Manila lace lay on the grand piano. When Federico Robles arrived, they were all already there. He entered as he always entered, his bullet Indian head, shaved to the temples, bent a little, acknowledging greetings with a slight movement of hand. Then, with his highball in hand, he straightened and waited.

"Progress has to have a buildup, or it isn't believed. And if it isn't believed, we don't get foreign capital. What pictures does a big North American magazine run? Not shots of sewers being dug, or streets paved, or homes lighted. No, they want scenic highways, hotels, the fronts of hospitals which may or may not have one bed inside. Anything that is smart and advanced and that will look good in Kodachrome. And Yankee investors are exactly the same. . . ."

"Look, Pepe, it all works together. We buy the lots at about a quarter of value, we buy them all. You sit tight, out of sight for a couple of years, and all suddenly the Government discovers that it's another earthly paradise, one of Mexico's natural beauty spots, and you'll have highways, urban development, public works, tourist promotion, everything you want. You'll at least double . . ."

". . . and the damn fool decided to go see for himself whether that road, which was already on the maps and which had cost thirty million, was really there. And of course all he found was cornfields . . ."

". . . why did Rio de Janeiro go down? Simply because they cleaned the Casino. Quitandinha became a white elephant. The same thing is going to happen in Acapulco if gambling isn't legalized there. The offshore gambling boats don't make enough to . . ."

". . . let's not deceive ourselves: the only organized force is the clergy, and they are willing to go along with . . ."

Chico ran among them, showing dirty post cards. Then he cried, "Saturday morning a hundred girls straight from Spain are coming!"

Lopitos added, "You hear, from *Spain*. No more Beverley Hills gringas, half fucked out at thirty. No sir, fresh imported . . ."

"And the children?" asked Robles.

"Gone back to the Dominicans' school in Canada," Pepe replied. "Sara misses them. Doesn't Norma like canasta?"

Chico appeared wearing a bra stuffed with oranges, a fruit bowl on his head. Robles moved toward the group in the middle of the room.

"Régules is the man to move for us. We stay on the side. If we have to oppose the operation publicly, Régules is willing to expose himself and be the target. It happens that he would enjoy a couple of years in Europe; things with his wife haven't been going so well, and . . . Hello, Robles."

Robles nodded.

"Look, we're just talking about the need to create the impression that a certain investment you know about is a public benefit. It's better if the announcement comes from a private institution."

Robles nodded again, and in the door he met Roberto Régules.

"Hello, banker. I just saw your wife at Bobó's. Will you be at the links tomorrow?"

Robles nodded, and with a nervous finger, standing very straight, he signaled his chauffeur.

Through all their brains the same alcohol and the same forgetfulness flows, along with the same dilute blood; now beggars are horsed, and now all those so important little details of pins and handkerchief points, perfume and gesture and quotation, are all swirled together in the common pool of mutual jelly; cling to each other, the Mexican hallmark of good breeding, cling together, cling together at the same spas, the same Cap d'Antibes, the same San Sebastián, the same Mexico City; change backdrops, but the world is not changed, we know all excellent secrets and values, we're something, brother, something. We have every right to stomp on whomever we care to.

Jungle rhythm flooded the party *píntame de colores pa' que me llamen Supermán, ay Su-per-mán, pa' que me digan ahhmi Tarzán, nené.* Delquinto downed his submarine chug-a-lug and Juliette followed suit, her arms high, her eyes unblinking. *me llaman loco, porque soy un poco, y también borracho, porque tomo ron* Cuquis dropped her eyes and shook her shoulders *eeepa, pa' que me llamen Supermán, caaaaballero.*

Silvia Régules left without good-byes, Gloria Balceta came in with her lips parted and her head high, Charlotte handed someone the telephone and ran to embrace Lally. "Before everyone I say it: this women is perverse, she has hurt me terribly, but . . . I adore her!" *así, así, a ver, gózala, caaaabellero, ay tu verá, nené.* Cuquis was dancing penguin style, her hands like flippers.

"Licenciado Tortosa," asked Gus, with a hand on his hip, "as a Marxist-Christian, don't you feel a little ashamed in this Armageddon atmosphere?" *ay minué minué minué, lo bailaba el siglo quince y ahora en el cincuenta y uno*

"Nihil humanum me alienum puto," Tortosa exclaimed ecstatically.

"Ooooo, always so indirect! The Greeks, you know, believed that harmony . . ."

quién es? quién es? Pachito 'e Ché, le dicen al señor

"Inderweltsein."

la televisión, pronto llegará, aaay, no, no, no, no

"The intellectual's place is in the field."

pabarabatibi cuncuá, neeegro, pabarabatibi cuncué

"He tries to make me sleep with my garter belt and stockings on, can you believe it?"

Delquinto was feeling up his Juliette; he kissed the nape of her neck, he exposed her breasts, squeezed her belly, while his watchers howled, Bobó and Charlotte and Lally and the young women wearing spectacles and the philosopher Estévez. "Look at her, my Juliette, do you think she's a mysterious creature with a past? She is simply an idiot, vulgar, ignorant, snatched by my own hand from the School of Odontology, and she is dying of fear here . . . grrrrr!"

Bobó, laughing until he cried, made the lights whirl dizzily, made them scissors that cut all profiles, brown, red, purple, while Countess Aspacúccoli headed for the kitchen and Cuquis mamboed a conscript strut and Supratous crawled after her on his knees. Smoke clouded, naked arms waved through it like the ganglia of other life, and Delquinto pawed her: "Infamous whore! May earth cover your grave with boils and your ghost never drink . . ."

ay Supermán, ay Supermán

"My dear, Mexico is the Nietzschean tropics!"
cuando se murió Dolores, murió siendo señorita, cero jit, cero carrera, cero error

"Propertius!" Dardo Moratto cried jubilantly: "Propertius! *Terra tuum spinis!*"
ya se va, la clave azul, se va al son del marabú

Squeezed into pajamas of a thinner time, Bobó finished the last bottle of cognac with the absolute sadness of a fallen Goth. He breathed in air sour with cigarette butts and liquor-wet rugs and grunted, "Fear the Greeks, Bobó, fear the Greeks."

Then on all fours he began to gather up matches sprinkled over the floor. Eleven in the morning. Cars roared by on Insurgentes, on Niza, where mansions from the epoch of Porfirio Díaz had begun the quick decline toward pharmacies, beauty parlors, shops. The sun beat down. No breeze stirred Reforma's graceful tree crowns. From the ninth floor of a rose-stone building which soared between two melancholy mansard roofs, Federico Robles stared over the unsteady city's pastiche. Vaporous glass façades showed him their backsides of painted brick and beer advertisements. In the distance, at the foot of the mountains, a whirlwind of dust collected its brown atoms. Here, near, laborers blasting, air-drilling a street away. Wreathes of secretaries and paunchy sidewalk vendors and skirt-watchers wove among files of beggars and elderly gringos in open shirts who told stories about Kansas City to other elderly gringos who told stories about Peoria. They ran, watching their watches, brave men dressed in gray, tattered brief cases under their arms.

One more, One more, signaled the fingers of peso-cab drivers. Cars raced, zigzagging, squeezed into packs, *tan-tar-ran-ta-tan-tan*. Their horns woke Rodrigo Pola; the city's impenitent racket filtered through cracks into his inside room on Rosales Street. On the roof of her home surrounded by the hills of Las Lomas, Norma Larragoiti de Robles spread cushions and made herself comfortable on them, took off her silk wrapper, and with care, aware of the smallest of her pores, anointed her body with an opal oil. Sun tan. Hortensia Chacón, forever in darkness, waited for sounds from Tonalá Street, waited for the moment when the school would let out in the afternoon, and for the sound of a key in its lock. And on Avenida Mixcoac men were opening a new way through wine stores and third-rate movies and little sals-stalls and the roar of steamrollers and air-hammers and asphalt heaters, slowly and dustily, but none of that reached the sealed room where Rosenda Pola slept, as always in delirium, captive of a lucidity that could not be put alive into the world, that clotted and stuck inside her trembling emaciated throat. Charlotte, Pierrot, Silvia Régules, Gus, Prince Vampa, Pichi, Junior, all were sleeping. Only Pimpinela de Ovando was ready for the new day, straight and perfumed, wearing dark glasses and walking along Madero toward Roberto Régules's office. From Robles's high window, Mexico City spread itself like a fanned deck of playing cards . . . the Ace of Spades at Santo Domingo Street, the trey of hearts in Polanco . . . from the dark tunnel of Mina, Canal del Norte, and Agentina, mouth open, searching for air and light while coughing up lottery tickets and gonorrhea carriers, to the straight but not strait propriety of Reforma, indifferent to the crowded minor vices of Roma and Cuauhtémoc's brittle-faced rising walls. From his office Robles looked down

40

upon ungainly cluttered rooftops and thought about pointless awakenings: bleary-eyed tubs, rickety flowerpots. Robles liked to lean out his window and smell the flea circus hopping below without being bitten by all the necessary nobodies and all the nonentity weavers of life who passed oblivious to skyscrapers and to Federico Robles. Two worlds: clouds and excrement. Encased in glass, isolated, privileged, he always traveled from his colonial-style home, grill-windowed, the entrance spumy with meringue stonework, to his auto, from his auto to the iron and nickel elevator, from the elevator to the great window and the leather chairs; and just by touching a button, he could reverse the trajectory. "I have a right to it, a right to it, I've earned it," he would say as he brushed off his coat. "It's not easy to isolate yourself in this damn city. They're all bankrupts, bankrupts forever." He looked at his rosy fingernails: those hands had scratched dirt in Michoacán with the tenacity of a fixed fate. Into distance again: from the smoke over the Buenavista yards to the bridge, and farther, to the Basilica of Guadalupe. Standing on the bridge, smoking, Gladys García let her stinky cigarette drop onto the roof of a tin and pasteboard yard shanty. And near the yards, at the other extremity of the dust, Gabriel was pitching coins while waiting for his buddies, Beto, Tuno, and Fifo, to celebrate his homecoming. While Rosa Morales was looking through the undertaker establishments of her neighborhood for a cheap coffin, and Juan, on a stone table in the Red Cross morgue, his lips crusted with blood and wine, awaited her.

A fist pounding his door jerked Rodrigo from lethargy. Groaning, protesting, he threw the heavy covers off and slowly swung his feet to the splintery floor. The pounding went on, accompanied by a detestable, urgent, and uncomprehending whooping. At last he pulled together effort enough to get up. Ixca Cienfuegos's coal eyes greeted him with that murky merry look, quite careless of all feelings, which always irritated Rodrigo. Cienfuegos came in, and holding his nose with two fingers, ran to open the little windows that let sun enter from a damp cookery-smelling inner patio.

41

"Gas?" Cienfuegos asked, and answered, "But not yours. Haven't you noticed it yet? You can't call your life you own." With bellowing laughter he hurled a midday paper at Rodrigo's head. Rodrigo ducked, fell on the bed face down. It seemed that Cienfuegos had seized that small bedroom between his hands and remoulded it, pushing the walls back, pushing everything back as it had been before, except that what had been gold was now copper. Murdering sleep. With one laugh wiping away the society of ghosts.

"Tell me, tell me about it," Cienfuegos insisted. "Cut loose and talk. Isn't that what you want, someone to listen? Don't hold back. Talk."

"Don't make me think," Rodrigo murmured. Face down, he was staring at the newspaper, which was slowly sucking up a little puddle dripped from the ceiling: three magnates stuffing themselves in a restaurant, the Pox-girl had been picked up, crime of passion. Hard, carcass hard and guts tough. Last night, gagging within four walls. And now just the same here, scratching my itch with my fingernails, looking at the faces of three fat bankers . . . Rodrigo jumped up laughing: one of them, pearl in his necktie, highball in his puffy hand, was Robles.

Norma opened her eyes in sunlight and wished that her pupils would burn to ash. She shut them and watched a fugue of blue points and yellow flashes that grew like waves in a stone-splashed pool. Sun gathered on her lips. The sun was kissing her. She wanted to remember, remember her kisses, and she opened her eyes and sat up abruptly: she had always wanted others to remember her, she herself had never thought of remembering anyone. And now she felt, not fear but abuse, depreciation: now she would have to begin to remember while others were forgetting. She spread her nostrils to breathe the honeysuckle fragrance from the garden. It was the same as the fragrance of that other, smaller garden where she had celebrated her seventeenth birthday. Did anyone, anyone except herself remember that evening? Was anyone at this moment or at any moment remembering any of her life? She stretched an arm and got the bottle of oil while sun attacked its own light reflecting back from her shining body, the shimmering brown points of her breasts.

Manuel Zamacona opened the windows of his little apartment on Guadalquivir and closed his eyes, moaning. He held his head between his hands and sat, short of breath, on a leather sling-chair. He wanted to put together the pieces of words left from last night, but all that danced in the memory of his astigmatic eyes was the black unstained skin of Negro drummers and the tobacco swirl of Miss Dior and deodorants. "Paradox, metaphor, imagination, to what a chasm you lead!" he muttered, and jumped to a looking glass framed by a tin star, to see his ears burn. He smiled and went to his work table. He took out paper and pen. He looked toward Reforma, trying to discover a new color, a new air in all that was familiar. He began to write, "Mexico," with spirit, "Mexico," with fury, "Mexico," with hatred and pity, and "Mexico" again and again until the page filled and he began another and filled it, too, and then he went out on his balcony, wadded the sheets of paper, and with all his might hurled them at the center of the sun, sure that they would hit it and be burned; and then he seized a flowerpot and threw it at the sun, too. He wanted rocks, a thousand of them, and all he heard was the smash of the pot on the sidewalk below, all he saw was one geranium squashed flat by a tire.

He sat at his work table. He recalled that this elegant and spacious corner of the Paseo de la Reforma had been modeled, at the suggestion of the Empress Carlotta, after Brussels' Avenue Louise. He watched the fugitive passing of a family of Indians, floating, unhappy. Heard the sobbing breath of a child, smelled chili-sprinkled corn on the cob, lemon-sprinkled slices of jicama, whatever came through his open window. At the level of his eyes a five-story apartment building hanging over its concrete piles, aerial in polychrome glitter of glass and mosaic. Contrast? No. He took up his pen:

Eccentricity rather than contrast. It could be our word: eccentricity. We do not feel ourselves part of any rational system we can feed or be fed by. Locked inside cloisters, backs turned on

43

the world, we Mexicans cannot feel that either our works or our soul enter any logical order comprehensible to others and to ourselves. Spain: eccentricity, yes, but within Europe. Its eccentricity is regret for not having taken part in all that by right belonged to it. What frustrated its realization? What closed the door to European participation on a nation that today lives shut off from all expressions of intelligence? And that is the pain, the regret, Spain's eccentricity, queerness. And Russia is queer in opposing Europe, affirming a Russian excellence based precisely on the pretense of standing before Europe and being different, and this makes Russia eccentric; to pretend that Europe's rejection of her is a *sui generis* being, Russia gives up such being and accepts the European challenge and learns the roads which will lead to equality with Europe . . . roads that wind after what is gone. Mexico is the only world radically cut off from Europe which has to accept the fatality of Europe's complete penetration and use the European words for both life and faith, although the being of her life and faith are of a different language. Thus is our fate worse than death . . . death is a natural happening. Murdered, brutally tortured, the forms which belong to her being lopped away. Everything since has been the search, locked, blind, marginal, for some meeting between what we are and the forms that must be used to express our mute being.

He examined his face, reflected in the window. A fine-drawn profile, thin aggressive nose, the lips almost straight lines. A silhouette lightly pressed upon thick bones and dark flesh.

"Not to know what our origin is. The blood beginning. But does such a thing as an 'original' blood exist? No: every pure element grows and is consumed in its own purity, does not develop; the original is the impure, the mixed, the mulatto and the mestizo, as I am, as all Mexico is. Which is to say, originality supposes a mixing, a creation, not a purity previous to our experience. Rather than born original, we come to be original; origin is creation. Mexico must find her origin by looking ahead, not behind. Cienfuegos thinks of going back, falling to the beginning, and that that meeting with the past will be our revelation of what we are. No: we have to create our beginning and our

44

originality. I myself do not know the springs of my blood; I do not know my father, only my mother. Mexicans never know the father! Besides, they want to know only tho mother, to protect, defend her. The father belongs to the hazy past, an object of scorn, the violator of our own mother. He who did what we may never do: conquered our mother."

He went on dissecting his reflected face. Yes, there his mother was: Creole, whose features were molded with care for the foreseen crossbreeding. And behind, the shaping, forming native being of his father. "The dark background flesh, self-creating, isolated. When will we rescue it? When will we give it name? A being no longer anonymous."

He stood and lit a cigarette. His eyes passed around the room: leather slingchairs, disorderly shelves, tack-boards covered over with reproductions of native art: realism concentrated in the throats of Olmecan votive axes, ceremony abstract in shaped stone from Oxkintok, the vital sensuality of primitives, the burning coldness of everything wholly Aztec. "Barbarism's summit," Manuel thought. "The barbaric not as a defect or by a defect but as the perfection of its mode, complete, anterior to and very far from the idea of personality. Being for the cycles, food for the sun, life under the sign of uncreated nature. No, they're all wrong, all this explains us only in part. And it is not possible to resuscitate it. For better or worse, Mexico is something else now."

He returned to the table and his pen. "Constants. The Mexican people's intuitive gestation, never surrendering to the forms imposed from without. Search for formal definition, juridical-political, which is the opposite to search for being filiation, historical-cultural. Affirmation of definitions of form in anti-historical projects based upon importation, the irrational imitation of prestigious models. Negation of the past as the first supposition of all proposed panaceas."

But what is the true model, the true form which can really cure, that Mexico must follow? he thought immediately. Which should he himself imitate? Not without humor, he thought of his religious possibilities, his artistic possibilities, his animal alternatives. He bit his pen and took a fresh sheet. "What is

45

the order of living values? If it were objective, we would have no problems. But it isn't; each of us gives first place to his own powers. But let us suppose, hypothetically, that the scale *is* objective and that the highest degree of human perfection *was* attained, let us say, in Leonardo da Vinci. What should be encouraging is that there is clearly less difference between any man and Leonardo than between any man and a chimpanzee. It would be easier for any man to attain the being of a great artist than for a chimp to attain the being of any man. However, now a good Christian appears and tells us that between Jesus and any man there is less difference than between Jesus and Leonardo. Would it therefore be easier to approach an imitation of Christ than one of Leonardo? Or are we in reality treating of two mutually exclusive lines of value? The fact is that we take any man as presupposed in both, and at moments one wishes to attempt the Jesus possibility, and at other moments, the Leonardo. The lines of one's own value are left trembling: five days of Leonardo against three of Jesus! As if my strength could be directed toward first one and then the other standard, without ever marching backward. Besides, why not direct them all toward the standard of the chimp? It is easier to fall than to climb, and, although there is less difference between your being and Leonardo's or the being of Christ, than between your being and that of a chimp, you will reach the chimp state before the others. Clearly, these ideas ought not to be expressed so crudely. We would better say, 'There isn't time enough for perfection. Time, indeed, merely moves us further from our original perfection.' This is what Cienfuegos must believe. *Ergo*, we allow ourselves to fall, with the rationalization that when we hit bottom, we will find our forgotten original Super-being. And this is what usually passes for progress, for spiritual progress rather than material, and one becomes satisfied with very simple propositions, much too sure of his basic goodness to need to apologize for what he is: the search for a measure which is neither Jesus nor Leonardo leads only to the chimp disguised as a Noble Savage, Siegfried, Scipio Africanus, or pristine communism. Progress must be found in an equilibrium between what we are and can never cease to be and what we may, without sacrificing our being, try to become. . . ."

A noise broke his thought. He put his nose out the window and saw with what strength a repulsive-faced, low foreheaded, greasy haired, thick lipped carrier was shouldering a water carafe; then the carafe slipped and shattered on the sidewalk. The carrier crossed himself piously and sat on the fender of the truck and began to sing as he wiped sweat from his tiny forehead:

> "You're a beauty, little woman,
> It would be better if you died."

Manuel wrinkled his eyebrows and returned to his writing. "Ours is a land which has had redeemers, its anointed, its higher-being men. But perhaps they disappeared because of the abundance of chimps they had to face. They succumbed. Mexico has never had a successful hero. To be heroes, they had to fail. Cuauhtémoc, Hidalgo, Madero, Zapata. The hero who triumphed, Cortés, is not accepted as such. This may be extended to the nation itself: has Mexico ever accepted itself as triumphant? No, we taste and take seriously only our defeats. Victories are converted into empty holidays; Cincode Mayo. But the Conquest, the war with the United States. . . . Who really won the war of 1847? Victory seemed to go to the United States, but without saying it, Mexicans see that as the triumph of brute force, materialism, excessive growth, and the downfall of human values. Mass-produced automobiles versus gourd drinking. Et cetera. Mexico's defeat, on the other hand, led us to truth, to honor, the correct limits of a man of culture and good will. What wins is not valor but the contrary. Consequently, what wins is not always good, and what loses is not always evil. Good may not be identified with victory, nor evil with defeat. For otherwise the United States would be good and Mexico evil. What is of importance is the intensity of feeling, not any practical result. But if the feeling of hatred is evil and the feeling of love, good, we fall back into a Manichaeanism based not upon practical but

47

upon sentimental considerations. Everything Mexican is, by sentiment, excellent. And everything foreign, judged as to sentiment, is evil."

He bit his pen and thought: a sense of inferiority? Smiling, he wrote: "What is a sense of inferiority? Only the awareness of a disguised superiority. In simple superiority there exists no anxiety about self-justification. Our inferiority is only the unrecognized awareness of an excellence which others have not learned to apprehend, a conjunction of high attainments which unfortunately do not as yet make themselves obvious and earn us respect abroad. So long as this real superiority of the Mexican goes unremarked, Mexicans feel inwardly that they must dissimulate and pretend that we have made others' values our values. The last accessible milepost of European progress, the Industrial Revolution, is being born in Mexico day by day. Superiority by fiat. Nevertheless there is some truth to that, for we have to look forward. It is only that 'forward' does not mean European and Yankee forms of being, which, although they are still vigorous, are really only the expressions of a last stage. Unfortunately, the Mexican *bourgeoisie* does not see this, and its only desire at the moment is to assume, as quickly as possible, the classic shape of a capitalist *bourgeoisie*. We are always too late to our banquets. And yet . . . today we could have open eyes and prepare ourselves, we need no different powers than we have and no point of view more basic than our present experience, to create from the root and in reality a new social structure and philosophy. Has not the Revolution brought us nearer such understanding? But what can we do when the Revolution gives itself over voluptuously to the tickling of a hedonism unprecedented in Mexico? This is the problem: real power. While real power has never been so great, at the same time it has never been so unproductive of human values. What does the 'real power' of a man like, say, the banker Robles, what does it represent except a gathering of power for its own sake, without the least admixture of value? The disjunction is monstrous, for if any value is a human value, it is precisely power in its broadest meaning. When power has not value, it becomes something very dangerous: its exercise, in whatever manner, ceases to be responsible. Value-Power-Responsibility are the great trinity, tied one to the other by nature and by God. Power without value and responsibility is wasted in dispersion. We stand at the crossroad. Which, of all the roads, shall we choose? Above all, Mexico, so weighted with confused events, with contradictory being and life. Will it be possible for her to choose, to choose her own road, or will she be spavined by the criminal blindness of those who choose for her?"

He did not want to write more. He stared at the sun. He felt small and ridiculous: small and ridiculous was how any man had to feel when he tried to explain anything about Mexico. Explain? No, he said to himself. One does not explain Mexico. One believes in Mexico, with fury, with passion, and in alienation. He folded the sheets of paper and stood.

"But I want to have some value in myself," Rodrigo said, looking under his bed for his shoe.

"What for? What a man is doesn't matter, only his label. Señor President. Señor Director. Señor Label X or whatever." Cienfuegos yawned and put the teapot on the electric hot plate. "On the other hand, does it make any sense to kill yourself? Here, in Mexico, I say? Unless you do it ironically because of the very good chance that at any moment you may be killed by someone else?" He crossed his arms and waited for the pot to boil.

Rodrigo slowly pulled his shoes on. The cigarette dangling between his lips bothered him. Smoke clung to his face, he squinted his eyes. "Words don't help, Ixca. Last night's temptation comes back now. But that's all it was, just a temptation. Two temptations. Last night's, and to go on living. I don't know . . . but I see everything. The thousands of petty days searching for the little throne, the quick short-breathed introduction, Lady X. Everything is so damn little and mean. I've fucked myself, Ixca. I really have."

"No. You've just had small successes."

Rodrigo's languid gaze went on scanning ink (THE HOPELESS

SITUATION OF OUR CATTLE INDUSTRY) with all the spiritual re-
sources of the Santa Madre church

> While the case was being clarified
> Susanah, her little girl with her,
> Was sent reluctantly to the Pen last night.

Speeding taxi smashes up. Juan Morales, driver of a cab, et
cetera, collided last night with a bus of the, et cetera, wife and
three children suffered superficial contusions, et cetera, autopsy
revealed he had been drinking, et cetera, a family left in poverty
as the consequences of this new proof of carelessness by, et
cetera, city cabdrivers.

With one movement he tore up the paper. But the jukebox on
the corner began to howl *pasito tum tum tum tum pasito* and
someone was noisily sweeping the corridor. He put out his arm
and found an open bottle of warm beer and turned it up to his
lips and then spat: a cigarette had been dropped inside. "No,
I'm really fucked. You were there, do you remember the days
in college when I published *Lavender Verse?*"

He couldn't go on. His excuses for not dying had become all
mixed; that was one he had phrased and saved and relied on
for such a long time, and now suddenly its name, two words,
Lavender Verse, had destroyed it. He fell on the bed, and almost
bouncing up and down, holding back tears, he roared at the
immobile Cienfuegos: "*Lavender Verse!* Oh, my God! Doesn't
that make you die laughing? And what else, what else, tell me,
what else?"

"Anything you want, Rodrigo. Even the crack-up."

"Don't you know that I can't sit down and string a dozen
sentences together without stealing ten of them from the last
ten essays I've read—or the last miserably translated novel?
Doesn't the whole world know that that is what Rodrigo Pola
writes, goulash, served up in yesterday's dirty soup bowl?"

He buried his face in the yellow pillow, and Cienfuegos
poured two steaming cups of tea. "Suppose you had always won.
With Norma, with the critics, money——"

50

"No," said Rodrigo, raising his head. "No, I would have smashed everything. That's the power of my weakness. Suicide! Sure, the biggest joke of all. Kill yourself, because at a party thrown by one Bobó, a character with peroxide hair, a sort of eunuch, they laughed at you, Ixca, they pissed on me, you saw them, don't lie."

"So you were pissed on one more time, Rodrigo. Not the first."

"And you know it. Who doesn't? What a goddamn laugh: the youthful bard, hope for Mexico's lyric future! Shit."

Cienfuegos placed the cups on the chair and took Rodrigo by the shoulders. "And today you have to decide, you understand, eh? Choose between one and the other, and no more living in between."

"What else do you offer? Who the hell cares!"

"They all care, even those who never understand us. Those to whom you can say *yes* or *no* by your silence. Those to whom you yourself deny your smile or forgiveness. Plenty care, Rodrigo, who will never know about your decision. Once you join us, your eyes will be opened to tears sadder and more naked than any you have ever wept yourself, you'll walk carrying lead inside your chest. Or if you choose to stand against us, you'll be clear-cut and shining and unique, alone and surrounded by the many and your own sense of belonging. With us, you will be anonymous, brother in solitude. There, on the other side, you'll have your own name, in the mass of names you'll be safe, never attacked by anyone. Choose."

Rodrigo squeezed his hands. "You don't understand, Ixca. I don't believe, I don't believe——"

Erect, Cienfuegos jerked Rodrigo's hands apart. "Choose . . . and remember."

"Memories . . . ." I am Rodrigo Pola.

And more, more.

The place of my conception.

And more.

"Success is always for others, not for me, Ixca. Isn't that true? Norma and Federico, even Bobó, Pedro Caseaux." Why is it for them?

And those who did not reach it? Who never had the chance to, who had to give Mexico more than life: their no-lives, their no-words? Who never had the chance to waste life? The opportunity to give up anything?

Two shores.

Which will never meet.

Jungle shore of feathers and knives and gold headdresses. And the hard shore of laws and whips, the shore of all Mexicans——

Dead.

And the other shore of all Mexicans who are——

Living.

Shore of the abiding dream, the slumber of many suns. And the shore of unfilled ears of corn, shrunken bodies, and dry water.

And in the middle, the city.

Treasury of monies and bones and titles, borne on rickets-warped legs. Here those who live, who have had to renounce . . . There, spreading their arms, those who never had the chance to renounce. My father.

Gervasio Pola. And will you die, Rodrigo, will you and Federico and Norma and all of you die without ever knowing those who spread their arms? Memory, Rodrigo. It is born and dies between two moons and a shocked gaze searches.

The spike with which we crucify ourselves; that spike is always a man, my father.

"Do you remember him?"

"My father." My father, my father.

GERVASIO POLA

A March night in 1913, the air heavy with dust, a bright moon scarring the Valley of Mexico. Enrique Cepeda, Governor of the Federal District, arrived at Belén prison: thirty armed men got out of cars, wiping their noses on their sleeves, rolled and lit cigarettes, polished their leather buttons against their thighs; the bald-head, Islas, yelled to the prison sentries, "The Governor of the District is here!"

52

Cepeda swaggered up to the first officer who appeared and bellowed, "The Governor of the District is here."

General Gabriel Hernández was in his cell, sleeping. Oil eyes and obsidian mask face trembled to the kick of a black boot. "Get up. Dress." Gabriel Hernández raised his small Mongoloid body and from the corner of his eye saw the squad waiting outside his cell. "To the yard!" ordered the subwarden.

Brown air, gray walls, Belén. The high bullet-pocked execution wall. Cepeda, Islas, Casa Eguía, offering each other cigarettes, guffawing while General Gabriel Hernández, boxed in by the firing squad, advanced across the yard.

"If I had a gun, you would not murder me now."

Cepeda's fat hand slashed across Hernández's face.

Fivo volleys, punctuated by the Governor's echoing laughter. With the last volley, he stopped laughing and touched his hand to the ground. "Build the pyre here." He leaned back against the wall.

As fire consumed the body of General Gabriel Hernández and the stench of roasting flesh darkened Cepeda's face, Gervasio Pola was leading three fellow prisoners in escape, hidden in a covered garbage cart.

During that journey from Belén to the dump, Gervasio Pola thought that the dead must feel as he felt, wanting to shriek that in reality they were living, had not died, but were only suffocated by mute pestilence and a transient rigor, the coffin should not be nailed around them, earth should not be clodding down upon it. Four men, four mouths pressed to four cracks between boards on the cart-bed, tombed under refuse, their lungs congesting with rotted vegetables and excrement, all their terror concentrated in the act of breathing. One of them alternately panted and sobbed, wasting air the others would have liked to steal. The cart rolled on. Finally it stopped. Gervasio Pola elbowed the man beside him. They waited for the cover to be thrown open, pitchforks to dig into the filth, night to breathe coolness on their sweat.

The two garbage men did not resist. They tied them to the spokes of the cartwheels. They were in a field near San Bartolo.

Mounds of refuse, soft, gray, crusted with flies, stretched all the way from the road to the first hill. Gervasio Pola looked at his companions' filth-smeared faces, filth-soggy bodies, and was overcome by dejection. "Between now and tomorrow to reach a Zapata camp," said one of them. Gervasio Pola stared at Froilán's bare feet, Pedro's feeble naked legs, at Sindulfo's ankles, rubbed raw by shackles, infected and suppurating. Moonlight glinted on their toenails. Jewels against the dark garbage earth. Wind from the hills passed across the hummocked dump plain. A route had to be chosen. Gervasio moved off toward the ridge.

In Indian file the three followed, followed both Pola and habit. Here on the level their feet sank deep into loam and grass; there, when the climb began, their flesh would be scratched, thorns would tap their blood. At the foot of the mountain, Gervasio dropped. A dry wind was creaking through the dry scrub. "All we can do," he said without looking up, "is split up. We'll stay together until Tres Marías. Then Pedro and I will turn off, easy going but we'll have the Federal outposts to miss. You, Froilán, you know Morelos better than the rest of us, you'll take Sindulfo and strike left. If we don't find the camp by dark, we'll split up again, every man for himself, and hide until dawn, or wait until a Zapata detachment comes along. If none comes, I'll be seeing you back in Belén."

"Sindulfo won't last with that crippled foot," said Froilán Reyero. "Better give me Pedro and you take Sindulfo, Gervasio."

"Better we stick together no matter what happens," Sindulfo interrupted.

Pola raised his head. "You heard me. One of us at least must save his skin. For us to die together isn't so important as that one of us not die. We'll do what I said."

Cold began to lash their chests, announcing the end of rotund midnight, the oncoming of small-houred dawn. Gervasio led them up a path that rose, twisting, through the wild cricket-voiced sierra.

Sometimes immensity does not make men little. Gervasio felt that with his band of three he formed a heroic phalanx and that their bare feet, now dragging up mountain paths, would come to thunder like a multitude, to clang like steel helmets until the sierra's vastness shrank to insignificance and cringed rather than towered before their advance. Pine trees scattered the rising sun, and the four men climbed on. Pola looked back at the dry Valley of Mexico; it was shrouded by distance. They did not speak, the climb was slow, but:

Look, Froilán: who could have told you that once you were in the mountains, you would feel even more alone and imprisoned than in your cell? What broke in you in Belén? I remember the night I heard the first shrieks. So many first nights, so many dawns. All the same, each new. A first night of shrieks. The first dawn of drums and volleys in the yard. They came to be all alike, those noises, the uniforms. But now I know that each was different. And I was never the first, nor the next, the hour never came for me to stand and tell them that I was ready, unafraid, that there was no need to blindfold me. Always waiting for it. I wish it had happened, so I could have shown them who I was. They never let me. Others died . . . sobbing, leaping, begging mercy. But they never let me show them that I was there in solitary, waiting to spit their mercy at their faces. And every man who went to the wall left me waiting, wishing I could go in his stead, with my head high, at the same time wanting to stay in my cell. I gave them death as a gift I would have liked to keep, and every time I' could have substituted myself. But the march from solitary to the wall never happened for me. It was never granted. And something in me broke.

Pedro cut his foot on a piece of glass. He bit his lip: Cut, let every blade and edge cut, let my blood spatter dust on the ridges; but don't let me be alone. Together, we'll make it. They caught us together, and if they catch us again, let us be together. It will end when they shoot the four of us together. But don't let me be alone.

And Sindulfo was not thinking, but only reaching his hands down time after time, trying to rub his ankles without breaking stride.

They stopped, at midday, near the highest summit, but not yet so high as the mist. They sat in the shade of a pine.

55

"We need water to bathe Sindulfo's ankles," said Froilán Reyero.

"Stop thinking about water," said Sindulfo, his head down.

"Stop thinking about food." Gervasio laughed.

Pedro murmured, "Food . . ."

"Cut it," Gervasio snapped.

"We're almost to Tres Marías."

"Yes. We must split up now."

"I don't like it, Gervasio. I don't like it."

"You know Morelos better than we do. Don't be scared. The one who will have trouble is me."

"Somebody's going to have trouble if we all four make it." Froilán rubbed his limp mustache.

"Every man for himself, we'll all make it," said Gervasio. His eyes stared down at boulders.

"There was an old man at home who wanted to die by himself. They said that was what he'd always wanted. He planned it, death would never take him by surprise, and when he felt it coming, he sent everyone out of the house so he could meet it alone, enjoy alone what he had waited for so many years. And that night when death walked around him and its voice fell on him like bits of plaster, he dragged himself to the door with his eyes popped out, trying to tell someone what death was like. I saw it myself. I'd slipped into his garden to steal oranges. It made him feel good to have me watch him die, his face in the dust."

Pedro kept silent.

"What's missing is someone to talk to. Before, one minute before."

"Talk to a Federal."

"They don't give you time. They catch you alone, and that's it. Or they catch you with a comrade, and all you can do is exchange one look as you fall."

"What's missing is someone to forgive you," said Pedro.

Gervasio reflected that vultures already were forgiving him, earth was forgiving him for the insult of his change into fragments of dust, as worms pardon us for the nastiness we contribute

56

to their banquet. On his feet beneath a pine, stretching his hand toward the Valley of Mexico, at this moment he understood that far away from the hurts of his companions, far from the dust-lunged valley shackled to mournful earth, farther still, high over the ocean of mountains furrowed by drought and destruction; on the far shore of Mexico's massively indifferent world, lay salvation for men like himself, men stained with filth and exhaustion, absent from the memories of other Mexicans, but loyal, loyal to others only when loyal to themselves: today I shall save myself, myself, my own skin, so I can save others tomorrow. They would like me to die with them, one death for all, impersonal, common; that would comfort my three heroes. They believe that I would fulfill my duty, falling with them. They would even like me to die first, softening their deaths. I'm willing to save them if they will let themselves be saved. But only by saving myself can I save them today, and tomorrow, others.

"We saw it from the tower," Froilán was saying. "General Hernández, shot and burned. That's what we can expect, too, if they catch us again. Better here in the mountains, the four of us."

"I don't want to die," Sindulfo sobbed. "Not alone in the mountains and not in Belén surrounded by those bastards."

Pola returned to himself. He picked up a dry branch and beat Sindulfo across the shoulders. Light reflected from the valley softened the fury in his eyes. "You yellow-gutted blabber! Why do you have to shoot your mouth off? Don't you think we've got enough putting up with your goddamn crippled feet? So now you want to cry and screw us right? Shut up! Shut up!"

"All right, enough, enough, Gervasio . . . don't——"

"That's enough, Gervasio." Froilán grabbed his arm. Thin wisps of smoke were spiraling up here and there in the forest. The smell of dry pine and leaves burning.

"All right, let's get moving. They're cooking now, look at the smoke. Any one of those smokes may be a friend or an enemy. If all you want is to eat, head for any one you want to."

Near Tres Marías they separated, Froilán supporting Sindulfo, an arm around his waist. Gervasio went on with Pedro following, dejected, shivering, squeezing his arms in the cold mist.

The earth beneath their bare feet was clammy. The face of the earth was damp, steep, boulders and fir trees, it fought them, opposed their feet. The Federal outpost had to be circled, cold-stiffened soldiers warming in the smell of frying beans; they had to work through the Federals to the first Zapata outpost. At sundown, Pedro grabbed his belly with both hands and fell on his knees. He began to vomit. Twilight shadows were lengthening in the tangled forest shadow. Pedro, his face and eyes convulsed, wordlessly pleaded to rest, for a moment to catch his breath.

"Night is coming, Pedro. We have to stay together a little longer, then we split. Come on. Get up."

"Like General Hernández. First they shoot us, then they burn us. That's what's waiting for us, Gervasio. We better stay here in the mountains and die alone and with God. Where are we going? You tell me, Gervasio. Where are we going?"

"Don't talk. Give me your hand. Get up."

"Yes. You're the leader, the strong man. You know we have to walk, so you walk. But what you don't know is where. To Zapata? And then?"

"We're in a fight, Pedro. We don't have to think. Just fight."

"Fight without knowing why, as if we had no memory and no eyes. What's going to come out of it? You think it matters at all whether you and I fight? Right now, we're alone here, lost in the mountains, and I with my fever. Think man: what can we do here, you and I? What difference does it make what we do or say? Will one more sacrifice mean anything? Let's get out of it, Gervasio. Get out of the whole mess. Let the free wind blow over our heads. Nothing is going to change."

"So. What do you suggest?"

"Let's go to Cuautla. We can get clothes and money there. And then each one head for home."

"They'll hunt for you, Pedro, and they'll find you. You can't get out now. You don't want to be pushed, but I can't stop. There's no home for me to go to. There's no hideout in Mexico City. After it's all over, we'll all be alike. Each to his own place. The place he belongs."

"Afterward. Just as before."

58

"Don't ask. When you make a revolution, you stop asking. You just do your duty. That's all."

"Who's going to win? Seriously. Doesn't that ever make you think?"

"We don't know who's going to win. Everybody wins, Pedro. Everybody who is still alive. Those who live through it win. Come on now. Get up."

"My fever is back, Gervasio. Bats are crawling around in my stomach."

"Come on. Let's go. Night is falling."

Pedro got to his knees. "I can't go on."

When air filled with crickets and began to sigh through the cold hollows, Pedro's teeth chattered and he rubbed his arms. Night climbed all around them. "Don't leave me, Gervasio. Don't leave me. Only you can take me where I have to go. Don't leave me, for the sake of your mother don't . . ." He stretched his arm out, scratched his fingers through earth. "Take my hand. I'm cold. We'll warm each other." Trying to reach farther, he rolled over, face against the ground. "Gervasio! Say something, talk to me, it can't be you've left me here."

He wanted to see his hands and know that he was alive. Heavy fog covered the mountain. With his round eyes whirling, he shouted, "Gervasio! Let's go back to prison. I'm afraid of this mountain, I'm afraid to be free, unchained. Let them put my shackles on again, quick, Gervasio! Gervasio!"

His fingers tightened around his ankles, and for a moment he felt himself as a prisoner. I want to be the prisoner of men, not of cold and pain and night. Put my shackles on me, little mother, so I won't roll down the mountainside. I want to stay chained. I was born chained. That's the shame. . . . "Gervasio! Don't leave me alone! For the love of . . . Gervasio! Help me, Gervasio!"

His voice floated among the boulders.

Far down the mountain, Gervasio Pola ran toward the yellow flames of the Valley of Morelos.

General Inés Llanos wiped his fingers on his shirt and sat at the camp table. The olive-yellow hats and black eyes of his men shone in the night behind him.

"Help yourself, don't be bashful. Dig in. So you got away from Belén?"

"Yes, *mi generál*. I escaped alone and crossed the mountains in one day," Gervasio Pola said, blowing on his frozen hands. "I saved my skin. Now I am at your orders, to join General Zapata and continue the struggle against the usurper."

"Ah, how late and pointless that would be," General Llano laughed as he took another tortilla from the brazier. "Perhaps you haven't read? What the true Plan of Ayala says? There Madero is shown up for his lack of honesty and his complete weakness. So it is written, so it is written, eh. And who got rid of him? Why, my General Victoriano Huerta, who is now our commander. . . ."

"And Zapata?"

"To hell with Zapata. You stand before General Inés Llano, your servant, sir, and loyal servant of the legitimate government, and tomorrow you'll be on your way back to Belén. Now make yourself a sandwich. The trip is long and hot."

Gervasio Pola passed again between the gray walls of Belén. Scorched earth in the yard showed where General Hernández had been cremated. He stepped on the ashes, and it was then that his legs began to shake. In solitary, he tried to fall asleep. His eyes had just grown heavy when two officers entered.

Captain Zamacona, blond and tall, with carefully waxed mustaches, said, "There's no need to tell you that you are going straight to the wall." He kept his eyes on the ceiling. "But before you go, you're going to tell us where we can find the escaped prisoners Pedro Ríos, Froilán Reyero, and Sindulfo Mazotl."

"You will capture them anyway. What difference does it make?"

"We prefer to execute all four of you together, as an example and warning. That, or tomorrow you alone. Make up your mind."

The door closed with an iron clang, Gervasio listening to their heels tap down the stone floor of Belén's long corridor. A clois-

tered wind swirled through the bars. He threw himself down.
Tomorrow I stand before a firing squad alone; tomorrow, a skull
always hides in the corner of tomorrow . . . my legs began to fail
me when I walked over General Hernández's ashes; we will be a
bridge of ashes for the shoes of the condemned, Pedro will walk
upon mine, Sindulfo on Pedro's, Froilán on Sindulfo's; alone
against the wall and no way to say good-by except with our heels.
Marched there down the corridor at a small feeble hour, trying
to forget what I have known and to remember what I have forgotten. . . . Will there be time for repentance? No: I would need
a new life for that. Ay! what a vengeance you take on me. Here
we squat, tossing dice to learn whether we shall be heroes, and
at the end are all with the same thought: how we will feel when
one lead ball and then another and one more nail us in the belly
and chest. Will we notice our own blood dripping, or our eyes
popping out like onions. Will we know when the man comes near
us to deliver the *coup de grâce* in the nape of the neck and we
cannot speak and beg mercy. For we have already drained mercy,
little God, and now that we have drained it from ourselves, how
can we beg it of you? I'm afraid, saintly little God, I'm all fear
. . . and you will not die with me and I don't want to speak of my
death with those who will not die with me! I want to tell it only
to my comrades, so that our voices will fall silent together and
we will wall ourselves together, together, together.

He stood and shouted for the guard. "Call that captain!"

"I left Pedro on the mountain to the right of Tres Marías. He
had fever and he must still be there. Froilán and Sindulfo went
left, rugged terrain, and Sindulfo crippled, they can't have gone
far. None of us had eaten, and with the cold . . .

At dawn one Sunday, earlier than the clang of parish church
bells, Gervasio marched with bent head down the long hollow
corridor of Belén. He touched his shoulders, face, stomach,
testicles; his body had more right to live than he did, but it was
his body which would die. His eyes were hemmed in by the
guards around him. He wanted to remember everything, to remember all his life; the memory which came was of a bird wet-

ting its wings in a tropical river. He would have liked to leap to other images, women, his parents, his wife, the son he had never seen, but all he could see was the dripping bird. The squad stopped. From another cell came Froilán, Pedro, and Sindulfo. He could not see their faces, but he knew it was they. He realized that he was marching at the head of a file. They would die together. Dawn bathed his face. He was thinking that now, just as in the sierra, he felt himself a giant. They marched to the wall and about-faced into the muzzles of the firing squad.

"We saved ourselves together," Gervasio Pola murmured.

"Fucking death," Sindulfo breathed beside him. "It won't separate us long."

"No, we'll fall together," said Gervasio. He filled his lungs. "Give me your hand. Tell the others to hold hands."

Then he saw their eyes and felt that death had appeared to them first, and closed his own eyes so that life would not leave him before its time.

"*Viva* Madero!" Froilán shouted as the volley rang.

The captain moved to give the *coup de grâce* to four bodies twisting on the dust of Belén. "When are you going to learn to kill with one volley?" he growled at the firing squad, and studying the lines in his hand, he walked away.

My father . . . my father . . . my father . . .

A wisp of gas hissing from the inner patio past Rodrigo Pola's room, past the roof, up to the center of the sky, where it mixed with all the smells of the city. Along Madero, Pimpinela de Ovando walked erect and perfumed, her eyes concealed behind tinted lenses, on her way to Roberto Régules's office. Precise numerals wrote themselves inside her head, as upon a blackboard of air: three hundred shares. Four hundred and fifty thousand hectares. For Benjamín, a position in Robles's bank. The dinner at Aunt Lorenza's had been arranged. Régules was the road to the regaining of at least some of their land. The neat numerals erased themselves and Aunt Lorenza's face appeared, stained by memory and by years, floating upon other images: Porfirio Díaz and a landeau in front of the Hotel Porters; the Zócalo shadowed by trees; bonnet walls and roofs; words: For many years I have waited, patiently, for the people of the Republic to become capable of electing and changing government officials at the end of each electoral period without danger or fear of armed revolution, and today, I presume that this time has arrived. . . .

THE DE OVANDOS

"Foreseen?" . . . a lovely day, the great house—those mansard roofs which, like a scutcheon, proclaimed their rank, their good taste, their propriety—the great home on Hamburgo and a great reception in honor of the Marquis of Polavieja (in Doña Lorenza's unspoken thoughts the long years of graciousness struck their brightest light at precisely that moment); and then, exile imposed by loyalty. To Doña Lorenza it seemed a hint of a certain weakness of pride not to accompany Don Porfirio Díaz all the way to Paris, and live there; but Joaquinito opined that such ocean-crossing loyalty seemed excessive, and Don Francisco, quoting something about the virtue of the Golden Mean, elected to settle the family in New York City. There they satisfied duty while maintaining prudence. No one was at all worried about the haciendas.

Exile, he would say under his breath, for such as we is rather the rule than the exception, and only my obligation to be present at the celebration of the Centenniel kept me away from the coronation of George V, interrupting my delightful sojourn in England. I have in mind a pleasant flat on Park Avenue. Lorenza will make friends. Joaquinito will enjoy, he is an eccentric boy, horseback breakfasts with the Vanderbilts, summers at Newport. We are all calm; the storm will in any event not be long in subsiding. If Madero wants to remain in power, he will have to continue General Díaz's peaceful and honorable labor of consolidation; if he does not, Don Porfirio's return seems inevitable. Don't even his enemies say as much? "Díaz's private life is beyond reproach. As the father of a family he has devoted himself to the wise rearing of his children, which is shown by his daughters' great virtues and the activity, modesty, and correctness of his son; as a husband he is a model, according to his distinguished life companion, with all the tenderness and consideration which she so merits." Is he not the very keynote of modern Mexico? Can such an exemplar be toppled? Our magnificent structure of peace and progress cannot easily be destroyed; the revolution will result in no more than a flash in the pan, a puff of dust. Civil servants know that never have they been more bountifully remunerated, families of the middle class are more decently housed and clothed and fed than ever before. The country cannot in any event prosper if it is deprived of its leadership elite. Be who may at the helm of the government, little by little those elements which have understood how to guide the nation, to hold it to ways of material progress and administrative continuity, will be recalled.

Don Francisco made mental lists and with satisfaction judged that there were not in all Mexico better men than they, and behind the men, the names, stood the great firms which testified to the country's stature; Don Francisco repeated and savored— they were like the first solid proof of international equality— Mexico's first acceptance as peer by the great nations of the world:

Doheny, Pearson, C. P. Huntington
Moctezuma Copper Co.
Palmer, Sullivan, Batopilas, Nelson and Waller,
Creston-Colorado Gold Mining . . .

They could take with them only their most treasured momentos, those which had brought brightness into the great house on Hamburgo: paintings by Félix Parra and Alberto Feuster. The rose-colored city was left behind, the fragrance of dust and afternoon showers. The exile was begun.

When news of the Tragic Ten Days reached Park Avenue, Don Francisco ordered the family to pack; when Huerta consolidated his position, Don Francisco reluctantly reversed the order. But Joaquín was, as always, at some country house, and Don Francisco had been called to Chicago to a board meeting of the Sonora Land and Cattle Company, and when they returned to New York, it was too late, and Don Francisco by now had other news: a sugar refinery had been burned in Morelos, a train dyna-mited in Zacatecas. And then Don Francisco died of pneumonia and neither Doña Lorenza nor Joaquín knew how to administer the stocks and properties which had been filed only in the old man's memory, much less how to make them produce an income. Near Paris, in Neuilly, they had a house, and to it Doña Lorenza and her son moved in the autumn of 1916.

How pleasant to be speaking French! sighed Doña Lorenza, and that year Spanish was in effect dismissed from service at the villa. Here it was possible, Doña Lorenza observed as she ordered her butlers about, to receive again, to have teas, to live with grace. Here there is time and place for life. New York! Suffrag-ettes and Protestants! Presidents who shoot tigers! There is some-thing known as breeding. I shall never tire of repeating it to my son, there is something known as breeding, and few can distin-guish and appreciate it. The United States . . . *toujours quantité, jamais qualité*. Our spiritual homeland is here in Europe. I shall never tire of repeating it.

Neuilly became a reunion place for those Mexicans who, flee-ing chaos, were maintaining national dignity and demonstrating to their European friends that they knew how to distinguish the years of a Burgundy. France is, of course, at war, but one knows the difference between war waged by gentlemen and revolution waged by a rabble of Indians, sandaled and uncombed. At one of his mother's teas, Joaquín met a Mexican girl who could not speak Spanish, a fact which persuaded Doña Lorenza to arrange a marriage; in a short time the wedding took place in the church of St. Rôche. The good old days seemed back: so many familiar faces! Reading, rereading her invitation lists, Doña Lorenza found deep pleasure at each name which here, in bitter exile, continued to stand upon the validity of permanent principles and classes. Sometimes she thought that they had never really left Mexico City.

Joaquín's wife, Fernanda, was a stiff, severe, pallid girl, edu-cated by nuns in Switzerland, and she soon tired of Doña Lor-enza's incessant prattle and of the reminiscences of their frequent house guests. "*Je ne peux pas supporter tes mexicains folkloriques et leur pitoyable d'épave,"* she said to her husband between clenched teeth. Benjamín was born in 1924. From his first week his grandmother took him to sleep in her room among the family portraits. "It's all right for him to hear French, but just the same he must not forget that he is an Ortíz de Ovando. Your father, Joaquín, would have observed intelligently that Mexico cannot tolerate much more from those bandits in sombreros who are tearing her to pieces. . . . Here, this letter from your uncle—look, it seems that now our lands were never ours. And even if these Señors Carranza and Obregón are not gentlemen, it is certain that as soon as everyone gets tired of it all, which will be soon, they will call us home, and we have to be ready to assume our places again." Benjamín played in the Neuilly park, and at the age of two was entrusted to a Belgian nurse; but every night Doña Lorenza carried him to her bedroom, showed him the photographs, told him about their illustrious Indian-subduing ancestors: "This portrait is of Don Alvaro, Captain General of his province, who settled in New Spain about sixteen hundred twenty. And your great-grandfather, the Emperor's Prefect. This is a photo of our home on Hamburgo; your father grew up here. Look, your uncle when he was sent to the coronation of Alphonso XIII. And this, do you like it? It's the Pro Ecclesia Pontifice order which was conferred upon us by His Holiness."

Benjamín grew up, rolling a hoop, without friends, and when he puffed his chest out and shouted, *"Aux aztèques, aux aztèques!"* Doña Lorenza could hardly contain her pride and satisfaction.

When the boy was in his fourth year, his mother died, and Joaquín came back to the villa in Neuilly. With happy synchronization, the lawyer who was their administrator died, also. Joaquín installed himself in the library to grip the reins of the Ortíz de Ovando patrimony. To his surprise and delight, he discovered that the estate, far from diminishing, had grown under old lawyer Leselles, and Joaquín, widowed, in his forties, and also in a Paris of vanguardist poetry and of courtesans who, if they did not quite glow so splendidly as in 1915, were just as diverting and far less expensive than then, decided that the moment had come to invest his fortune in new interests, blessed be Lesseles, blessed be Don Francisco, blessed be haciendas and stocks! His administrative stint lasted only two days; it took no longer. Soon he was the famous South American millionaire in the gray hat who could both hire "Le Sphinx" for a whole night and recite Victor Hugo in a most *"épatant"* accent.

The year 1935 came. The family had to sell the home in Neuilly and start back to Mexico. Montparnasse wept two weeks about the departure of a gentleman who soon knew no other pleasure than the soft-sprung sofas in the house on Hamburgo.

The house on Hamburgo! The night she re-entered it, Doña Lorenza sat on the great staircase and wept. That very mirror had greeted her in front of which, so long ago, she had said farewell and fixed her veil and departed with a smile of sweet resignation. Now, something unreal showed in the glass, on in her lips, something Doña Lorenza did not want to think about but that was stamped on her whole being, as to final relief without more doors on life, a certainty definite as a memory which being remembered, may no longer be sought for. And only the search had made it possible to believe that the memory still existed. Eyes fixed on her hands, she decided to forget. To forget that she had remembered. She would just go right on feeling herself a great lady. "Joaquín, have you seen? Yesterday I looked for Geneva's house; it is now a pastry shop. The stables are in ruins. Rodolfo's is a Spanish social center. They say that there are only Masons in the government now. And that isn't all . . . religious education is no longer imparted in schools! No one has money for receptions. All our old friends are public accountants and shopkeepers, traveling salesmen and lowly civil servants and the luckiest of them are history teachers." In home after home she encountered, like specters, blank spaces on the walls where ancient paintings had once hung; now they were in the hands of antique collectors. Cheap flowery cotton print covered the sheen of thread bare silk upholstery; there was linoleum instead of rugs. And no one gave them any importance at all: Francisco would have said, How is it possible for important decisions to be arrived at without consultation with the legitimate ruling class? And how can it be that the children of my sister have a blouse shop and pass their days behind a show case? How can it be that the niece of a Minister of State announces in her window that sweaters are knitted here? That will not happen to Benjamín Him I shall hold erect, aware of his station and his duty. Through him the name Ortiz de Ovano shall be returned to its rightful elevation.

And Joaquinito: This damn mess isn't my fault. I insisted all along that we ought to get out of the provinces and buy real estate here, as our cousins did, and they are well enough fixed now. In short, I find it much more pleasant to spend my days on a sofa sipping cognac than to follow the example of my old schoolmates at the British Academy and sell neckties in some department store at a slave's wage and with a damn Spaniard over me.

Many, many of their old friends stayed on in Europe. Others, though they still had money, began to drift back to Mexico and, Doña Lorenza muttered, to betray their class: to associate with the thieves and to close their doors to impoverished aristocrats. Even to make in-laws of priest-killers! The house on Hamburgo was broken up, first the garden, which went to some Lebanese as a site for apartment buildings; then the stable, which became a grocery; and, last, the front of the house, the drawing rooms and ground and second floors, which became a women's clothing store. They were left with only four upper rooms. A bedroom was converted into a living room. Joaquín's room. And the room in which Doña Lorenza and Benjamín slept, although he was eighteen now; and the kitchen . . . and a diet of meatballs and rice. Doña Lorenza wanted to cling to her furniture, and it was piled up grotesquely in the bedrooms, surrounded by crystal and porcelain and cane rockers; only smells hung in the walnut wardrobes; in the cabinets stood the tiny porcelain courtesans with their white wings, the cameos, the music boxes, the bucolic landscapes; everything lost grandeur by compression, and there was no sun. At night the green blinking of a neon beer sign on the roof. They had to enter quickly and silently through the shop below, the glorious drawing room where Polavieja had been feted was now taken over by clothes dummies. But in Doña

Lorenza's bedroom the old life persisted. There everything was preserved, both the past and the future. And Benjamín! Docile, most courteous, with his enchanting French accent. It was not possible for him to hold to tradition by studying in Europe. But neither did he have to rub elbows with the herd at the university, as did his cousins . . . who preferred to be architects, rather than Ovandos.

Long suspended hours Doña Lorenza, erect, eagle-nosed, in a silk shawl, her yellowing hair carefully dressed, opaque stockings, ribanded high shoes, would spend talking with Benjamín, with him would revive the dead names of their former properties in Bajío, Sonora, and Morelos, the titles of Spanish nobles who had received hospitality under that very roof, would relive visits to Chapultepec Castle when Don Pofirio's lady, Doña Carmelita . . . . Docile, courteous Benjamín, with his charming French accent. His mouth always half open, his eyes groggy, his soft-haired beard badly trimmed, his stride hunchbacked by a crook in his neck that already was permanent. Benjamín, without women, paralyzed behind glass. Benjamín, the last cameo. When his grandmother left him to himself, he would read newspaper classified sections and wave his arms each time he came to a French name.

When Benjamín was twenty-four, their cousin Pimpinela de Ovando (also, Doña Lorenza thought sadly, pawned to the whims of the new rich and to the band of adventurers who called themselves, without the least shame, The International Set) came to dine. Before the meal she whispered in Doña Lorenza's ear and then, at table, said with an eyebrow arching, "What have you thought about doing with Benjamín, Aunt? The fact that you have lived thirteen years on the remnants of your fortune doesn't mean that he can do the same until *he* dies."

"What do you propose? That Benjamín should go out of this house and sell socks? Benjamín is a model boy, we may almost say the last who has been reared as a gentleman, and some-day——"

"I believe that Benjamín would be very lucky if he sold even one sock. Obviously, he isn't prepared for anything at all. . . .

We'll have to see. But it might be possible to get him into a bank."

"Into a bank! My dear Pimpinela! Francisco always used to repeat to me, 'Be sure that bankers serve *you*, have them depend upon *you*, or otherwise you become their slave.' And that was then, when the directors of banks were well-known gentlemen one had to breakfast. But today! They have all become revolutionists and communists. Ah, no. Benjamín was born to use bankers!"

"Oh, Aunt, forgive me! But look . . . pardon, pardon . . . you are going to invite Norma Larragoiti to dinner. She's the wife of the banker Federico Robles. She's an upstart, obnoxious, vulgar, a classic anything you care to call her, and Robles is a savage from God knows what jungle. But Norma melts at the mention of an old name, and dinner here, among your mementos, will put her out of her mind. Don't worry, we'll buy everything you need. And the next day, Benjamín will have a position in the bank."

Doña Lorenza's protests were useless. Norma Larragoiti! Daughter of some sheepherder! Nevertheless, I will have to show her what it means to be what we are, and surrounded by this genteel poverty, make her feel that she favors us by visiting us.

It simply was not possible. Doña Lorenza felt a final passing away when Norma, radiant, wrapped in mink and playing carelessly with her pearls, visibly affirmed the sense of security in this new world, of freedom and belonging, which had used to be their own feeling. The pedestal which for forty years Doña Lorenza had believed was vacant, waiting for their return, turned out to be occupied . . . by vulgarity, on that the old woman insisted, by an upstart vulgarity without the least trace of sweet graciousness.

"You know, Doña Lorenza, my father lost all his haciendas in the Revolution. I tell Federico, who holds to revolutionary principles, that I married him only for revenge. But, moreover, that trivial circumstance puts us more together, well, a little on the same level, you and I, doesn't it? So many old families suffered! But the important thing is to preserve the old true dignity, isn't it, and that at least we've known how to do! Now what really can't be forgiven is that they won't let us bring Don Porfirio's remains back to Mexico, and . . ."

The following week Benjamín began his employment in the Savings Bank of Mexico, addressing envelopes. Everyone seemed enchanted by his penmanship, so French, as elegant as that taught in a Sacred Heart Academy.

Pimpinela, disguised by her dark glasses, just escaped meeting Ixca Cienfuegos face to face. A carrier providentially passed between them, his forehead blackened and corrugated by the hempen headband which drew the arch of the frame on his back. Cienfuegos smiled and went into the pink stone building which soared high on Avenida Juárez between two old nineteenth-century homes bonneted with their mansard roofs. He went to the office of . . .

FEDERICO ROBLES

"You ask me to go back to a very different time and place, Cienfuegos," Federico Robles said, standing in front of the large blue-tinted window behind his desk. He looked at his hands, then raised his eyes and tried to see his image in the glass, drawn on cold thin air. "I hardly remember that I began there."

. . . A trickling creek and beside it a hut leaned together of sticks and dust and air; the forest sickly, some small corn patches; children came one after the other, until to have another was a cause for neither regret nor happiness; and the mother gave each of them the tight feaures and squat bodies of that race of Indians which probably still is there, features no longer true but memorial and picturesque; the father came to the hut to eat and sleep and to get out of the sun, an old man with earth mummied in his face, terrible eyes, and tender hands, who would have liked to be able to speak without opening his mouth because words confused him and made him angry. It was only out in the fields and his hours in them were the hours when his words came.

"Get up, you goddamn *cabrona* mule, get up, the sun's going down."

71

Sundays in Morelia: candy and bunting and men on horse-back. Beautiful churches rising up like arrows through the green sky of leaves. All of them together to hang at the altar of their favorite saint a votive painting by the eldest son, who now was working in Morelia as a carpenter.

"May the child be born easily."

"May they give me the just-born baby-blue dove."

"May the corn ear be full."

"May we always be together."

"One feels free and happy, Father, working here in the car-penter's shop." And again back to the hut surrounded by flatness, by the stink of rotting corn stalks and burning leaves and thin hogs. . . .

"All that has to be forgotten. We came up too fast to have time to think about being the same men who just half a century ago were working under the eyes of hacienda overseers. Now there is still so much to be done. More jobs. Raise the nation to greatness. The old time is dead forever."

"Don Ignacio de Ovando owned the whole country there, but he rarely visited it. His name and his figure were almost legend-ary. Now I remember my father's figure, I remember it because it had been there since the beginning of my world. I remember that when he finished a day's plowing, he always stomped his foot in the last black furrow for the good luck that there would be sunshine the next day and the clay under his sandals would dry. Saturdays all the men got together to tell stories, and then my father also remembered what life had been before."

". . . In the time of my grandfather Serafín this land still gave for all of us. Then came the land laws, and that was when Don Ignacio began to buy up our plots. Then the foreign soldiers, and many of us were killed. I went on working the land. I still be-lieved that the land was here to feed all of us, as always. But after the war the Government gave us new laws, and Don Ignacio began to swallow us. But we can't complain. Everywhere else they make you buy only at the hacienda store. Here you can go into Morelia and spend whatever you have, any way you want. . . ."

"Yes, I think he was satisfied. By himself no Indian would ever have made the Revolution. To make them make the Revolution, my first cousin Froilán Reyero came. He had lived since babyhood in Mexico City. I remember him wetting his long mustaches in a gourd dipper while he patted my head and told us that in Morelos he had heard that young Pedro, Don Ignacio's son, had made a mess of the sugar refinery. Young Pedro would inherit when the old man died."

". . . There in Morelos he has organized riding parties for his friends. They gallop along and lasso peasants' wives. You should hear the screaming. And no one wants to step outside, but they have to go to the river for water, or to wash clothes, and then they're lassoed. After they finish with the women, they turn them loose."

"Froilán told us other things he had learned on his travels. About the National Valley, from which no one escaped alive in those days, and the strikers in Cananea. And he had been at Río Blanco."

". . . Just as men have organized there, so must you men here organize. Señor Madero is beginning his campaign now, and they say he is going to put an end to all mistreatment."

"I remember that my father just scratched his head, poked at the fire, and told Froilán to leave them in peace, that they could take care of themselves."

". . . In Morelos the Zapata brothers are recruiting. I was at Río Blanco and I saw the Government finally go too far there. My friend Gervasio Pola is in Mexico City now, raising money for Zapata. If Don Porfirio doesn't honor the elections, no one will wait any longer."

Federico Robles sat on the sofa and smiled. " 'Keep the peace, keep the peace,' my father said in his bird voice, and Froilán went on and told us about the strike at Río Blanco."

"I had a friend working there. His kid died, and that was why I went to Río Blanco, for the funeral. The factory and the company houses there are on level low ground, and behind them the forest and the mountains begin; you feel shut in, as if inside a palisades. There's a deep sadness, it comes down from the moun-

73

tains, and with it, a wind that keeps the road dusty. The factory has little balconies. A company store. The workers' houses. They told me that the kid had died because he had been put to work in the vats when he was only eleven. He didn't live a year there, swallowing lint and fumes. I saw him in his coffin with his white shirt and no pants, skinny and innocent. And he wasn't the first. Old men die for the same reason. It is only by some miracle that they live to die old. The workers are always having children, and who can tell if a baby will live or not when the father earns fifty cents a day; as soon as they can, the kids go to work, too, at twenty cents a day. Add it up, Albano. Remember that they have to pay two cents a week house rent. And as they get their pay in company script that is good only in the company store, God only knows why they haven't all starved to death long ago. Most of them just wither up. Working thirteen hours a day, they just shrivel up like a pile of roots in the sun. I used to watch them coming home from work, not strong enough to speak, as if their mouths were sewn shut, stumbling and falling down, so exhausted they couldn't even ask for food. But I was telling you, there was the dead child, and my friend just couldn't stand it any more and went out, dragging the child's body by the feet, down to the factory, screaming until all the foremen crowded out on the little balconies, half afraid, half laughing, too; and I was sure he wouldn't be able to stand that they were not really afraid and that they were laughing at him. He picked his son's body up and threw it at them, at their faces, while they slammed down the windows. Right then the Workers' Circle was born, and Gervasio Pola, who can read and write, came to tell them to hold back for a while and get ready. So when the textile strike in Puebla began, the men at Río Blanco took up a collection, though it hurt them, and sent that money to the men at Puebla. The company understood and ordered the factory shut down.

"Then the strike was on, and everyone knew that the store would be shut, too, and there would be no food. For two months they wandered through the mountains, hunting food! You ought to have seen that, Albano, how hunger struck those people down. Their hands were raw from digging among cactus for roots. All of them walked with their eyes gaping. Sometimes you can tell from a man's face what is going on inside him, and this was true of them, their eyes wide, their heads craning, looking just for something to eat. They held out two months. Even if what happened afterward hadn't happened, and all I had now was the memory of those faces, I would still never be able to sleep in peace again until I see Mexicans free. They ate their fingernails, Albano, some of them even cut off their arms and tongues so that others could have food. If you had seen that, you'd know now that you are not really alone. And that because you aren't alone, you must live in sorrow. I was full of sorrow and fury, and I still am.

"The strikers appealed to Don Porfirio. They begged him to have mercy and promised to do whatever he ordered. Don Porfirio said only that they should stop striking and return to work as before. Those are men of their word, and when they surrendered, all they asked was to be given a little corn and beans for the first week, until they were paid. We won't give the damn dogs water to drink, the foremen said. You can do anything you want to with hunger, Albano, except laugh at it. So long as you don't laugh at his hunger, a starving man will hang on, just from pride and dignity, until he dies. So long as you don't laugh.

"They went to the company store, six thousand workers, and took everything and then set both it and the factory on fire. There was no rage in their faces, nor hatred either. Just hunger, something that is like a birth or a benediction before death, something inevitable . . . it happened without anyone planning it.

"That was when Rosalio Martínez's troops came in, firing one volley after another without stopping while men dropped dead in the street, with neither strength nor desire to scream, with nowhere to run away. The soldiers followed them into their homes and killed them without questions or remorse. And those who ran up the mountain were hunted down and killed without a word spoken. No one opened his lips the whole time, neither workers or soldiers. There was no sound except the guns. They died in silence. One battalion of country-boy soldiers refused to fire and was wiped out, too. Afterward you saw the flatcars moving off, stacked with bodies, and sometimes only arms and legs. To be dumped into the sea at Veracruz."

Robles went to the ebony cigar box on his enameled desk. "My cousin Froilán did not live long. Huerta had him executed. Sometimes I wonder what would have happened to him if he had lived through the struggle."

His eyes lost above the pale outline of the Alameda, Ixca Cienfuegos murmured, "We all wonder. Those men who were called 'pure revolutionaries,' what would they be doing today? The Flores Magóns, the Felipe Angeles, the Aquiles Serdáns?"

"They would doubtless be underpaid schoolteachers, a little wheezy," Robles grunted as he turned his Havana in his lips. "It is one thing to attack injustice and another to build, and to build is the only real way to end injustice. I had the good luck to fight first and build later. But who knows. . . . We are trying to build a capitalistic economy and at the same time apply protective legislation to the workers. The plain truth is that capital is bought with lives, like those of the children who died breathing lint dust at Río Blanco."

Cienfuegos stared at the copper-red blushing dome of the Palace of Fine Arts and then closed his eyes, inviting Robles to continue. The banker sat, the plump cigar between his mouth, and pulled his shirt cuffs down and made himself comfortable. "When I was ten, they took me to live with the priest of a small church in Morelia. I learned to read and write and to assist at Mass. For a while my parents would come to see me, or I went to eat in the hut on the bank of the creek. But later I almost never left Morelia. My father died of diphtheria, my brothers stopped looking me up. I found out that my mother had been lassoed and raped, and when my oldest brother, the carpenter, went to avenge her, the Federals captured him and the others didn't say a word. They went on farming their little patches. Don't believe that I wanted vengeance either. I understood nothing.

"Even if I had understood, that alone wouldn't have sent me to the Revolution. A revolution comes . . . like sun or moon, rain or hunger. You stand or you lie down. You get out of the rain, or you get wet. That. I never knew where it came from, but once I was in it, I had to take the bull by the horns. Afterward, a few of us found reasons."

"Others did not find any, and they were those who knew why. . . ." Cienfuegos interrupted.

"Correct. But that is corn from another crib. Such men always know their whys, but what does it get them?"

"You were one of *those*."

"As corn is grain before it is meal. But when it is meal, it is no longer grain."

As he watched Robles gravely puffing his cigar, Ixca thought, Who were "those?" To what extent had Robles known perfectly, to what degree did he still feel himself one of "those," like "those," as anonymous as "they."

The banker spoke. "The curate told me that when I learned Latin, he would send me to the seminary; all the boys he had ever recommended had known Latin, and they had risen to bishop. When I was fourteen I knew my routine very well, and I must have been an attractive kid because everyone gave with pleasure when I passed the basket." Robles smothered a laugh which was lost in the thick cigar smoke. "I had a few friends, but many of them had gone to join Madero's revolution, in the north, and others had gone south to find Zapata. The curate used to talk politics and he was very pleased when Huerta won in Mexico City. I simply waited for the famous trip to the seminary. Yes . . . I hoped for it. . . ."

". . . He is a delicate, docile little Indian fellow who at an early age understood what separates him from his betters and has found his niche in the wise Orderliness and the rest of his life will serve God and the Order as a sexton, yes, even after I leave you to pass to the last parish, you will still see him polishing glass and marble the day long, intent upon only his duties, far from temptation, with few friends and the dream, poor boy, of going to the seminary."

"I hoped for it . . . until the day he asked me to attend a novitiates' ceremony in the cathedral. You should have seen them, their small porcelain faces alive against the darkness of their hoods, not one of them older than eighteen. I had never seen such girls before, and when I realized that they were going to be buried forever, I was very bitter. I wanted to kiss them, Cienfuegos, to ask their forgiveness in my name and above all in the name of everything that I was not. I believe I even wanted to offer myself to them for a purpose I did not understand well. To give them my love? The church was as dry as bones, and the rustle of their long skirts over the flat stones of the nave was very loud. You know how such moments happen. You begin to understand. To know what you can do. So when the curate took me along to his family's hacienda, near Uruapan, I went already decided. Their name was Zamacona . . ."

On his feet again, Robles stopped in front of his portrait by Diego Rivera, which hung above a steel file cabinet. On an indigo-blue background the banker's figure had been painted dark and dense, crammed into a maroon cashmere suit, and with two left feet. Taller, more aggressive, the Robles of the portrait seemed about to fly apart, shattered by a bow bent inside him.

". . . the family name was Zamacona. Revelations happen that way, you know. They invite without being invited. Not one second has passed but you know that you will never be what you were before. The mother was at the hacienda, an invalid, with her eldest daughter, thirty, unmarried and dressed in black, and another daughter who would soon be sixteen and whose dresses were very tight across the bust. Mercedes. The father was dead, the younger son was a captain in the army. . . ."

He stared at the date painted legibly in the right-hand corner of the portrait: 1936. He passed his hands over his paunchy waist and wished he could see, behind the face on canvas, that of the boy of fifteen. Who remembered that boy? With precision he recalled that his first photograph had been taken when he was twenty-one; he would never be able to recapture the boyhood face. He turned his back to the portrait and met Ixca's white teeth exhaling a gray and thoughtful spiral. He observed him with irritation and clasped his hands behind his back.

"I left the hacienda, and you may explain that any way you care to, and spent a couple of days in Uruapan, working as a water boy, and then the Federals grabbed me as an enlistment and took me to Querétaro. I stole one of their horses and headed north, traveling at night." Robles stroked his neck, the thick veins, the soft fat under his chin. "In Aguascalientes the horse died and I slipped aboard a train, a train packed with men running away from one army or hurrying to join another. In a village in Coahuila I happened to fall in, wholly by luck, with a Carranza general who knew a few words of Latin. I turned eighteen in his company of calvarymen, singing 'Valetina' in Latin for the general to laugh." Now Robles's fingers slipped along his gray wool arm, seeking, below that softness and the silk lining and the thin cotton shirt, his nervous muscle. "I slept on the ground and fought in the sun, had a strong back and hard arms and the legs of a horse. God knows how many towns, how many names and battles . . ."

Santa Rosa Guaymas Orendain now really drunk Huerta and your heart pounded Zacatecas Lucio Blanco Felipe Angeles Herrera the deaf one on learning that they had been defeated in Zacatecas to Barron Diéquez Iturbe and Buelna

Where the Federals took off
Nothing they could do
Except borrow petticoats
And hide as women

". . . the sun, like a copper pitched high every day in a game of heads and tails no one could win. My homeland was my general, glory was my sombrero full of bullet holes and all my memories run together, and the color of the mountains and of percale skirts, too . . ."

Twenty-five hundred shaved-head recruits
Were gathered in like sheep;
They learned to drill
And died just the same
And none of them ever killed anyone

across plains and mountains, fighting night and day and suffering a thousand hardships to destroy tyranny ". . . we crossed and recrossed the country inch by inch and foot by foot, Cienfuegos . . ." from Monterrey to Laredo and from Laredo to Torreón, Carranza troops flooded over the Republic ". . . and we learned the country, we really learned it. A dry, sad land, linear as the horizon where powder dust exploded between heaven and earth in the great fireworks merrymaking that always accompanied us. Our trains full of camp followers and ammunition boxes. Goats roasted on the bank of a river . . ." *she was curly-haired, curly-haired, curly-haired, and her papa and her mama were curly-haired, too* "Days of cannister and blood, lived on yellow battlefields that seemed to gallop past of themselves."

Robles's eyes looked beyond the window, beyond the tree silhouettes in the Alameda, beyond what could be seen of the churches on Avenida Hidalgo. The leathery pouches below his eyes glinted opaquely, and he told himself that he had to get more exercise, but that golf would only make the veins of his legs swell. "The brown virgins you fucked just once. The night we set fire to a shack where a corporal's woman and their child were sleeping." *How the hell could I know that was your home?* Robles sat again and puffed on his cigar while he loosened his garters and examined his calves for signs of inflammation. "And then they shot the corporal for howling too much. In the evenings, the general would call me in . . . Come in, my Latinist. Now the time of the fat kine is coming, ready to be milked. Exert yourself just a little and you'll go far. Balls is all it takes to handle these people, they don't even notice it when you're raping them, you can do whatever you want. If you try to be honest, they'll think you're a hypocrite. Beat them, steal from them, they don't mind so long as you have a good-looking broad with you and plenty of balls. They'll honor you most when you make perfect fools of them. So why try to go against the sovereign will of the people, eh? . . . "and then he would roar with laughter and go out to sing with his troops, squatting on his heels against a bullet-splotched wall. And so it happened that in April of 1915 we found ourselves on the front at Celaya."

Ixca did not interrupt. He merely nodded and wished that he could get inside Robles and learn at what moment Robles had ceased to be Robles the soldier, Robles the obscure ambitious lawyer, Robles who had known how to swim through the deluge, Robles of the name Robles, Robles of a destiny which could be exchanged for no other and which no one could know. Robles was silent, his eyes stared into Ixca's, he forgot his hands, his body, let his arms fall and let the heavy curtains inside his eyes slowly rise and reveal the inner pupil of memory, liquid, pin-point. Ixca Cienfuegos did not allow one muscle to twitch. Like an eloquent idol, rigid, silent, he invited Robles to open, not his lips, but his life, the slit eyes to spread the curtain more and permit a revelation, always a memory, that would ripen and become the fruit of all the days memory could not bring back. And now Robles's eyes were fugitive with light, trembling like turquoise wings aflame in darkness.

"Maycotte has dug in in Celaya! Villa has him surrounded!" A river of infantry poured aboard a train to the rhythm of trumpets and steam; from his saddle Federico watched the figures of General Hill and General Obregón as they ordered the lines to form; they would wait here, opposite Celaya, the town to which Villa would return, drawn back by Obregón's tricks once the seige at Guaje had been broken. Between sun and plain, on foot and on horseback, as thick as ants, men with copper faces and drooping mustaches and big sombreros pulled down almost to the eyes or cocked with a rolled brim, the officers' kepis, neckerchiefs, boots muddied by yellow clay and eyes glassy under the blaze, clenched teeth, sad stares from faces like sun-darkened gold; and the squat Yaqui Indians digging foxholes and planting the wheatfields with barbed wire, all the vast hot plain bristling with movement while they, the cavalry, standing in ranks immobile under the sun, waited, smoking loose-rolled cigarettes and receiving jugs of fruit-flavored water, saucers of rice from the women who, gathered under tarp flies were poking up little fires and mashing up green chilis and squeezing juices for the water in great clay crocks. All day in the saddle, waiting for orders to carry out. Federico blew smoke over the horse's mane and watched the flight of clouds journeying, weighted with their days like spongy blankets, toward the mountains. All his muscular instincts were collected in one tense point, ready to charge against General Pancho Villa's columns. The level wheat fields were inundated, and at three in the afternoon, the train returned.

"Villa attacked when he heard the whistle!"

"Maycotte slipped away around the right flank."

"They have reconcentrated in Celaya."

Obregón got down from the locomotive, frowning angrily, his mustache jerking as he shouted orders, inspected foxholes and the flooded wheat fields and the ranked cavalry and the barbed wire. The Yaqui, red neckerchiefs dancing in the wind, moved into the foxholes, carrying rifles with bayonets; there, buried in clay, it was as if they had found where they belonged by nature. Hill commanded the infantry to deploy. A fat afternoon sun wrote dark lines under every movement, under men and cannon and horses. Villa's infantry now had occupied the opposite ridges and, with a howl, suddenly descended while the first charge by Villa's cavalry was firing the plain with gallop and whinny and the rearing of horses roweled by singing spurs, stung by rifle fire from the Yaquis who, immediately after firing, ducked into their holes and stuck their bayonets straight up, stabbing at the horses' bellies from the wet sanctuary of their clay burrows, until blood and intestines dripped down on their Indian faces, and Villa's cavalrymen toppled off on other steel fingers while the infantry, advancing into the lake of wheat, found their feet sucked by mud and their testicles torn by wire, grape ricocheted from splashing water, their mouths bubbled red: men packed into a heap and wall of flesh and screams, caught and trapped by the wire. That afternoon and all night Villa's cavalry mounted charge after charge, twenty-six in all. By noon the next day horse-carrion stank the battlefield and the little bugler Martínez, who had blown bullfight *dianas* at the height of the battle, called Obregón's flanks in upon his center. Villa's new assault met a new defense, led by cavalry. Federico Robles galloped, brandishing his machete, firing his pistol among the enemy infantry; the horse's blinders tore loose and flapped near its ears; faces petrified by one second of terror, bodies washed in blood, raised arms and flailing weapons, all blinking past while his kepi blew off and his hair danced in the wind although there was no wind except his gallop: and then he felt glory-thirst come to life, his machete rose and fell on the skulls and necks, the shoulders and arms and the sweat and blood of men of the Northern Division; drenched with his own sweat, his penis stiff, his legs gripping his mount, his teeth biting the reins, Robles cut and fired, oblivious to counterfire, to the dying screams of voices from bodies already dead. Villa's wineskin infantrymen squashed, chopped, squirted beneath the hooves of Robles's horse. Only fleeing backs were in front of him now. He trotted back, toward a camp throbbing with bugle calls and the smell of cooking, sure proof of victory, throbbing with the return of those who had survived. For the last time his eyes stared over the battlefield of Celaya, stained wheat fields murmuring hymnally in the evening wind, smoke floating up from the guts of dead horses, tangles of arms and legs, the unmistakable embraces of cadavers, stiff hands protruding from the barbed wired, flooded fields, white eyes holed by sunlight, lips crying good-bye forever. General Alvaro Obregón stood erect among the fresh troops advancing. At a light trot Federico returned, he looked at his hands, the lines of his palms drawn dark by blood and dark earth, please may the wind always blow over me as it is blowing now, blowing now forever.

Trembling like wings aflame in darkness. No more than two minutes had passed. Robles again knew that he had a body, a manner, middle-aging glands. "April, 1915. We reached Mexico City in nineteen hundred seventeen, Cienfeugos. The General was not allowed to write constitutions in Querétaro; for consolation, he was given a mansion with a marble stairway, on the Plaza del Ajusco. The fighting was over and I didn't know what to do with myself. The General invited me to his banquets, which at first were just for us, his veterans; but presently young lawyers with long noses began to come, too, and women of definite class, and I had to swallow many humiliations because of my ignorance, my cheap clothes. That merely spurred me. I had to move ahead to a point where people would respect me in spite of my ignorance and my clothes. And I had to work hard to serve my country, because that was why we had made the Revolution. Not to sit and dream about the victory of our ideals, but to work, every man in his own way. Our emotions when we marched into Mexico City with Carranza and Obregón were contradictory. But we all felt that the time had come to attempt everything, any goal, no matter how high."

Robles eyes were narrowed to slits. "The nation had been destroyed. Ten years of disorder, no plans, nearly a million dead. The General realized how matters stood, and in nineteen hundred twenty, after Carranza's death, he disbanded his troops at a moment when everyone was sure that without support by troops, the Government could not withstand the attack of a single dwarf. . . ."

"I DO NOT SEEK THE PRESIDENCY," SAYS HUERTA

VILLA MURDERED

> Pancho Villa is dead
> They murdered him from ambush
> Poor little Pancho Villa
> You must look for him now in the graveyard

"'But not the General, he moved straight toward what he saw coming: business . . ."

the spot which has remained a center of style and wealth
in the capital: the Hotel Regis's cabaret Don Quijote

". . . he knew that the day of private armies was ending in Mexico . . ."

ESTRADA'S TROOPS HAVE TAKEN GUADALAJARA . . . "that it had known its high noon during the Revolution; and that if Mexico wanted to progress, it had to permit the sprouting up of the bourgeois seeds which had been incubating since the wars of the Reform . . ."

The stylish waist is clasped these frowthy days by wide colored sashes, richly fringed

a n   o l d   l o v e   neither forgotton nor abandoned

Lupe Vélez appeared on the stage to a delirious ovation

CARRILLO PUERTO

". . . to welcome that *bourgeoisie* and make it master of the coun-

84

try in reality and not merely in skeletal ideals as Juárez and Ocampo had done . . ."

four patches of corn
four alone
they left us

"The Plan of Agua Prieta put praetorianism to the knife once and for all. The rebellions by de la Huerta and Serrano and Escobar were only drowning kicks."

GOVERNMENT FORCES TRIUMPH AT OCOTLÁN

farewell little girl
don't cry for your Pancho

"The Revolution emerged with two distinct heads: Obregón and Calles . . ."

"Schoolmaster, veteran of 1911, commissioner of Sonora, provisional governor, friend, citizen, and statesman seem forever united in his creative autonomy, always most Mexican, all side by side at the moment of action . . ."

". . . who, with all their excesses . . ."

"What time is it?"

"It is whatever time you prefer, Señor President."

". . . still defended what was essential and ended the ancient anarchy. And I moved straight to what was mine . . ."

MY SPIRIT WILL SPEAK FOR MY RACE

". . . in three years I was a lawyer, I began to go to Sanborn's for breakfast, to see theater. I went into debt to tailors. I even took dancing lessons . . ."

Rudolf Valentino
Isabelita Faure's Company
María Tereza Montoya at the Principal
the Chapultepec Race Track Son-Sin L'Orangerie

'Tis you   just you
I've loved you and never knew

"When General Calles became President and began to set the country in order in all seriousness, I was ready . . ."

After many years of armed struggle, the nation now is offered the rare opportunity to assay the bravery of those leaders of the

85

(General Obregón is now devoting himself to farming in Huatabampo)
    Revolution, to judge the sincerity of their ideas and their popularity among the people
"... Those were undertakings for titans ..."
            MORROW NEW U. S. AMBASSADOR HERE
    Article Twenty-seven of the Constitution not retroactive
    ARCHBISHOPS TO MEET WITH PRESIDENT
"... and we had to move slowly ..."
            Gorostieta rises in arms
            SERRANO AND GÓMEZ CANDIDATES
"We may be criticized on many counts, Cienfuegos, and critics say that we of the old guard, a handful of millionaires, have gathered our wealth from the sweat of the nation itself. But when you remember what Mexico was before, things take a different light. Gangs of bandits who never stopped shooting, the economy paralyzed, generals with private armies. No prestige abroad. No faith in industry. The countryside full of fear. Public institutions gone. And it was our lot to try to defend the principles of the Revolution and at the same time make them work toward progress and order and the national good. It was no easy task to reconcile those purposes. To proclaim revolutionary ideals is easy: land reform, labor laws, whatever you please. But we had to face reality and accept the only political truth, compromise. That was the moment of crisis for the Revolution. The moment of decision to build even if it meant staining conscience. To sacrifice ideals for the sake of tangible achievement. And we did it, and well. We had the right to take what we wanted, because of what we had suffered, gone through, to earn it. One man had been forced into the army, another's mother had been raped, another had had his land stolen. Don Porfirio had given none of us any way up, the door had been closed on all our ambitions. Now our ambition could grab what it cared to. Yes, but always working for the good of the nation, always taking only what was ours and taking it not for ourselves but for the nation."
    On his feet in front of the window, Robles spread his hand

86

across the anarchic expanse of Mexico City. "Look outside. There are still millions of illiterates, barefoot Indians, poor people starving to death, farmers who don't have even one miserable acre of their own, factories with no machinery, nor parts, unemployed workers who have to flee to the United States. But there are also millions who can go to schools that we of the Revolution built, millions for whom company stores and hacienda stores are gone forever, and there are some factories in the cities. Millions who, if this were nineteen hundred ten, would be peons are now skilled workers, girls who would be cooks and maids are now typists, there are millions who in only thirty years have moved into the middle class, who own cars and use toothpaste and spend five days a year at Tecalutla or Acapulco. Our plants have given those workers jobs, our commerce has given them time-payment plans and savings accounts. For the first time in Mexican history a stable middle class exists, the surest protection against tyranny and unrest. Men and women who do not want to lose their jobs, their installment-plan furniture, their little cars, for anything in the world. Those people are the one concrete result of the Revolution, Cienfuegos, and we made them. We laid the foundation for Mexican capitalism. Calles laid it. He did away with the generals, built highways and dams, organized banking. What if we did get our percentage from every highway contract? What if the collective farm directors do steal half the appropriations they are given? Would you prefer that in order to avoid these evils, we had done nothing at all? You want us to have the honesty of angels? I repeat, because of what we went through, we are entitled to everything. Because we were born in dirt-floor shacks, we have the right now to live in mansions with high ceilings and stone walls, with a Rolls-Royce at the door. Only we know what a revolution is. A revolution is fought by flesh and blood men, not by saints, and every revolution ends with the creation of a new privileged class. I assure you that if I had not been a man able to take advantage of his breaks, I would still be scratching corn-rows in Michoacán, and just as my father was, I would be satisfied. But the fact is that I got my breaks and I am here, and I am more useful to

87

Mexico as a businessman than as a farmer. And if I hadn't, someone else would have seized what I have seized, stand where I
stand now, do what I do. We, too, were of the common people,
and our homes and gardens and automobiles are, in a way, the
people's triumph. Moreover, this is a land that falls asleep
quickly and can wake unexpectedly, and who knows what will
happen tomorrow? We have to protect ourselves. To get what
we have, we had to gamble. None of today's easy politics. You
had to have, first of all, balls, in the second place, balls, and in
the third place, balls. To do business, you had to wade into
politics up to your neck and to change when the wind changed.
There were no North American partners to protect against any
eventuality. You gambled everything, and every day. And so we
grew powerful with the true Mexican power which does not
consist of a show of strength. Today no one tyrannizes Mexicans.
They don't need to. Mexicans are tyrannized by what they are.
And for thirty years there has been no other tyranny. What we
have had to do is very different, to kick the country in the ass
and keep kicking it, not give in, never let it go back to sleep.
Which has produced, far from upheaval and protest, admiration.
In Mexico no one is more admired than a perfect son of a bitch,
you know."

Robles's arms fell. Exaltation had darkened his skin, Indian
color, the Indian so carefully disguised by cashmere and cologne.

"We know what the country needs, what its problems are.
There is nothing the country can do except put up with us, or
fall back into anarchy, which the middle class won't permit. You
know, Cienfuegos, you're very sly, you just listen. Don't think
I've told you any real secrets, or that I've been talking just to
hear my own voice. You know more than you pretend to, maybe
some day you'll want to try to scare me. Well, don't . . . that is
why I've been talking. So you'll know just what you're up against.
That's all."

Cienfuegos smiled, friendly and open, and in spite of himself
Robles felt his hard face soften. Cienfuegos silently recalled the
words of another man who had also created great power, another
great and well-admired son of a bitch: "Mexico now has a middle

88

class. The middle class is the active part of society, here and everywhere. Men of means are too worried about their wealth and their place to be of use to the well-being of the nation, and on the other hand, the lower classes are, for the most part, too uneducated to develop strength. Democratic growth rests upon the strength of an active middle class, hardworking, determined to rise." Still smiling, Cienfuegos reflected that with his flared nostrils, reptile eyes, and puffy, carefully shaven cheeks, Robles strongly favored His Excellency, the other great son of a bitch, Porfirio Díaz. For the last time the banker puffed on his cigar.

"Cienfuegos, what I tell you is so true, is so exactly the instinct of the country, that even our most leftist administrations have had to join the movement toward bourgeois stability. Mexican capitalism is indebted to two men: Calles and Cárdenas. Calles laid the foundation. Cárdenas brought it to life by creating the possibility of a large internal market. He raised wages, gave labor every conceivable guarantee, protected workers so there was nothing for them to agitate about; he established once and for all the policy of Federal investment in public works; he broadened credit, broke up land holdings and on all levels tried to stimulate a vast circulation of stagnant wealth. Those were permanent accomplishments, still living. If Cárdenas hadn't given the labor movement an official character, administrations since would not have been able to work peacefully and increase national production. And above all, Cárdenas ended Mexican feudalism. Mexico might become anything, but never again a kingdom of great absentee landlord estates ruled by a perfectly useless agrarian plutocracy. Plutocracy we may have, but thanks to *this* plutocracy, markets are created and jobs are provided and Mexico moves ahead. The Mexican Revolution has been wise; it understood early that to be effective, the time of militancy had to be brief, private fortunes had to be large. Not one important decision has been left to chance; all that has been done has been done after meditation. Each time the right man has become president. Can you imagine this poor country in the hands of a Vasconcelos or an Almazán or a General Henríquez? It would, to be blunt, be flushed down the drain by the rhetoric. Mexico's

89

technological and administrative maps are drawn, and cannot be changed by newcomers. And here the story ends."

Federico Robles filled his chest with air, buttoned his double-breasted coat, and said, "Let's go. My wife has cocktails waiting for us."

He drew the window's gauze curtains shut.

Two cotton pads on her eyes, Norma Larragoiti lay naked under a dry and enervating sun. Sun came through the pads, through the eyelids, and glowed inside her eyes like two diffuse egg yolks. Sun: her first memory, the flat desert northern sun and then the high vague dusty sun of Mexico City, dark in a dark sky. First memory and also first wish: she wanted to be the sun, felt a seed of sun burning in her breast and repeated, in the heat of the sun, her name, once, twice, over and over.

NORMA LARRAGOITI

Norma was born in Torreón. Her father had a small store which failed soon after the proclamation of the Plan of Agua Prieta, when Norma was five. Her father committed suicide, and with what little money was left after the burial, Norma's mother sent her to Mexico City to live with a comfortably well-to-do uncle. Christmases she spent at Santa María del Oro, to which the family had removed because her brother, its sole support now, worked in a mine there. But when she was fifteen, she refused to give up Christmas parties in Mexico City, and her aunt and uncle, understanding her, bought her a ball gown. Norma was already an object of attention, her eyes were very green and her skin very white; she rinsed her hair in manzanilla tea and fox-trotted gracefully *in some secluded rendez-vous,* always resting her youthful hand on the nape of her partner's neck. Her aunt and uncle's small home, with a large garden, was in Colonia Juárez, and occasionally they gave parties. Many young men came, and Norma learned how to keep their respect while exciting them harmlessly. "The boys say that Norma is really hot," her smallest cousin shouted, sticking his tongue out at her, and Norma pretended to be angry, but inside was not displeased. For her seventeenth birthday her aunt and uncle gave her a dance, and she met a college boy who was already talked about as a poet and whose black soft eyes looked at her tenderly. His name was Rodrigo Pola; he was penniless, but she was happy just to listen to him talk so beautifully, to have ice cream with him in a soda fountain on París, to go with him, Saturdays, to talking movies starring Greta Garbo, Charles Farrel, and Janet Gaynor. He told her about his papá, who had been a great Zapata general and had been executed by Huerta, and about the sacrifices his mamá had made to give him an education, and how he was going to enter law school soon and about his plans to write poetry and how he had discovered the universes of Rimbaud and St. John-Perse, and about the national university and about the labor movement. Later he became bold enough to kiss her. There is one thing I just won't stand for, and that's for anybody to look down on me, and that is what Rodrigo has done, kissing me and talking about falling in love with me, thinking I'm a pushover and will take anything just to have the thrill of his hand on my waist when we dance. The idiot! What does he think we'll do between kisses? Hasn't he noticed that I want to really live, and in the company of people who are not his sort, for there *are* boys better than he is, convertibles and expensive night clubs and week ends? Well, he can enjoy himself alone now, ten and fifteen days waiting for a kiss, a kiss hiding in the garden . . . the kitchen garden! If he thinks I am going to live in this dead atmosphere forever, he insults me! *Ja!* and then Norma felt that she had gotten just what she wanted to, but Rodrigo kept looking for her and whispering in her ear. Her aunt remonstrated, "No one is going to think well of you for this. How can you stop loving someone between one evening and the next morning? Boys will think you don't know your own mind."

But Norma reflected that it was better to give and take all tenderness from all men, from each storing up more for the next, or for the last: love was an affair of her will, not her heart. Her uncle had good luck in his business and they moved to the Lomas, where people were richer and they belonged to a new

91

set and quite forgot her little crowd on Reforma; and when a politician's son began to stop by for her, she informed family and servants that if Rodrigo Pola telephoned, she was always out. Then she met another rich young man, Pedro Caseaux, who brought her orchids, and on his arm she moved into a circle addicted to week ends in the country and she was invited to the loveliest haciendas, Thursday night until Monday. She was in Cuernavaca when her mother came to Mexico City to see her, and returned too late: God help me not to lose my pride, it's all I have. Why did that old half-breed come? How could my father, so blond and Spanish, ever marry her? Thank God I take after him, not her! Wandering around all day in her aprons and shawls. And that hulk, my brother! Digging rock, and that's about all he's good for. Even Aunt and Uncle have begun to be ashamed of them. And Aunt and Uncle themselves aren't much to brag about. I've pleaded with them not to peep out the window when Pedro comes for me, I die of shame. Neither my mother nor Aunt and Uncle understand that I am going to go up until I am the best that Mexico has to offer. Not just to have the gold and the elegance, but to be, I myself to *be* gold and elegance! Is there some law that ties me to mediocrity? They'll all be happy enough when I finally marry a millionaire and arrange for them to have . . .

At the haciendas there were often people who spoke harshly about the Government. There were foreigners who played artificially with words and made jokes about everything her aunt and uncle most respected.

"We'll see how long this country lasts without the oil companies."

"*Ils sont bêtes!* A land of savages governed by a savage."

"What they need is another dose of foreign intervention . . . an emperor, or the Marines."

"Well, why criticize? At least there's a pleasant climate, cheap whisky, and women who are eager to go to bed with us."

"*Çà, alors!* Fornication at an altitude of two thousand meters. . . . Only goats and Mexicans, you know."

Screwballs, but with an indifference that no amount of frivolity could quite free of its solemn sadness, a longing for snuffed-out candle glow, Biarritz, Jean de Luz, Ischia; words like "our sort," "our set," "new rich," "sensitivity," and the heavy sun, domesticated stone, scarlet blocks of air, the deep blue of the greens in the Valley of Morelos. Exchanging wives and husbands, daring fully-clothed swims in tile pools, the monotonic pop of champagne, arched eyebrows, small-houred nights inventing new cocktails; morning hangovers, skin offered in silence to the golden sun, contests between busts, the blasé endless enumeration of names famous in the arts, in politics, the wandering nobility; the retelling of long stories about someone's reputation; Evaristo and the Countess Aspacúccoli, who in Paris had believed each other to be, respectively, a millionaire oilman and an heiress, who had married and in Cuernavaca had discovered their respective poverty; Count Lemini, originally of Dallas, né Thomas Schwartz, insistently prospecting for sulphur in the south of Mexico; the ancient millionairess, Mrs. Melville, who was always accompanied by an always different, always young and astute nephew, Don Efrén, the old *Porfirista* who had known, so opportunely, when to sell his haciendas and buy urban real estate; Lally, the exquisite model for all Mexico City's new painters; Bobó Gutiérrez, a young man so full of life and practical jokes; and the girls, the girls, the girls from every corner and nook of everywhere, admitted to the Holy of Holies because of the etherial force of their singing laughter, their potable capacities, and the exclusive taste of the priest of the temple and lord of the manor, Don Luis Verdaguer, self-styled last true prince of Elsinore: Yorick on the auction block, Hamlet already knocked down, the palace in Avenida Juárez, knocked down diplomatic appointments in Europe, knocked down the substance, *hors commerce*, of a great name. Knocked down, Saturday teas with Díaz and Díaz's doña; knocked down in one word, all elegance. Now he was only an old cask, a pool: San Fermín.

And the woman in black slacks whose cigarette holder was Chinese, an ivory serpent of intertwined elephants and pagodas. "*Chère* Norma," she said, sitting beside the pool to enamel her fingernails, "are you still a virgin? Look what a face Pierrot has now! Knight of the Round Bed!"

Norma had to strain to seem unconcerned and to avoid blushing.

"And that's why you have conquered our conquerors, you're the only one who can still blush. If you knew what you will lose when you lose that! Ah, *liebchen*, you and your blushes have Pierre roped, and I. . . . And you always have to keep just a little on for after the show, like a striptease; there, *voilà*, is the only true beautiful . . . discovery. Give me a loincloth and I'll raise the world! Mexican men have a wonderful theory about feminine shame; if they see you naked just once, even if they don't touch you, they become mystics about it. But if you wear only a grape leaf when you go to bed with them, your honor is saved. And that's perversion. Better a Rousseau at the feet of a Madame Basile, respect and panting at once."

Norma would always smile nervously and never know what to say. Moreover, Natasha's dark glasses always bothered her.

"How old do you think I am, Norma?"

"Thirty, a little more, maybe."

"How faintly ingenuous. If I were thirty, do you think I would be sleeping twelve hours every night, wearing dark glasses all day, a scarf to hide my baldness? Raw carrots, bran crackers, two hours of cream, massages! all the rites between chic and agony? And you should see me in bed. Guignol."

"You're very attractive, Natasha."

"Bah! Five years more and I'll have to make a fool of myself with a gigolo or play poker with other painted old women, like a character by Colette. What's that tune? 'Better to die already.' Oh, but how macabre. And here you are, hesitating before love. Do you think you'll always be as you are now, so willowy, blushing? Wise up. And he is, after all, something . . . golden, eh, and muscles, too. Well . . . *Ja*."

Natasha whistled for her Great Dane and walked off into Cuernavaca. That night Norma went to Natasha's room to borrow fingernail polish and found a mummy, powdered and goose-fleshed, with wasted arms laced by blue veins. All her hair had

94

been braided into three braids, and double chins dropped like a marsupial pouch. On the bureau shimmered another, the languid jeweled Natasha of twenty years ago.

"Rasputin took that picture of me. Nobody believes it. Someone said . . . someone . . . that not to believe in the supernatural is to give the Devil a running start."

Natasha sucked her bran crackers and Norma left, nauseated by the teeth shining in a glass of water: One thing I really believed and that was that I have to reach marriage still virgin, but no, that's to render far too much honor to a husband, and to wither in agony meanwhile. Some of these hot nights in Cuernavaca I feel like selling myself to the whole plaza. I'm going to go crazy if I don't get a man to paste myself against, if I have to go on with no kicks except looking at myself naked in the mirror and feeling myself with my fingers under the sheets. . . . The following week end she went to Pedro's room, using some pretext, and it happened, impatiently and without fear. A servant was collecting empty bottles when she left Pedro's room at seven in the morning, and he observed her with a half-smile she had seen directed at most of the guests at all hours. Pedro was rather sickened by the way she had bled, and he stopped seeing her, but now other men asked her out, though they did not send her orchids and they felt her up in the car and did not date her again unless she kissed them. Once again her mother came from Santa María del Oro, and now Norma was not so thoughtless as to go out on the street with the old woman who was always dressed in black and who often said *pos* instead of *pues* and could not carry on a conversation. The old woman went back to the mining town, weeping, leaving behind photos of herself and of Norma's brother, dedicated to Norma in an almost illegible hand. Norma soon threw the photos out. At the railroad station she happened to see the de Ovandos as she was putting her mother onto the train; she pulled her furs up around her nose and afterward told them that she had been seeing off an old servant, What democracy, Norma!

When she was twenty-six, she was much talked about; her picture came out in society sections frequently, taken in all the night clubs and always with a different man. At an official Government reception she was introduced to a swarthy banker, tightly encased in his swallowtail, to whom everyone bowed and scraped: He has tone, that's sure, they fall down in front of him. Really that's all I need . . . a man men bow to. Love, as Natasha says, by definition excludes sincerity.

"If that old boy would tuck me in bed, we'd have our fortune back," someone said. "He's the local Rothschild, never says a word, and a bachelor."

Federico Robles asked her to dance. After two turns he stopped and took her to the buffet. She talked and talked, about how Mexico City had grown and changed, the new night spots, the Casanova, the Sans Souci, so many interesting people had come from all over everywhere, and now we had, indeed, an international capital, what with Carol and Lupescu, and about the green hairstyles of Fernanda Montel: ah, one had to enjoy this wonderful cosmopolitan new Mexico City, didn't he agree? Enjoy it, yes, for everyone has a right to play after working hard all one's life, but the problem was that a girl needed a real man with whom to enjoy it. A girl met so many stuffed shirts without the least character, and so few real men, men a girl could help, why in a thousand little ways, social life, clothes, taste, the true enjoyment of the true riches in life; didn't he agree? Robles found it pleasant to laugh with her. He regarded her with affection, and in one year, they married.

When the maid appeared on the terrace, Norma had just sat up, hastily, dizzied by the sun, and was thinking—not thinking, rather, wanting to know what she felt—that she could not cry; the more images of pain or fear she conjured up, the less willing tears were; they would not come, would not come. She covered her breasts with her robe.

"The *Señor* is here with his guests. They are waiting for you, *Señora*."

"Tell him . . . tell the *Señor* to excuse me. I don't feel well. Anything. Tell him."

"Yes, *Señora*."

RODRIGO POLA

Rodrigo breathed deep, and Ixca, beside him, covered the orange flame of a match with both hands and slowly lit a cigarette. Twilight was settling upon the blue treetops of Paseo de le Reforma; here near the corner of Seville, traffic at this time of the evening was light. Two men: one of medium height with delicate features and pale greenish skin that darkened around the eyes; the other with burned almond eyes, thick lips, brushy hair, and features somewhere between pure Indian and equally pure Mediterranean European sunburned. They were strolling along the soft packed-earth walk beside the Paseo. Rodrigo looked at the dust on his shoes; he was conscious of every nervous movement. Cienfuegos was as if he were not walking at all, but were being drifted along by a light summer wind, as if he did not have legs, nor the powerful hands which so disturbed Pola. Ixca snapped his match into the air and let smoke rise past the wings of his nose until his eyes were hidden.

"You and I have lived many moments together, Rodrigo. We think that we know everything about each other."

"No, but I know something about you," said Rodrigo. "Look at the dust. You can't walk ten minutes in this city without being covered with it."

"You know as much about me as I know about you. We're what are called the watery Mexicans."

Rodrigo felt all hands and feet, awkward, clumsy, in every posture ridiculous. The Monument to Independence was pulling itself up by the calves, and on Florencia a cluster of goats were crossing, shooed by a shoeless Indian. "You know that my father died in Belén prison, executed by Victoriano Huerta in nineteen hundred thirteen. I was born after he went to prison . . ."

Did you remember me, father, just before you died? Did you think about me?

A bag of semen, warm thighs, that was what I remembered. You had fired mother's blood, and about me.

No. Only a cold dawn, the image of a bird dipping, wetting its wings in a tropical river. And then the lead that comes in without your feeling it, to bleed you inside.

". . . They refused to let us have the body, I mean to say we found out, my mother did, but only years later, that my father's body had been heaped with others from the Revolution, all unknown. . . ."

"And now the dust cloud is coming, son, and I shall close my eyes and swallow dust. It comes from where your father lies."

". . . and we were always thinking about him, Ixca, as if there were really three of us living there. I had nothing to help me remember him; from the very beginning I tried to find something to use to form a true image, that photograph was never enough, cracked and yellow, a man in uniform with a light soldiery smile, glistening mustaches; and my mother never wanted to recreate the image I needed, for it wasn't hers, for her my father was some other man, outside her, who had gone away and left her a widow just one year after their marriage, a repeating rancor, to have also lived so briefly, but surrounded by something extraordinary, as he had been, and she never had been, and that, the absence of contrast and relief in her life, more than anything, made her compare herself with my father and wish that she could be him, but a different him, and that he had been her. But I didn't, I just wanted to be the continuation of my father, in some way, and I believed that the continuation ought to be moral (I believed that without knowing how to explain it, even as a baby), yes, that was what I knew all along. But I think that today is the first time I have understood it. My father lived in another land, another city: Mexico and Mexico City die completely every time a man gives his blood with passion; it is as if we were waiting for such a man, one who could give everything, so that we might make a sacrifice of his giving and die with him; and I believe that when he went to death, I was just being born, and I knew only the corpse that belonged to my mother, seated on a cane-bottomed rocker, knitting baby clothes to sell in the neighborhood, and later when my grandfather, who had helped us a little, died intestate, his other sons, who had exiled Rosenda my mother from the family because she had married a Revolutionary, fell on the poor patrimony and by every possible means tried to keep her from touching one cent. And that is when my memory and my life begin: dragged along by the hand, downtown streets, from shop to shop, looking for work and my eyes staring at the laced buttons that squeezed my mother's feet. Finally she found work in a department store, her hundred and twenty-five pesos a month plus her commissions (and knitting more baby clothes at night) just let us get by, and I spent my days alone on the roof of our little house on Chopo Street because there wasn't money enough for a church school and she didn't want to send me to a public school; and I would look far away to see the steel cobweb where the Museum of Natural History was, and listen to the whistles of balloon men and to organ grinders who trooped through the neighborhood every afternoon and would see me peeping down at them and hold their hats toward me and I would begin to whistle and to examine the sky, as if to tell them that I hadn't asked for their music and moreover could make my own. How strange, to remember like this, spontaneously, all the little details, and you see yourself as if seeing someone else, so far away, it is almost a drawing or a photographed landscape seen as you thumb through a magazine; you remember the stocking the kid wore every night to make his hair lie flat, but you see him only as a boy drawn on a rooftop hours and hours, quietly watching people pass and listening, sometimes, to the racket of cavalry over the city's paving stones. Those were men from whom one had to hide, they frightened the boy, and I'll never forget my mother's face, pale as a winter sky, when she came home from work the day Villa's men marched into the city; she hid me under the bed and for several days pretended to be sick to avoid going downtown. Above all, she must have felt that one of those ferocious men was my father, my real father, who had not died but gone on galloping across plains in disguise. It's useless to remember that; he was not what the memory was at that moment, and we shouldn't have even the right to remember the memory. Now the coyote is coming to eat you up, eat you up, with a big stick. And comings and goings on Chopo Street were my only amusement. All day long on the roof, and during the short night hours at the foot of the cane rocking chair, watching my mother knit. "Poor baby, we've been left all alone, you and I, in a world without men. What's going to happen to . . . go to sleep, to sleepy, to sleepy . . ." When I was eight, I started in the Fathers of Mary school, and my mother worked harder than ever at the store and knitting at night. I had two pictures, one of Father and the other of Mother, and if his was always the same, so that even as a corpse I saw him still in that uniform and still with that martial smile, hers was sometimes two pictures, the photograph portrait and a new one which I discovered as I did my homework under the lamp with the green velvet shade, watching her from the corner of my eye. She was seated at the window, trying to hold the last faint rays of sunlight on her yarns; the first portrait always said, 'Everything will be better soon,' but the new one surprised me; I watched her pass her hands over the cheekbones reflected in the window, and she must have seen, too, because she stared at her cheeks and her chin as if trying to remember beautiful words: it was her eyes that had changed, they were far away from the wrinkled knitting, a little sunken, and they had a new expression. She saw it herself at the same time I did, and from that moment, every night, when she saw herself reflected in the window, my mother's stare grew fixed and she peered, trying to understand that new expression. I pretended to be writing in my copybook, but I didn't miss anything, not the slightest detail of that nocturnal ceremony, and my mother, the deeper into the glass her vision moved, the more she became aware of the world of reflections, became aware at last of me, and suddenly, like a flash of lightning, her eyes whirled around on my hunched figure while I, with an electric jerk, tried to get back to my homework; but she was not deceived, she realized that I had been spying on her, that she had not grown old alone, that someone noticed things not noticed by her, that there was someone else in her life with whom she had to share; that was what she must have been feeling then, and very straight, with her shawl flying, she fell upon me and slapped my face and spilled my ink bottle, and I dropped to the floor and hid between the legs of the table and from there watched my mother grow taller and taller until she reached the ceiling, like a dark, shadow-ruined column; I watched the nerves in her fists dancing and the way her hand grew skinny as she opened it imploringly and said, 'Come boy, come, if I don't protect you, who will?' And I ran and hugged her knees, weeping with a new bitterness, happy to have learned something about her, to have discovered that I could understand her without making her angry, but very ashamed of myself."

Rodrigo looked up, awakened by insistent horns from the Circle of Cuauntémoc, opposing streams of vehicles which flowed up and down Reforma and gushed out of Dinamarca, Roma, Insurgents, and Ramón Guzman, twisted into amalgamated snakes, not to be solved; the horns never stopped, cops whistled fruitlessly, heads popped out of car windows to shout and disappeared inside again to hit the horn again one-two-three-four-five times.

"You learn what you are very young. I had learned. Afterward, I always knew that I was what I had felt myself to be then: a spy. That is to say, a looker-on, destined to make my life of the lives of others. And that was all. And I made something shoddy, because of my ability to understand all my defects, my inability to rise above them."

"You resemble the nation," said Ixca as he took Rodrigo's elbow to cross the avenue.

"No, Ixca, no. Why did my father know how to throw himself into the struggle, to overcome his defects, and I haven't known? Why was there a path of honorable action open to him and his men, while for us there is only conformity, burning inside and secretly, and the goddamned hopelessness? I tell you, from the time I knew anything about anything, I knew that I am less his son physically than morally, and that today I ought to act, that I have better reason than he had, that he *would* act today, one way or another, that he wouldn't live at second hand. And I've wanted to, Ixca, I've meant to, I've always fought against myself to learn truth, to discover morality; but what help has it been? You tell me."

"Manuel Zamacona would tell you that you fulfill the moral struggle in yourself, that if you think and in all conscience feel yourself joined with other men, that is enough, you are taking part in everything. . . ."

"Do you believe that?"

"What do I believe? Your own life will tell you someday what I believe, or I will have been of no service at all to you."

"Look at Norma's husband. He's balanced, directed, he knows what he wants. He is convinced that he is serving the good of the country. Would it be enough to do what he does, feeling as he feels? My God, Ixca, what *is* this country, where is it going, what can be done with it?"

"Everything."

"Everything, but what? What do we have to do to understand it? Where does it begin, where does it end? Why is it satisfied with half solutions? Why does it abandon its best? What formula makes it intelligible? Where can you grip it? What happened to the Revolution? Did it serve only to create a new group of potentates, sure that they control everything, that they are just as indispensable as Díaz's clique believed themselves?"

"Nothing is indispensable in Mexico, Rodrigo. Late or soon, an anonymous and secret force floods and transforms everything. A force that is older than all our memories; as compact and concentrated as a grain of gunpowder. The beginning, the origin. All the rest is masquerade. There, in our origin, Mexico still exists, is what is, is never what it can be but what it is. And what Mexico is, is fixed forever, incapable of evolution. Mother stone cannot be shifted. Any sort of slime may grow on that stone. But the stone doesn't change, it is the same forever."

"No help, Ixca. That is no answer for me."

"And your own life?"

"Yes . . . we were talking about my life." A line had formed in front of the Cine Roble. Rodrigo and Ixca made their way through. Men and women bored by the snail's pace at which they were moving toward the illuminated ticket window.

"At seven-thirty every morning, I walked to school, and one block before I got there, I would begin to drag my feet and play hopscotch. The class in morality terrified me. Our teacher said that it was the most important of all. 'If you don't know geogra-

102

phy, you will only be an ignoramus; but if you don't know your catechism, you condemn yourself, and you'll go to a place where you will be all alone, with neither your parents nor anyone, for ever and ever.' And I could never learn it. In other subjects there was something—not much, but something—that I could learn by understanding and thinking; but in morality, everything had already been thought."

"And the theological virtues?"

"Faith, hope . . ."

Rodrigo was made to blush by words he understood too well to understand. His deskmate was Roberto Régules, and once Roberto invited him to take chocolate after school. He lived in a turreted home near Chapultepec Avenue and had a room full of lead soldiers and big notebooks. Rodrigo asked him what the notebooks were and Roberto said that they contained secrets; he climbed up on his bed and took one of the notebooks down from the shelf and sat on the floor and opened it gleefully, awaiting his companion's admiration: "You know what a mess morality is. But really it isn't so hard. It all depends, because here are the secrets. . . ." And he opened the notebook; it bristled with pictures cut from magazines, with religious prints and writing in Indian ink. "The trick is to figure out what everythng really means, so when Valles asks you, you'll remember the answer and he can't mix you up. See, this is hope." A print of the Crucifixion, next to a photograph of an Italian movie actress. The word *hope* was written across the top of the page in red ink, and across the bottom was written: CROSS, AN INTERSECTION, JESUS COMING AND THE DEVIL GOING. "But if Jesus doesn't come, then what? Or if the Devil takes you or if you are more a devil than the Devil himself, then it's the Devil howling. You see?" Rodrigo didn't see. With his head twisting, he inspected the page called HOPE.

"You must be thick. Don't you see? Everything means something, and you pick out the meaning you like. Look, here is chastity."

The page was blank.

"And why is it empty?"

103

"That means two things. Nobody talks about it, and if you ask, everybody stops talking, that means that chastity is something bad and therefore it is forbidden to you."

"But the catechism says we have to be chaste . . ."

"Then why don't your mother and father ever want to talk about it? No, it has to be something bad, but because they forbid it, at the same time it's got to be something pretty good. All you have to do is pretend to have it, and see how it goes. Well, would you like to play the game, too?"

Rodrigo said *yes* and they shook hands on it, and Rodrigo signed a wrinkled scrap of paper with an *X*, and in morality class they looked at each other furtively when the Father talked about hope and Roberto remembered the Italian actress on the tiger skin, and every time the Father said one of the sacred words, Roberto wrote it on a piece of paper and slipped it to Rodrigo: the dry flower, the cat, the Cross and Blood. When he got home Rodrigo sat in the green light, opened his copybook, and pretended to be doing homework; in reality he was trying to think up code equivalents for the magic catechism words; he searched his small memory feverishly, looking for formulas, shining voices that the next day would earn Roberto's approval. The Holy Ghost: the flag of the Black Pirate. Theology: the black death-crêpe on grandfather's door. . . . As lunch hour neared, he felt an intolerable weakness in his legs, he chewed his pencil and wished for the moment when his mother would sit in her rocker in front of the window and begin to read his copybook; then, very swiftly, he filled the pages with senseless numbers that meant nothing and hid the holy sheets of their game inside the jacket of the copybook.

"And thus, Ixca, my friend Roberto Régules and I invented a secret game based on the catechism, a game that swallowed up time and imagination both at school and at home. I wished I could have my mother in the game, too, not for her companionship and understanding, but because I felt superior to her because of the game, the game only Roberto and I knew about, only we could explain and allow others to enter; and I felt sorry for my mother without knowing it, sorry because of her old shoes and her face that every day was further from the elegant youthful wife in the photograph, and I wanted to present to her the game in which all mystery and companionship were concentrated; but my mother never knew, she believed that she dominated me naturally, without asking leave to do so, that I would always be a part of her, the only spectator at her day-by-day life and her night hours next to the window, seated in the cane rocker with the ball of yarn on her lap and her eyes sinking deeper and deeper into her skull, further and further from our portrait in thick baby clothes; and she had no desire to help me with my life, nor I to help with hers, but without her I couldn't finish making the game, without her astonishment, her awareness that I had created another world: that was what I needed, for her to take part so that she would know I lived for my own reasons, I didn't need hers; but she never got into the game, because one morning . . ."

Father Valles, who taught morality, silently drew near Roberto and Rodrigo and opened the top of their desk. His smooth pink cheeks shook violently when Roberto jerked the top down again, smashing one of the Father's fingers. He opened the desk a second time, twisting the boy's ear all the time, and found the slips of paper full of incomprehensible code, and took them out. When the class ended, he called Roberto up to the front and advised him to stop the tomfoolery or he would have to talk with the Director.

"What are we going to do, Rob?" Rodrigo asked when they were walking home along a street of old elms and old rose-colored homes.

"You'll see what I do. We're going to let him into the game, too."

One week later the whole school was called together in the Assembly Hall. Boys in knickers and tan knee socks gave off an odor of soapy necks, sour breakfasts, and drowsy flesh; there was pine scent of the benches and dry dust smell from pencil sharpeners. At the end of the hall a blue altar shone, a statue of the Virgin dressed in white and blue, suffocating among white lilys. The bearded Director entered; at his side, dejected, wear-

105

ing lay clothing, was Padre Valles. Scuffing and blowing and joking stopped when the Director's whiskers opened on the curve of his tongue: We are here to confirm a serious charge. The father of one of our students has informed us of grave irregularities on the part of a teacher. I want Señor Valles, before he departs from our cloister, to stand before all of you and ask your forgiveness for his unforgivable conduct. You, my dear boys, will point out to your parents how sensitive we of the school's administration are to every aspect of honor—how, although risking the loss of new students next year, we nevertheless comply with the wishes of a father of a family . . ." Rodrigo felt a lump in his throat, he could not hear the Director's speech; he knew now that Father Valles had entered their game all right: Father Valles was the third. He tried to whisper to Roberto, in the row behind him, but Roberto's smile, the triumphant gleam in his eyes, stopped him. The Director made nothing quite clear. The boys' guesses accused Father Valles of every kind of crime.

"They must have caught him with a woman."

"Don't make me laugh; you know fathers don't go in for women."

"He was stealing from the money we gave for . . ."

With sweating hands Rodrigo approached Roberto Régules, with a shaking voice asked, "So you let him into our game?"

Roberto laughed, howled. "And how, I let him in! They found the notebook in his room." And with his hands in his pockets, he rocked back on his heels.

"*Our* book? But how could it . . ." He wanted to cry. He bit his lips.

"I put it there. And then I told Papa the screwy ideas Father Valles was putting into my head, and Papa asked the Director to get rid of him or he would stop the annuity he gives the school. Since the annuity is more than forty tuitions, well, you see, eh?"

And so the game had not been sacred, that was what Rodrigo wanted to say, still facing his friend, but he didn't say it, didn't say anything. Roberto began to toss a coin. "Now I'm going home to Guanajuato; some of my nitwit aunts live there and they'll get me a tutor. This place disgusts me."

Rodrigo, his eyes watching the acrobatic coin, felt as if his whole body had gone into his throat. "And our pact?" was all he could say; and wanted to say, You were my friend, my only friend, you invented the game, and now there will be nothing except the long hours on the roof and my mother knitting. I can't play the game by myself; you were my friend; don't go away. Roberto walked off, tossing the coin, and Rodrigo stayed, scratching the yellow point of his boot against the patio tree, now without any sacred code word, plain words danced inside his head. . . .

The tube-squeezed light of neon advertisements, beer, rum, insurance, newspapers, flickered over their faces. Charles IV stood royally erect in the middle of the circle, commanding the whirl of busses and cabs, while an electric billboard, high on the white building which was surrounded by ticket vendors come back to turn in the numbers they had not sold, flashed the winning lottery numbers. Yellow streetcars squealed along Rosales, and on the corner of Colón, a group of women stood patting dabs of spit on their eyebrows and stockings while a dozen newspaper boys who had just finished sharing a skimpy evening meal, ran teasing a dog, trying to slap its haunches; and soon those kids would begin to look for a doorway bed, a place to sleep, a bank or one of the churches on Carmen. Rodrigo hesitated, then crossed Bucareli. "Let's go in Kikos and have coffee. I still don't want to go home."

Overweight men in green gabardine. Unshaven bums. Women with their oily hair up in knots. Teen-age boys in blue jeans, using their combs over and over, feeding the juke box. Ixca and Rodrigo looked for a table.

"Any kind of whore you want, at Chayito's they got her."

"Jive, boy, jive!"

"So what objection you got to make to his *pase por alto?* Cunt, man! That's one little bullfighter who knows what he's doing."

"And just because he's your boss, he thinks he can get away with . . ."

"Jive, boy, jive!"

"A pay raise? Really?"

"Then my mother got a promotion in the department store. And at school I was all alone. Roberto left, and he had been my only friend. Now all the boys, seeing me unprotected by Régules, the rich boy whose father practically supported the school, began to tease me and to kick my shins . . ."

"Pola! Hey, kiss my ass, Pola!"

". . . and I would pretend to be sick to keep from going to school. I began to buy books with money saved from my allowance and to read on the roof as long as there was light enough; I would go downstairs before Mother got home, eat, and shut myself up in my room and read, and then she began to make me sit at her knee at night, and while she knitted, she would complain, 'You never tell me about your plans, child, what do you want to do?' But I didn't answer, but thought about magic words that no longer had meaning or about *The Three Musketeers* or about the kicks that had bruised my legs. What was it she would say? 'Remember that even if you are left alone in the world, you will always have your mother to tell your secrets to and be honest with. Now you are beginning to be a man, and if you don't tell your mother everything that happens, you'll be full of questions and unable to explain anything.' And I looked around that familiar little living room, a room lived in by the two of us and inhabited by my father's ghost: the green-shaded lamp, the table with its rickety chairs and smelly fruitbowl, the cane rocker in which mother knitted every night; the sofa, cane too, unraveling; the wooden floor, painted rose, the window with its cotton curtains, the door with its little bronze bell. And only now, hearing my mother's words, did it occur to me that I would someday have to leave that home, and I thought, without giving it importance, that my mother would not be left alone because the ghost with glossy mustaches and the martial smile would companion her forever, never so far away as I would be, and she must have understood my thought . . . as she understood so many things, but only one minute before I did, as if in my idiot eyes she divined everything. I thought and some things knew always one minute before I knew them; and because of that, she never realized just what she said to me that night, those gratuitous words I did not understand, refused to believe were true, and that now I see as her desire to drink me up completely, squeeze me between her thighs and be forever, to the end of our three lives, giving birth to me without rest in an endless birth of days, an eternal vocal birth which would always tell her what she wanted to hear, squatting huge on the placenta, words like a monument, living in her thick need to be always the mother, always giving nature flesh. So when I asked her, 'Was father good to you?' she bit her lips and dropped her needles in her lap. Gratuitous nature, Ixca, like her great mother's words, the opened outraged mother, torn by something that existed no longer than the prolonged, true and truthful moment of birth; words that were explicit but I shall never understand: 'Your father was a coward who betrayed his comrades and died like a fool, leaving us in poverty!' "

Rodrigo concealed his broken face behind his cup. Ixca Cienfuegos began to hum the juke-box tune: *si Juárez no hubiera muerto, la patria se salvari.* Rodrigo returned his cup to its sugary saucer.

"And I remember myself afterward as having greener skin, eyes more sunken. I began college when I was sixteen. The church school had been closed and my mother was very afraid that I would be contaminated at Prepa. We could no longer speak to each other, not after that scene, except to ask for something or to say we were going out, when we were coming in. But she watched me, she spied on me. Now she spent her solitary hours in the cane rocker, knitting and trying to speak to me with her silence, and I carried silence to my room and every night took my pen and wrote because at last I had found my solid stone. I wrote feverishly, tense, not always knowing what words were spilling across the paper, but sure that no matter what they were, they were important. Important because the paper wasn't paper, nor the words, words, nor the writing, writing: important because everything was my own way to say, Here I am. I. I, who am not everyone, nor any other. I who am I. Unique. God himself cannot change me into another. If I were anyone else, the world would fall. The moon would be the sun, day would be a different light. They could not change me into anyone else, nor anyone else into me. I read Garcilaso and felt I had moved into a more perfect world of harmony in which everyone could love and live, see and be seen, without shame and above all, without apologies. And when Rimbaud fell into my hands, I believed that I had met my true brother and friend, he would know how to understand and share the great discovery, the great sadness. I clenched my teeth and wrote, slapping the hanging light so that I could feel my head whirl with the swinging shadows and that the room was not just as space around me, but my brain itself, great and at the same time sick, illuminated and dark and dancing to a fatal disordered beat. Afterward, I would fall, drained, on my bed. Undress in silence, with closed eyes pull the covers up and wait for the headache that came every morning when I was getting ready for the terrible moment of departure to classes.

"In Prepa I met a group of young men who were interested in literature. They were headed by Tomás Mediana and they were planning a new review which would bring all the unknown new European writers to Mexico. They laughed a little at my enthusiasm for Garcilaso, but when I mentioned Rimbaud, they looked at me attentively and decided I might take part in their sessions. Tomás asked me if I had read Gide, and promised to take me to see his library. 'I subscribe to *N.R.F.* and get all the new work. Here they haven't even heard of Marcel Proust. There already exists a new sensibility that is truly ours, of our century.'

"Those friendships stimulated me. All of them were taking, just as I was, law degrees, but no one read law. 'It's the nearest to what really interests us,' Mediana would say. 'And as our fathers think that a degree is equivalent to honor and bread at the same time, down with Bohemia!'

"I began to cull my verses to show them to Tomás, and when he said one day, 'When will we see some of your things?' . . . what didn't I feel, eh, Ixca, what didn't I feel! You were there, you remember. We felt capable of everything. Art, literature . . . the new code, the new magic words. I remember that Orozco

110

was painting at Prepa and I used to stay after classes and watch, a spider filling the old walls with new form and color, nailed to his scaffolding, hour after hour, working with only one hand. I felt that his colors were mine, that their coming out into light was something important; they had appeared to speak and tell every man who he really was, where his ideas were, what his character was. I began to be late getting home because I would spend hours with my new friends, the new group, in downtown cafés . . . you remember them, Ixca? Pablo Berea, formal, he had already triumphed in poetry and in government. Luis Pineda, who had brought out a satiric review. Jesús de Olmos, tall and gummy, always punning. Ramón Frías, modest, handsome, precise, never said much, forever at work on a mysterious long poem. Jorge Taillén, the oldest of them, had traveled to exotic places and published three volumes of peculiar lyric poetry. Roberto Ladeira, the most secretive and brilliant, the idea man. And Tomás Mediana. Small, pale, always in black, full of humor and satanic comparisons. I used to say their names over, Ixca! They were the high priests of a new cult that would take us, through poetry, each to his own salvation, and allow us to leave beauty behind us."

Rodrigo sniffed the rancid air and was carried back to those coffee tables on París:

DE OLMOS (*murmuring as he watches Mediana's opaque silouette enter*): *L'Ange Heurtebise! Je te garde, je te heurte, je te brise . . .*

LADEIRA (*eyes lost in smoke*): Gide asks if there is being first, so that there may be appearance, or if the condition is to appear first in order to be that which is appearance. . . .

MEDIANA (*sitting*): There exists an uncertain but apprehensible geometry of time. Time and man are the only elements which can juggle themselves. Maybe that's because they are the only elements that do not touch, even when they envelop each other reciprocally. *Les jours s'en vont, je demeure.* But also: I go and days remain. Why does time seem, is it that I am? Or is it that time is, and I, only a perception of it? There, in infinity, the parallels meet. Here . . .

111

DE OLMOS: A Rose is a rose is a rose. Mirror of a mirror of a mirror, every being is that: the illusion of itself, the continuation in a looking glass of a simple *I am.* Until when? (*pounds floor with pearl-handled cane to summon a waiter.*) *Tu,* Tomasso, and also I, why not confess if the confession can be voluptuous . . . you profess friendship, not the cult, a horrid word, of elasticity. Now you know quite well that our immobility is in this instant charged with imminence! From eminence deliver us! There is no immobility except by a subtle process of self-hypnotism which we cannot analyze.

PINEDA (*round-eyed, from behind his milkshake*): Always that greedy *leitmotiv.*

DE OLMOS: Knopf you, too. Today's slogan for the academy.

BEREA (*coughing and clearing his throat*): It seems to me that the conversation has lost its way. This disparity and opposition between time and man are really between one time and some men. Let me enjoy, if only by memory, those epochs in which time and man coincide! Today coincidence is broken and we must find it again. I mean to say, the right coincidence for this time and these men. A coincidence which I dare to say is synonomous with sensibility. And there we have the magic word which at once explains our promise and our purpose, too.

LADEIRA (*without abandoning his uncomfortable posture, the back of his neck on the back of his cane chair*): In a way Iago is right. Something unites us, and it is only that we are apart.

MEDIANA (*rising, then afraid to speak, or perhaps feeling that he is selling something to the wrong market*): Our solitude, our non-being for no one.

LADEIRA: Yes. There's no doubt about it, a community of poets, of men with lofty preoccupations. But their community is determined not by values or common pursuits but precisely by the divagation and loneliness of individuals who day after day carry out labor further removed from the collective interest, the needs of the mass.

MEDIANA (*lowering his eyes*): Cocteau's unhappy phrase is not fortuitous. Poetry in our time preserves the beauty of martyr-

112

dom. Poetry: the desire for communion. Martyrdom: a solitary experience, unique.

DE OLMOS. To cult is to occult.

"Under those stars, I began to write. 'Dedicate yourself to discipline from this moment on,' Tomás Mediana said when we came out of the café about seven in the evening and walked together toward the Puente de Alvarado. 'Above all, we must determine our ground and then never leave it.' We said good-bye at the corner, and I walked home to the window on Chopo Street where my mother sat knitting. It was dark, her window was dark that evening, and I went in with a presentiment of evil, a sadness that was waiting to show itself, a sickness that still gave no fever, although the germs were already at work. That night I found her in my room, seated on my cot, with burning eyes and a sheaf of papers in her hand. My manuscript. I wanted to run and grab it, but that glow of deceit, that petition of hurt in her eyes stopped me. 'Be careful,' her eyes said (but not her eyes, they were saying something else, something terrible: *deceived*) every time I moved near her through her name. . . . Mother, Mother . . . each time I suggested she come have dinner. My mother's eyes that night had changed into calm ponds of still fire with two sharp points, and they and her lips, too, told me, as she had not discovered it when I played the code game, that the cord had broken, that her legs had come together and closed, and the son had escaped from the warm entrails that had nurtured him and that he in turn had to warm and nurture.

" 'So this is what you have been doing all year! These verses!' and I knew, I understood then that she had finally found the opportunity she had never had to speak the old accusations she had never given voice to; I knew and was afraid, and now that dark figure on the bed was shaking my manuscript and saying, 'And I have been killing myself in the department store to make you into a useful man, did you know that? Look at me: a woman who has lived without blood, and now without love, either, no, always without love from the moment he stopped wanting me, to provide you with food and an education, your mother, but you haven't understood anything.'

"And to me it seemed just . . . just incongruous to be hearing those words in the same room where I had written every night and had discovered the bitter heaviness of words and ideas that were mine alone and unless I expressed them, would never be known by anyone (I learned the monstrous weight of the mouth that insists it must speak words and shape them into the strongest form, that this is the heaviest mouth of all to open, but only by opening can it earn its bread and win fame with its sold words), and because of this I felt myself suddenly drawn with a life line of my own (as my father must have seen the silhouette of his life for one moment on that mountain to which he fled after escaping from Belén and again later, in the blood splattered from his face as he fell in front of the execution wall) and the son not so much of my parents as of my own brief but unique and unchangeable experience, and I said—what were my words? 'Mamá, I have my own destiny,' while my mother's hands tore my manuscript and she repeated my words with bellowing laughter, 'Have I had my own destiny? Has anyone ever had his own destiny? Your father had no destiny; he had death. His native land ordered him executed; he gave more than blood, gave everything except the absurdity of one love who went on waiting although forsaken. And you have no destiny either, learn it now. You have responsibilities and a mother who has never had nor, for that matter, wanted a destiny, who has had only shame and bitterness struggling to make a man of you, well educated. Yes, well educated; rich, yes; well married, yes, with children, a good Catholic, yes, yes, who would know the right people and receive them in his home, yes; without conscience, yes, a conformist living with neither tenderness nor pain, neither grief nor fury, yes.' Her voice trembled, it was both thunder and lightning, in a bitter grimace of held-back tears. I fell at her feet and embraced her knees and wanted to ignore all the inner voices crying for me to be cold. Then I got up and sat beside her on the cot, and caressed her hair. She did not give in to her tears, she held on, held herself shut like a boxed storm, with that mournful face, and I felt satisfied with myself (as when you raise a hand in class because you're the only one who knows the answer, or as when you are waiting, on the street, for people to watch you give money to a beggar, or as when you know that someone is eavesdropping on you and you don't allow yourself to be understood, but raise your voice and choose your most brilliant words); I felt most satisfied with my filial tenderness, but my heart was shrieking rebellion, and a sob kept trembling my mother's throat, and I saw her then, I saw her . . . how shall I say it, Ixca? well, as a woman, just a silly anyone's mother woman, that was all. I put the torn manuscript in my pocket and ran out of the room to hold it next to the night light and I put my palms over my eyes and felt an uncontrollable endless urge to laugh: where would I store her words, inside the days and happenings of my real life, that scene with my mother? What did one have to do with the other? Maybe she was right and no one has a right to his own being, and life is a continuous ebbing away before the wishes and acts of others; that room was from then on no longer mine; it would be forever shared with a woman begging pity, offering wrath, demanding apology, seated on the edge of my bed. Mediana's words came back to me, and I hated him. I no longer wanted to believe his serious, unctuous voice saying, 'Our generation has the duty to create in Mexico the dedication to labor without which no creative work may become more than a passing style.' No, no, no, cowardice, a man has to be crazy to attempt what only leads to defeat, and my lips spoke clichés and crippled verses sacred only because they said what I wanted to know and what I had wanted to believe, that I and the world were, to say it somehow, there, and that this was what was important; but I knew no way to say that to Tomás."

"Yes," said Ixca Cienfuegos. *Juárez no debió de morir, ay, de morir.*

"A few days later I took the manuscript to the printer Mediana and de Olmos had introduced me to. I had no money to pay him, but he agreed to take his chances and I didn't ask for a single copy. The book was called *Lavender Verse*. When I told Mediana, he wrinkled his eyebrows and informed me that nothing would have been lost by showing the verses to our group before firing them off to the printer, that there was a certain solidarity in the group, that what one published affected all. But all along I had felt that need; the book would be the only proof I existed and had a right to think, to doubt, on my own account and without asking permission; I had to do it alone."

"He gave the bull two derechazos, *and by then he almost had no belly left."*

"Just because I'm so damn weak, I found myself in that motel with him."

"I'll be seeing you, kid, I told her, so she wouldn't think I didn't have no pride at all . . ."

"The meetings in the café on Paris went on. Now they were all talking about a new theater group to introduce Cocteau and Pirandello. De Olmos had been photographed wearing a shroud and a three-cornered hat to illustrate his magazine article about the new literary sensibility; he jeered at the old graveyard of modern and romantic poets and he adapted several remarks by Gide and Ellis to a Mexican setting. One of these (Let us end our milky habit of placing our poetry within reach of women and children: Baudelaire, you bawdy liar, though the women like you, you don't belong to them) brought letters to the editor and protests. Taillén was on a walking tour in the Holy Land and sending back exalted sonnets. Berea was working in the Department of the Interior. And the famous South American poet Flavio Milós had just arrived in Mexico City. The group decided to honor him with a dinner, and chose Mediana's home as the most elegant; everyone pitched in with spirit, and the night of the fête we appeared, wearing black suits with carnations in our lapels, and lit candles on a table decorated with tulips. Mediana's family had once held some important government positions, and the house, although a little shabby, still showed memory of greatness, plaster cornices and gold-framed Empire glasses. But the furniture was cracked and rickety, and on the pier tables Tomás had placed copies of *N.R.F.* he had brought down from his room. Hours passed, and Milós didn't show. An old maid servant kept popping in and declaring: 'Young Tomás, if I water that wilted salad again it will wash away.' "

Rodrigo smiled and ordered another cup of coffee. "Finally we gave up talking and stared at the candles, which were getting shorter and shorter. Ladeira began to smile ambiguously, and I had an overpowering desire to laugh. At last, exactly at midnight, the bell rang and a fat young man with no necktie, wearing a corduroy jacket and a three-days' beard, came in. I remember very clearly his first words. They smashed the intellectual composure of the group like breaking teacups: 'Good God, what asses the whores here have!' And without saying *hello* to anyone, he grabbed a bottle of wine and sat on the floor. Ladeira's smile widened and Mediana turned chalky white."

DE OLMOS (*glistening with pomade, trying to save the situation*): There is, in Max Jacob a sentence so "posterior."

MILÓS (*howling, spitting a mouthful of wine on the rug*): Two days and two nights in a whorehouse!

MEDIANA (*groaning*): Roberto, an introduction is necessary.

LADEIRA (*rolls his head back on his chair, intently observes the obese poet*)

MILÓS (*now on his belly, with his nose in his glass*): Those women are like flowing lava, Jesus, what scissors! All of them with blue bedsheets. Blue sheets and a bottle of tequila, so you can feel like an eagle. You have to know how to hump, boys, hump like the dolphins near Talara, flash up out of the water for just an instant so that everyone can see them and miss them and then dive to the deep bottom. Oh my God, what asses, what asses. . . .

BEREA (*straightening his tie*): We were thinking, Señor Milós, that a little chat about the influence of Pound and Reissig . . .

"Berea and Mediana sat very straight on their Second Empire chairs and sipped wine mechanically. Milós was stretched out on the floor. De Olmos opened his mouth and at once shut it again. I was just taken by laughter, a fit of it. I remembered all the questions we had prepared, the careful collective review we had made of Milós's entire works, his probable influences, the illumination we had expected. And now that drunken whale, rolling about on the floor. I was happy. I thought about my book and I was glad I hadn't shown it to Mediana. I laughed so hard, I

117

had to get out without saying good night. While Tomás, very pale, went on sipping wine, and Flavio Milós stretched and roared on the rug. . . ."

Rodrigo stopped and emptied his cheap pack of cigarettes on the table. With his head down, he began to build a tobacco pyramid. "But Milós was only an amusing tourist, Ixca. He departed; I remained, accused by Tomás Mediana's hurt looks. When *Lavender Verse* appeared, he led the criticism. Doubtless it was well founded and honest, but I considered it malicious then. Verbal criticism, of course. Not one single review of it was published. The jokes and puns multiplied. Would *Lavender Worse* be next? My mother gave away most of the copies to the salesgirls in her department. And that was the outcome of my sleepless nights, my ambition, my presumptuous claim before my mother to my own destiny. She understood, and said nothing. The group grew cool to me, I decided to cut them. That was when I met Norma and believed that having her love, I could do without the group and literary glory. When I lost her love, too, I tried to find self-justification in university politics. You were in that. In nineteen hundred forty I was an underpaid minor civil servant who spent everything he made in whorehouses. Mediana was right. The group produced, they wrote, they persisted, they held to their purpose. My mother was right. There is no destiny. There are only responsibilities. The——"

"Closing time, gentlemen. Have to lock up, if we don't, we get fined."

Rodrigo emptied his glass of water. Ixca paid their check.

"We finish some other day, eh?" Rodrigo said with his head down.

A great silence, now and then broken by the kiss of neon lights, rolled around the frozen bronze head of Charles IV.

PART TWO

That Sunday the old man with a yellow mustache and a copper-handled cane went to Edison Street, to a dark house, and got his nephew and took him to the Little Horse Monument on Reforma. There they boarded a Lomas bus. The old man, intermittently trembling, sat his nephew next to the window, and with jabs of the heroic cane, pointed out the places that were no longer—Iturbe's mansion, the Limantour home, the Colón café—and those which, in stationary exile, deserved an elderly gentleman's recollection, although they still existed. "This was one long street of palaces in the old time," he told the boy, and rapped the window with his cane, paying no attention to the protests of the fat bus driver, who would occasionally, at intersections, lower his bottle of pop and his sports page. "After General Díaz, my child, this country stopped, stopped forever," and the boy licked his popsicle and craned his neck to see the height of buildings going up on Colón Circle. The old man did not see the buildings, the years of the past lay before his eyes, his mouth was half open in expectation of the next important Porfirian palace: a chill plain of steel and concrete hemmed in those lonely, barren islands of the past, lonely in his memory and taste, and after the Cuauhtémoc monument, where twenty teen-age boys wearing red sweatshirts came aboard, footballs under their arms, the old man's eyes grew animated and he jabbed the cane right and left, describing gardens he had known, how coaches had sounded, the liveries coachmen and servants had worn, the mansard roofs and, something he found hard to

121

say, the old-time rhythms, different footsteps, different smells, the so-different air people had had. "We have maimed this city forever, my son. Once it was the City of Palaces! Here, there, pay attention to what I am telling you and stop licking that ice cream." He would have liked to mention Governor de Landa y Escandón, but he suspected that the boy would not understand. And now they were rising, in the Lomas. With horror the old man saw a colonial-style residence, rich with lacy stone carving and niches and yellow stained-glass. He hit the floor with his cane. "There were only empty fields here!"

CITY OF PALACES

Federico parted gauzy curtains and entered his wife's dressing room, heavy with perfumes, with rosy powder puffs. Norma was at her looking glass, carefully doing her hair; as he entered, she covered her breasts with her silk gown and smiled lightly. Robles stood just inside the curtains and tried to find her eyes in the glass. He looked at her shoulders, her auburn hair, her hips.

"Yes?" said Norma, with a voice empty of all intentions.

"No . . . I've come only to ask what you're doing today." Federico reflected that the absence of inflection in their questions and answers was now natural and obligatory. Courtesy would never again be wanting between them, there would never again be scenes. She looked so useless and feeble. Her back was very thin, very easy to break.

Norma's puff raised a pink cloud around her throat. "A wedding, Pérez Landa's daughter. On Sunday, like any servant. I can't imagine what they're thinking about. And with all the old man's money. Obviously, it's going to be as common as——"

"Then why are you going?"

Foolish question, he thought. He knew himself that she had to go, to this and all weddings, to be his complement so that tactily or expressly his presence would always be felt in both worlds, the social as well as the business world.

Norma in turn looked for his face in the mirror. "We have to keep our obligations." She smiled. "And one can gossip. Sometime we'll have to go together. Sometimes you can learn things even at a silly wedding. At least you have a chance to see the bulge the groom is selling."

"What? Doesn't he love the girl?"

"Ay tú! You think any man could love that bony old maid? I saw her in her wedding gown, sweating to make you sweat, too. No, he's loading, that's all, loading up to the teeth. He'll never again have to lift a finger the rest of his saintly life. And the girl is so bewitched by the compliments she reads about herself in newspapers that she doesn't know what's happening. She thinks she's God's gift to bachelordom . . . with a face to stop a clock. Some things money can't change."

"And Pérez Landa understands?"

"Well, what do you think? He doesn't want his blimp dwarf to stay at home, forever toddling the paths of their so lovely garden. He thanks God a simpleton finally came to take her off his hands. Look, they say the nuns at the school in Canada didn't want to accept her because they said she would demoralize the other girls. And it's true, she's ugly enough to demoralize a school of apes. Full-dress birthday parties, a trip to see the scenery at Cochinchin . . . the wider outlook, you know. So the moment some halfwit wants to burden himself with her, her father grabs him. And that's how it happened."

Scented powder drifted to Robles's nostrils. He recalled—without wanting to, for he preferred those other moments to consume themselves alone, on the other side of his life—the absence of such scents in the bedroom of Hortensia Chacón, and he wanted to leave these penetrating fragrances and return to where the only smell was joined bodies and separate sweat, the attenuated moment of unrepeatable meeting when every movement endangered the stability of all creation; then one could reach for air and grasp it, shoulder the crust-earth and carry it to another region, liquid and incandescent, among stars. He was feeling, now, the great difference between the two women. To go to bed with Norma was not dangerous. With Hortensia, to make love was a somersault in air, you never knew what veil was tearing or what fire-glass burned your tongue, what support

123

beneath either life, his or hers, would be destroyed or created when the moment ended. With Norma, the ceremony was always as precise as the four quarters of a watch dial. With Hortensia, it was time, the unmeasured hours. Untouchable and mute, she demanded an answer without words, file and iron, held and enclosed inside her life, waiting for the moment when the reins loosened . . . for two minutes, for four minutes, joined. Federico put his hand on Norma's shoulder.

"Please," she said, gently removing his hand.

Wasn't she his creation, too? Or was she merely the other part of him? He was searching the mirror now for Norma's real features. Her face, which had belonged originally to those called adorable, had gradually been refined until it more and more resembled the mask worn by all internationally styled models: arched eyebrows, cold, brilliant eyes, thin neck, high cheekbones, the mouth full and stiff. Federico wanted to remember her first face (and before he had met her, the first time he had known of her, two men talking in a restaurant, back about 1940, when a simple "I am a believer" could relax tension, and when Norma's face was only something drawn by his imagination from the moment that he had heard the two voices and learned that there existed a beautiful woman named Norma Larragoiti); and he realized now that these features before him this very moment were what he had imagined her as possessing from the beginning. Her mask had been shaped by him, imperceptibly, into a face he had invented, or at least willed. Her profile was the work of his will. Without knowing it, she had molded herself to an imagined print until her true face had been made over and lost forever. With a shiver, he wanted to touch his hands to her cheeks; but the inner fury in Norma kept his hands away . . . fury concentrated in an invisible atom while her smile remained just the same, just the same the movement of the slender arms. Always the same. Federico would have liked to believe that he needed only the gift of one second to listen to her thoughts. His eyes moved over her silk dressing gown and her fragile body and scented throat to his own livid hands and solemn stiff carriage and his own face reflected also in their common looking

124

glass: what could be the point of union between that diamond mask which had reproduced the glossy pages of feminine style until it had changed from a species of unique elegance into a common example of clandestine vulgarity; between it and the thick dark face of heavy flesh and cockroach eyes and shaved temples bulking beside her? No words had to be said; words would never have to be said. And this evil obliquity—Robles understood without thinking it, although he lived it naturally— this Mexican reticence which could not use words for an idea that was submerged and arrested and at the last currupt: are we all of us like this? he asked silently. He wanted to believe and knew that he could not, that the feeling was strange: we all of us merely pretend courtesy, very slowly we squeeze something out of ourselves, and as it appears, it is called spontaneity, and after two or three minutes we are empty; we are afraid to judge, we want to be singular, and in that penurious singularity, sacrifice the great singularity, the oneness of the many, the great one which is the union of many, the point at which "I love you" may not be spoken because to love you is to love someone else and to drop all defenses, surrender all rottenness and vanity and power into the guts of her who knows us and dominates us and parts us, pair by pair. Nor could he and Norma ever do that. He would not build with her, as he would not build with men who put obstacles before his ambition. But he loved her as such a person: she was what he had wanted and searched for: the counterpart to his public being, the continuation and spreading of the streams of his triumph, a fellow comrade in the true revolution. He fixed his eyes on her reflection again. Across it danced a rosary of cocktail parties and weddings and dinners where she was respected because she was the wife of Federico Robles, accepted because she was the wife of Federico Robles, a man who had triumphed and was wealthy and Norma was consequently elegance and chic and all that. And he liked her as that; he believed, he was thinking now, that he had searched for her to be exactly that. And nothing else. He had no right to demand more of her, or other of her. She had fulfilled their tacit bargain.

"Look how I impressed the de Ovandos, Federico. They live like church mice, in another epoch, without comfort, so poor."

"We ought to invite them to dinner sometime."

"Mmmm, I know they're dying to come. Well, why not? Right away. But maybe we'd better wait until they call on us. We have to let them know our place. Doña Lorenza is a proud old woman, but she'll see, by and by. Her home is a coffin. She behaved as if she were doing me a great favor. But you should have seen her face when she saw the bracelet you gave me Christmas. *Ja!* And I swear that great lady is going to come to *me* and beg *my* favors."

He felt a slight movement of rebellion. What had Don Francisco been in the old time except an adventurer who had had the enormous good fortune to be liked by General Díaz and had taken advantage of it to steal land from poor farmers? What had Pimpinela's father, Don Lucas, been except a peddler who had gained control of customs agents by paying graft to Limantour?

"Think how it would feel to have everything and then to be a Don Nobody," said Norma as she pursed her lips and used the lipstick.

"Don't worry. If I should be ruined tomorrow, the day after I would build my fortune back again."

Norma squeezed his hand. Robles again felt her as his continuation and spreading and no longed cared to remember moments with Hortensia Chacón, moments that had no place in this closed life which only Norma could share, silently, with shut-in hatred and a conjugal fiction. The fullness of his power swelled in him like a hot sphere, lighting all that showed in the foreseen corners of his life. Power had begun on the Celaya battlefield; power to this very moment when his continuation would be evident by all her elegance above the aristocrats of a wedding. He erased, automatically, all that could still tie him to the time before his power, his forgotten and hidden life. Mercedes. Hortensia. Two names that sometimes still danced on the empty stage of rejected memory; while Norma stood, sighing, "My love, the things one has to do! I think now and then that this isn't really life, so complicated, so busy socially. I believe I do it only for you."

Federico, with a slight, cracked smile, agreed.

"But what a commonplace wedding!" Charlotte García growled between her teeth as she waved good-bye to their hosts, in the Mercury pulling away from Monte Líbano toward Reforma. At her side, Pimpinela smiled and freed her hands from long black gloves. Charlotte brusquely flipped off her little rose-feathers hat and let it fall on the seat. "I'll never understand, my dear . . . why such a garbage of champagne and turkey and canapés, violins, silk trains; because afterward, we all just go home and . . ."

The Avenue descended, undulating, shadow-striped by oblique sunlight. "I can understand why a confessed social climber like myself gets into these holocausts, but you, Pimpinela! How can you tolerate their *smugness,* their self-satisfaction! Presenting their bourgeois as if it had begun in the garden of Eden! What a horror!"

Pimpinela's enchanted smile, the point of glitter upon her golden body, did not change. "I remember my grandmother said that just as the Porfirian aristocracy were horror-struck when Villa and Zapata marched into Mexico City, so she and the old families were horror-struck when Díaz marched in a century ago. In those days ladies and gentlemen were all Lerdists. Even though they, too, had become ladies and gentlemen by stealing church properties."

"You're divine. I suppose we have to be loyal to our prejudices." Charlotte laughed hoarsely. Green shadows from Chapultepec Forest danced over her face, held in unchanging elegance by creams and massages and, above all, by her strong will.

"Well, think about it, who will the aristocrats of the Revolution see marching in and be horrified by tomorrow? Mexico will always be Mexico. And while it is, we may as well put up with it. When I see Aunt Lorenza shut away in memory, still believing that Don Porfirio will rise from the grave and chase off the bandits and trash with his horsewhip . . . And anyone can make the same use I do of this hunger for prestige, for the aristocratic veneer, that the new fat fish have. One has to have a little common sense in this new common-sense world, don't you think?"

"Ah, Pimpi, you're always intelligent. But I see only the aesthetic side, and how can I feel, surrounded by so many weeping, sentimental parents and sniffing girls in tulle? If one can live in the center of the world, in New York or Paris, with people who talk and dress as we do, what are we doing in Mexico City?"

"Masochism, my dear," said Pimpinela, widening her clear honey eyes at the same time that she softened her voice. "And the pleasant axiom that in the land of the blind——"

"You're insufferable." Charlotte groaned, patting her hair. "Did you see the dressmaker watching from the kitchen? Eulogizing his creations to the servants?"

"I saw something much more interesting. Norma Larragoiti for the first time old."

"Well, with the husband she has. Imagine how afraid she must be that they might have a son who would look like him."

The car stopped in front of a bar on Liverpool. Sunday afternoon groups of maids were passing, their lips painted like big damp cherries, wearing cotton and imitation velvet and patent-leather slippers, arm in arm with soldiers. Their *rebozos* tangled upon military buttons, some of them sucking lemon popsicles, others humming. Wide, brightly colored skirts, kinky, oily permanents. They came and went, along with vendors of ice cream, and balloons.

"Enough of zoocials," Charlotte sighed, getting out.

"Are you sure Silvia will be here?"

"Every Sunday. *L'amour, tu sais.*"

Four guitarists were crooning beside the table where Silvia Régules sat, her mink on one shoulder and her eyes fixed on one of the musicians. "What are you talking about, this is an old-fashioned?" Bobó was shouting at the headwaiter. "You want me to tell you, Nibelung, what an old-fashioned is? Place: Nassau. Year: nineteen hundred forty-two. The Duke of Windsor ordered my old-fashioneds while his morganatic mate was being photographed for *Vogue.*"

Silvia kissed their cheeks. "His Highness, the Prince," she gestured, and Charlotte half curtsied. "The others you know. Countess Aspacúccoli, Cuquis, Bobó . . ."

Cuquis was trying to work her hand between the Prince's ribs

128

and bicep, and he, just as persistently, kept removing her hand. Pimpinela sat beside Silvia. Charlotte sat facing the Prince: "I knew your august parents, *chez la Comtesse de Noailles*——"

"Those deplorable events of nineteen hundred eighteen," sighed royalty, allowing his enormous jaw to tremble.

"I'm giving a cocktail party this afternoon at seven in honor of Maryland Ainsworth, 'Soapy' Ainsworth, you know, and in honor of her horse, too, if it wins the Jockey Handicap, and I would be honored if——"

"Today my ancestral homeland suffers beneath Red tyranny."

"Pinky, do you remember those last dances, when you and I peeked down from the musicians' balcony," Countess Aspacúccoli's misty voice said.

"*Liebe* Zagreb!"

The Countess swirled her drink. "Pinky, Pinky, everything is over, *kaputt*, here there is only a kingdom *des épiciers et commercants*, oh *damn!* I feel like crying."

The Serbian prince, on his feet, lifted his glass and cried, "*Vive l'Empereur!*"

"Sure, even though we murdered him," Charlotte interrupted. "I still offer you my party in honor of Soapy Ainsworth and Tennessee Rover Boy."

"But who is Tennessee Rover Boy?" the Countess asked.

"Soapy's horse, which, God willing, has just won the handicap."

"We don't know the pedigree of your Rover Boy, my dear Charlotte, but if you are referring to the line of the Reiffersheidt-Orsina in the same breath, rulers of Aachen since eleven hundred forty-seven and connected with the oldest families of the Holy Empire——"

"Pedigrees, to me, *Señora?* Read your Bernal Díaz, you'll meet my great-great-grandfather, who was Marqués of Aguasfloridas and a relation of Moctezuma when *your* ancestors were hoeing beets beside the Danube."

Red with anger, the Princess upset her glass, and, standing, aimed her index finger and fired off a volley of incoherent words. She threw her stole across her breasts. She flared her nostrils and impotently shrieked, "Daughter of galley slaves and criminals who crossed the ocean with scurvy!" She grabbed Charlotte's hair. "I'm going to show you the ass where the mole of Charlemagne is engraved!"

The guitars stopped. Only Royal Intervention prevented the furious princess from raising her skirt and pulling down her panties. "*Liebe* Sophia, *je t'en prie . . .*" With a deep bow, and with his princess wriggling in his arms, His Highness retired.

"They spoiled my romance!" Cuquis complained, putting her daiquiri on the table. "I was about to hook him!"

"*J'ai le cul de Charlemagne!*" the Princess howled from the door.
siempre que me preguntas, que dónde cuándo y como, yo siempre te respondo

Junior came over to the table. "Well done, all!" Charlotte smoothed her hair and said, "*Viva* the victory of trade over tradition! What can you expect of people who don't know what bathtubs are? Did you whiff the Holy Archduke? Phew! Sit down, Junior."

Cuquis ran to embrace the columnist who laboriously was swaying up from the bar. "My eight columns, darling! I tickled a crown! You can put that only pure nobles were present . . . the Serbian prince, Aspacúccoli, Charlotte, who, it turns out, is descended from Cuauhtémoc, and I, Queen of Spring, once . . ."
quizá quizá quizá

"Your little problem has been taken care of," Silvia whispered to Pimpinela. "My husband spoke with them and they agreed to return the Chihuahua hacienda."

"Silvia! This is so unexpected! Aunt Lorenza will be speechless . . ."

"Tut. I owe you rather more than that, don't I?" Silvia squeezed the hand of the curly-haired, long-mustached guitarist.

Tennessee Rover Boy, by God's grace, won the handicap. First by a nose, his triumph spread waves of rising exhilaration from the Hippodromo stands to the chilly tables, high above the race track, which constituted the Jockey Club. Maryland Ainsworth raised both her arms and spun them in ecstasy. Beside her, Gus and Lally suffered collapses, and Gus recovered with quick common sense and ran to the telephone to inform Charlotte. From the

130

hall he watched the confusion of young women, some fat, others lean and birdlike, who ran in nervous clusters from one corner to another, bored dandies who slid sidewise glances at one another and at the demimondaines Sunday-adorned in violet dresses, eyelids, and lips, while dried up elderly members of the Old Guard and elderly wives and survivors of that company made ready, setting up their folding chairs, to play canasta.

"Rover Boy!" Gus breathed into the mouthpiece, and hung up and ran back to the whirling arms of Maryland, who was now weeping.

"My old mammy should have seen this! She raised Rover Boy on clover and alfalfa, she did!" Maryland was of course speaking English.

"Don't worry about it, darling," Lally, choking, said in Spanish. "I was raised on straight mystics, from Plato to Fulton Sheen, so I'd be able to tell cosmetic stars from cosmic ones, and it hasn't hurt me a bit."

"She understands your feelings," Gus translated.

"Oh, you're sweet," wept Maryland 'Soapy' Ainsworth, infinitely freckled.

"Soapy, this is Mister So-and-so, the most divine man in Mexico!" Charlotte whispered as she led the heiress to an empire of suds from guest to guest. Her orange-silk-lined apartment boasted autographed photos of celebrities on its walls: Shirley Temple, Doctor Atl, Somerset Maugham, Elsa Maxwell, the Windsors, Joe Louis, Ali Chumacero, and Victoria Ocampo. Satin taborets, scattered like toadstools, formed nuclei: Lally on one, Junior on another, Pedro Caseaux on a third. Los Panchos, a quartette, and Jacqueline François alternated from a hidden phonograph. A crown made of gardenias, with the name Rover Boy written on it in forget-me-nots, drowned the room in the three-pronged scent of nuptials, repentance, and fresh moss.

"Julia of Bulgaria," Paco Delquinto presented his now thinner, always silent Juliette, and Soapy responded, "Charmed, I'm sure."

"That party at San Fermín last week broke all records," Pierre Caseaux observed, and Cuquis, at his knee, sighed, "The Serb!

Pichi was after him, but it was me he invited to the Te Deum Friday. In honor of the defunct kings of Montenegro."

oh, je voudrais tant que tu te

"Furstenberg Place is full of dead leaves this time of year," said Pimpinela de Ovando.

"Yes, but it doesn't make Frenchmen any less grouchy nor Paris any less disagreeable," Junior said. "You know, Pimpi, they talk about their City of Light—where the hell is the light, eh? If they wanted to give a fiesta, they'd need all the lampposts on Insurgentes. Which is all right, if you go there the way I do, once a year, but to live . . . give me Mexico City. Where in France do you ever see the like of what we have here? From public baths, eh, to homes—everything. Do they have any residential districts like the Lomas or Pedregal? No. Napoleon and museums, and that's all."

les pas des amants désunis

"Soapy says she's been married seven times and she still can't understand why she never gets pregnant," said Lally with her dentifrice smile. "Isn't that right?"

"Kee-rect! Daddy has three million a year after taxes. But he likes to keep in touch with the finer things, so he pays for a traveling culture-trailer. Records and books and all that jazz."

"Gus, you're just a homosexual."

"*Homo*, yes. *Sexual*, who knows?"

abre el balcón, y el corazón

Rodrigo Pola moved near Cuquis's quite visible perfume. She was rubbing the back of her head, her auburn hair two waves that swept back from the temples and disappeared, exhausted, on the nape of her neck; conscious of the two soft folds of her shaved armpits, of the rounded muscular line that accented her breasts and made her at once both heavy and feather light. Caseaux, Delquinto, and Juliette were chattering around her. Rodrigo mentally blocked off every cultured phrase in his vocabulary; that was the only way to please Cuquis, he reflected; culture was what had made Norma run away. Didn't he want to succeed in everything? Success was to be attained passively. Enough just to meet the moment on its own terms, to submit to events which no

132

one puts in movement either intelligently or passionately. And moreover . . . what the hell, it seemed damn pedantic and not at all democratic to climb a soapbox or a podium every time there happened to be a crowd. His eyes watched Cuquis, her catlike passivity alternating with reptile tension.

"Don't you think the Scrb looks like Rock Hudson?" Cuquis was asking, when Rodrigo finally decided to break the wall of Miss Dior that surrounded her.

"Who's going to win the Royal Handicap?" he chuckled. He sat cross-legged on the rug, strongly suspicious that his remark had not been opportune. Cuquis pursed her wide Joan Crawfordish lips.

"Well, why not, didn't I introduce you to him?" said Pierrot.

"Ai, my angel," said Cuquis, and put her lips near Caseaux. "What would we do, abandoned here in Catusco, without your *savoir-faire*."

. . "*Oyez, oyez*," Junior cried from his taboret. "Those nobles are okay for bed, Cuquis sweet, but when it comes to here's your little convertible and here's your little apartment, who puts up the dough, eh?"

"Ai, Junior, you enjoy us, don't you? It's not just because of our big soft bras that you take us out, either. As if I didn't know you!"

"Ah, leave the occult pleasures to nuns," Junior said, licking the rim of his glass. "Who's going to go anywhere with a girl except to be seen with her?"

"You're divine, Junior!" Cuquis twisted her head around to place her transitory lips up to the kidney-shaped, rosy mouth of Junior.

"Well, there's no phony who is worth a damn without his props," Rodrigo observed, with difficulty holding back a quotation from *Love's Labour Lost*.

Cuquis's positioning movement stopped short. She made a face. "Listen, *Señor*, you've opened your mouth twice, and each time you've put my foot in it. You know me or something? Why are you talking to me?"

"Norma introduced us once at Bobó's," Rodrigo said, without conviction. His yoga posture felt offensively foolish.

133

"Oh! so you're the famous drip! Hello, my love!"

Rodrigo struggled to recover face. *"Vous n'êtes si superbe, ou si riche en beauté, qu'il faille dédaigner un bon coeur qui vous aime."*

He observed that his agonized expression and his waving hands were not helping much. Pierrot smothered a convulsion of laughter which immediately infected Cuquis and Junior. They rose and retired, shaking, to a dark corner.

que yo también, tengo una pena muy honda

Like a pouchy-eyed fish rising from the floor of an aquarium, Natasha sallied from her corner, displaced by Cuquis, Junior, and Pierrot. In the aged wisdom of her eyes there was a wish to pour her slowly accumulated experience over new heads. The double image, one sumptuous, the other corpselike, of the first times in Cuernavaca, had now resolved into only one: an ashy mask which lay hard on her face. Rodrigo felt a rouged touch on his cheek and turned his face into two open lips painted two tones of orange.

"Will you let me visit with you? No, don't say anything. I was watching. There's impertinency and there's also fatuousness. Someone . . . someone said that an impertinent man is only a fatuous one magnified a little. Fatuousness is tiring, boring, disgusting; impertinence galls, irritates, offends. One begins where the other *finit* . . . ends."

With melancholy, Rodrigo gazed at her high velvet collar and her peacock-plumed turban; her face was both green and rosy, like the ancient and thin moon of creation.

"And which do you think I am, *Señora?*"

Natasha widened her eyes and made a wrinkled *O* with her lips: "*Usted! Usted!* Only a Mexican would go on saying *usted* to an unknown woman who comes up to tell him a lovely observation by La Bruyère! *Usted!* Always that courtesy! Which do I think that *tu* are, my love?"

She pointed her long Russian cigarette at Rodrigo's chest, in her favorite give-me-a-light-my-dear pose. He did not understand until she waved the cigarette impatiently. Sheepishly he searched his pockets for matches. Natasha held her pose.

"It's all a question of wings, my love. With wings, a butterfly. Without wings, a caterpillar. *Voilà.* Take me to a drink."

With great ceremony he took her arm; she creaked as he pulled her up. "*On n'est pas ce qu'on était . . .*" She sighed while blinking smoke out of her eyes. They went to the bar. Charlotte had dimmed the lights. Cuquis was kissing Junior while Pierrot offered comments on her technique; Lally was rubbing Soapy Ainsworth's thigh while Bobó looked on and praised the advantages of bisexuality. Juliette, as if grown accustomed to a ceremony which she had judged sinister so many times that it now meant nothing, let Paco Delquinto's cataract of words pour over her. Natasha touched her glass to Rodrigo's: "Cheers!"

Her face grew paler with every sip. "That's all, my dear, just let your wings grow. They don't carry you high now because . . . you clip them every so often, or let them be clipped . . . who knows. Am I right?"

Rodrigo nodded and sucked his manhattan, feeling good. He did not want to interrupt her. His body joined the party; he felt his thighs waking, his neck excited; and Natasha, on her bar stool, reminded him—why, he didn't know—of some upside down scene in *The Blue Angel.* She began to whisper a song, with a pasty accent,

Surabaya Johnny, warum bist du so roh?

Du hast kein Herz, Johnny und ich liebe dich so

She was a female Emil Jannings, and he, a frightened Marlene. He thought about that and pulled up the leg of his trousers. Natasha covered her eyes with her hands while her song struggled on, quaking through her laughter.

Du hast kein Herz, Johnny und ich liebe dich so

Rodrigo took her hand and kissed it; she rubbed her wrist over his tingling neck. They asked for more drinks.

"Do you know you're sweet? I don't, don't say it . . . it isn't easy here. Mexican women of our class are either sour hypocritical saints or cheap whores. We want security, or to be laid, but not a relationship . . . how shall I say it? human? . . . *Il faut savoir mener les choses,* you know."

"And whose fault is it?"

135

"Mexican men's, *bien sûr*. What did that little nun write? *Hombres necios*, and so on. You want your women to be saints or whores, something simple that doesn't require much imagination. And what more? Shall I tell you? *Ecoute:* no one can stop me from saying what I want to about Mexico. New rich who don't know what to do with their money but just have it, like the carcass of a bug or the rind of something, with none of the circumstances . . . how can I say it? none of the gestation which gives the European *bourgeoisie* a certain class. Well, the *bourgeoisie* in Europe *is* a class. It is Colbert and the Rothschilds, and it's also Descartes and Montaigne, and it produces the Nervals and Baudelaires who reject it. But here, my dear, it is only a little unexpected gift received by a few, *on ne saurait pas se débrouiller.* . . . There aren't any, as they say . . . any ties; there is caste without tradition, without taste and without talent. Look at their homes, their furniture. They're an approximation to bourgeois, they are *toujours les singes* . . . little Mexican monkeys playing in imitation of the great *bourgeoisie* . . ."

Natasha made a face and drained her glass. "And the intellectuals! *Cher, cher,* they are to intelligence what spit is to a letter—a way, *tu sais,* to lick the stamp and make it stick. They love prestige and they want to be valued, my dear, *et ça suffit;* they don't love ideals nor labor nor the passion of creation; all they want is to show themselves off; their conversation is unhappy when it isn't pompous; they are ugly, ugly in the worst way, without character or greatness—ugly like bad breath or jaundiced eyes. In short . . . shall I go on? The newspapermen who with one hand hail the Virgin of Guadalupe, and with the other pocket bribes! *porco Dio!* If you have even half a brain, you've a right to read something in your newspaper besides movie ads! This country is more remote from the rest of the world than . . . than Jupiter! Everyone has his own little set of prefabricated ideas which allow him to feel himself an honorable and good sort of fellow, a good father, a good nationalist, a red-blooded he man, *ça pu, mon vieux!* And what sadness! And the petty Mexican priesthood and the pettier Mexican Catholicism! Why get upset, eh? But really, it's important, my dear, if you *really* are a

Christian, or if you prefer really a Buddhist . . . it's a serious problem . . . how shall I say it? A burning problem, eh? *Il faut avoir* . . . steel kidneys. It isn't just a matter of sending your daughters to a nuns' school to learn shame and avarice, nor just forbidding them to criticize the Pope at meals, nor teaching them to weep at post cards of the Vatican, to give beggars bread, and to beat their breasts until they feel that their consciences are clean; to be a Christian is to know agony *tous les jours,* you know, and to live every day feeling yourself at once the greatest pile of shit and the most blessed of beings because you have to beg forgiveness in all seriousness and be truly humble. It's such a pity Catholic ritual is so much more impressive than its dogmas."

"Why do you live in Mexico?" Rodrigo wanted to laugh, and now he winked an eye, tacitly agreeing to all she had said with those orange spumy lips, yet in reality feeling offended.

"Why do *we* live here, *cheri?* Why do we live in such a hor-rible city, where we feel sick, where the air's too thin and there's nothing except snakes and eagles? Why? Well, some because they're adventurers and social climbers and for thirty years this has been the country which has given first place to adventurers and climbers. Others, because vulgarity and stupidity and hypocrisy are still better than bombs and concentration camps. And others, others and I, because beside this repugnant show and false courtesy of people like you, there is also the incredible real courtesy of a child or an old servant; because alongside this scab of pus called our city, there are also a few people who are . . . *ça va sans dire,* unbelievably out of place, sweet, full of love and true ingenuousness, who never think they're downtrodden, *comme la puce, hein?* and exploited. Because under the cheap American leprosy, there are living bodies, old man, the most alive in the world, the truest in their loves and hates and sadness and happiness. That's all. *C'est pour ça, mon vieux.* Because one can feel at peace with them. And over there, we have the best of what you believe is best, not the best of what you believe is worst. *Ça va?*"

Rodrigo stood with his eyes lost inside an empty bottle for several seconds. Wasn't Natasha trying to say what Ixca had

137

said: choose, choose your world and then turn your back on the cities of salt. He looked up. "Paul Gauguin crusading again? the search for the Noble Savage and local color and primitive truth, this time among the bootblacks and scullery maids come down from the Puebla mountains?"

"Could be, my friend. At least we Europeans always have the possibility. To s'enfuir, to find our là-bas, our El Dorado across the sea. But you? Not you, mon vieux, you're inside your là-bas, you surround yourselves. And you have to choose, no?" She smiled with explosive warmth that tried to be truly concerned and interested in him. "It needn't be hard for you. Just let your wings grow. It's very easy. Just a matter of floating. Look around you. You think they have the least moral scruple, or that they even understand that they have no moral scruples? Look how easy it it, my friend . . . just look." Natasha's voice went far away with her hands and her body, from Rodrigo, from the bar; the party's shadows, darker because so much more complicated than mere night shadows, had swallowed her; until the last second he kept his eyes on her, and then he was alone, while voices and sounds and the tedium began to whirl, to spin away from the spinning unholding center.

Ixca Cienfuegos walked through the old Juárez Market on his way to Librado Ibarra's small room on Abraham González. He passed stalls empty after the morning trade, where venders sat eating leavings of resinous meat and vegetables in the ruck of gutted chickens and fish-blood staining paving stones and mixed with rivers of sudsy water splashed from buckets by fat women with vaseline hair and black moles, while dogs howled and other women, silent old women, counted and recounted their little handfuls of sweet marjoram, laurel, thyme, wild marjoram, parsley, peppermint, and camomile, left over and now to be carried on the long return to their far-away neighborhoods, Contreras, Milpalta, and Xochimilco, to wait and to be brought back to market again with other handfuls, next market day. A hidden guitar could be heard: sleep strummed it with drowsy fingers; and the birds on sale, their cages covered with cloths, neither chirped nor fluttered their wings, but slumped, heavy, in sleep. It was almost five in the afternoon. A great silence lay over the market. Afternoon sunlight boiled in Ixca's eyes. Compunctious organ-grinding music began to rise on every corner. Kids joined the organ grinders and sang the old songs . . . *rayando el sol me despedí peregrina de ojos claros y divinos . . .* Cienfuegos looked for the house number on Abraham González, entered a long patio full of abandoned flowerpots, and climbed a winding stair to the fourth floor.

LIBRADO IBARRA

"Hard to talk about Federico Robles? Pah! It's hard to talk about yourself or someone you love or hate. Pah! Federico Robles is not one of these, that would be like loving or hating a headline in a newspaper, something that's just there, part of something else that doesn't concern you."

"I think I understand," Ixca Cienfuegos said. "But it seems that Robles has——"

"My foot? Pah! A piece of machinery did that, not Federico Robles. No, I want you to see that for me, my own experience is enough and more; I'm content with what I've seen and lived, and Robles has had very little part in my life. Look, I met Federico in law school when we were both about twenty-five. He was secretary to a general, I was a lawyer's clerk with just as much ambition, if not more. That wasn't the problem. It may be that Federico has done what I couldn't do. Or that I've done what he couldn't. But then we were in the same boat, two poor law students twenty-five years old, both facing the same Mexico. Obregón President, thousands of youngsters just like ourselves, full of hope and confidence, sure great things were coming. How we used to knock ourselves out, studying and arguing, my friend! Long November and December nights in a stinking little room on Doctor Vertiz, smoky, full of coffee cups running over with cigarette ashes, Planiol's *Civil Law* and Duret's *Constitutional*, until our heads swam and our eyes were like hard-boiled eggs. What friendships form in school, those small-houred nights, until afterward you are so close that seeing your friend is as hard as seeing yourself. As if there were too much closeness, until you know each other's way of thinking, even his way of pissing! And so we had to shell ourselves, always keep a distance between us, try to make it seem we weren't really invading each other's privacy. That was how we were, my friend, and what could we do? I knew Federico to the lines of his palm, and he knows me. Except that today he's in a position to screw me and I'm in a position that exposes me to it, exposes me even sometimes to hunger, and with hunger you don't argue, you shut up and give in. But then we were the same, in the same boat. To be secretary to a general is good experience, but in those days it killed few flies. And I was pleading civil cases for a quarter of the fee I ought to have had. So we'd go together to Chinese cafés and to whore-houses in Dos de Abril, we'd buy used books on Avenida Hidalgo, and all that. I told you I knew him even to how he pissed? Pah, I understated it. Sometimes we'd share the same whore in the same bed. Eh? You see, eh?"

He scratched his bald head and blinked his bulbous fried-onion eyes. Light entered through small windows full of flower pots. With his leg in a cast, Ibarra tried to get comfortable on the bed. From time to time he would spit at a brass spittoon. His small round belly poked out like a casserole. A water pitcher. An old wardrobe. The cracked wooden chair on which Cienfuegos sat. A bureau with a marble top. That was all.

"Yes, we were just the same, the same roads lay before us, the question was to choose. It was easy to say. Mexico had to be made over and was waiting, and obviously one had to find what was sure. But what was sure in those days? The new roads to success weren't mapped yet; all looked alike. Everything was possible. Yes, *Señor*, we were going to build Mexico. Remember, the new government was pulling in everyone—workers, capitalists, farmers, intellectuals, professional men, even Diego Rivera. Unlike Díaz, who had organized from above downward, the Revolution first gathered in all the living forces in the nation. That was the situation when Federico and I were twenty-five: opportunity in every field, promise for everyone. That was why the Revolution had been fought. Lawyer, banker, farmer, worker—all would have the same chances. Sure . . . why not? Anyhow, we believed it then. The question was to choose and get at it. First and last, a man becomes powerful in Mexico by living down his errors. English empiricism was talked a lot in Caso's school. Pah! what is there in Mexico that isn't empirical? But we saw things differently, we were young. I decided to specialize in agrarian law, because of the chances that offered a young man with talent. I told the law office to go to hell and set out to see how the agrarian world worked. Federico took another direction. The General, when he had a deal, would let him in on it. He found out that some ruined Porfiristas and other asses were selling some downtown lots at about a fifth of value. So by and by Federico himself offered those lots for sale, and they were not his yet, to some gringo bankers . . . at three times the value. The gringos balked at the price, so he showed them a forged check from the General for five times the value of the lots and told them the lots were going to be bought by the Government for Government buildings. So the gringos gave in and paid, and then Federico went to the owners and bought at their price . . . a fifth of value. And I, what was I discovering, *Señor?* Well, that the experts sent to the old haciendas were being murdered by the landowners' gunmen, sometimes with the help of local politicians. Where the big estates had been broken up, the politicians had turned against the sharecroppers, used the public-private law enforcement forces, and exploited the land just as before. Or a governor's brothers and uncles turned out to be needy Indians entitled to one farm after another. You see, eh? I was disgusted with Mexico, and all I wanted was to live again in Mexico City and not even smell what was going on outside it. It was very impressive, my friend, how many times I was run off estates, accused as a Government spy. A hard life. So back I came and married the first skirt I ran into, a small skinny repulsive woman, but then I'm no Jorge Negrete myself, and I believed—at that age, imagine—I believed that I would be able to grow old peacefully with her beside me. Well, the old law office told me to go to hell this time. But a union took me on as attorney. I had to deal with the

Prophets of the Proletariat in their mansions in Cuernavaca, arrange their chorus-girls parties, their dinners in honor of this or that Old Regime aristocrat. But I was an idealist and didn't play ball, and ended up drying my bones on Islas Marías, the prison island. With Communists, honest union leaders, kids from socialist youth organizations, and with this and that sly Vasconcelista. Yes, *señor*. And there you have me, until nineteen hundred thirty-four. My wife left alone here in the city; I had no more than gotten used to her when pam . . . Islas. Not even time to have a child. Pah! That's what the fruits of the Revolution were for me . . . as if the Revolution and the Inquisition were one and the same."

Librado chuckled and put his handkerchief to his nose. "And Federico Robles?" He blew his nose and went on. "Well, there you see him breakfasting in Sanborn's every morning, and then, with the money he had made on his very first deal, he bought a big stable in Toluca. But he soon got out of that, and he told me that there was nothing to be gained in Mexico farming, that the agrarian laws had destroyed speculation, and above all, that Cárdenas was going to be President, a man you don't play with, and now the land that was worth something was in the capital. Then he went north for a while . . . you didn't know that, did you? He's kept it quiet. He was mixed up in some gambling joints in Baja California; I believe he tried a little everything . . . bought and sold, shipped and received, got to know gringos and to get along with the customs thieves at the border. When I came back from Islas, I found him at the head of a real-estate development company, in partnership with gringos and Mexican politicians. He was one of the first to build apartment buildings . . . the sure thing, you know. In nineteen hundred thirty-six there was no one to stop him. Money makes money, my friend, and the gringos trusted him. They made him consulting attorney for their companies and then board member, and presently he could call his own tunes and finance his projects alone. What a nose he had for loans! He understood that not one cent was available for agriculture, that now everything was building in the city, or business or industry, all in the Federal District. He was one of the first to offer credit on a large scale to the building industry. As the value of lots went up, so did rents; if not, he would demolish a building and put up another. The city grew and grew, and he with it. You've seen the files of farm workers coming into the city because here there is work in construction and in the country there is nothing any more. Or the wet backs. Or the many upper-class families from Orizaba or Mazatlán or wherever you please who come to Mexico City and join the middle class, thinking that here they're going to get rich overnight. They end up with little shops, or as typists. Robles always played it safe. In politics he had connections with Washington, but in Cedillo's time, with the Golden Shirts and the Nazis, too. Anyone who was useful. Pah! Trips to the United States, a society wife, everything that gives prestige. He's known how to take care of himself.

"And I? Well, when I got back from Islas I found my lonely ugly wife damn bitter. It was hardly surprising. I had lost touch with everyone, but finally Feliciano Sánchez, my friend in the union, got me on in the Department of Education. I was assigned to travel inspecting to enforce the socialist compulsory education law. You know how that was sure to turn out. Off I went. I couldn't take my wife with me. A teacher in Villa de Refugio had been kidnaped by a gang of paid goons and beaten to death. Another had had her eyes gouged out. Others had been hung up and tortured with coals against the feet. The country politicians, *Señor*, the rural political bosses, and the priests. That was rural education, and I was supposed to do something about it. So, the same beginning, you see, a great opportunity, great promise, everything for which the Revolution had been fought, land reform, labor, now education. And you observe what my experience has been. And what was sure was something else, and Federico Robles got it. So it follows that what Federico Robles got was what the Revolution was fought for. That there might be more subdivisions in Mexico City."

Ibarra began to laugh. Great guffaws that seemed to have no reason, great explosions of laughter like a blown-out tire. "And my old woman? Well, what could I do? Could I send her money when I had none, and was traveling the back country in constant danger? But Felciano Sánchez, my own union buddy, took pity on her and let her live with him. Obviously she had to repay him in kind. But I'm not bitter toward her. After all, I gave her reason enough. Since I've been in bed with this cast, she's come to see me. And on a fifteenth of September, they killed Sánchez. He was locked up, they told him he could leave, and shot him as he ran. My wife preferred to stay with the children she had had by him. Now she's an old woman. When I remember that I married her thinking we would grow old together . . . My friend, don't believe you don't need someone to grow old with. Everything that can be shared is never lost; it's like having it twice, eh? So! Back to the Department of Education, where I stayed until just a short while ago. Workers have a hell of a lot more protection nowadays than a civil servant. The middle class is far worse off than the masses; they not only have dreams, they have to keep up appearances. They have to maintain a certain decency in homes and clothing, they can't go walking around in sandals and serapes. Even if they starve to death. So they have to move, rise. We live in a free enterprise society, Señor, and a man has to go up; but the middle classes can't go up. They just stay where they are, with their sordid routine jobs, as I did for fourteen years. One day I wanted to burn all those damn file cases and never see another dusty ledger in my life. Every day the same useless work, the same bus with the same wooden seats, the same little room, the same goddamn nothing to do after work except look for a woman or take in a foolish double feature at the Colonial. And at eight the next morning, marking up bits of paper again. Pah! While Federico Robles . . . Well, who wouldn't begin to weaken under it? Six hundred pesos a month. And who did I know in the new plutocracy except Federico Robles? I got out, borrowed three thousand pesos to buy into a little company, apparently as an associate but in reality to be foreman of a bunch of miserable workers in a factory equipped with broken down machinery. The whole business was a violation of law. And there you have me, the brilliant specialist in labor rights."

He roared with laughter again.

"And now Robles talks with me in *usted*. He grants me that

144

courtesy! But it doesn't matter. What's important is for every man to have his own life, eh? There he is on top, and here I am on the bottom. Two lives, that's all. And who's complaining? Pah!"

Before he honked his nose again he shouted, "Ignacia! Ignacia! She's the servant for the whole building, my friend. One of these pretty little Indian girls. Say, would you mind getting me some cigarettes and a Pepsi at the corner? I'll be obliged to you. Here's the . . . man, I don't need anything, why do you have to treat me? Well . . . well, thanks."

At ten Saturday evening the cheap whore went into a lunch room on San Juan de Letrán and ordered a pork and sausage *torta*. As she gobbled it down she looked into the mirror and with three fingers greeted other women who were hurriedly eating or patting spit on runs in their stockings or puckering their lips in front of their compacts, the whole while never stopping jabbering. They were all "sisters" and well known there, and when hard up, they would come for something to eat; but the girl with the *torta* did not mix with them and they believed her new to whoring or maybe standoffish. But she found it endlessly exhausting to be forever telling and hearing the same old lies, to make up, as they all did, the same fairy tale about hailing from Guadalajara and having a husband to support; it was too much trouble to make up fairy stories just to break the timeless monotony of her work, and it was only her work, with no apologies, with no old mother or newborn baby or crippled brother to provide for, work done for the simple pleasure of being a whore, because to be a maid or a clerk in a store was just too boring and now even whoring had begun to bore, too, and hoping that she would be able to sleep all morning but at eleven already awake, counting the hours until ten when she would go to the lunch counter and eat her *torta* and go to the hotel cabaret and see if she was given another *torta* and wait and dance and order one tinted-water drink after another and get rid of her customer in ten minutes. She tightened her pony-tail, powdered her brown cheeks, and went out on the street, eying where men strolled in T-shirts and

145

peg-leg pants, sassy queers edging up on a soldier boy. She was not aware of the lean air or the steam floating from alleys and sewer covers nor the laden sky that nuzzled flat rooftops, nor the neons lighting a trembling night profile of a city that wanted to make her its own, one living drop of city essence, carry her to the beginning of itself and all its living drops: where city and its men and women learn wisdom; and so Ixca was thinking as he watched the cheap whore cross at the corner of Mesones, never looking up from the sidewalk, walking with a forced wiggle that had now become natural to her. Ixca dragged his feet along the street beside the cheap whore and she stopped and stopped him, and put her hands on her heavy, gaudy hips: "If you ain't buying, don't spoil the market, Mac." He lost her on a side street off Vizcaínas. On Niño Perdido he went into a smoky bar full of voices and guitars and a blaring, rasping cornet and the coming and going of slopping beers on bronze trays, to the little table where Beto the cabdriver, with rolled sleeves, sat with his arm around Gabriel's dark neck hollering at the lost, whining voices of the *mariachi* singers.

MACEUALLI

"Heya, Beto. What's new?"
"Hey. Nothing, nothing new."
"Business?"
"Okay."
"Your friend?"
"Gabriel."
"The wetback?"
"How you . . ."
"Teódula told me about you."
"Yeah?"
Ay ay ay ay ay! unas vienen y otras van
"Listen, the *Señor* here is a friend of Widow Teódula, Gabriel."
"Okay."
"How was it in the States?"
"Well . . . what can you say?"

146

"Drinks?"

"Sure."

Ay ay ay ay ay! unas van para Sayula

"Tequila?"

"Whatever you say."

"Up there, you miss it, don't you?"

"What?"

"In the States, you miss tequila."

"Miss tequila. Yeah, I suppose."

"Why did you leave Mexico City?"

"Who knows?"

"You didn't have a job, or what?"

"Oh, you know how it is. They promise you this, that . . ."

"Another?"

"Sure."

Ay ay ay ay ay! y otras para Zapotlán

"Life is hard here in Mexico City, Gabriel."

"You said it, *patrón.*"

"What's this *patrón?* I'm your buddy, Gabriel, the same as Beto."

"You said it . . ."

"What's your neighborhood?"

"Here and there, no special place."

"Boturini, *Señor.* Boturini and Jamaica."

Ay ay ay ay ay! Allá va mi corazón

"Man, don't be so suspicious."

"Well, I am and I'm not."

"So?"

"So help me."

"Listen, Gabriel. He's okay."

"Well, the plain truth, the plain truth is that talk's cheap, and the plain truth is that we're here for something else."

"Another drink, Gabriel."

"Sure. Hey, Beto. Where's Tuno?"

"He's coming."

"Smooth, smooth."

Ay ay ay ay ay! Sobre una viga nadando

147

"I imagine that in the United States things are . . ."

"Hey, Beto. What gives with Tuno?"

"Later, I told you."

"What you mean, later?"

Gabriel whistled sharply, and a youth with long hair and a short-sleeved shirt came toward them through the smoke and the music and the bowed heads.

"Hi-ya boy!"

"Hey, Tuno, you old son of a bitch!"

"This is Señor . . ."

"Pleasure, Mister."

"He's okay, Tuno."

"Eh? Watch out for him, Mister. Ha-ya, boy! I haven't seen you since L. A."

"Not since . . . Ah, Tuno, fuck 'em!"

Ay ay ay ay ay! Qué dice ese amor engreído

"Check! Well, I'll be seeing you."

"So long, *Señor.*"

"Be seeing you, Mister."

"Thanks, *patrón.*"

Ay ay ay ay ay! con el que me estás pagando

"Boy, how sweet and perfumed we're getting to be."

"Don't kid yourself, Tuno. He's okay."

"Yeah?"

"Yeah. He's one of my customers. He's okay."

"He's a pain in the ass."

"No, man, he's a good guy."

"A pain in the ass. You doing good, you doing bad? All of a sudden the bastard begins to pity you."

"No, man. You got him wrong."

"Wrong my ass. What's he think, I'm going to open up what's inside me? Shit, what would he understand if I did?"

"Sure, Gabriel. You don't have to talk if you don't want to."

"Hell, no. Not except to my buddies, like you and Beto."

"Hell, no. And sometimes not even to us."

"Hell, yes. Sometimes not even to you."

"Sure, *mano.*"

"What's he trying to prove, eh? He think I'll tell him anything he don't know already?"

"Drinks!"

"And now that that bastard is gone, they'll taste better. Shit."

"Sure, Gabriel."

"That's how it goes. Who wants to be remembering things? Bad enough to be fucked by every bastard you ever knew without——"

"Brother, you have said it."

"Shit, man, I don't complain. When I started working, in that barber shop, it wasn't so bad. But you don't stand no chance. You get a good deal and you go looking around, sticking your nose into where it don't belong. What the hell can you do, *mano?*"

"Who's kicking?"

"Some guys get the breaks. Win the fucking lottery. Everything they do, it rolls seven."

"Yes, shit."

"What can you do?"

"What can you say? God's will."

"Yes, shit."

"And the bastard who gets the breaks, what the hell can you say? It's the plain truth, nobody ever told me I had to do nothing. But when I looked at them . . . the old man and the old woman, *mano* . . . I knew they were waiting for me. I had to do something. And then you're the oldest and your brothers are dead and the damn girls are no good, and your folks get older and more and more pissed off until they're no good, too. What can you do?"

"Nothing."

"Nothing! It's okay when you're a kid. Then you run around, enjoying whatever the hell you come across. Even dogs know the neighborhood better than you do, so what the fuck, you just follow. You begin to feel that the whole neighborhood is yours, everybody says, Hey kid, when you go by, they tell you come on and pitch pennies, *mano*. But you grow up and son of a bitch, it all changes. You begin to catch dirty looks."

"Move on, kid. Don't step on my toes."

"Women, they're scared you'll knock up their sisters or steal their teeth. Then some smart bastard decides to beat you up, just to see if you can take it, and what the hell can you do?"

"Take it, *mano*, while your ass shakes."

"The smart boys. You get so you walk looking in front and behind at the same time, watching they don't come at you with a razor. And if they want to get you, boy, they get you. And then they find a way to tell some really tough guy about you, and you've had it."

"Better just shut up and play ball."

"And then if *they* want you out of the way, you've fucked, *mano*. You try to get even, but you can't. Better just take it. You know, I had it made waiting tables in that cabaret. But after a while the old waiters began to snap at me and I felt like shit. They didn't make nothing. I was stealing their bread. They're just goddamn bums. And those slick-talking bastards who come there night after night, looking for a fight. No, *mano*, not this boy. But what the hell is there left? You push an ice-cream cart, it's the same fucking thing. No, *mano*. All day at work you get screwed, and, come evening, you take off and go looking for a screwing. You head for the States. They give you dollars, you come back to live it up at home. To hell with them. So what if the damn gringos treat you like shit? That's why they pay you."

"God damn son of a bitch!"

"Son of a bitch! And jeez, the way they make you strip and they look for your lice, you feel like——"

"Like grabbing something . . ."

"Cut hair laying around the cow-stall to your ankles, everybody naked and stinking like whores with that fucking——"

"D.D.T."

"Shit, yes. And a two-meters-tall gringo hollering 'greaser' at you and snooping through everything you got. But what the hell! you'll never see the bastard again, nor any of the rest of them. And when you finish a day's work, you can sleep in your cot as long as you want to and you got dough for a drunk or a lay. And then the harvest is in and they kick you out on your ass. And when you come back across the border, *mano*, you remember those rich fields. Here there ain't anything but desert and dirty Indians. Nothing grows but the kids, and they don't grow much. But on the other side——"

"Fifo tells me that when they get the dam, there's going to be good land in Sonora, Gabriel."

"We'll see, Christ, what wouldn't you give to be able to work and make a living here in Mexico City?"

"Yeah."

The following Sunday, as every Sunday, they gathered, survivors of that short-lived phalanx known as the Northern Division, in the home of their comrade in arms Pioquinto. The woman soldier, Doña Serena, her seventy yellowing years. The ancient lieutenant, Sebastian Palomo, for whom it seemed that time had stood still, although his gleaming teeth were gone; he was now a switchman in the Indianilla yards; and Don Pioquinto himself, as sleepy-faced as ever. Today there was a special feast, coast-style tamales, *tacos* with yellow sauce, red pulque, for Gabriel, Don Pioquinto's son, had come home from north of the Río Grande, his hair crew-cut, wiry, with fistfuls of dollars. All of them sat around the table in the little one-room apartment, the wooden door open to let in midday light and the far away clang of church bells. Gabriel knew by heart everything that would be said, the old stories, the wrinkled old photographs that each of them always brought along.

"To the boy's health!" Doña Serena cried, lifting her head of blue hair as she tilted the pulque jar. She drank and went on, breathing hard, "Youth ain't what it was in our time, my lieutenant! But what can we do about it? And even we weren't the equal of some! Remember, *compadre*, we all started just alike, from the same ranchos and villages, off to the same Revolution. And now, how many are rich, and we no different than when we began. But let's not complain. What's over and done with, neither man nor God can . . ."

With the baseball cap Gabriel had bought him stuck on the back of his head, Don Pioquinto bent, refilling their glasses. "Do you remember when they crossed the border after us?"

The other two survivors raised their arms and roared with laughter.

"Listen, my chick," Doña Serena said to Gabriel, who knew every word she would say. "They almost caught us right in the middle of Mapimí. Your old man, Palomo here, myself, and three scared privates. But we knew that country like we knew our asses, and the gringos got lost."

"Five days we hid out in the desert," said Palomo.

Doña Serena raised both arms and let her hands fall on her squarish knees with a sharp slap. "And then, my God, our water gave out!"

They united in a chorus of gleeful laughter. "You tell it, Palomo."

"Well, it was just that our water gave out and we went twelve hours with our throats drier than the desert scrub. Then we saw one of the horses pissing and . . . whose idea was it, Serena?"

"Yours, who else would have . . ."

"So it came to me that *there* was water, and like a flash I held my canteen between the horse's legs."

"And with water from six horses we stayed there waiting under that Chihuahua sun."

Doña Serena took a packet of ancient stained photographs from her big market bag, and they passed from hand to hand.

"Look, Serena, here you are on your horse with your rifle, on Cinco de Mayo."

"We never ought to have left Mexico City. They tricked us."

"Gabriel, did you know that your old man once sat in the President's chair?"

"And what a kick in the ass he got when General Villa saw him there!"

They were silent as they gulped their complicated tamales, and when the northern-style wheat-flour tortillas and beans were brought out, Sebastian Palomo choked and Doña Serena had to pound his back. After coffee, Palomo began to strum the guitar, and all three of them, smoking cigarettes they rolled, began to sing:

152

> "The Carrancistas retreated
> One July twenty-fifth
> Leaving the battlefield littered
> With their dead."

Doña Serena became sentimental, felt a tickling in her navel, and jumped up, weeping. At that point Gabriel rose and said that he was going to the bullfights.

In the bar called Cuauhtémoc's Loves, Fifo and the cabdriver, Beto, whose cab they were going to use, were already waiting, Fifo in his open-throated yellow shirt, with his unraveling palm hat. Tuno arrived. He also had just returned from the United States, and his black-as-midnight hair was cut as short as an army recruit's; he wore peg-leg pants and a jacket of yellow checks. At four, they were high on the sunny side of the bull ring, pushing past the knees of fat women whose hair smelled of vaseline, past the raised arms of soft-drinks and peanuts vendors. They sat. The solemn moment of the bullfighters' entrance procession. The band became silent and Fifo put his fingers to his teeth and whistled while Beto launched paper airplanes at bent necks below. Tuno put on a bored expression. "Boy, baseball is dead, but it ain't this dead."

The *torero's* miserable first passes provoked the storm of a hundred thousand jeering whistles. Fifo enjoyed it, and Gabriel shouted, "We didn't come here to drink tea!"

"Piss on him, ox!"

When a famous movie actress arrived, swirling her fox stole, a murmur of resentment swelled slowly all over the sun-side of the ring.

"You want a horn between your legs, stay at home!"

"Ay, little mama, here's your lovin' lover-boy!"

Fifo took off his hat and extracted from it a small yellow half-suffocated snake. "Pass it along, it don't bite . . ."

The snake began to pass from hand to hand, to the shrieks of the plump women and the obscene gestures of their men. Its route was visible; its contortions were imitated by the files of spectators among whom it passed.

Boredom increased. The bullfighters were no good; the *picadors* leaned over the ancient necks of their horses upon the powerful necks of the bulls; the *banderilleros* leaped, frightened, over the barrier; a volunteer *torero* jumped down from the crowd and was tossed three meters high and lost his tennis shoes. The snake returned to Fifo, dead now. Everyone tilted their beer bottles. Whistling was general, cushions and bottles began to arch through the air. Paper bags full of urine sailed down and splashed on the heads of front-row spectators.

"Savages, savages," a man seated behind them growled.

"We sure are," Fifo sighed, and Beto turned and squirted a mouthful of beer upward. The man began to shake his shoulders while Fifo dug him in the belly button and Tuno jerked his hat down to his ears. He got up and left, wiping beer off as Fifo began to pinch, with the points of his shoes, the round ass of a girl in the next row.

"You keep on and I'll call the guard," the girl shouted.

"Boy, we'll be screwed then, won't we?"

"Gringos, piss on the gringos, piss on the gringos!" Gabriel called.

The tourist couple were just about to sit in front of them; Fifo quickly placed a banana vertically upright beneath the man and he stumbled and fell as the woman took movies of the four savages. Tuno began to tickle her with his beer bottle while Beto dropped the dead snake into her purse and removed her wallet in exchange.

"Police," she was about to scream, but when Fifo let her see his razor, she could only gasp.

Cushions continued to sail, a shower of urine descended on the tourists, and the beer-squirted man came back with five friends and began to swap punches with Fifo and Beto. Tuno and Gabriel clipped two of them behind the knees and kicked them while Fifo, with one swipe of his razor, cut the shirt buttons of the beer-squirted one and Beto buried his knee in the crotch of another. The guards picked their teeth with their knife blades and looked on and laughed, and the beer-squirted man and his

154

companions retired, defeated and humiliated, shouting, "We'll see you at the gate, you bastards."

"I wanna fuck," Tuno mused, and they left, bumping their elbows against spectators' heads and hawking spit toward lower tiers and shaking the dead snake over women's breasts. Before they got away, they had to swing a few punches.

"This is the life," Fifo whooped, and Beto hollered, "How do you like my uppercut." In Beto's cab they went on, whooping and singing and yelling at passers-by.

"I wanna fuck," Tuno insisted, pulling up his suspenders and adjusting the pleats of his pants.

"It ain't time yet. First, we got to get drunk."

They parked in front of the Margo and got out and walked down Santa María la Redonda, already gray with twilight, and at the corner of La Libertad found a bar and went in, kicking at brass spittoons and showing tough faces. They sat at a small marble table. Tequila began to flow.

"You going back to the States?" Beto asked Gabriel and Tuno.

"You damn right. Hey, Tuno, what do the broads up there call you?"

"*Puro* Latin lover," said Tuno. "You know, instead of fucking their women, gringos just piss inside them."

"Aw, Tuno, you son of a bitch. And you, Fifo, how's it going?"

"Shit, it ain't going. That goddamn ice cream pushcart you left me when you took off to Gringoland is a pain in the ass. Even the goddamn cats laugh at me. There ain't anything worse than a steady job with a pushcart. You got to be ready to go in the morning, and when they want something, they look at you, suspicious, and say have you got this or that."

"Sometimes I wish I had a steady job here in Mexico City. Something with a future, you know. And what's the chance? Hell, I already been a shine boy in a barber shop, I pushed ice cream, I've done construction work, I was a waiter in a cabaret. What's left?"

"It's a hard life," Fifo grunted. "Only Beto, with his cab, has it good."

"Don't believe it," said Beto. "Sure, there's some advantages.

You can pick up broads or give a buddy a lift. But pretty soon you're spending all you make and you get tired of running all over the city all day long, half the time by yourself. Sometimes I feel like taking off with Tuno and Gabriel."

"Don't complain, Beto. You've had it good all along. Hey, what happened to that broad you had at the Bali-Hai?"

"Gladys? The damn bitch had forty plus syph and she never told me. If it hadn't been for that doctor on San Rafael . . . and you remember that after Gladys, I was taking a blonde out, and I couldn't do a damn thing."

"Why the hell is it some broads are always saying you got to be faithful to them? Don't they like a little change themselves now and then?"

"Well, they don't know how to respect a man and they're afraid to be compared with other broads. But us, now, men, we're all buddies, we're ready, we don't give a damn. Like you, Fifo, you my buddy, goddamn it."

Fifo and Beto embraced and pounded each other's backs.

"There ain't nobody like a buddy."

"Who the hell else can you talk to? You got to talk to somebody. If you didn't have a buddy, how the hell would you ever get it off your chest? In this fucking life, if you didn't have your buddies, what would you have?"

"Shit, yes. Your old man and your old woman, they don't give a damn about you. Kick you out on the street when you're nine to sell newspapers or carry parcels, or dance with a cup."

"Well, that's how you get to be a man, Beto. You get to know the faces and the tricks the bastards use. Until I was thirteen I had a job leading a blind man around, and I learned, *mano,* I really learned. Even the way they give the money you beg, you get to tell them by that. And what that old blind man didn't know! It was like he had eight eyes in his ears and his fingers and another right in his belly. He could tell who was coming by the smell, or who was going to give a peso and who would give five cents. He never let anybody know where he kept his money, and when he stepped in front of that bus and got killed, nobody knew where it was and I was left with no work and no money, either."

156

"Yeah. If you don't get screwed one way, you get it another."

"Waiting tables is good work. I wanted to get on at the Aztecas, but they got a union there."

"Well, let's get out of here. It's about that time."

They went out arm in arm and crossed to Organo, among rows of jammed busses. Green-lighted open doors and windows showed their brass beds and blue sheets to the crowds of soldiers, laborers, drivers, who walked with their hands in their pockets between lanes of squat puffy-fleshed women, coated with lipstick and rouge, their cheeks brown, or white with layers of powder. Like dancing puppets, they performed the traditional movements: some pranced, swaying and wiggling; others showed themselves, wrapped in cotton gowns, from their windows; others darted out and grabbed men's sleeves and explained that one more would be enough to pay for beans and busfare. They pushed out their breasts and their buttocks; their bellies, too, were distended, and their knees were wrapped with adhesive tape. Eyes like feather tufts, quick and dancing; or eyes like stones, hard and bored. Tight lips painted into curves of petals and arches, full lips with red gums and rats' teeth. And in all of them sex shone, mysterious and soft, like a gash filled up with trinkets, with fugitive welcome, swift and sweet, loose or tight, friendly, leisurely, or impatient. Some like waterfalls and others like single drops of rain; some new and others ancient; some hoary, wise, and decaying, others fresh, tearful, and without knowledge; some shamed and others shameless, some given to play and laughter, others serious and formal. Some like overripe strawberries offered one last time, others as firm as fresh apples. Some who could sing and speak melodious words, and others who could merely groan and quiver.

"Let's take in the Tívoli first," suggested Gabriel.

They sat in the balcony and chewed popcorn. A blinking spotlight played upon a tenor in a red-lapeled smoking jacket. Dancing girls all in a line bumped into each other, weaved their hands, gracelessly hopped. Hennaed, with great navels and flopping breasts, they bumped and ground, and one of them whirled on her heels. Then the tiny star came on, wrapped in black velvet and wearing a huge feather hat.

157

"Hair! Hair! Take it off, take it off!"

Her dress fell away as its zipper slipped. Then the bra, and the dwarf's enormous breasts quivered on either side of a Virgin of Guadalupe medal, while, with her tiny legs spread, she edged toward the audience and gyrated as the theater roared, "Hair! Hair! Hair!"

Her hand dropped to her crotch-patch and pretended to jerk it away and the lights went out and the orchestra mounted a furious crescendo.

Outside, darkness lay its hands on broken streets and sidewalks and spineless walls along Santa María la Redonda. Cars entering the Plaza Garibaldi were swarmed upon by *mariachi* musicians dressed in chaps and metal-spangled sombreros, and guitars and violins were playing from one end of Tenampa. Girls in red stockings rose to dance as their glasses of tinted water were renewed. Greasy fingers and plump mouths folded around *tacos*; dancing neon tubes displaced the sky, and in shadowy corners where straight-haired men and women walked arm in arm with nowhere to go, dirty postcards were being hawked, along with envelopes of magic medical drugs and powders. Hand cards advertising neighborhood doctors lay on the sidewalks, along with upset garbage and bits of tortilla, with rickety old dogs and big heaps of thrown-away Sunday newspaper. Small bodies in overalls and striped T-shirts and satin blouses loafed around the food stalls and the newspaper stands and went into smoky cabarets where dance music softened and restrained their shoes while their pigtails whirled to the mambo. In Bellas Artes the nocturnal fair dissolved and gained a new impetus, more secret, not so heavy with sequins, along San Juan de Letrán. The human river flowed on, indifferent, searching its Sunday rite, faces never seen, forever seen, molded each alone yet all the same, dark and stony.

Fifo palmed his oily hair down and took Tuno's arm and cut across toward Organo. Tuno tightened his belt and puffed his chest out.

"Okay," Fifo cried to Beto and Gabriel from the middle of the street. "We'll see you at the Basílica tomorrow."

"That's what pisses me off about gringos," Tuno said. "They're always asking who the hell is this Virgin of Guadalupe. I don't let them get my goat, I keep right on wearing my medal even if they all laugh at me."

Night swallowed them. They walked to Meave.

"Here's what we need," Gabriel said.

Pale lights showed the way to the big glowing juke box, from which a dance called *"Nereidas"* was moaning tiredly. "Got me a cigarette?" asked girls in white linen with draped sequins. Beto moved past them and headed for one of the little alcoves which were separated from each other by thin partitions. A table with a roll of toilet paper, a bottle of disinfectant, and the single green linoleum divan. He lay down, sure that a girl would come. He didn't look for them, they just appeared. And he knew how to give all of them something they wanted, from the oldest and cheapest to those who were new to debauchery. He put the light out, lit a cigarette. Presently he felt breathing near him, an oily scent. He put his hand out and touched the girl's invisible neck. He pinched her nipple.

"I didn't see you," he said.

"I saw you come in, and I knew you'd come to . . ."

"A little water, that's what I'm going to put in you."

"Like I always said, the joker. There's nobody just like you, Beto." Her voice softened until it became the shamed voice he remembered.

"Gladys," he said almost silently. "So you've ended up here."

She lay down beside him, took his cigarette and lit hers. Silence whirled coldly in her abdomen; and without knowing it, without power to express or even to grasp her certainty, all through her body ran the understanding that no matter what Beto might say, he was feeling it too, and tonight they would not be able to touch each other. The two glowing cigarettes rose and fell from lips to relaxed resting arms.

"The room is twenty-five pesos," said Gladys.

"In the morning, when we leave."

"You been doing okay?"

"Working, like always." Beto closed his eyes.

159

"And what happened?"

"Nothing happened. You remember when I broke up with you. That blonde, so we stopped seeing each other. I didn't do it, Gladys, it just happened. To all three of us. They say some men got strong wills and get what they want. But you and me . . ."

Gladys closed her eyes with her hands and wanted to say something; prayers, words. A deep fear of sleep trembled between her breasts.

Ask: but what are we going to ask for; the sky falls on us and shuts our lips. But we don't need to do anything or say anything. Just look at each other . . . you ever noticed people like us, that they're a flood, they pour along the streets and markets, all just like us, and they have no voices . . .

Beto pressed his butt out against the cockroach-stained wall. He didn't know what to say, but he was thinking: I was born and someday I'll die and I won't know what happened in-between. . . . Days go by, Sunday comes, all dressed up. We go to the bullfights and then to a beer joint to get drunk, and drunk, we take in a strip show, we fuck a broad, and the truth is that we are always just waiting with our heads bent for whatever God sends us.

"You ever notice, Beto, the people who have a name?" She kicked off her shoes, and they fell like two blows on the splintery floor. "The Pope. Silverio. The President."

Gladys, I don't want you to talk. I never talk with nobody. I take what comes and I forget it; how can I talk to you when I don't have memories? All I remember is my mother and the way her face made me sicker day after day, until the last day when my face finally made her sick, too; but don't ask me to tell you what happened in-between; I'm cold and I want to turn over and open my arms, I'm sleepy, I just want to go under.

Gladys closed her eyes and let her cigarette fall into the bronze spittoon. There are so many of them, like ants, and it makes you think, they're all alive too, they all have souls.

"I'm beginning to have to count the number of men I've fucked, and I don't know any of their names."

Don't talk, please, Gladys. Today is a holiday, we're enjoying ourselves, it's our holiday of shadows, not like it used to be, the black fiesta now, and before it was all sun.

We don't have names, Beto, any more than mongrel street dogs do. There are so many people and none of them has a name, and they all just dream, like you and me now.
We dream together
and alone like this I remember what has happened to me and all the colors and days one by one turning over. There's a bridge in Nonoalco where nothing grows except birds in cages, waiting to be sold, and a corner to kneel to the Virgin. Don't do that, little girl; belly don't go away, and I left them with just my heart to eat.

Their eyes closed and both saw red under the dark city of the whorehouse; a dog began to whimper near their feet.

They're dwarfs with long oily hair who hug us and dance on our bellies; the turkey talks to us from his amethyst throne and with his feathers we make faces for dance and for sleep; music is the voice of the stone woman who stirs the waters of the lake and strangles herself with a noose of flowers: flowers chew the jewels of the moon that on fiesta day will dissolve us in a liquid sun, cupped in the guts of our destinies, the destinies we make and those that make us, the rabbit and the water, the snake and the crocodile, the leaf and the jaguar. Our home is the turquoise diadem, ours are the fates that speak, ours is the black mirror of premonitions. In the womb of the past the pistiled flowers wait for us, so that the sun will rise when we give them the secrets of our wombs: Take the yellow corn path of the *papagayo*, the white yams, the blood-stained well . . .

We go there by any road we take, to the water eyes

And it was said at the beginning, so everyone had his kernel of corn, and they built the city . . .

And from pupil of the water-eye the command issued, that all should seed red corn and cover it with a handful of suns . . .

And the suns sprouted and opened their stone maws and called together the grandparents to take their places, and then the water opened and burned with red fruit and the snake

161

walked erect until the high corn fell back into the furrows and the water watered them

Then we knew that the sun had hunger too, and that it was feeding us so we could return its swollen hot fruit to it . . .

And then those who carried burdens were created, those who scratched the earth with their fingernails and with nets trapped forest birds and scaly fish

But fiesta day came and the garden throne was touched by all fingers and turkey feathers fell out of clouds and water turned to stone and nothing issued from our lips . . .

Then we could offer open veins before the journey with the spotted dog

Then without shame we could feed of one another

But the metal wind changed stone to fields and mud

And the day of weeping and futile search came, when we sat in the dust and looked for ants, when we opened our hearts and found a sun in ashes, the day of orphans came when no word could be spoken

"O alms-takers, O little brothers, eat your ants, for the age of water has dried, seas come back over the mud and cave the cities: dance barefoot and clap your arms about walnut trees, nail your hands to the wings of hummingbirds while the sore-infested dog smells his belly; weight your words and your eyes, too, with slime; sink to the bottom, to the mother of waters, the ancestor of moth-winged butterflies . . .

"It's gotten cold," Gladys said when she woke.

Beto opened his eyes to see the last glimmer of a flicker of yellow on the ceiling.

"Another day," he said between his teeth as he rubbed his eyes. And beside him on the sofa Gladys lay with small and frightened eyes.

"By our patron," said Beto, with his stomach hot and his hands tense, "by our patron San Sebastian of the Apparition, I swear, Gladys . . ."

She moved her face near his. Their lips met in a deep secret kiss.

"No need to go to the Basílica," Widow Téodula murmured to

162

herself, "the Holy Mother slips around everywhere." She was sweeping the dirt floor of her little hut. Slivers of afternoon sunlight came through the walls, which were made of old boards covered with reed mats. Two yellow crocks, a flat piece of sheet-iron to cook tortillas, a bunch of dried chilis hanging from a nail, tortilla *masa*, a basket full of rags. Widow Téodula dropped her broom and began to sprinkle the floor with water from a pitcher.

"Lie still, dust, go to sleep . . ."

It seemed that she was held upright and straight by the balanced weight of her heavy earrings and bracelets and gold collars. She fluffed her red cotton gown out, and her jewelry clinked in rhythm. When she finished sprinkling, she knelt and said aloud, "You don't need an altar, because I give you my heart, ay, cloth of roses, skirt of snakes, mother of suffering, ay heart of the wind. Be good to old Don Celedonio, who died when I was so young, and be good to the children you took from us. I'll soon be with you, it won't be long."

Standing, she caressed her jewelry. Suddenly she wrinkled her eyes and put a hand to her ear. "Have you come? Come in, my son, I'm alone."

The rickety door opened, granular evening light fell through it, then the tall profile of a man. Widow Teódula sat on one of the floor mats and gestured him to do the same. "Don't dawdle," she said. "I can feel my blood slowing, beginning to thicken."

"It's true, your day is near," said Ixca Cienfuegos as he made himself comfortable on the mat, crossing his legs. He patted the widow's white hair.

"You should know better than anyone, my son. Now whole days go by and I can't urinate. My tortillas stick in my throat."

"Soon you'll begin to cough blood and to count minutes on your fingers. You know that if you want to, you can choose your time yourself."

"That wouldn't be any better. But what I do want is a sacrifice, a sacrifice, my son, if only a little one." Teódula's voice changed, and she lay down on the mat until her fingertips touched Ixca's knee. "Even if only a very tiny one. You promised, my son. There in the country, before I came to Mexico City, I offered sacrifices for my old Don Celedonio and for each of the

163

children. I adorned their bodies, I gave them gifts, I offered what I could. Now that I am going, too, I can trust only in you not to let me go alone."

"Don't doubt me, Teódula," Ixca said, breathing deep the smells of dried chilis and the fire in the brazier. "There will be someone to do it for you, to give you what you want."

"A sacrifice, my son, that's all. All I need is that. My jewels don't matter."

"Has anyone here tried to steal your jewelry?"

"What are you talking about? The other day Tuno was telling me that I am like a part of the buildings here and everyone has agreed to take care of me, and to use a razor on the person who fails to respect me. Of course, it isn't the same as in the country. There I could show off my jewelry on fiesta days, and how much prettier they were, too, with flowers and leaves all around. And the dresses girls wore were prettier, too, and the sun was higher than here, and golden light flew through the air until it seemed endless . . ."

"It's good you have never wanted to sell them."

"Hush, son, don't even think such a lie about me. They come from the old times, before the time of the oldest man I knew, Don Huismín, and he was over a hundred when I wore my first hair ribbons. When I married, they pierced my ears and hung my jewels on me, and I have never taken them off since that day. If I didn't have my jewels on, I wouldn't be able to pray, nor go on thinking that soon I will be with Don Celedonio and the children again. Like the wings of a hummingbird or the scales of an armadillo, take them away and you have something, yes . . . a red worm or a hairless dog, but not what you had before. You'll say I'm crazy, Ixca, my son, but these days I can remember all my life. When you're busy living, you don't have time to remember what you have gone through, but now I can, and I know I am sure that I am Teódula, the Widow Moctezuma, only because I have always worn these jewels and never let them leave my body one moment from my fourteenth year when I married and was given them . . ."

"Come in, Teódula, come in and warm me."

164

"I'm coming, Celedonio, but I smell of peppermint and sage, and I want to cool first, so you will feel me cool and will want to make me hot."

"Let me look at you there, near the door. Just a year ago you were still a child."

"Last rainy season. When my breasts began to swell and the hairs to come. And now I am your wife."

"I like you like this. Naked, wearing only Don Huismín's jewels."

"I shall never take them off, Celedonio, and when I am with you, they are all that I shall not take off."

"Are you ready now?"

"Yes, Celedonio, I'm coming now, the stars have washed me."

Ixca got up and lit the candle stump in a little jar which hung from the thatch roof. Shadows flickered over their faces. Teódula went on, although this was not the first time Ixca had heard her story; her voice caught flame from familiar sparks.

"In those days there was forest everywhere, and I would walk in the woods, wearing my jewels and watching blue hummingbirds. I wanted to make a snakeskin skirt for fiestas, but when I went through the forests, all animals crouched in front of me, frightened by the glitter and noise of my jewels, and I could not bring myself to trap such innocence. The jewels seemed to belong to everyone, like sunlight and color, and it wasn't until I came here to the city that I realized they belonged only to me and I might be robbed. Here, I have been protected by Tuno and his friends. There, I didn't need to be protected, the jewels belonged to everyone, and more than to anyone, to the forest animals who loved them so. When a baby was coming, I would put a gold collar on my belly for the birth to be easy and for good luck to follow the child. That was why they lived so briefly, so that I could enjoy first their lives and then their deaths. So I could give them jewels at birth and gifts at burial. I can't complain, my son . . ."

She lit an Elegante and puffed on it, rocking her shoulders. When the first child died, I remember soldiers of the blond king were passing through the land, seizing young men for his army.

Or was that later? I am no longer sure. When they brought me to Mexico City, the Miracle Child Fidencia was going around making prophecies, and I didn't know when many things that my neighbors told me about happened."

With a grimace she put out her cigarette and sat beside the charcoal brazier while Ixca stretched his legs across the mat and a concentrated light came into his eyes, more distant than the ancient widow's hundred-times-told ancient story. Teódula prepared tortillas, raised her voice over the slap and spank of her hands as they flattened the dough. "First we'll eat. Then we'll take them out and pray over them. You will excuse me, my son, for not making as many tortillas as other times. My arms ache."

The old woman finished patting the tortillas, and in silence, after splitting two chilis and sprinkling them with onion, she offered the *tacos* to Ixca. Very solemnly she chewed the hot-seasoned concoction, and then she washed her mouth out with fruit-flavored water and spat. She stood and wiped her hands on her red gown and gestured to Ixca. Both knelt and rolled up the mat and with their hands scraped until they uncovered a wooden cellar cover. Ixca jerked it up in a shower of dust and the little hut was flooded by the smells of damp pottery and dry flowers. Ixca dropped down into the deep hole.

"First Don Celedonio's, it's the biggest," said Teódula. A long rotting wooden coffin rose vertically and crashed on the dirt floor. Teódula dragged it to a corner and returned, puffing, for the smaller coffins which Ixca now set out of the death cellar. The smallest boxes tinkled musically as he swung himself up and out, covered with dust, and ranked them beside the big coffin. Teódula continued: "Here the ground is all water and wood rots quickly." She dropped to her knees and raised the cover of the large coffin. A confusion of clay idols and dried flowers was revealed. "Kneel too, my son."

He placed himself beside her and she removed the idols.

"Here you are, Celedonio, and right on top of you is the *nahuaque*, so your bones will sing forever." She raised an idol and kissed it and pressed it three times to her chest. "And the *ixcuina* with four faces to lie on you and cover you with mold so you won't forget who you are, and the two-faced one, so you will see them and us, too, and never be either going or coming. And this *patecal*, whose medicines couldn't save you, here, even though you don't need medicines now, so that you may be called and nothing can hold you back. And all the little rabbits, to let your bones drink the earth, to let you have fiestas . . ."

When Celedonio's skull appeared, Widow Moctezuma clasped her hands and wept, "Ay, my old Celedonio, you left me when I was so young and had no more than learned how to enjoy you. Now the *huahuantli* has you and you are just as naked as he is, your skin is gone and you are in the heart of the mountains where there is no air! Ay, Celedonio, see what you have become!"

Cienfuegos put an arm around the old woman's shoulder and held the skull up to the light. "Now we'll touch it up," said the widow, drying her dark face on her gown. "Bring the things."

He found a jar of blue paint in a corner, with a small brush, and he gave them to the old woman. She wet the brush in the jar and passed it over the skull's cheekbones.

"Now you, my son, for you can write . . ."

He took the skull in one hand and brushed large blue letters across the forehead: CELEDONIO. Teódula's angular face smiled broadly. "Good, good. It's a shame I can't put his flowers in now, too, but you'll bring them from the country, you promised."

On her knees, she touched the small boxes.

"And here are the children, who never knew what happened. . . . Here they are, sleeping with the black face that cures all evil. They were painted the last time, and their flowers are fresh. Just pray over them, Ixca, and don't bother them. Ask the four hundred in the south to give them light, for it is to the south that my children stare, painted fields and the moon."

She lowered her head and abruptly fell into a deep vigilant sleep. Her gold collars and gold bracelets glowed upon the clay figures standing in file in front of the coffins. Motionless, her eyelids denser minute by minute and darked, she remained there with her dead ones for a long time. Ixca stared at her, but her eyes did not open. She went on sleeping, and he waited beside her as a new light fell through the thatched roof on Celedonio's

167

painted skull, and make the candle pale. The widow stirred in her nest of dust and idols.

"It's time for me to go, Teódula," Ixca said softly.

Without opening her heavy eyelids, she whispered: "Will I have my offering, my son, my sacrifice?"

"You are near it now."

"Blessed be the Holy Mother," Teódula said with closed eyes.

At that very moment Teódula's neighbor Rosa Morales was looking at her hands and feeling sick. She wanted to vomit, she could hold it back only by staring at her blunt hands, day after day more chapped by steam and suds and hot water. A soft noise from the boys' cot made her turn. She put her fingers to her lips as Jorge rubbed his hair and blinked his oval black eyes. Slowly the child got down and in a hushed voice asked, "Are you going away again?"

"I've been with you two days, Jorge, baby. They don't give us all week off."

"Why can't you stay with us all the time the way you used to?"

"Because Papa went to heaven and now I must work for us."

The boy nodded and stopped asking questions.

"Remember, Jorge, to get your brothers up, give them breakfast, and take them to school. I'm going to ask Doña Teódula to look in now and then to see if Juan's chills come back."

"Mama. Are we ever going to hear the *mariachis*, the way we did the night Papa went to heaven?"

Rosa embraced the naked little boy. "We'll see. If they give me a little extra Christmas, yes, I promise you."

"Do you like them?"

"They're very rich people, Jorge, but the cook runs everything. Señora Norma leaves it all up to her."

"Aren't you going to take me to see the house sometime?"

"Yes, someday, but Señora Norma says she doesn't like children. I'll take you when they go on their vacation."

Juanito began to breathe quickly, short of breath. Rosa got up from her chair and ran to the cot. She lit a candle and kissed the boy's forehead.

168

"Not until next Sunday, Mama."

"Not until Sunday. If your brother gets very sick, you know the telephone number." She hurried out and did not look back at Jorge, standing in the door, waving his hand. As she passed Teódula's hut, she called, "I leave the children in your care, Doña Teódula."

On Balbuena she took a bus packed with laborers and with women on their way to market plazas, carrying baskets of chickens and vegetables. Far away, pale haze crowned downtown buildings; street lights had just gone out on Fray Servando Teresa de Mier and a line was forming and lengthening in front of a hiring window. Marques of theaters and cabarets were dark, and a cluster of weary *mariachis* were eating *pozole* on the corner of Salto del Agua. The city's faces whirled past the window of the bus, and Rosa, her cheek against glass, remembered only her baby's choked breathing and, an unconscious part of the same image, the wreck, and Juan dead on a mortuary slab at the Red Cross hospital and all of them, herself and the children, staring at him there with the taste of red wine still on their lips. What good would it be to punish anyone, that wouldn't bring him back to me. . . . Ay, Juan, I can't tell you everything now, I can't tell you about the suffering. I don't hurt any more, it doesn't bother me now, all I want is for you to come back and warm our bed once more before I forget your face and your body . . . because every day now you are further from me, I can't touch you with my eyes the way I could at first: now I have to close my eyes and fold my arms to smell and feel you near, and I want to smell and feel you near, that's all, just once more I want you, just once more, even if I never see you again in paradise. . . . Then the bus was climbing between the high walls and wide lawns of the Lomas and Rosa made her way to the door to get off and walk four blocks to the home of her employers, Don Federico Robles and Señora Norma, to wash dishes and make beds and wait for next Sunday, when she would go back to Balbuena and see if her son had died.

An Indian in sandals and a light-blue home-woven jacket

169

turned his face and showed his corn-kernel teeth. Gabriel wrinkled his nose, shifted his weight from foot to foot. The line twisted along Fray Servando Teresa de Mier. Fifty men at least were ahead of him. The sunless heat of the cloudy sky prickled and tingled his skin. He loosened his shirt collar and began to whistle. The Indian in front of him turned and smiled with a wisp of mustache, crinkling his broad nose. Gabriel made a gesture of impatience and felt through his pockets. The Indian offered a match; Gabriel shook his head, he wanted a cigarette. But the Indian had no cigarettes, only matches. "We're screwed."

Who knew if he would get hired? They needed only fifty men on this job, and thirty had already been hired. A *taco* vendor passed along the line wrapped in rags and baskets. Gabriel chewed, filled his mouth with sweet slivers of spiced meat. He straightened his shoulders and scratched his ears. "That's all," the hiring man yelled, and immediately shut the window. The line of men came apart, growling displeasure. Gabriel toed a puddle.

"No luck," the Indian said.

Gabriel spat a piece of tortilla and waved so long. He clewed up his belt and at the corner hopped a moving bus and made his way to a metal hand-support and continued whistling. "Where's your fare?" the driver called, narrowing his eyes in a mirror covered with religious cards, pictures of naked women, and miniature altars adorned with paper flowers. "Eyes on the road, *mano*," Gabriel said cheerfully. He stopped whistling. He spat a fiber of meat on the floor. When the bus turned a corner, heavy women burdened with fiber bags rocked against him, little kids with dirty faces and patched overalls grabbed him and held on. He jumped off the bus and headed for a blue, half-cellar bar with big Pepsi-Cola bottles painted on both sides of the door. The Conquests of Sóstenes Rocha.

It was noon. Two drunks leaned against each other, mumbling meaninglessly. Gabriel ordered a mezcal and looked at himself in the mirror. His skin in the glass was mustard yellow, his curly hair was cut close and shaped box-square, his half-open lips made a sneering, challenging arch. Presently the doors swung open and two men wearing gabardine suits and felt hats came in.

170

They looked at him. The tall one approached. "So you come back."

"How's it going?" Gabriel said. "Yeah, I come back."

"So now what you planning?"

"Stick around. Look for work."

The two men elbowed each other and drew their lips back. "So you're going to look for work?"

"Sure I am. I got to eat, don't I?" Gabriel raised his arm to drink his mezcal. The tall man pushed his arm and the drink spilled on the bar. Gabriel closed his fists. "What gives, *mano*? What you trying to prove?" He heard blood in his ears.

"He says what are we trying to prove, Cupido, just listen to him," said the tall man.

His companion opened his mouth and sighed "Some people just got no memory at all."

"I just stopped in here for a drink," said Gabriel. "I was here enjoying myself. I wasn't looking for you . . ."

"We ain't talking about you looking for us, *mano*,. We're talking about us looking for you, to make sure you ain't forgot us. You ain't really forgot your old buddies, have you?"

The other opened his mouth again. He rolled his eyes and tipped his hat back.

"Because sometimes a guy does forget his old buddies who took care of him and then, bang, they got to look him up and get even."

"Look, I'm not bothering nobody," Gabriel grunted. He signaled the bartender. "Give me another."

The tall man jabbed a finger into Gabriel's navel. "Don't you see what we mean, *mano*? You're slow, boy. Who told you you could have another drink? Be better if we would treat you, wouldn't it? Ain't that right, Cupido?" And he elbowed his companion again. "Hey, a mezcal for my buddy here, and two beers."

Flies buzzed around their heads: there was no other sound; the two drunks, arms around shoulders, had slumped into sleep. The bartender came and went silently, opening the bottles.

"Well, *salud*," said the tall man, tasting his beer. Gabriel raised his arm to drink, the tall man hit his elbow. Very slowly

Gabriel wiped his arm while the two men watched and grinned.

"Now you begin to understand, *mano*," said the tall man. "Tourist in California or no tourist in California, you're no different than you were before. Don't forget it."

Gabriel moved his face near the tall man. "Listen, I stood up to you once just so you'd know that no matter what a wheel you are around here, and no matter how they lick your ass, so far as I'm concerned, you can go fuck your mother."

The tall man sipped the foam in his glass. "Understood, *mano*. But nobody catches me twice with my pants down. Ain't that right Cupido?"

The other showed his teeth and, very relaxed, hit Gabriel behind the knees while the tall man buried a knee in his belly and beat him on the shoulders and face with the beer bottle.

No! the bartender tried to shout. But he said nothing.

Gabriel doubled on the floor with one hand over his face and the other at his crotch. The tall man went on kicking him, at the same time straightening his tie and saying, "Now everybody knows who's boss."

They paid their check and went out, elbowing each other. Gabriel, on the floor, tasted blood running over his mouth and tried to stand. He knocked a spittoon over and fell again. His blood mixed with the spilled contents of the spittoon.

"Them guys, you don't fool with them," said the bartender.

"What are we going to do . . ."

His mother held a hot cloth to his swollen nose. His oldest sister was in a corner, singing. On the cot, his father slept.

"You'd be better with your brothers. They're only dead," said his mother.

"All I want is to work. I swear I wasn't bothering nobody. I wasn't looking for nothing."

His mother sighed and went to get the other hot cloth from the kettle boiling on the hob. "It's always the same here, Gabriel. Some got more than others, but we all got troubles. Every time I confess, the Father tells me about people's troubles. And he ought to know. I stay there three hours listening to him tell me, so beautifully, the troubles of everybody in the neighborhood. And I confess for myself and for everyone else, too. You'd feel better, believe me. Why don't you go?"

With a gesture of impatience Gabriel took the cooling cloth off his face. "What will confession give me? Is the Father going to bless me with a job?"

She put the other cloth against his skin. "You spend everything you make. But you still got some, you don't have to go to work yet."

"I'm beat, that's all. It's all right to wait around, but that ain't my way. All my buddies got work to go to every morning, and what have I got? Fidelio away all the time. The old man working in the yards. What's left for me? You know, I'm thinking about just staying in the States. There's always work there."

His mother let the clothes fall and held his head in her hands and did not want to speak but only to hold him close, to put her own tense, deep-hollowed face beside his, while the girl hummed in the corner and the old man snored heavily on the cot.

A big-boned, flabby-skinned, humped man walked along Avenida Mixcoac with a little white dog in his arms. The dog wore a suit of yellow and blue ribbons with small bells around his neck and on his paws. Behind the tall humped man walked another, dark and tight-lipped, older, carrying a cardboard cylinder, a dented cornet, and a small stepladder. The two men both wore faded felt hats, open shirts, and coats and trousers that did not match, and they walked listlessly, as if the street itself were moving under them. But even in his weariness the big man had a certain theatrical assurance about him, while the other hardly raised his shuffling feet, and if he had fallen and lain there, no one would have been surprised or thought it unnatural, he would just be rolled out of the way for people to pass. His eyes shone without luster, his mouth was shut and yet hung, his features were long and stretched as if by the hand of a sculptor using gray clay lacking strength. They walked along past cheap shops and cheap movies and yellow streetcars and new lampposts, like two mummers in a perpetual carnival that never stopped to celebrate but ran on and on, chasing the receding consummation of its decreed merriment. They had come from Colonia Portales, had left very early, at noon had been on Generál Anaya and then on Noche Buena. Houses were the same everywhere they went, the same people. They would stop and go to work for no reason except that they were tired of walking. The big man honked his aquiline nose and wiped snot away. They crossed left to Once de Abril, and the big man protected the little dog, held it tighter in his arms. They walked toward Héroes de la Intervención. The small man fell behind, his face gray, his lips sucked in. The big man stopped and took his hat off and extracted a red cardboard megaphone from his pocket. The weary little man tooted the cornet, groaning sounds which the big man accompanied with *tah-rah-rahs* through the red cone. Several servant girls appeared on the roofs of powder-gray houses. Ixca Cienfuegos, about to go into one of these houses, stopped to watch the dog walking on the rolling cylinder. The big man put down his megaphone and bowed to the servant girls. "I present that great little mutt Josué, who after years with an international circus has come to visit the land blessed with more beauties than laurel has leaves . . . Mexico!"

The small man went on tooting the dented cornet while he very slowly, in the middle of the badly paved street, set up the stepladder. The big man led the dog to it. The animal climbed quickly and haunched down on the top, frightened and whimpering. "And now, watch him descend, ladies and gentlemen, that great little dog Josué, late of the Barnum Circus, who has circumnavigated the earth itself!" But whining and tinkling its bells, the dog refused to start down, and the big man finally gave up snapping his fingers and took the dog by the collar and forced it to climb down while the trumpet groaned crescendo and the little dog's ribbons fluttered and his frightened bells tinkled in the sunset. There were no servant girls watching now. Beneath closed windows the big man walked with his hat held out. The small one sat down on the curb, with his face as dark as on-coming night. Ixca Cienfuegos moved along a hall to the room of Rosenda Zubarán de Pola.

"Get up now, Portales is a long way," the big man said, but the little man just sat on the curb as if deaf. "Listen, we haven't made much, we don't have enough for a bus, let's get started. Come on. I'll buy you a *taco* at the corner." But the little man did not move. The big man folded his great frame down and sat, too. "So here you are. Aren't you ashamed of yourself? Do you think I'm happy with this red megaphone? Come on now, I promised you, didn't I? Only don't spend it all on one drink, don't be that damn silly." And they rose heavily, retrieved the cardboard cylinder and the stepladder, and caressing the frightened little dog, made their way back toward Avenida Revolución.

ROSENDA

"No, I won't tell you everything."

Because all truth is measured by our own days and falls into a thousand fragments in the light of every glance, every heartbeat, every unforeseen turn, and you have never, no more than he, known what those days were, passing veiled like forgotten dreams in rooms of silk curtains and damask and velvet armchairs and porcelain figurines and landscape paintings in a world of peace and tranquillity. When we were a family, we went outside with little flags in our hands to salute Don Porfirio as he drove through a city which was not then what it is now, deformed and scrofulous, humped with cement and holed with secret abcesses, but small then and pastel, a city easy to know, clearly understood. Now you see riffraff everywhere, on all the avenues, seated without the least respect in the Alameda, with the vomit of their obscene meals staining the length of what was our street of silver. Now you don't know what will happen next. The windows, suffocating among their damask drapes and silent unctuous varnishes, let in a storm of words which I don't want to hear, like those words, no, not even then, when they were a mist of truth that dried afterward but was preserved in something more secret than the yellowed pages of a book or the most cloistered cabinet or locket: in the heart of a woman who loved, words from the mouth of a flattering, lying gentleman seducer, tall, small in my

175

arms, almost candid in his innocence, faced with what we women know even before we know anything about love. And now I am going to die . . .

"I am going to die, *Señor*."

. . . and he will not come to see me because I might tell him to look around him—he doesn't make anything, I know that, but even so, even so—and think about that palace he took the perfume from and he will begin to see everything—how a life passes, preserved inside a woman whom everyone protects from common people, and above all how when she is the daughter of the family, with little snow-white dresses and a nana with leaves of marjoram on her temples who knows stories about witches, and a sideboard open to the pretty baby throat, a sideboard of cookies and candies and creams, milk candy more than anything, and it seems that nothing, never, ever again will disturb the palace of games and the the words come in shaking crystals and saying what in spite of ourselves we want to know. That was what he was like, Gervasio Pola . . .

"My husband's name was Gervasio Pola."

One word, a word I did not want to hear and its sound made me pull the sheets over my face and call my old marjoram nurse: Gervasio, who appeared ready with seduction on a black horse and silver harness to tell me that now life had changed, the head of the family had gone away on a German ship (and I in my house of dolls, stealing candy silently, stealthily, and never noticing anything) and that now he, Gervasio, was a colonel and able to provide the life to which I was accustomed and which I deserved, his pomaded mustaches glistening against the living-room hangings and my parents eavesdropping from the dining room, but not so far away as to miss the shine of his buttons and boots and his pomaded hair, parted down the middle and outlining his face, the olive almond shape of his skin. But that was only one year, a year that they tolerated him because he was a colonel and Madero was still President and they were living high and had somehow to hang onto their little palace with its varnishes and velvet, the year during which he filled my head and belly with enough to last me forever, yes filled my belly, which he never knew because it came out into the world when he was rotting in prison and then they pointed out to me just how stupid and careless I had been, saying, "Well, and this is what you wanted, eh?" and all my brothers, too, sharing the same sense of disgust to see me pregnant, even though I was married, that they would have felt no matter who I had for husband; they would keep quiet if the marriage were convenient, yes, if it didn't shake their quiet worlds and if everything continued as before; but now that was not the case, Gervasio was in prison and Madero assassinated, and I with a womb boiling with what Gervasio had left inside and with the one lone word I put there, Rodrigo, the word inside my belly, which I had to accept, alone, enjoying alone the first small kicks and trying to understand what it was I would give him, alone all the long slow gestation of a little being created by my thoughts and my blood, knitting baby clothes, sure that by the time they were finished, he would be back to touch my hair and tell me that all was well, I could rest now, go to bed with him and feel how big my womb was becoming with something that was ours together, let night pass in silence trying to feel the child's life, making love to me without touching me, with caresses of my hair, with holding hands, with our warm cheeks; but no, it couldn't be, he was never beside me while his child was growing round and heavy in the middle of my entrails, he was never there and he never knew because I never saw him again; and if he had been there, I would have known that there were three of us, three; but no, we were always only two, I and the father-son, I and Gervasio-Rodrigo, one single continuation but made now not of him but of my silence and lonely decisions, you see. But the only decision ever presented me was just to go on eating; years later I understood that when Captain Zamacona came and told me, when I was working, merely in order to go on deciding to go on eating, working in a downtown department store, and he wanted to take me away from that, three years after the death when I still believed that he would come back and by sheer force of will had kept my figure, his figure, so that he wouldn't think of days and years but go directly to the moment when we parted, the bittersweet welcome would come in another moment when we would recapture all that long lonely time of ignorance and desolation and gestation; and so the Captain learned my name and told me the story: "I myself gave the order to fire, and I was there myself that daybreak in front of Belén's pockmarked execution wall, in front of four faces who had preferred not to be blindfolded, and at the last they held hands and shut their eyes, and I myself walked forward and delivered the *coup de grâce* to the rebel Pola, who writhed before me in the dust, your husband, for the privates of the firing squad never could shoot to kill but only to half kill. So your husband has been dead for three years, *Señora*, another of Huerta's crimes, and he has paid dear for each of them, and now that I have joined the Carrancistas, I find that I can provide what you deserve to have provided you." Yes, almost the same words, and again a cocked kepi and curly mustaches and a soldierly bearing, the same as always, he who had come now to inform me that Gervasio was dead; and then I understood that my decision had always been only to go on eating, and that I needed to have sat in wake over Gervasio so that afterward I could prepare our (Rodrigo's, mine) meal on the coffin table and blend the scent of candles and gardenias with those of grease and butter; but it couldn't be, three years had passed, and not knowing where his body lay, I could only breathe in wind-blown dust when whirlwinds would spiral across this valley I have watched become arid and bone, but which I can recall as green and flesh, hoping it might be my husband's dust; but the Captain insisted, "Don't mourn for him; I don't like to say it, but the truth is that he did not die well. He could have gone to death alone, but no, he had to tell on his comrades, he did not know how to go alone, but had to inform us where the others were, so that he wouldn't be frightened. That is what he did, *Señora*." And I refused to blame and reproach his cowardice (cowardice? wasn't he their leader? didn't he have the right to demand everything of them? He did well, and this is not what I reproached him for), but that he had not let me know so that I could have fallen beside him, because if he was captain and leader of those who died with him, he was also my man and the father of my son and he ought to have summoned us, demanded it of us; oh no, he just left us, telling us that we might take care of ourselves, that he could give me life but not death; that was his real cowardice and the gall I felt and preserved, that after offering me so little of life, he had refused to offer me death, too; he would have done better to give me something whole, one or the other. And my bitterness, my feeling that I had been deprived of death, made me forego forever understanding certain things, but not one: that Gervasio had never really existed, that the child had been engendered by my own will and to my own purpose, I had inseminated myself with a dream, a man who had known me only in sleep, who possessed me only in the dream hour two hours before dawn and was not really there. And the child, the seed of my dream, he didn't want that, *Señor*, he didn't want to be any part of my life (my life, mine, formed by those two moments and of which he ought to have been part forever, forever tied to the cord, engendering the dream which in turn engendered him), and without his saying anything to me, his transparent child's eyes let me know that he was not as I wished his own father, not in the way I insisted, the father-lover, but only as the father-critic, not the father who would accept me forever, but the one who would spy on me, saying with his eyes that *now* I was no longer the woman I had been before; now you are changing, now the sockets of your eyes have hollowed and your eyes have sunk into them, your skin has loosened, you are a miserable widow who is growing old and toiling futilely after having been created for the little palace of toys and the nurse-maid who told you make-believe and the sideboard scented so unlike this moldy home; I couldn't tolerate that, my face was, it had to be, just as always, it had to belong to the loved words which had changed it originally into the face of a wife. But Rodrigo didn't know, he saw only that my skin had little wrinkles and he spied on me, and what was worse, he obliged me to see myself, and so it was that that little boy who was seated doing his homework under the green-shaded lamp, instead of entering my life, had withdrawn from it in order to look at me and tell me: I'm not you; I may be with you, but I am not you and I will not be you.

"My son, my son!"

"And you never told him everything, everything you thought? You just wanted to live, without explaining to him, expecting him to understand?" asked Ixca Cienfuegos.

"Yes, that was what I wanted."

. . . Because I couldn't cheapen myself and vulgarize all my world, for my world was already cheapened in all that could be touched and measured and I couldn't cheapen it more by bringing out into the light all I thought, too, because before, in my own home, everything had always been clear and understood, we had no need to explain ourselves or to ask forgiveness for what we had done or what we were or felt, our home and our place were both already explained and justified by the natural order of things; and that was how it ought to have been now, but now my work was vulgar toil and my home and my clothes were vulgar and I couldn't let my soul be vulgar, too, nor my words, nor the life I was giving my son; but his alienation from me obliged me to go back and look for Gervasio, and just as the child had forced me to know that he was different from me, so now he forced me to feel that Gervasio was changed: the child had canceled and ended all that I had held to, my rancor, the lukewarm memory of a body, the father-son solution, the need to have joined my death to Gervasio's; but now my days were gray monotonous days of toil from which there could never be a recompense, for it is possible for labor to be as graceful as idleness, yes, but if it isn't, then, Señor Cienfuegos, it is empty of everything; and those vulgar hours all I learned was to reproach Gervasio, which had nothing to do with the beginning of our life together or its consummation in our intercourse and the fruit of that, but which had to do only with my new life and the new city growing up around me and the new people who had sprung up; and from my dishonesty, from my wrenching away from all our own experience, the new Gervasio sprang up to be reproached by me, and from that new image there came forth also the destiny I planned for Rodrigo because the other, the true destiny, had lost its voice (my true life) in that mountainous accumulation of vulgarity, and I had to form new purposes and relationships and

180

justifications; and it is only now, when I am alone, that I understand this, but it is not just because I am alone that I understand, nor is it because I'm dying. Ten years had passed since Gervasio's death, and I went back and compared myself physically with what I had been then and took his photograph, sitting near the bed where my widowhood had passed and now was ended because I had stopped thinking of myself as a widow and had stopped remembering that something had gone deep into my body so unscrupulously and with such gathered and trembling strength, but at the last reverently, which is something not everyone knows how to do, but he did; he was a good man, I know it now, very late, good and generous, and those are just the things that escape us because we make our thought and our body complicated. I held the photograph beside my face and stood in front of the looking glass. I thought that now I was like his mother, and speaking aloud, I accused him with words which were not mine, but belonged to my disillusioned toil and the new city and its new people. And which came like a storm and clouded my heart. You, you have stayed always the same, dead or wherever you are, now you are still no more than that thirty-year-old idiot, half an idealistic hangman, and don't you understand, Gervasio, that a man has no right to follow his own destiny if he has a wife and son to take care of? Fool, fool, executed in prison and now, ten years later, you could be rich; and I let my arms fall and remembered the store where the new people came out to buy furniture for their new homes in the new *colonias* where they lived, all who had not died in Belén prison, all of them flooding in a multitude which filled me with shame, and the old aristocrats forced to move over and give way, and you, Gervasio, did not have the right to set yourself apart, you ought to have protected yourself as all the others did who today are rich and powerful. You didn't think about me. You didn't think about your son. You abandoned me to dry up little by little. I would like to forgive you, Gervasio, but I can't, for you gave me neither your love nor the little I would need to live comfortably. But I will make your son (and this was the lie, the lie born of my reproach, and only now, too late, I know it as a lie; tell him, the poor boy, tell him before it will be too late for him, too, that there are neither victories nor defeats in this country, that no man can leave the print of his foot upon this land, that all have been and all shall be, without intending it, ghosts before birth, because in the heart of Mexico's hearts only ghosts walk, only they carry battles well fought; our gymnastics in the dust are a struggle which has no resolution: tell him that); but I will make your son victorious as men are victorious here. I will educate him, I will teach him to search out the mighty and submit himself to them so that they will not assassinate him against walls, and he will learn to give normal life to the woman he will choose and to be beside her at the birth of his son . . .

"The glass, *Señor*, quick, the glass on the bureau . . ."

He reached, two movements, one which touched and raised the glass to the transparent lips of the old woman, the other to raise her head, groaning, disarticulate, on the bed, with her eyes measuring by an infinity of expressions the unpronounceable words and thoughts flickering behind them. The gray, opaque liquid danced for an instant between the trembling veins of Rosenda's throat. "Do you understand me?"

I couldn't make myself vulgar, too, you understand, I couldn't say anything to the child, but only to the portrait of the father (because at the back of all my perceptions and memories I continued identifying them as one and went on confusing them) because the child was only an object of scorn at his school, and every day he hid himself in his bedroom more, and I, downstairs sewing, thinking of what he might be up to, thinking and sneaking to his door and waiting for some sound and thinking that now he was a big boy, going on thirteen, and the temptations were beginning; thinking that I had to tell him about his father (about his failure) so he would not waste time but understand (Gervasio, I was going to tell him, gave me only pretty words and then let himself be murdered) and the lie was shouting in me: I don't want you to turn out the same, Rodrigo! But he, you, has to do things, and this I resolved in my lie, and because of my lie, because of my day in and day out toil and my feeling of being in exile within the city which had once belonged to me without my asking for it, and which could have been the kingdom of our domestic happiness and then, for a moment, my heart jerked with love and abandonment and widowhood, and because of my worry (why, why a love so cruel, so needing to be destroyed just to survive, so determined to suckle an escaping child and draw him back into the womb) about what was mine and only mine, I told him instead that his father was a coward who had abandoned us to poverty: that was what I said, a coward who had betrayed his comrades, and all the boy had asked was whether Gervasio had been good to me, and now I had lost, in my lonely bed and my days of widowhood and my hours of toil, the truth, what I have already told you, Gervasio's goodness and generosity . . . I was the fool, I, the coward, mine, the child, mine, the dark flesh. . . . And it was to his schoolmates' scorn for him, not to my love, the love I told you about, that I attributed Rodrigo's silence and distance, the impossibility from that night on of returning to what had been before, even if he had been as before; neither of us would ever again know the other. They have deformed him at school, I said to myself, we are not rich and they laugh at him and take away from him the self-confidence he needs to triumph, they make him hide in his room and write instead of thinking about the so much he has to do. And Rodrigo grew larger and I added to the lie: he was a man now and the moment of decision and danger was nearer than ever, and I watched over him from my cane rocking chair, I repeated to him silently, and he never heard me, how much I feared the absence of a man in the house had harmed him, and after midnight I would slip silently into his room where he did his writing and had begun to smoke in secret and was sleeping while I knelt by the head of his bed with my eyes wide to speak to him and tell him that now he was not a boy any longer and other things and to tuck in his covers while he slept so restlessly, moving his head as I repeated my words in a singsong below his sleep and into his sleep. It was enchantment, a spell, and it was all I could do, for he was far from me now in the glitter and pride of new friendships, joining together with other sons now, not to forget me, but to create the illusion that he was independent and had become alone, which for him was true . . .

"Are you his friend?"

. . . he would come home late while I waited with my sweating hand on the doorknob of his room, as if an ogre had been concealed there, a dark monster which would whisper to me about my son's secret life, the new relationships he did not permit me to understand, and when I finally decided to face those sheets of paper, his new love (more than I, more than his friends, more than himself, he believed and felt then; I don't know now, he has drifted so), those verses, and then I culminated the lie, I gave the lie full possession of me, and maybe without realizing it, let it consume me and so return me at last to truth . . .

"He . . . did he tell you about it?"

And what did I say to him then? I thought that no man has a right to destiny, and I wanted to consummate the lie: he was so big now, the desolate field between my destiny, my life in the linen department, and my widow life, that I refused to believe it and I refused him to have his own destiny, he ought to have only responsibilities, as I did; I told him that, and in reality all I wanted to tell him was how much I wished that it were possible for him to have his own destiny, but one that would be a continuation of mine and the destiny of his dead father, too; but I couldn't hold back, I didn't understand, I just let the lie take me, and I ran out of his room, bumping against the narrow walls of the hall, and locked myself in my bedroom. I saw both of them for the last time, and knew I had obliged Rodrigo to go away . . . not yet physically, that day or that year, but someday, yes, to go away with his spying eyes and the soft pulse in the veins of the hand which went on caressing me as if I were a child or a mute ancient monument, in his abstract courtesy which prevented me from ever knowing anything about his real life, to go away, too, in his measured distance from me until the day when he would never come back, never come back except amiably and without scenes and without even saying one word of blame that might have saved me, you understand, indeed would have saved me; never to come back then at all and never to know me again, not even to this day, the day of my death . . .

"The glass, Señor Cienfuegos."

... and ... and ... Gervasio, if he should return covered with clotted blood, what could I say? For the boy was pretty at birth ...

"You should have seen him at ..."

... there, in the wardrobe, suffocation among the dusty photographs of yesterday, when he moved his hand over my head, he was small, he was tiny, he was born of a mite of dust and I knew, never understood ...

"Tell him, Señor ..."

... that there is neither victory nor defeat, that he must go on, he wanted it, didn't he, until he meets his tiny destiny and all the land fills with old ghosts, where I lived as a girl with my nana and the milk candy; tell him that it will never be said because truth is measured by our own days and falls into a thousand fragments in the light of every glance, every heartbeat, every lineament of destiny, and you will never know those dream-veiled times were, but they couldn't last, nothing lasts here, we bide only a moment before the whirlwind seizes us and we suck our teeth ...

"The glass, Señor ..."

... tell him, tell him to come, just once ... I know he's poor, that he can't help me ..."

"... to come, to ..."

Rosenda's pointed tongue came out between her straight lips and an almost soundless sound, of her throat choking, brought Ixca to his feet. He covered her face with the sheet and blew out the candle on the bureau, and left the room.

"Add it up yourself, Luis. The way I figure it, we can't ..."

A blonde, thin young woman, both sharp and irregular in profile, with straight hair and uneven teeth, seated on a rose brocade sofa. Tonight as every night the fifth floor apartment on Miguel Schultz smelled of gas, of cooking, of the animal-like half-modern made-in-Mexico furniture. A dark cube gave passage to a dark hall floored in gray mosaic and then to the unpainted door which opened on this living room. Dining table, two chairs, the sofa, a woven easy chair. The décor was finished off by several religious chromos. "Don't get excited, Josefina," the man said, also young, puffy as to mustache, wearing dark glasses and a white shirt with rolled sleeves. He was writing numbers on paper. "If you wait, you'll see . . ."

"We still haven't finished paying for the bedroom."

"We will soon. Look. I've averaged it out. After December, I'll be out of debt. If they give me the northern territory, I'll be making plenty. Cotton farming is getting better, lots of farm machinery is going to be sold up there . . ."

"Ay, how I'd like to take Luisito out of that school and put him with the Brothers."

"Sure, we will. That's the first thing we'll do, don't worry. Then, I'm thinking about an apartment in another neighborhood . . ."

"How much, Luis?"

"Six hundred pesos, my heart. Two hundred more than here, and in a fine *colonia*, Nuevo León."

"I'm so tired of San Rafael now. You can't help having to do with the neighbors. You run into them in the market, in the park, and they aren't like you, but . . . you know. Sometimes, Luis, even though I love you and have faith in you, I'm afraid we'll never be able to live like decent people, and . . ."

"Ahhhh."

"Your boss won't change his mind?"

"Not a chance. You see how it is with the head of the department now. Talks to me as if I were a big shot, too. It's all arranged, I tell you. In December they'll put me on the road, you'll see."

"And if you don't make a lot in the north . . ."

"Don't worry so, Josefina. Have a little faith."

"Luis, I want a car so much. Luisito is going on seven now, and it would be so nice to take rides Sundays. And then I want another baby, because it isn't right to . . ."

"Please. We can't take on another mouth. There's hardly enough for three of us."

"But I tell you, it's not right. I do it only because I love you and you ask me to, but I was taught that it's a sin, that we have

186

to have as many children as God wants to give us. If you would ever go to Mass with me, you'd understand . . ."

"What the hell can a priest know about our personal problems?"

"Don't talk like that, Luis. You know I respect my religion . . ."

"Okay, okay, but cut out the worrying. I'm going up all the time. They like me, I swear it. Maybe in ten years . . ."

"Our own home?"

"Dead sure, Josefina. We can't miss."

"Look, I cut some pictures out of an American magazine. You know what I'd like better than anything? One of those breakfast nooks next to the kitchen so I wouldn't have to carry so far. And they're more intimate, too, don't you think? Maria de la Luz Rodríguez has one, and she was telling me that . . ."

"What the hell does Maria de la Luz Rodríguez know? You stay away from that broad, she just puts ideas in your head."

"But you have to admit that they're very well off. Señor Rodríguez has made a pile in his variety stores. Such friendships can mean a lot to us. . . . Luis, this *colonia* isn't good enough now. Put the pressure on your boss, tell him that . . ."

"Sure, sure. Just you take it easy. Everything will be all right, you'll see."

MEXICO IN WATERS

Seven in the morning and rain. Ixca Cienfuegos, wearing a black gabardine raincoat, arrived with the hearse. A home of two storeys in the depth of scattered homes in Mixcoac. He breathed glassy air, thin and cutting, and jumped from running board to door sill. The small street was deep with yellow mud. "I'll call you," he shouted to the men in the hearse. With long jumps he went upstairs three steps at a time, to Rosenda's room. All her scents met him at her door. It was as if every word she had ever said had become ash and odor. She was just as he had left her: tongue protruding, eyes wide, her vegetable skin more transparent. One knee on the bed, he folded her arms, not easily. He lowered her eyelids. To hold her chin up, he had to tie a handkerchief around her head. He went downstairs.

187

"All right. I'll wait here."

The windshield visor dripped. He turned the lapels of his raincoat up and listened to the noise of the casket descending the narrow stairs, the splash of feet in rain. Women watched from windows. Some kids, who had been carrying bundles from one curb to another on Revolución, came running as the casket appeared. "Mister, Mister, five cents to walk with the corpse." One kid neither ran nor begged; barefoot in water, he stared silently as the men from the hearse struggled not to fall in the mud. Hair flopped down dark and wet almost between his eyes. His hands were continuously making the sign of the cross and his lips moved. Ixca called him, "Kid, aren't you a neighbor of Doña Teódula's?"

"Jorge Morales, at your service," the boy chanted.

"What are you doing this far so early in the morning?"

"Making money from the rain, Señor," said the child. He went on crossing himself and murmuring as his eyes watched turbid water.

"You want to earn more?"

He nodded *yes* and scratched a knee. His eyes did not meet Ixca's.

"Run, take a bus. Go to Doña Teódula. Tell her, The mother is dead. That's all. Can you remember?"

He nodded again. "The mother is dead. That's all." Ixca gave him a peso and the child ran off, curving water up from his bare feet. The hearse began to move.

Between Mixcoac and San Pedro de los Pinos, morning came into its own. Rain fell heavy and warm now, warm vapor rose. Ixca thought about the cadaver which, wrapped in her shroud, at last had become the fruit of life of which Rosenda had always dreamed, the gestation of a father within a son, Gervasio and Rodrigo; that gestation which she had repeated for so many years, death had finally ended. The city passed. Gray, squat, splotched with rain which could not reach into the earth, but remained between soil and sky, in mud and the regurgitation of gutters. By his thought about Rosenda the city was changed into a great placenta, swollen with firing-squad volleys and by demanding love and unasked-for sacrifices and indifference. Four million were standing in line without touching hands, each stiff beside his neighbor, the long length of a wall flaked by gunpowder. Four million were coming to birth with closed mouths in the light of every morning, the darkness of every nightfall, birth repetitious like the painful movements of hurry, hurry, and every man was born of human proliferation to follow his hurried timetable and disappear with his memory, without resurrection. Here was the cadaver; there was the city. All Rosenda's gestations gave birth at last to only one: death.

A path oozed between files of cypresses. Rain ran down his face as he walked with his head down and his eyes on the heel tracks of the men carrying the casket. The open grave was full of water. Rosenda's casket sank into it, gurgling. Spadefuls of earth effervesced.

He left.

Floating between dark garments, Teódula Moctezuma closed the door of Rodrigo's room on Rosales and he remained in front of his bathroom mirror, looking at a reflection which was pale but, at that, brighter than its living face. He began grimaces. Laughter, interest, aloofness, a stage of faces until his face and his reflection became actor and audience and as far apart from each other as the moon and its trembling image in a puddle of rain. He sniffed the scent of dried flowers Teódula had brought into his room, and then the dried flowers which she had left. The muscles of his face pained, but he could not stop making faces at himself. What had he looked like when he told Norma Larragoiti that he loved her? This? And what face had he worn when Mediana cut him away from the group? He wrinkled his forehead and made an *O* with his lips. And what was his official writer's face? An eyebrow arched, the blade of his nostril trembled avidly. Then he let his shoulders droop, grabbed his head, and felt a real urgency, far from the comic moment before, to sit and write . . . somehow to communicate with himself. He felt in the upturned drawer on the bureau and found a pencil stub. He sat on the edge of his bed. He rubbed his nose and wrote:

"The problem is to understand how one sees one's own face. What it really is, ugly or lovely, doesn't matter. The point is to believe that it is interesting, strong, clear-cut, or that it is ridiculous, foolish, and gruesome. I have my seasons. Some times when I leave a movie, I imagine that I have been remodeled by the strongest of the faces which for two hours have been blinking at me. I arch my brows, put out my lower lip until it dries, puff out my chest, and am sure that everyone must be aware of and impressed by my extraordinary strength of character. At other times I wake with an uneasy emptiness in the pit of my stomach and stop my razor in midstroke before a lather-bearded effigy in the mirror. I walk with dragging feet and my head is down and I am sure that everyone looks at me and names me 'poor devil.' All depends on the state of soul, and that depends upon external impulses. Consequently, it is enough to control those impulses correctly to arrive at the states of soul and personality which are desired. But the fact is that usually I prefer to be seen as a poor devil, to be pitied. Why should this be? Perhaps that later I may surprise with a sudden leap of character that will make liars of those who name me poor devil. Which doesn't mean that it does not happen sometimes, my contact with people being so fleeting that I have no time to change the impression; and such persons must carry away the conviction that they have been acquainted with a jackass. Because of this I try to elaborate acquaintance across time and toward precisely the impression I want to leave. Someone might say that this is foolish, that men are objective and one's true character shows through all disguises. I'm not sure. Perhaps the game, the pretense, through long repetition may become authentic and the original personality be lost by the atrophy of disuse. What I do know is simply that I, carried along by my personality dialectic, no longer know my true face.

"Examples: Let us suppose that I have, or had, some special talent; for writing, let us suppose. I began manhood showing myself as a writer, presenting myself to the world, my first introduction, with a card on which was written: Rodrigo Pola, Writer. As others announce themselves Fulanito, Civil Engineer, or Perengano, Restorer of Oil Paintings. Except that civil engineers and

190

restorers of oil paintings may at once and tangibly prove that they really are what they call themselves: here is the physical work, you may apprehend it with your five senses. But how can one prove to others that one is a writer? No matter how tangible a book is, to see, smell, or touch it does not prove anything or say anything about its stylistic excellence but only its primitive existence. It is so hard to apprehend the intrinsic being. Very different from the apprehension of a concrete and steel building, or of a fifteenth-century oil painting, restored, shining, smelling of varnish. Definite proofs that one is a writer do not, then, exist; at most, there may be a little prestigious noise. As a college student I wrote a volume of verse and I exploited it well, not to write another book aided by the first, but to see what I could do to get a more concrete job. But obviously, if one pulls a rabbit out of the silk hat, the rules of the game indicate that the magician may not, after his act, stew the same rabbit.

"In effect I had no alternative than to seat myself at a desk as the director of an office in government service and dictate words which became letters, memoranda, and reports. But then my original point of view intervened. Because I needed to prove I was a writer, I would dictate badly in order to correct well. Except that this, carried to its extreme, produced hatred from my subordinates and the conviction in them that I was too slow in my work and slowed them down, too. And all I wanted was to create an initial bad impression in order to surprise with a following good one. Such a plan, unfortunately, needs time to develop and the assurance that there will be enough time for the later twist, and this is hard, for men and business prefer and demand a quick, clear portrait, and if one does not give it, they get along with the first impression. What a lack of patience! And wisdom, too. If my government superiors had possessed both, they would have ended by seeing the usefulness of my literary genius. But they were in haste, they judged the vine by its first fruit, and I was fired. They lost, not I. Such are the consequences of spiritual haste.

"As it is impossible to force anyone to forego haste, the public display of an attitude such as mine is self-defeating; the only remedy is to limit its scope and practice alone. One day, in this manner, I decided to ignore certain organic necessities. I refrained for a number of days from going to the bathroom, taking delight in the progressive malaise which ensued. Delight changed into a serious illness . . . peritonitis, no less, and I had to call in a doctor and feel, upon being saved from death, that in my cure I had a triumph which had come to me through and over the monotonous daily act of defecation.

"It is clear that such heroism, to name it truly, may not be repeated frequently; its heroic quality is precisely in its rarity. This requires one in daily life to seek substitutes which, if they also are named truly, can only be 'pathetic,' 'pitiful.' The category of the 'pitiful' deserves a broad, careful study. Why is one 'pitiful?' Why should one seem so to one's fellow men? Perhaps 'pitiful' is the definition of my version of 'heroic.' If, as is the rule, there is not time enough for the long-planned and deceptive parade before an observer, it is enough to seem 'pitiful' to prove that one is capable of moving people, making them feel something. So, when in government I used to order my typist to sharpen a pencil and when she gave it to me, I would let it drop and break the point again. This led naturally, at last, to the disappearance of the pencil itself and then I felt justified in accusing my typist of neglecting her typing, and if the confused woman dared to tell me—she didn't often—that she had spent the whole morning sharpening pencils, I would always reply that her job was to type, not to sharpen pencils, and if she herself did not know the nature of her job, it might well happen that she would find herself transferred from her typewriter to the pencil sharpener.

"These are, then, the little expressions of my general attitude. There are other occasions on which I play the fool. A few evenings ago I consciously made an ass of myself at a party. Ixca Cienfuegos was present and witnessed it. I came back to my room, preparing, as was logical, for a later triumph before the same people who had watched my debacle. I put water to boil for tea and by carelessness let the tongue of my belt touch the coil of the hot plate and didn't notice until an unsupportable stink of burning leather reached my nose. If my attitude in the face of events is understood, it will not seem surprising that I let the belt go on burning, and then retired, wrapped in that pestilential stench. When Cienfuegos came to wake me the next morning, he at once thought that the smell was gas and that I had intended suicide—my motive, doubtless, the ridicule I had suffered at the party. Men are so used to judging me weak and impetuous. I confess I did not enlighten him. On the contrary, I kept up the deception and spoke pitifully of my innate suicide, the failure of my life. That same afternoon my friend took me walking the whole length of Reforma, so I might take the air after breathing in so much gas, my God. He insisted I talk about my childhood, it being the style nowadays to believe that we are determined by our childhood. I took good advantage of the chance and gave him a version which added to his feeling of pity. Who knows . . . ? Maybe I told only the truth, but stained, I am sure, by such an air of humility that it seemed I wanted to portray myself as a 'good boy.' I don't know if he swallowed it all. Neither do I know whether now, and in spite of my firm intention to be honest with myself, I am not at the same time holding to self-pity. In any event, none of this is serious, much less culpable. What is culpable is the absence of generosity. But to be generous, one must possess something worthy of being offered to others. A capacity for work, love, talent, understanding, knowledge, what one has. And when there is nothing to give, when one is empty, can one be blamed for a lack of generosity? I believe that this is my case. By the same reasoning, if there are no obstacles to overcome, is it wrong to do nothing, to sit quietly in a corner? I, for example, have no temptations. Therefore I have none to withstand. I imagine that Christ, led by the Devil to the summit of a mountain and shown all the temptations of the world, knew very well first, that it was the Devil who was with Him, and second, that as God He could not, if He held the least sense of congruity or even a regard for appearances, succumb to the Devil's temptation. He was immune in advance, and the poor Devil made a great fool of himself. God cannot be tempted; temptation does not exist for Him, and therefore He can never be blamed for not overcoming

193

it. The same is true of myself. I feel no temptation. I may at most sometimes feel enthusiasm, but that is not the same.

"Fundamentally, I am interested only in fulfilling my dialectic. Sometimes, as I have noted, a thesis fails and nothing happens. But each time I fail one way, I try the opposite. For example, my college friends mocked my book of verses; I cut their friendship away and went to the opposite extreme; if they were aesthetes, I would be a man of action. I fought for the autonomy of the university, I joined the Vasconcelists, as if proclaiming, 'I don't need you, I can betake myself to the other side, and the better for the move.' But at the least gesture of impatience on the part of those in my new circle, back I would go flying to where I had been before. And so on, ad infinitum.

"What will be the end of one who lives and thinks as I? Very simple: fraud finally exhausts itself and one comes to one's limit. Yes: the limit. And there, incapable of changing anything. The man who always wants to pass as just and forever changes in order to appear what at the moment he supposes is just may be supposed to lose finally all possibility of justice. He becomes the slave of his own game, the movement overcomes and chains the mover, and afterward only the movement matters; he is not carried and raised by it, no longer an agent, only an element. And this is neither good nor evil, redeemable or irredeemable. Maybe it can be called to live remote from grace. That is all."

Six in the afternoon. Ixca Cienfuegos unbuttoned his black raincoat in the entrance to the cathedral. The Zócalo was emptying, the last overloaded buses pulling away; but students were beginning to pass, hurrying to their night classes at San Ildefonso and Santo Domingo, their hands in their pockets and their books and notebooks under their arms. On every corner there was a lottery ticket vendor crying his numbers and the prizes. Newspaper stands were being folded up, peddlers whistled as they collected their rags and little boxes of glass diamonds and copper gold. A few small boys danced down Madero and Cinco de Mayo, shouting the headlines of the evening *ess-traaa!* Teódula Moctezuma's unmistakable bulk at last appeared through the gate, slipped along the front of the church to the dark twilight door.

"You saw him?"

"Yes, my son." Teódula blew her nose silently and took a crumpled cigarette from her bodice and gestured for a light. "Your mother died last night, I told him. I've been looking for you all over the city. Where was she? he asked me. By now she is buried and I don't know where. Where had he been when his mother died? I asked him. At a party, he said, and he began to shake. You should have seen him, my son. What next? I said, and then, Well, the poor soul is beyond old age and hardship now, and do you know what he did, Ixca?" She took the cigarette from her lips and began to laugh. Her face, like an old tortilla, wrinkled square.

"What did he do?" Ixca smiled.

She raised her arms and let them fall on her stomach. "He asked me what right I had to address him with *tu*. My God! My God! I told him by what right, Ixca, don't worry!"

She flipped the cigarette away and floated toward the central entrance. There she turned and looked back at Ixca. She smiled and covered her head with her *rebozo* and went into the cathedral. Leaning against the façade of the cathedral, Ixca continued smoking. When he finished his cigarette, he felt that it had distracted him, unconsciously, from someone's stare, a gaze which had produced, without his noting it, sensations both of anticipation and discomfort. From the sacristy he looked around, his eyes oily in the twilight. An old man with a flexible face selling religious cards. Two crawling women with big scapulars hanging between their throats and knees. A child's eyes almost covered by a thick fringe of dark hair; he was near the gate with a couple of newspapers under his arm, barefoot, rubbing his knee. Jorge directed a questioning look at Cienfuegos, a tacit invitation to be informed of his wishes, the promise to try to carry them out. He put his hand on a fence bar. He seemed ashamed, not very sure of his piety, his small body covered by too-large gray overalls. Ixca walked to the gate. The sun had hidden behind Zócalo buildings, its rays were thrown up from the distant level earth through a gray intermediate zone, every second narrower, between the buildings and the dark dome of descending imminent night. Ixca felt shadowed by that imminency. He coughed, tousled the child's head. "You get around, kid."

Jorge tried to smile. *"Esss-straaa?"*

"Night is coming. Doesn't your mother expect you?" Ixca could not take his hand away from the child's head. And the sun vanished.

"She doesn't live with us. She works for some rich people." He wiped his nose on his forearm and snuffed his nose, trying to smile.

Ixca moved his hand to the boy's shoulder. "You live a long way from here. Do you want to . . ."

Jorge, smiling and with his eyes still questioning, went on rubbing his knee. His eyes shone as they moved up Ixca's height, over his black raincoat.

"Your father's dead, isn't he?"

The boy nodded *yes.*

"Don't you want . . . some candy, or supper, yes, that's better, something hot to eat and then to go to sleep . . ." Ixca took the boy's hand, felt it cold, its coldness repelling the warm sweat of his own. The boy's spontaneous smile was paralyzed. His eyes stopped questioning and turned toward Ixca with a magnetic certainty, he tried to get his hand out of the man's fist. Ixca squeezed the little hand harder and harder; he could not control his eyes, and he bent his head near the child's while the child threw down his newspapers and fought to get loose, and finally, sinking his teeth into Ixca's hand, succeeded. He crossed the square, running, and stopped on the distant curb. There he looked back at Cienfuegos one more time, and then ran on, the length of a dusk-dark path, until he became a tiny moving point and then disappeared down Veinte de Noviembre.

Ixca covered the bleeding mark left by the boy's teeth. He crossed the pavement until he stood on the center of the great square. He sucked blood from the wound, and, whirling where he stood, let his body drink in the four shores of the square, which now was deserted. The last oblique ray of sun profiled across the sky like a shield. His blood moved with the shifting quickness of mercury. He waited, his face turned into the last ray. Palace, cathedral, Ayuntamiento building; the other, disequal side of arched legs; half shadow forming an area of transient light, opaque, between the natural shadow of gray stone and worn marble. Across his eyes another scene hurried, violent, in flight: the flow of a dark canal to the south, filled with white tunics; on the north, a corner where stone broke into shapes of flaming shafts and red skulls and still butterflies: a wall of snakes beneath the twin roofs of rain and fire; to the west the castle of albinos and hunchbacks and peacocks and dried eagles' heads. Both images, both scenes, were strong in his eyes, and dissolved back and forth, each the mirror without background for the reappearance of the other. Only the sky, the tiny shield of light, was the same in both.

He looked down and shook his bitten hand over the soft earth until one drop of blood fell, turning to a dry color when it touched the dust. He bit his hand, driving his teeth into the same wound the small teeth of the boy had made. Warmth dripped down his lips. He closed his eyes to let the acrid metallic taste of his own blood fill his mouth. His head swam with that taste; blood whirled in his ears like two breaths, united by an hour of terror: the breath of a man, the breath of a ghost, one standing in front of the other, and both invisible.

He opened his eyes. Night. The sun had gone. In darkness, with a surprised face, he felt a multitude of shadows dance over his chest. "I need another night, not this one," he murmured. "Not this, another, a night when pieces of moon may be gathered up, all the broken fragments of origin, and can be put back together again. Another night." Lampposts came on. A few pious women appeared, leaving the cathedral. Blinded, he raised his hands to his eyes. A bee was buzzing around a lamppost lantern in shadow and light both, its yellow body gleaming, its black body lustrous. Buzzed without penitence, enamored of its own sound, its possession of night and its enslavement to the fictitious sun. Ixca spread his arms, anxious to conjure away darkness. His pupils flattened and spread, trying to penetrate night, to pass

197

through it, ignore it. His eye sockets larger and larger and injected with light, he searched the sky for one star sign.

One tear, at least one, he was thinking with an intensity of which he had believed himself incapable, as he slowly descended the stairs. Taut air. Irresolute, premonitory. The storm was readying, loading, trembling with dry lightning. Electric sky signs were made dark by intermittent sky flashes. Under the vastness of the firmament, Rodrigo walked along Rosales to the Puente de Alvarado. It was as if the earth were standing on its head, an ocean was where air had been, agitated, intent upon the creation of a storm of lightning and liquid clouds without bases from which darkness rayed out like the black nerves of an octopus. He was oppressed by the menace in nature, and reflected that his reality, his person, was like a cliff, drowned by a tormented flood but remaining a cliff and singular even when the anonymous, mighty but nucleus-lacking cataract poured over it. Nor was that the only fantasy which came to Rodrigo during this nocturnal walk: he was more than ever obsessed now to find some support for his belief that his agony was obligatory, the illusions that he had been rejected because those who rejected him sensed and feared his superiority, that Tomás and the group of young writers of the twenties had attacked him because his youth and promise threatened them, that Norma Larragoiti had refused to love him because he would have dominated her and demanded of her a very different honesty and devotion from those demanded by a boring banker without ideas. Greatness, honor, and power had escaped him, Rodrigo reflected, not because of his deficiency, but his excess. He reflected, and smiled. In reality all his many defeats reduced to only one, another cliff, as singular as himself: Norma. He stopped on an intersection in front of the San Fernando cemetery and savored his thoughts, his rationalizations. A moment before, the news of Rosenda's death, the terrifying old woman who had brought it, his resolution to settle into his destined role and in truth discover the deepest explanation of his life; all seemed far away and unreal. To line the important salients of his life he needed gentle moments and that sensation of the absolute which only a moment possesses. A long file of buses and streetcars inched along Puente de Alvarado and Avenido Hidalgo, almost all of them empty; it was nearly eleven. He crossed the park, nodded to a greenish bronze, eagles-guarded Vincente Guerrero. San Fernando building, anchored to earth of imperturbable dignity, reflected on its stones the movement of trees within the cemetery. The long gated gallery of statues and trees sighed in a wind that passed, incapable of reverence, over the illustrious marbles. Memorial legends shone during a lightning flash: *he lived and sacrificed his life, at the battle of Soria, 1863, for his homeland . . . she came to the marriage altar full of happiness and there death struck her down . . . here lies . . .* Sleeping pigeons reposed in the niches of the great stone caskets, on a decapitated saint. Rodrigo continued along Guerrero. He walked beside the dry flowers of the chapel. Buildings lost height; cabarets, crumbling façades, catch-all shops, sandwich stalls, hardly visible in the dead light, acrid in their smells. On the corner of Violeta he rocked his stare against the surrounding world of all the city's trades and lives: a small cheap family restaurant, vegetable stores, hardware, shoe, tortilla shops, a bar, flophouses, a hospital for dolls and religious statuettes, a carpenter, car batteries, the rose gurgle of the Garden Cabaret, a trinket shop, Gold Glitters and its cavernous billiard depth, books bound, jokes, magic tricks, puzzles, the glass gallery of the engraver Tostado; Insurgente Pedro Moreno Street, Mina, Magnolia, Esmeralda, and Moctezuma. And the wizened bodies, the eternal Mongoloid faces of some forgotten race hunched over their hot meals, hidden behind their face masks. And in the center of the square, anchored, he, Rodrigo, who was aware of the middle ground, planted between two worlds, both of which refused him. He half turned, and through the essential and impenetrable darkness of this Mexico City in which he had lived, he tried to make out the lights of Juárez and Reforma. He stood between two lands in a city of physically invisible but spiritually high and barbed frontiers. Had the city itself created those barriers, or were they the work of its inhabitants? One time only had he sensed the need, not dictated

199

by intelligence, to be without his own barriers: with Norma. He had wanted to open himself to her and to pour out all that was in him and receive all that she wanted to give him. But the manner they met, their style together, had created new barriers each time they saw each other. He realized that with Norma he had felt the need to define his love, fill it with words and echoes of words, fix it, insist on the abstract fact of it in every conversation and in every embrace, none of which had ever been enough in itself; while Norma on the other hand had wanted only the isolated and complete experience of being loved, with no need for Rodrigo to prepare an inflexible word-prescription by which they must both live. "Give me what you don't know you have," Rodrigo was thinking now; for to live is only to open the ground of the unknown, that which has never been traveled before. That had been her request, her challenge to him yesterday and a few days ago at Natasha's, too. Now, walking slowly among the fecund smells and the silence of tropical trees, Rodrigo wanted to believe this. She had offered the challenge, and he had not accepted it.

The sky opened, a green oxidized sheen at its vertex, shafts of colors rising toward that focus. Rodrigo sheltered himself under the awning of an oyster bar. Water drummed on the parched canvas; drops filtered through and splashed on his shoulders.

What he had never known that he possessed. What he had never offered. And therefore did he still have it? Or had it withered, annihilated forever? Yes, he had his prepared rationalizations: at first he would seem what he was not in order to surprise later. Plain cowardice would have been braver, however, than this intellectual fakery. Norma first. Then Rosenda, his mother. How many times, over the years, had he gone to a door on a little street in Mixcoac, knowing beforehand that he would not cross the threshold and was going only to fool himself and let himself think that he could freely will himself to go inside and visit his mother; when he had known from his first steps that he would not go in. "I'm too proud," he had said when he reached the door; "she must come to me first." And so almost eleven years had passed without their seeing each other, without their much noticing that they had not seen each other, for nothing gives time such wings as indifference and littleness. But his mother had been proud, not he. He had merely played at pride. He had played at pride when he refused to accept Norma's challenge, when he abandoned his vocation because his friends had criticized him: he had been able neither to prove their criticism wrong nor simply to go on, ignoring their criticism. He had given up everything, to prove . . . what? He questioned himself again: to prove what? What had been proved to others or to himself when he had peeped from his room and spied on neighborhood boys and girls, going to a dance or on an excursion, holding hands, walking with arms around waists; hidden behind his window curtains, he had hurled the cheapness of his spirit toward them. To prove what?

He abandoned the protection of the awning and walked swiftly toward Rosales. The storm enveloped him in an implacable liquid drumming; overhead, space was imprisoned by its own clamor, light was dim. The sky resounded to a sadness removed from all conditions.

He climbed pale-blue tiled stairs to his room. He lighted a cigarette and his eyes jerked: in the flare of the match he had seen a figure posed before his door. Ixca Cienfuegos smiled from the shadow. His raincoat and black hair were lost against the dark background; his pale, smiling face seemed to float. Rodrigo raised a hand to his mouth, touched the burning cigarette, and burned his hand.

"You had to come, eh?" he said as he put his fingers in his mouth and wet them with spittle. He opened the door. Ixca went in and sat with his legs spread and the raincoat dripping on the floor.

"Don't ruin my parquet," said Rodrigo, and he began to pace back and forth, five strides to the small opaque-paned window, five strides back to the bathroom door.

"The rain caught me!" exclaimed Cienfuegos. "I thought a cup of tea would be good for me. What's happened?"

Rodrigo shrugged. He took his wet jacket off and threw it at the bed. "Put on the teapot, if you want."

201

Cienfuegos observed him for a while and winked one eye. "Tell me about it, man."

Pola stopped and shrugged again. "We have to fake, don't we? We are taught to do that." He lifted the burned finger to his chin. A blister had appeared on the tip. "My mother died last night. An old servant buried her this morning. I didn't see her. I was . . . I was trying to make a girl at Charlotte's, I was trying to prove . . . shit!" Rodrigo tried to smile. "I wasn't even invited. Crashed it, as at Bobó's the other night. But I have to have at least these moments, Ixca, if I didn't . . ."

Cienfuegos was silent. Rodrigo's face did not correspond to his words. As if he had read Ixca's thought, Rodrigo turned his back and took the teapot to the sink.

"What?" he said above the splash of water. He thought that Ixca had said something. He returned and put the teapot on the hot plate. He sat on the edge of the bed; then he got up and opened a window. A damp corruption, formed of soggy garbage and growing plants, old newspapers and cockroaches, rose from the cube of the inner patio. Rodrigo let himself be hypnotized by rain, held by it, controlled by its destiny as it dropped into the patio, losing transparency. This, he said to himself, is the nature we know: occasional and contaminated rain. He thought that he had begun to love nature and silence now. To hear only those sounds nature offered without being asked to. Creation breathes: it does not speak or think, it merely breathes in grateful reply, murmuring as a glen descends, breathing flavors of grass and myrtle and earth packed by the hooves of masterless horses, and the death of a wild ass leaves a scent to the new vine. Only that. At night, a colt and a cricket, visible breathing complemented by heard breathing. No other sound. Rodrigo turned his face to Cienfuegos; he had the feeling, unconscious, violent, and forgotten, that Ixca's features reproduced the same dark flat view the patio afforded, and that Ixca's face was falling upon him like rain upon mountains of swollen garbage and upon roofs of tin and roofs of tar and gravel and the city's pavements. Like the streets, that face swallowed up nature and destroyed it with a gesture, an expression, that was equivalent to noisy juke boxes and auto horns. "'City of Palaces! Street of Roses! Eternal Spring!" Rodrigo imitated a wolf growl. He was thinking that they needed changes of seasons and skin to know themselves, and also others. With his eyes held by rain that already, in mid-air, was sewer dust, he wanted to create a hot, heavy summer inside himself, growth weighted with sweetening fruits, heavy gold branches beside a river where bodies swam, cooling; a visible sepia and red autumn, with harvests and harvest season festivals; a winter of white coasts, stripped of deer, covering a strength-recuperating earth which was getting its seeds ready . . . and a spring: rebirth, not the continuation of anything, unland-marked, uncalendared, a time of repose. "We lose our bearings here, Ixca, because all days are the same. Rain or dust, and always the same sun, and that's all. What can resuscitate this unchanging world, Ixca?"

Resuscitate. Cienfuegos again felt the night's weight, the sun's traveling arch locked away by the padlocks of darkness, as he had felt it in the Zócalo earlier. He stared at the cover of the teapot, which had begun to dance in the steam. "I can't help you. You have your own stars. Your life is traced already. What do you want me to do? Tell you what *I* believe? What is valid for *me*?"

"Why not?" Rodrigo put two tea bags in the cups and poured the pot.

"Because you won't understand me. Your life, the life you told me about a few days ago when we were walking along Reforma . . ."

"Has nothing to do with what you believe?"

"The world isn't just given to us," said Cienfuegos, com-pressed into the black raincoat. "We have to re-create it. We have to keep it going. Support it. The world is blind and brutish. Left to its own forces, it wrinkles up like an apple fallen from the branch, holed by worms. The trunk and branch give it sap and life, yes. But the hand which takes the apple must preserve the apple, or die with it."

Rodrigo sat on the bed. "You know, I believed that when . . . when I tried to cut free from my mother. The day I left with no good-bye or anything . . . I felt I had freed myself from the trunk, that now I was my own trunk. Afterward I thought . . . that my mother's attitude had controlled my leaving, more than any decision of my own. You understand me? Isn't there an implicit invitation in the trunk, in that creative force, for us to fall away from it? How can the creator misunderstand? Doesn't he have the obligation to himself to support what he creates? Why does he permit the apple to rot?"

Ixca blinked in the smoke that hung around his nose and eyes and thought about Rodrigo's father, Gervasio Pola. "Yes, it is possible that he feels shame and regret" he said in an even tone which contrasted with the nervous excitement in Rodrigo's voice. "What did he raise in the first place, by making the least gesture of creation, the tree or the apple? But maybe all his shame and regret is not enough to undo what is done. If creation is divine, it will carry that into its corruption. Nor may the same creature go backward. He himself cannot cancel what he has created: the creation of God is final!"

"But he could foresee that his creation would be corrupt, couldn't he? How then could he knowingly engender evil? Where does evil enter into creation?" The rain spattered slow and unevenly now. It fell in heavy drops.

"Yes, where does evil enter in, Rodrigo? For God has to be apart from evil, or it isn't really evil, eh? Look . . . some time back I knew a parish priest here in the city who was talked about very badly . . . first in the gossip of women, but later by their men, too. His conduct as a priest was admirable, he was a good confessor and preacher, but his conduct outside the temple was very different. He would go to the plaza Sundays in an open shirt and some sort of gray suit, smoking and looking at people cynically; they watched him go into bars, heard him use strong language, get into arguments. But once back in the temple, his unworldliness, his devotion, his indisputable sincerity at Mass . . . just by his presence he changed a social process into a living and relived rite; the depth and warmth of his sermons, the purity and dignity with which he heard confessions; all these earned him the love and respect of his parishoners.

His superiors naturally knew all about this and they reprimanded him for his frivolous and scandalous attitude apart from his strictly ecclesiastical duties. He was forced to control his worldly appetites. But to the degree that he achieved that control, his interior religious life changed also. His cynical words on the street became cynical maxims cloaked with ecclesiastical trimmings and delivered from the pulpit. It is believed that a young woman killed herself following confession to him. Nevertheless, his conduct outside the temple was now irreproachable: he always wore his cassock, he walked very slowly along the loneliest streets with his palms pressed together in a posture of continuous piety, and he did one good work after another. Until at last, one Sunday, he leaped up on the altar, shouting blasphemies and spitting at the chalice. He was carried away to an insane asylum."

Ixca sipped his tea. "This is the lie; evil and corruption are also divine works. God devised them, foresaw them, carried them out. For if God is infinite good, Rodrigo, He is also infinite evil: He is the perfect mirror of all that He created. Both good and evil, we are His creatures. Our destiny may be varied, but if it is to be a true destiny, it has to be carried to its consummation in one of the two realities, good or evil. We have to let ourselves go all the way, no matter which way it is . . . the passage is so brief."

Rodrigo, getting to his feet, did not want to accept that brevity, and still less, such destiny. He wanted to reject Cienfuegos, to recover, by two or three words, his faith of indifference, and then, clinging to the words, to use them as a talisman. But he felt he did not know how to pronounce those words now and that this incapacity forced another reality: their two bodies, his and Ixca's, face to face, his broken and nervous, sterile to engender any physical explosion which would level the tenacious presence and enduring power in Cienfuegos.

"Just the same, God is one," he murmured, without conviction.

Cienfuegos narrowed his eyes, concentrating the light of his powerful body in the slits of his eyelids. "And that is the other lie. God is many. Every god was born of a pair, and each pair of two pair, and each two pair of four pair, until heaven was populated by more gods than there have ever been men." His voice rose, came to Rodrigo as insulting, affirming and swaggering. "Maybe there is one point of contact, quite nameless, for which singularity may be claimed. But from this point flows a river of men who receive creation and are obliged to maintain it and another river of gods who create. Every man feeds the creation created by a god, Rodrigo, every man, every succession of men, reflects the face and colors without form of a god who makes and controls him and follows him until death reunites him to the original duality. It is necessary only to know whether this passage between creation and death, this short passage, fulfills the nourishment of a creator, or whether it is spent in compromise in a simple and unconscious passing. Which do you prefer?"

Rodrigo did not reply. He didn't understand what Ixca was asking: Was it a great augmenting of value to life, or a solitary sacrifice, a renunciation which in a final burst would give significance and rescue him from mediocrity. "There are so many things that hang over us that we feel as if others have already finished that part of our life. Only my father, you know, could live as he lived, not only for himself, but for my mother and for me, too. It is as if all the possibilities of life have already been lived by him, in the Revolution. No, I don't understand what you ask, Ixca."

Ixca opened his lips and moved them neared Rodrigo. "It was a leper, yes, a leper, who first leaped into the brazier of original creation in order to feed that flame. He was reborn, changed into a star. A motionless star. One sacrifice by itself, even one like that, isn't enough. Daily sacrifice is needed, daily feeding so that the sun will give light, and in turn feed us. No, I don't see one God, nor isolated sacrifice. I see the sun and rain. I see visible and immediate things joined without intermediary to every man's life. I see true proofs, sun and rain, of higher power, and on the earth I see my thin reed of flesh and bone. This is where we meet. Higher, the gods.

Lower, the remnants of life, hidden in frightened eyes. That is all. Which do you want?"

"I . . . I don't know what to say. I know that I have failed. I couldn't attain the literary fame that I was obsessed by as an adolescent. I could not gain the love of the only woman I wanted . . . I couldn't give my mother the two drops of tenderness which would have been enough . . ."

"And if this were all to be renounced? If you had renounced fame, love, and generosity?"

"You mean that they would have given birth to sacrifice, Ixca?"

"They might have. But you didn't renounce them, you accepted them in half measure, you understand me? You diminished them. There is a limit for men like you. At that limit, to contemplate suffices . . ."

Rodrigo felt himself justified: the words he had written that same day seemed repeated and come to life in Ixca at this moment. "Yes, yes . . ."

"Or you attain the triumph of a caged squirrel. You trot the treadmill of your little state prison, creating the impression that you are going somewhere. And one day it all stops. The end. And then only sacrifice can save you. Then you have to face the worthlessness of your life and undertake the only thing that can prevent your destruction, with the hope that something may be born of your sacrifice."

Rodrigo felt himself shivering.

"There isn't even that. I need only one word. I don't know which, nor would I know how to speak it. I believe that my mother more than anything else demanded only a hard strong word from me. Perhaps in that we would have met . . . we would have found my father. I didn't know how to pronounce it. I left home, you know, Ixca, like a light-fingered servant. I didn't tell her why I went, not what I thought of her, nor anything. And everything was that way. Nothing was ever said or done completely. You're right. But let me be what I am and don't . . ."

"You want the sacrifice," Ixca breathed between his shining carved teeth, between his straight, drawn lips. "That can redeem you. Come with me, I will teach you . . . forget all the others, what you have been until now, the trappings of a faith which you have not even known how to live faithfully, which has merely added to your self-pity. Spit out what is sacred, if what is sacred is that crude mercifulness which only accentuates your mediocrity! Spit out the cowardly God mouthful. Tremble and feel the terror of sacrifice, yes, sacrifice. Come to be ours, smother the sun with your kisses, and the sun will seize your throat and devour your blood to let you be one with it."

Rain and yellowing, darkening light chinked Ixca's voice and profiled his figure, as if each word were stone; his eyes and mouth glittered with something that trembled, they demanded everything, they were eyes and mouth which were ready to devour. The wind had changed; rain fell into the room in broken gusts, lashing at both men. Ixca stared at the lost, the useless, unmoved face of Rodrigo Pola.

"Don't you want the destiny your father and mother had?" he whispered over that inanimate face. "Don't you want defeat and humiliation, as they had? Tell me: isn't that what you want and what you told me the other afternoon that you want? To be the continuation of your assassinated father and your mother who was squeezed empty of life and deprived of everything, love and everything else that was hers? Ah! 'I want to be the continuation, morally, of my father!' How easy it was to say then!"

"Yes."

"Well, your father was a sacrifice, death faced alone . . ."

"Oh, no, Ixca. That wasn't what my mother meant. He was incapable of dying alone. He had to betray three men to be able to die. Even in death he wanted to fall with others and not alone . . . not alone. He asked exactly what my mother begged of me: Protect me, don't leave me by myself. He begged as he died; she begged living. To belong. That is what they really sought, and it is what I wanted to tell you the other afternoon. That *I* want to belong, I want to get out from this mud-hole of failures that I have inherited from them. I don't want to fall in the dust as they did. That's what you must save me from. From humiliation, from defeat. I told you that. Didn't you understand me?"

Ixca's mouth slowly lost its rigidity. He lit a cigarette, trying to recover his usual manner. He would have liked to laugh at his mistake; the ghosts of Gervasio Pola and Rosenda, thought Ixca, were probably laughing. Yes: he had to go back to that long walk down Reforma. Rodrigo had said that he wanted to be the continuation of his father, but in reality he had confirmed that is was men like Federico Robles who knew what he wanted. He wanted a safe, quiet place in the center of a balanced and directed Mexican world. Therefore Federico Robles was the living image of Gervasio Pola, in Rodrigo's eyes.

"That's very easy," Cienfuegos said. "Haven't you noticed the sort of society in which we live? Opportunities are plenty."

"To belong," Rodrigo said, still suspended in the moment before. "Yes. That's what she told me. I ought to have done what they could not do: belong. 'Your father should have looked out for himself, like all the rest who today are rich . . .' that is what she told me."

"As Federico Robles did."

"Yes, like Federico Robles, who also came out of the Revolution, but who knew how to survive it, to serve Mexico, to create . . ."

"Wealth and prosperity. That's what you want?"

"I don't know how to explain it, Ixca, but . . . I see no other way in Mexico today. My father did what he had to do then. Now . . ."

"I'm always late to my weddings, eh," Ixca whistled between puffs of smoke.

"What?"

"Nothing. Sure, I'll help you, old man . . . why not? I was talking with some movie producers. They need script writers. Interested in meeting them?"

Rodrigo nodded *yes*. The rain had stopped and a cutting dampness steamed up from the patio. Ixca stretched his legs in front of him, whistled, and smoked.

From Federico Robles's blue office windows Ixca Cienfuegos stares over the length of Avenida Juárez. He stares at everyday men and women . . . office girls, law clerks, salesmen, salesclerks,

209

chauffeurs, doormen, typists, samples-distributors; white and mixed and copper, some wearing coats, other shirts and home-spun jackets; girls in their approximations to high style, inspired by the movies, underlined according to the local taste for breasts and buttocks; and he would like to strip them all away. History, alias memory, calls up of this same Avenida an August day when an old man, weighted like an old oak, hidden behind smoked glasses and a huge curly beard, marched into the city at the head of the Constitutionalist Army, touching the campaign hat which had replaced the senator's old derby; and the incredible days and the burned-star eyes shining with all the passion of Ayala and divining the passion of Chinameca: the sadder, clearer eyes looking down the Avenida from beneath a sun-faded sombrero, and the same day, Doroteo Arango's great corn smile and riding pants and leggings and gray sweater and Stetson; the July day when the Caballito flowered with huzzahs! for the small sweet man, too small on horseback, incongruous in his dark Prince Albert, flattered by a surge of voices which wounded a little saint's continence, a little man with neither feet nor hands to strike with, seize with, or ward off; and another July day when an old black coach of state, dusty with all the dark dusts of Mexico, rolled past like an insomniac image caught in the mask of an inviolable wakefulness; the June day when the splendid deluded royal couple passed beneath arches of flowers conveyed by a Napoleonic marshal and a Pueblan archbishop; the September day when the old man with the face of a caged lion stormed down the Avenida, waving the flag of stained stripes and stars to the San Cosme sentry line, on Chapultepec and Churubusco, while his regiment of Carolinians and his battalion of marines marched, squeezed together by night and grasping beggars; the May night when Independence donned Mardi Gras costume so that an imperial sergeant and his dark rabble and his aristocrats could pass past palaces illuminated to light the way for a Momus who had trafficked in all seeds, all hungers and all flags; and farther, the last, the long ago August day when the waters divided and all was confusion and shields and cries and plumes and the crash of arquebuses and brigantines and Señor Malinche

210

climbed to the roof of a house on Amaxac and watched the conquered canoe approach. And ever since then, Ixca Cienfuegos thinks, there have been two symbols, that of the beginning and that of destiny, both planted on the same Avenida, whether it is water street or pavement; from Yei Calli to 1951. Always two, the impeached eagle, the nocturnal sun.

He took the newspaper and left the window, for Robles's voice was raised with urgency:

THE EAGLE BEING ANIMATE

"Just read the newspaper aloud to me, friend Cienfuegos, and don't worry about a thing."

Three stenographers formed a chorus around Robles's steel desk. Hunched and tense, he paced from one end of the office to the other while Ixca read aloud and the steady light of midday filtered through Venetian blinds, drawing stripes on the banker's gray flannel. Unexpectedly, Robles stopped and jabbed his forefinger at Cienfuegos: "Your idea was a good one, friend Cienfuegos. The Monterrey group seems to have blown up, their statements hint that they have removed their leader. But where the captain sinks . . ."

Robles chewed his cigar with satisfaction and burnished his nails on his lapels.

"They'll eat the bread they have baked. If I don't sell, they will. We'll see who sits on whom. A good idea you had, Cienfuegos. That's called the nose. They must have felt rather strange, finding themselves partners in Couto's group so quickly. Now, no matter how they smile at each other, they know that either they eat Couto or Couto lunches on them. And we are out of it, with the best price."

Robles pounded a fist on his hip and grinned. Cienfuegos read on: with an ironical smile, he reported the statements of the Monterrey financiers. Robles narrowed his eyes. Until now he had been too attentive to the words to notice the voice.

"Come home and eat with me as soon as I finish giving them

their instructions. We have to celebrate. Norma is going to bring one of her cocktail-party intellectuals and I'll be left out."

Folding the newspaper, Ixca stopped reading. "Who, *Licenciado?*"

"His name is Zamacona."

"From Michoacán?" Cienfuegos asked quietly. Robles looked at the floor. "Eh?" he said, pursing his lips. "Perhaps. No, I haven't met him, he's a friend of Norma's." He turned his back on Cienfuegos and stood before the large window. He was afraid that Ixca would go on with questions, as the other day, and he did not want to fall again into that trap. He believed himself very sure of his purposes and he had consented to tell his past only to convince himself that he could face the facts of his early life, his father's name, Froilán Reyero's, the curate, the young woman at the hacienda, with no more feeling than if he were looking up names in a telephone book. That was enough now. There was no reason to repeat.

"All right, *Señorita.*" He turned to the nervous girl whose sweating hands had not left her dictation pad. "The bank is authorized to make the loan to the development company, and the lots will be insured by the insurance company. Memo for the Board, in reference to the Prado Alto deal, the same procedure." His fingernails vibrated on his lapels again. He observed Cienfuegos and directed his words to him. "*Señorita*, remind Juanito about the box of cigars for the Minister. He'll understand." He began to pace the thick rug like a cat. "All out," he ordered. The three girls soundlessly departed while Robles dropped with spread legs on the leather sofa. He let a heavy hand fall on Ixca's knee. "You begin to understand. The bank, which is mine, lends to the development, which is mine, and the land is bought with spit alone. Ten pesos a meter to that blockhead who thinks he is taking us. I can sell this minute at thirty, or wait a year and sell at seventy. In any event, we are insured, by a company which is also mine. A profit of three hundred thousand pesos now, or more than half a million if we wait." Robles sighed and dropped ashes into the floor-tray. "These days you can shuffle the cards yourself. I still remember the time of the General—to make a little you had to meddle in every possible split with go-betweens. There were some men who made five or six thousand a month— and those pesos!—from the governors of states just to look after their interests with the President. Now, as always, you need their moral backing, because that is how life is in Mexico, but you gain it with friendship and trust, Cienfuegos, because they know that you are working for the good of the country and in accord with the national policy of progress."

He stood and began to pace the rug again, tense as a puma. "No, if there is anything that makes me laugh, it's to have sold my part of the damn chain without saying even 'excuse me' to the rest of them. The fits they are going to throw! Come on, let's go home and have a drink to celebrate. Part of this victory is yours."

Cienfuegos did not lose his grin, and Robles could not take it away. "I'm sorry, *Licenciado*, but today I can't. Anyhow, you'll enjoy talking with Manuel. He's an intelligent boy and will show you the thinking of the younger generation."

"What does he do with himself?"

"Poetry."

"Ouch!"

"But he makes his living writing editorials and articles for a newspaper. He's worth your while, *Licenciado*. You haven't concerned yourself much about these new men who also have prestige now."

Robles grunted and chewed his cigar. "Every monkey to his own tree, Cienfuegos."

"Well, at any rate," said Ixca, spreading his grin, halfway between a smile and a yawn, "they say that to talk with youth is rejuvenating. And you have no children."

Robles blew smoke and grunted again. "Ah, friend Cienfuegos. We're too old for dances. In ten or fifteen years I'll be tired of working and there will be no pleasure left for me except to see the results of my efforts measured in the progress of the country. That will be my son. Don't believe it . . . there is still plenty to do, and this is a country of loafers. Here a handful of men have to do the work of thirty million drones."

"Good. That is almost to feel yourself a savior."

"No, no salvation . . . just duty. . . ."

"But Mexico always looks for a savior." Ixca's smile sharpened. "Now you and your group have had to shepherd all the sins of the whole country. To you, in particular, it has fallen to be part of all the important events of half a century. From the strike at Río Blanco to the sale of your shares in the great consortium. From Zapato's straw sombrero to the flat-top Panamas which J. P. Morgan bequeathed his universal admirers. From *A* to *Z*. Tell me: how do you feel about it? I have always been curious about these radical transformations. Do you feel yourself still, in spite of everything, the same person you were in the beginning? Or what has changed? All these scrambled pieces, your beginning in a cornpatch, the battle of Celaya, your ambition and steadfastness, the talent for business; how do you put them together? Where do they meet, how do they fit? Does one feel as at first, or does one even remember how one felt then? Does one become better, or merely go on as before? Are we from the start what we are at the finish? Is our first decision, in reality, our last one?"

Robles was not listening to Ixca's words. He went to a file case and got his summer hat off it, and with a calm face jammed it on his square head and said, "I'll be late. I must go, friend Cienfuegos."

As they rose from the table, a servant wearing a white jacket and black trousers came up to Norma. "Today is Friday, *Señora*. The poor people are at the gate."

"I'm coming," said Norma, forcing an enchanting smile. "Poor people come Fridays," she explained to Manuel. "Don't think it's pure philanthropy. I get rid of old clothes, even old newspapers. Excuse me. I won't be long."

Norma's exits were like lightly hiding a perfume. Zamacona and Robles prepared for conversation. Robles opened glass doors onto the garden and invited Manuel to precede him. At the end of the garden, behind the kitchen gate, a dozen brown faces were squeezed together, some shaded by straw hats, others wrapped to the mouth in *rebozos*, all motionless. Manuel tried to

214

discover some individuality in them, but none revealed more than mute fixed waiting: closed lips, dark eyes wiped empty of glitter, high cheekbones. He thought of them as identical in all epochs, all ages. Like a subterranean river, indifferent and dark, flowing far below idea or change. The servant and Norma reappeared, he carrying paper bags and she with her chin up and the air of a person about to confer great favors on her fellow man. Hands touched *rebozos*, as if to cover up more and become still more anonymous; other hands stretched through the enameled bars, all heads bent. Without opening the gate, the servant distributed the bundles. A child with lips sticky with mucous began to cry in the arms of a yellow-skinned woman. All said thanks, mumbled or chanted, anonymous also, and they left with their paper bags, some of them whistling. Norma, from the gate, gestured with thumb and forefinger that she would rejoin them soon.

"So you're an intellectual?" Federico Robles said, with no more preamble.

"Yes," smiled Manuel. "I imagine that doesn't especially impress you."

Robles shrugged. "To hell with what impresses me. What matters is doing things."

"There are many ways." Manuel smiled again.

"Correct." Robles found a cigar wrapped in cellophane. "But not here. Here in Mexico we can't give ourselves the luxury of intellectualism. Here we have to look to the future. And poets are of the past."

Manuel lowered his head and put his hands in his pockets. "You have to define what you mean by 'past.' "

"The past is everything that is dead, friend, something that makes you feel in most cases great or pious. That's all."

Manuel raised his head and fixed his eyes on Robles. "And Mexico's past?"

Despite his concentration on unwrapping the cigar, Robles did not hesitate. "It doesn't exist. Mexico is not the same country since the Revolution. The past is done with, forever."

"But in order to look to the future you mention," Manuel insisted softly, gazing into sunlight which fell on Robles's shoulders and head, "at some point you have to recognize that there was a past which at least must be dealt with in merely being forgotten."

"Perhaps."

Sun silhouetted Robles: one solid black figure, opaque, crowned with light.

"And when you observe that past, *Licenciado,* what do you feel before that past? Do you feel made great or made pious?"

At last he got the cellophane off and the first aroma of the fine tobacco rose, fresh and virgin. "For me the past was poverty, friend. My past, I mean to say."

"And Mexico's, *Licenciado?* You have your thoughts . . ."

"All right. For me Mexico is a backward impoverished country which has struggled to become progressive and to join the stream of civilized nations. The past century it was thought that to have laws patterned on those of the United States and England would be enough. But we have discovered that we must create industry, give impetus to the economy, also, create a middle class which is the direct beneficiary of progress. Now tell me your version."

To speak about Mexico. He did not know where to begin. "I envy your clarity. I wish I could explain Mexico's history as neatly as you do. What I feel, precisely, is that I can't find the syllogism. . . ." He bit his lower lip. A word, any word. "The magic word or the single explanation which will clarify a history so stained with pain."

Robles widened his eyes and his match burned out before he raised it to the cigar. "Pain? What pain? Take it easy, friend. Ask a European if this is not paradise. Pain is to have gone through two world wars, bombings, concentration camps."

"No, no, you don't understand me," said Manuel. He sank his shoes into the soft garden turf. "Because those men who suffered bombings or concentration camps could at the end assimilate their experiences and thus wipe them away, give an explanation for their own behavior and for that of their hangmen. . . ." He wanted to summon up the face of a man tortured, marked with the yellow star, but he could recapture only the faces of the moment before, anonymous and beseeching beyond the garden gate. "The most terrible of experiences, Dachau or Buchenwald, was only a development of the ancient formula of attack against freedom, human dignity, as you may care to name it." Like an underground river, he was thinking, dark, indifferent. "But for Mexiso there is no formula. What justifies the destruction of the ancient civilization? Or our humiliation before the United States? Or the deaths of Hidalgo and Madero? What justifies the hunger, the dry fields, the plagues, the assassinations, the rapes? On the altars of what great idea may they become sacred? By reason of what measure are they rational? All our history hangs heavy upon our spirit, in bloody integrity without which none of its facts or its men is ever really past." Without noticing, he had taken Robles's sleeve and tugged it, forcing him to move forward two steps. "Apollo, Diogenes, Faust, *l'homme moyen sensuel,* what devils do they refer to or explain here? None. Everything smashes against an impenetrable wall of heavier blood which has sprinkled our land with injustice. What is our key, and where? Will we live to find it?" He took his hand from Robles's arm. "Something has to be brought back to life and destroyed before we will understand Mexico. And we can't live and die blind, do you understand me, live and die trying to forget everything, to be reborn with each new day, knowing that no matter how we try to forget, everything is still present and living and presses against our diaphragms. Quetzalcoátls and Corteses and Iturbides and Juárezes and Porfirios and Zapatas, all lumps in our throats. What is our true image? Which of the many?"

"You intellectuals like to kick up dust," said Robles, opening his mouth and blowing smoke. "Here there is only one truth: we make the nation prosperous, or we starve. The choice is between wealth and poverty. And to attain wealth, we have to push on toward capitalism and subject everything to that effort: politics, ways of life, styles, laws, economics, whatever you care."

With full intensity the sun shone, slanting, on the garden, less rotund than at midday, but more penetrating. Soon it would be gone.

"But surely you know that that is what we have always done,"

217

stammered Zamacona. "We've always tried to imitate models that were foreign to us, to wear clothes that could not fit, to disguise our faces to conceal the fact that we are different, by definition different, with nothing in common with anyone, a country popped up like a mushroom in the middle of a nameless countryside. Don't you see Mexico wounding herself by trying to become Europe and the United States? But you yourself told me that just now, *Licenciado*. Didn't you point out that Porfirianism tried to ape laws, to conceal what we are? Don't you see that everything, monarchy, reform, liberalism, centralism, capitalism, has always been a mummery?"

Robles let a pool of smoke fall on Manuel's lapels. "And what do you want, friend? Shall we wear feathers and eat human flesh again?"

"That's exactly what I *don't* want, *Licenciado*. I want our sleep to lose those shadows. I want to understand what it means to wear feathers in order not to wear them and in order to be myself. I don't want us to take pleasure in mourning our past, but to penetrate the past and understand it, reduce it to reason, cancel what is dead, save what is living, and know at last what Mexico really is and what may be done with her."

Robles moved away from Manuel toward the gate. "Don't be presumptuous. The only thing that may be done with Mexico is what we, we of the Revolution, have done with her. Progress."

"Progress toward what?"

"Toward a higher standard of living. That is: toward the individual happiness of every individual Mexican. You will agree that is what matters."

"But how can you talk about every Mexican's happiness without first understanding every Mexican. How do you know what every Mexican wants, or that he wants what will be prescribed for him?"

The industrialist turned and faced him. "I'm older than you, friend. I know human nature. Men want property. A car. Their children educated. Plumbing. That's all."

"And do you believe that with these things men feel really satisfied? Do you think, for example, that the richest nation in history is precisely happy? On the contrary, isn't it oppressed by a deep spiritual sickness?"

"Possibly. But that is secondary, friend. The important thing is that the majority of gringos live and eat well, have a refrigerator and a television set, go to good schools, and even permit themselves the luxury of providing for Europe's beggars. Your cackling about spiritual sickness, I think, doesn't worry them very much."

"You may be right." Manuel took his hands out of his pockets. His eyes narrowed as he looked at where sun and air joined, and he shaded them. "I don't know. Maybe I stated the problem badly. Our hatred toward the United States may be sickness, too. After all, I'm a Mexican for something."

Robles smiled and placed an obsequious hand on Zamacona's shoulder. "Come on, don't run away from me now. I enjoy an argument with you youngsters. After all, you are sons of the Revolution, too, just as I am."

Trying to return the smile, Manuel realized that he was merely grinning. "The Revolution. Yes, that's the problem. Without the Mexican Revolution, neither you nor I would be here talking as we are; I mean without the Revolution, we would never have faced the problem of Mexico's meaning, its past. All Mexico's history, its great men, seem to reappear, carrying their burdens, in the Revolution. I feel, I sincerely feel, *Licenciado*, that they all come back in the faces of the Revolutionaries, living, with all their grossness and refinement, their pulse and throb, their voices, in their true colors. But if the Revolution discovered all Mexican history for us, it did not insure that we would understand, or that we will move beyond. That's our sad legacy, more than it is yours, who could give yourself up to action and think that just to do was enough."

"Your generation has a duty: to carry forward the work we have begun."

"Not the same for us, *Licenciado*. You had something urgent before you and you rose to it quickly. We find ourselves in a very different land. Stable, rigid, everything is more or less settled and taken care of, where it is very hard to intervene in public

219

affairs. A country jealous of its *status quo*. Sometimes I think that Mexico is living a prolonged *Directory*, a formula for stability which procures a notable internal calm but at the same time impedes the just development of exactly what the Revolution proposed in the beginning."

"I don't agree, friend. The Revolution has lived up to itself in every way. And it has done so most intelligently, by indirect methods sometimes, if you care, but the accomplishment can't be denied. You don't know what Mexico was in nineteen hundred eighteen or nineteen hundred twenty. You have to keep that in mind in evaluating the nation's progress."

Garden eucalyptus trees covered the sun; its rays tangled among branches and leaves and were lost, but still tinted the trunks.

"And where do those indirect methods lead us?" Manuel Zamacona said. "Isn't it rather a contradiction that we should be striving toward capitalism just when we observe that capitalism has lost all vitality and hangs on only as a kind of fictitious vanity? Isn't it clear that all the world is searching for new moral and economic formulas? Isn't it just as clear that we could be taking part in the search?"

"What are you asking for? Creole communism?"

"Give it any tag you want to, *Licenciado*. What interests me is to find solutions which are suited to Mexico and will permit us for the first time to reconcile human and cultural being with lawful forms. A true integration of the scattered members of what this country is."

"Well, well." A great rose wound lay over all the tree tops. "You were discussing what the Revolution proposed in the beginning? What did you have in mind?"

Zamacona did not want to argue more. He thought, uneasy on the dampening grass, that there is never one but two of everything, two, three, an infinity of truths which explain, and to hold to any single one is dishonesty. Perhaps honesty itself was merely one variety of conviction. "What I just said: to reveal Mexico to all Mexicans. Rescue the past from lies and forgetfulness. Porfirianism, also implicitly, believed that the people are happy only

220

when they can forget. That was its lie, the reason for its mummery. Díaz and his collaborators thought that for us to become European, all we had to do was wear clothing cut by Auguste Comte, live in a mansion designed by Hausman. The Revolution made us aware that the whole past was present, and that if remembering it was painful, trying to forget it did not destroy its power." What did all these words mean, he thought. How did they help, really, concretely? Or did they, merely by being thought and said, carried into the air, enter men's hearts? Yes, that was it, that was what was behind his words. "Specifically and expressly, on recovering the threads of our historic experience, the Revolution gave us very clear objectives: land reform, unionization, public education, and above all, to get rid of the human collapse of economic liberalism, anticipating the collapse of totalitarianism of right or left, the need to reconcile personal freedom with social justice. The Mexican Revolution was the first great popular movement of this century to face the basic problem: how to insure the community protection and growth without sacrificing personal dignity. Economic liberalism sacrificed society and the state on altars of individualism. Totalitarianism sacrifices society and the individual on the altar of the state. Faced with this problem, you'll agree, the Mexico Revolution found the way to go about solving it. But why didn't we develop it? Why were we satisfied with half solutions? I can't believe that the only concrete result of the Revolution had to be the rise of a new privileged class, economic domination by the United States, and the paralyzing of all internal political life."

Robles snorted three chuckles, separated by puffs of smoke. "Take it easy, friend. In the first place, the class you call privileged is so only by reason of its labor and contribution to the country. We're not talking about absentee landlords with great estates any more. Second: Mexico is developing industrially, but lacks capital. We have to let North American investments in for the good of the country, and when all is said and done, they are well controlled by our laws. Finally, the paralysis of internal political life is not the result of the Revolution, but of the notorious incompetence and lack of popular support of the opposition parties."

"No, *Licenciado*, I don't accept your explanations." Manuel felt his nostrils quiver before the showdown with Robles and, above all, with Robles's world. "The new plutocracy has not risen by hard work, but by taking advantage of their political situation to organize prosperous businesses, and its quick rise frustrated the very heart of the Revolution. This class has not only grabbed economic, but political power, too, and this power is reactionary. You know that the principle of 'limited' foreign investment is violated over and over and that there are many firms which are Mexican only in letterhead. You know, too, that foreign investments are good for the country only if they help to build an internal Mexican market. Above all, you know that the market for our farm and mining industries, with the possibility of developing our own industry and indeed the whole balance of our economy, do not depend upon us. I agree that our 'one party' is better than the so-called opposition parties. But what I reject is the sleep our one party has imposed on Mexican politics, preventing the birth of political movements which could solve our problems and make good use of elements which have lapsed into somnolence and indifference; good elements that have never associated with either the clerical reaction or the Soviet reaction. Must the party go on accepting a *status quo* that gives no solution at all? Which is the same as saying to the Mexican masses, You're quite well off as you are. Don't think, don't speak. We know what's best for you. Just lie quiet. Isn't that precisely what Porfirio Díaz said?"

"You speak like an irresponsible. I see that we do not understand each other, friend Zamacona."

"Nevertheless, it is important that we should understand each other, Licenciado Robles." Manuel folded his hands and walked toward the gate, through a garden vague and pale in autumn twilight. One of the last showers of the rainy season had washed it a few hours earlier. At every step he could smell the scents of eucalyptus and laurel.

In darkness the swollen electric pads of Hortensia Chacón's

fingers caressed Federico's arms. Her soft hair crackled lightly as oppressive air came into the room through curtain cracks. A storm was approaching. Federico's eyes opened from sleep heavy and sweet as the body lying beside him. Today, after so many times in this room on Tonalá, he found her body new, he felt something about the woman who had offered him her body, something he had not understood before. He looked at her and thought of his conversation with Cienfuegos, digging up the past, and of the subtle rejection in the conversation with Norma the day she had been getting ready to go to a wedding. He had wanted then to understand what Hortensia really meant to him, but he had had to be with her again and to sleep beside her in stonelike depthless slumber before he could give the truth words. He thought now of the moment before his sleep had begun. Her silence, her darkness, her lack of words and groans, his entering her without her making any sound, yet a furious and concentrated entrance, and at the moment of culmination he had taken her hair in his teeth and bitten and his teeth had summoned up the memory of the battle of Celaya, the day when he had bitten the reins of his horse and felt all his body erect to fight, men in battle around him, the crashing around him which from his saddle and with the reins between his teeth he could dominate. Robles closed his eyes. Cienfuegos's questions returned, asked by the voice of the young man who had dined with him in the afternoon and had dared to say what he thought and to address him as a living man and not as the figurehead of the success of the Revolution. He stared at Hortensia, trying to discover some link between her body and his memories. She moved with exaggerated caution and Robles murmured from the pillow, "I'm awake."

"All right."

Soft and submissive, directed to him, her voice; pointed in its desire to be directed only to him from darkness, from silence. She was all this: silence and power, the direct quiet power which is the consummation of individual actions that lie below the exterior and daily pomp forms of power. Earth, sap, air. The bloody battlefield of Celaya. Her damp open flesh. His chest filled with air. His pulse ran fast, swollen with blood. He lifted his hairless thin legs and sat on the edge of the walnut bed and Hortensia's fingers caressed his back.

"Do you feel good?" she said.

He tried to tense all the muscles of his body at the same time, to make physical the strength which he felt. Good? Strong, clean, renewed . . . but tomorrow, he reflected, all he had gained here would be used up again. He looked at her brown body, at the darkness of her sex triangle.

"Hortensia . . ."

Her hand lay on his shoulder.

"Do you remember sometimes . . ."

Her fingers touched his neck. "A little . . ."

He scrubbed his face with his knuckles. A world trimmed in chrome and neon crossed behind his eyes; behind him lay another world, flat and rosy, full of songs and names and tree colors and furious horses; and he stood planted in the center of each of these worlds, in one his figure was transparent and pale, in one it was dark and burning, representing a life without breaks in its line from birth to death, heavy, unified, and weighted, beyond any possibility of fracture. But now he did not want to think any more. All he wanted was to get up and leave her, with his richness of strength gained from her ready to be thrown at a world which demanded candies from the man of strength. He got up. He stopped thinking.

Hortensia's blind eyes tried to see his shadow. She smiled at the sound of his garments being picked up and put on, at his breathing, at the scrape of his shoes on the floor.

A man in a northern hat and a woman wearing cotton got down from a mud-splattered bus at the Ramón Guzmán terminal with their ten-year-old son, a skinny boy with a dirty face. The man wrapped his thick lips around a black cigar and observed the setting down of their baggage from the tarp-covered rack on the roof of the bus. The woman, who, without being fat, was shapeless, let her shoulders slump even more and held the child's tugging hand as he shouted and pointed to the street.

224

"All right," said the man. "Here's our bags, so let's go, I'll show you our capital!"

"Yes, as if you had been here before!"

"It is true that I have never been here, but a man knows more about such things than a woman knows."

"Look!" cried the child, who wore short blue pants and an open shirt. "Look, ice cream! I want some ice cream, I want my ice cream!"

"Silence, you noisy half of nothing," said the woman. "My God, how I wish he would begin to get his growth."

"Yes," said the man. "Then you'll be complaining that he has abandoned you to run after whores."

"Be quiet, Enrique. Someday you'll be asking who taught him such words."

"Well, let's move along," the man with slant eyes and lopsided mustaches said. "Just look around! Tere, look what a city! That's why they call it the capital, eh! The City of Palaces! Just look what an avenue! Look across the circle there, that's old Cuauhtémoc! Felipito! Who was Cuauhtémoc?"

"The fellow who made Isabella pawn her jewels. I want my ice cream!"

"So, Tere, that's why we're sending him to that so-called school. Felipito! Tell me who Cuauhtémoc was!

"Ah, piss on Cuauhtémoc. I want my ice cream!"

The man threatened the boy with his hand, while the mother looked on accusingly.

"Well, well, here we are," said the man placidly. "Beautiful Mexico City! You'll just see how I get on my feet here in the capital, Tere. In no time at all I'll be making money right and left, you'll see. The way I make a belt, and with the flock of gringos here to buy them, in a year, we'll be rich!"

"You said the same thing when we left Culiacán and went to Piedras Negras, and now look at us, not even enough for busfare."

"Woman, don't talk to me about those hick towns. Here we are now, in the capital! I'll set up with our little savings, I'll even have me an apprentice, and in a year I'll be clearing three thousand pesos a month. You'll see."

The shapeless woman made a mouth. The child kept pointing at things, and the man in the northern hat, standing at the intersection of Reforma and Insurgentes, breathed deep. "This is my capital! Yes, *Señor!*"

PIMPINELA DE OVANDO

"Yes, you're quite a practical joker, Cienfuegos. You ask me to meet you in a bar and now you want the story of my life."

"And what were you expecting of me?"

"At least you're frank. Shall I tell you my list of possibilities?"

"Why not?"

"First, Cienfuegos is a friend of Robles's and that might be useful to me. Agreed?"

"Agreed. But may I tell you something? The powerful banker is on his way to the old folks' home. If just one depositor should demand his money, the House of Usher would shake."

"So? It doesn't seem quite so."

"It doesn't seem so because it hasn't occurred to anyone that Robles might have all the deposits tied up in fantastic land schemes. But just the same."

Pimpinela pressed her lips and affected complete unconcern.

"Second, Cienfuegos believes *qu'il peut coucher avec moi* and I'm never far from the temptation to give people lessons. I was reared to give lessons. Agreed?"

"All right, but you're wrong again."

"Third, not so likely in your case, but my *métier*, nevertheless, you'd like the luster of an aristocratic name, my friend, so here I am. I think you said it once yourself . . . give me cash and I'll give you class, give me class and I'll give you cash. But as this can't be true in your case, I imagine the situation is that my life is important to you."

"Precisely yours, no. Lives in general, yes."

Pimpinela smiled, uncomfortably, and took off her gloves. She looked around, searching for familiar faces. The little bar was obviously a rendezvous for lovers and mistresses and flirtations and blushing sweethearts. Avidly she sought faces she knew. But

226

a dying bit of candle, shaded in vellum paper, was the only light on each table, and faces could not be distinguished. Booths made secrecy easier, and a tenacious pianist softly drowned the imperceptible voices of men and women scattered around the little room.

"Thirty years ago places of this sort at least offered chaise longues and other conveniences."

"We live in the epoch of the finger-fuck, not the chaise longue, Señorita."

Pimpinela squeezed her glove and let her eyes shine coldly.

"I forbid you . . . there are certain words which immediately reveal the class of the person who speaks them."

"What are you drinking, Pimpinela!"

"Don't you hear me speaking to you? I say not to sit here blinking at me like a beggar!"

"My dear Pimpinela, with this lack of flexibility you won't get anywhere, much less your haciendas back." . . .

"What do you know? It's very easy to judge. What do you know!"

She rose and turned her back as she pulled on her gloves. She forced a smile and left. In her Opel, she drove straight to her apartment on Berlín. She felt that she had to be, just be, inside an adequate setting, a place carefully made to preserve and to display the imponderables of which she felt herself the depository. She opened the door and waited for a moment before turning on the light: she wanted to smell the ridged rugs, the pots of perennials, the light perfume which her own body had left there, suspended in the air, every day of her life. In the darkness she felt over the red velvet chairs, the glass cabinets, the frames of paintings. She turned on the record player and set the needle on the record that was already on the turntable. A river of insistent strings flowed into the room. She lay down on the velvet divan and closed her eyes and allowed Vivaldi to create a world both intangible and deep, made of sea-green glass. Full creation, Pimpinela repeated without speaking aloud, wounded by music, inert, without even one living and taut cell: she felt the music was softening her; she wanted to give herself the pleasure of a world which she could feel destined for herself alone, like a sort of providential prize which falls to those who are well born, to those who have a station in life. She was also telling herself that she had never wanted nor asked for her birth and station. She felt more than recompensated, defined, whole, absolute, and at the same time that she lived broken and fragmented, that she herself was only the fragment which had labored and worn herself out trying to restore other fragments which could not be brought back to life. For a magic second Pimpinela touched and smelled and remembered, her memory flew back and at the same time forward in a double movement, sprung from her desire to recover and preserve, while her eyes filled with opaque and volatile smoke.

" Little Pimpinela doesn't want to eat, *Señora*."

Señora Ovando floated her mass of noisy silk toward the tiny girl with red curls seated on a walnut high chair and sniveling over a bowl of oatmeal. The child was like a golden brooch lost in the vastness of the dining room, on the expanse of the Persian rug, under the two great chandeliers which never ceased their crystal tinkle, before the great copper-inlaid table where twenty-four places could be set. Mirrors at each end of the room reproduced the world between in accordion-pleated reflections. Walls hung in green damask, a sideboard of mother-of-pearl marquetry, white marble vases on stands carved into garlands with cold white pears, flowers, peaches, nuts. Pimpinela opened her eyes for an instant on everything inside the huge home surrounded by formal gardens. Tapestried chairs, a cabinet of blue Sèvres porcelain, a *rocaille* clock crowned by a plump cupid whose bow and arrow rose higher as the hour mounted; table legs carved and capering over four lion's heads. Cabinets full of big picture plates, reproductions of Watteau scenes; arabesque chair backs, flutes over doors, candelabra of silver with cold cups. The entrance hall with its enormous double stairway. Identical busts of Marcus Aurelius on either side in niches. And the infinite reflections of the gold-framed mirrors.

"One for Papá, the other for Mamá."

She held to her mother's neck.

228

"And what does my little precious want? Doesn't she care for her ugly oatmeal? Come with Mamá, precious."

A quilted landau waited at the door. Her blue eyes stared at the sky and watched it pass between two green shores of tree branches. She waved her feet in the air and pressed against her mother's soft, almost electric silks. Homes of two and three storeys, rose, pale-green, with balconies of wrought-iron trellises and high roofs. Men with enormous painted sombreros passed, carrying water buckets. Candy stands, cobblestone streets, stiff gaslamp posts. And again the sky through the foliage. The landau was trimmed in yellow inlay and its smell was dusty and penetrating. The measured *click-clack* of hooves over stones lulled her drowsy. She smelled the yellow trim, her mother's clothing, hid her head on her mother's lap, and slept.

"We shall certainly defend what is ours, Angélica."

"The child is growing up. She deserves other things. The atmosphere for which we have reared her. You can't deprive your daughter of that. You can't condemn her to live in hiding in a land destroyed by revolution."

"We shall defend what is ours, Angélica. Observe your cousin Lorenza. She and her son live in hiding from, not in, their native land, and from their duties also. We shall save what we can from this orgy of barbarism . . ."

With a finger hooked behind the red chain which hung across his vest, Don Lucas de Ovando paced the dressing room. With his other hand he stroked his full iron-gray beard. His chin was heavy and strong, like his metallic eyes, like the two ridges of his cheekbones, like the compact rigidity of his short body. Tall, pale, and languid, Angélica sat before her mirror, combing out her long copper hair.

"I do not understand how, Lucas."

"Do you think that this latest revolution is different from all the others? No. We have known too many revolutions in Mexico. Our families suffered the Acordada and the Proclamation of Pío Marcha, the Plan of Casata and the Plan of Ayutla, and then the Noria and now the Guadalupe. All the same. To survive, one must deduce from which direction each of these economic rebellions issues, and then step aside. Now the danger is from the Zapatistas and their kindred agrarian reform ruffians. It is from that side that the blow will fall."

"But that's our income, Lucas . . . our haciendas. What can we do?"

"We shall get rid of the haciendas. Sell them quickly to Americans. Exchange them for properties in Mexico City. There will be no agrarian reform in Mexico City, my dear."

"But that's not what worries me. It's the lack of the right atmosphere. . . . Poor Pimpinela . . . when I think of my life as a young woman! . . ."

"I prefer my daughter to have an empty scrapbook rather than that she die of hunger. It is settled. I have looked over some lots at the end of Reforma. There is more than one nitwit who is disposed to offer his downtown corners for a hacienda. You will see that I am right, Angélica."

"And did you go to lots of balls, Mamá?"

Angélica caressed Pimpinela's head. The girl's throat, arms, and face almost shone in contrast to her loose dark gown. That nose, so like Lucas's, the mark of her birth. Nevertheless, as a child she had been snub-nosed: "Yes," said Angélica. "Life was different then." She tried to laugh. "Now, you have to be from Sinaloa or Sonora."

"Wouldn't it be wonderful to give a ball for my nineteenth birthday?" On her knees, Pimpinela leaned toward her mother's legs. The dressing room was the one of before, a little decayed now. There were no maids to speck-clean sleeping dust from marble vases and plaster stands. "Wouldn't it be beautiful? Now that we are almost out of mourning for Papá . . ."

"But almost no one is here any more, precious. Whom would we invite?"

"Why did our cousins and so many of our friends go away?"

"Well, our situation is the fault of your father's very clear purpose. Yes, he rescued something, just as he said he would. But life isn't just real estate. It is also atmosphere, it's being with your own sort, it's . . ."

Pimpinela thought of all the balls to which she was forbidden to go. But why mention them; she knew what her mother's answer would be: "And as there are no balls given by people we know, none to which your mother would be invited too, and no well-bred young men to escort you, you must just stay at home."

"There is a boy, Mamá. I met him with Margarita, at a tea. He's a lawyer." . . .

"And what is his name?"

"Roberto Régules."

"Régules? Régules? This is the first time in my life that I have heard that name." Angélica sat on an uncomfortable brocaded armchair and slowly munched *marrons glacés*. Pimpinela frowned.

"But Mamá, he seems a most acceptable sort of boy. He dresses well, and he is very polite."

"Cowls don't make monks, my dear! You know that what I do is for your own good. Your father was one of the most intelligent of men, and has left us comfortable, while others have lost everything. We can live quite satisfactorily on our income. There is no need for us to have to mix with this new set. We have saved, through your father, some of our wealth. We must also know how to preserve our breeding. It is our duty, in honor, to the memory of your father, to be loyal to that also."

"Yes, Mamá . . ."

"We cannot sacrifice loyalty for a ball! Still, I understand . . . I understand." She lowered her head near the girl's. "How can I help understanding? When I think of my own youth, so different. . . . Oh, you should have seen the uniforms they wore in those days, my dearest! Such plumes, such hats! The quadrilles . . . and then, then the waltz! With skirts swirling, in the arms of young men who . . . It was quite like a ritual, you know, one certain day every year, this family gave a ball, and another certain day, that family, and so on . . ." Angélica touched Pimpinela's shoulder. "And suppose we go to Europe?"

231

Pimpinela leaped up with waving hands. "Mamá! Mamá! Europe!"

The mother gathered her black skirts and ran to the little wardrobe. Excitedly she fingered through yellowing papers, titles, contracts, until she came upon the one she wanted, a lot: "Cinco de Febrero and Bolívar . . . fifty pesos a square meter, and today we can get a hundred! This is it, child, this is it!"

"Do you recall the Régules boy, Mamá?"

"Régules? This is the first time in my life that I have . . ."

"The first time! Yes."

"Well, and what has happened to your Señor Régules?" Angélica coughed from her frothy bed, drowned in embroidered cushions and pillows.

"He's married now." Pimpinela's fingers slowly passed over the gilded board of the bed. She could feel in the older woman's manner, even now, in the debilitation of sickness, a certain glow which she herself, lowering her eyes, opaquely reflected in her own body. "He married his secretary. They're going to New York for their honeymoon. Remember that I met him . . . six years ago, when he was a young lawyer. And now he's . . ."

"Yes, I can imagine." Angélica cautiously smoothed her hair under its white nightcap. "Careers are made overnight nowadays. That's something else changed between nineteen hundred ten and nineteen hundred thirty-five. Speed, modernity, yes, that's it, all that. . . ." She coughed again, arching her eyebrows.

"They have a home in the Lomas, a big garden, a car. Roberto's the lawyer for a lot of new companies."

"Yes, yes . . . modernity . . . in my time only men of maturity were vested with great responsibility." . . .

"I could have married him."

Angélica's head jerked impatiently. "We are all right as we are, child. We don't need anything."

Pimpinela gripped the side of the bed with both hands.

"Am I pretty?"

"You are more than merely pretty. I should say that you are also distinguished. That you appear to have inherited——"

"What good is it to me? Mamá, I don't want to make you suffer, you know that. But tell me what good it is to me to be a lady and respected, with an old name. Tell me, please . . ."

"Child, compose yourself. You are still quite young enough . . ."

"That's what you said when we went to Europe. But did anyone come close to the poor little Mexican girl? Does anyone come near her in Mexico?"

"If you could have had my youth . . . the balls and promenades . . . the life of the past century . . ."

"But I couldn't have it. And it isn't just that. It's belonging, knowing that you are accepted. . . . I don't know, Mamá. I swear I don't want to make you suffer. But I want to know, what good——"

"It wasn't our fault." Angélica stretched her hand out and caressed Pimpinela's hand. "Our world just went under. You can't blame us. . . . They closed all our doors. . . ."

"Roberto has married his secretary."

"Let him go. It's better so, that's his world, not yours. Content yourself. We're all right, we don't need anything. And if we do need anything, you know that we can sell a lot or two, for traveling again."

"Pimpinela de Ovando."

"No, man! The real Ovandos?"

Pimpinela spread a shining smile. Her eyes traveled around the drawing room with a delight that her hosts could not mistake. A California-style home—colored windows with wide frames, an abundance of wide doors, floors of blue tile; modern furniture, nickeled table and chairs, foam-rubber cushions, red-lacquered tables, a dozen mirrors of all shapes, stars, a half-moon, wings, stairs. With obvious enthusiasm the hostess worked the venetian blinds.

"But Mexican decoration has become adorable," breathed Pimpinela.

"Your home, my dear."

"What a delicious painting."

"Do you think so? It's one of the first things I bought."

"A Tiépolo, I should think. Some of that thick twilight, Venetian grace . . ."

"That's it, that's exactly right: Venice at sunset, the twilight . . ."

"Hmmmm." Pimpinela's smile included everyone. "How pleasant. It's been a long time since I've seen anything so chic."

"That's it, that's exactly it."

"You who are a connoisseur, General, would be interested in some paintings I have. Of course they are seventeenth century and have come down from generation to generation, but if you'll come . . ."

"We can use *tu* can't we?"

"Pimpinela! I've learned to love you so . . ." Silvia Régules served two steaming cups of tea. "Lemon?"

"Thank you."

The afternoon slanted into the Lomas mansion through narrow windows and fell, an intangible coronation, on Pimpinela's head and shoulders.

"Your suggestions for the party the other night were wonderful, just wonderful, Pimpinela. I don't know how I'll ever repay you . . ."

"Forget it," Pimpinela said, playing her small palms over Silvia's hand. "It is so pleasant to know someone like you in Mexico City. Distinction can't be acquired, Silvia, my dear. You know, after losing everything in the Revolution, it's like finding wealth again to meet people like ourselves, with whom one may make believe for a while that nothing has been lost. That the gifts of good taste and elegance . . ."

"Pimpinela, my dear . . ."

"In a word, to meet kindred souls . . ."

"Knowing you means so much to me," said Silvia, raising her nose a little and touching her throat and earrings. "Roberto is always loaded down with work, you know, the poor man. Every little while they call him from the Presidency. And now he is on the boards of who knows how many companies."

"Yes, I know how it is. My father had exactly the same kind

234

of life. But it's all over for us, Silvia. We were somebodies for a while, you know."

"Pimpinela, it was horrible." Silvia raised a hand to her throat and slowly widened her eyes. "All the assassinations, the priests murdered, and the stealing, the stealing, all those lovely haciendas."

"Yes, that's true. But I repeat: what is important is to hold to friendships, not property. Friends, elegance, distinction. Spiritual wealth."

"Yes, yes, Pimpinela, that's what I feel in you. Sometimes I get so hopeless, so lonely here, the children in school and Roberto working until ten at night."

"Count on me. Whenever you care to, we can go out and drive around, or go to a movie or have a drink together . . ."

An insistent horn sounded outside. Pimpinela opened her compact and powdered. "That's Pierrot Caseaux, he's come by for me. We'll see each other tomorrow, eh?"

"Yes." Silvia turned her bracelets and wiped away a make-believe tear. "Pierre Caseaux? The one whose picture is always on the society page? Very good-looking?"

"That's him. He's quite adorable, and all the more because he has nothing to do except to take his friends out. He's lots of fun. Want me to introduce him?"

"Norma, Norma, if it weren't for our friendship . . ."

"Precisely because of our friendship, Pimpinela. That's all that's needed. Why shouldn't I help you with your problem, it's mine, too, I've gone through the same thing. I had the luck to marry Federico and that solved everything. How can you think I would hesitate to help a friend of my own class . . ."

"Yes, Norma, that will always save us, that loyalty to what we are. There are some who don't understand it."

"You may count on me. This very day I'll talk with Federico. He doesn't like me to meddle in his affairs, but for you I'll do anything."

"You enchanted Aunt Lorenza, you know."

"She is so sweet. She reminds me of my mother, may she rest in peace."

"She keeps saying she wants you to come see her as often as you can. You seem to remind her of her youth."

"So sweet! There's no doubt at all that people bred alike must stick together, especially in this immoral city. By the way, what do you think about Silvia and Caseaux?"

"I don't blame her. She lived alone without the least attention from her husband, above all in the little ways that mean so much . . ."

"I live just as alone, *tu*, but you don't see me looking around for a lover."

"That's exactly the difference, of course. You're not an ex-shopgirl."

"It's certain that he has taken her to that hacienda, isn't it?"

"Of course. They go every weekend."

"Live and learn. How pleasant to have you as a friend, Pimpinela. You're so above all this bawdiness."

"There are some things that can't be acquired, Norma . . . they are just the way we were reared."

"Don't worry about anything. Your little affair will turn out all right. Jot down exactly what you want me to do, won't you?"

Pimpinela got up from the divan and turned on the lights. The needle was stuck on the record at the sharp whine of a violin, and yet that also was Vivaldi, she reflected, and let the noise go on repeating to infinity while she stood before a mirror and observed her blonde elegance, her thin body, her severe black suit, her hands tense on her hips, her aquiline nose, the two metallic eyes staring at the reflection, the small wrinkles that had begun to harden around her proud chin. She wanted to recover, looking through, into the glass, her childhood home again, to begin the memory: "Little Pimpinela doesn't want to eat, *Señora*." They have no right to judge me, she said, and put off the lights and let the phonograph needle go on squealing over the scratched record.

236

The hatchet-faced Catalan woman stared at the man with a florid worn face. She was seated on a chair as stiff as her shoulders. On the little bookcase, photographs, a single row of faded volumes: Prados, Hernández, García Lorca, León Felipe, Altolaguirre. "So you saw him?"

"In a manner of speaking only, I saw him. You wouldn't have known him yourself, he was so changed."

"Where?"

"The outskirts of Tarragona, *Señora*. But a different man. Nobody would have known him."

"You forget that I will soon have been thirteen years in Mexico."

"Not just the years. A different man. Not the man he was. Someone else."

The rigid tall woman knew that the ruddy-faced man did not understand. She meant: his face can never change, face of a militiaman, sun-darkened, rusty Mauser on his shoulder, lost face coming back to say a last good-bye, snapping off its military cap while Mediterranean and Pyrenees mixed in the air of San Feliu and in their joined voices, militiamen and people, singing . . . *to the front at Teruel, to the firing line* . . . and Pablo's ashy eyes raised above the stomp of march and song and the swirl of mountains and sea, and they marched below where she waited on the balcony with her finest smile and sang their rasping trench song to her . . . *if you love me, write, you know where I'll be, the front at Teruel.* . . . No: nothing could change that face. "I spoke of time only," said the Catalan woman with the blade profile.

"Thirteen years, *Señora*?"

"Soon, yes. At first a candy store. We got along. No one denied us anything. Now we are both here and there. Two homelands are always better than one. And you? You escaped? How?"

"By walking like a camel. By walking by night to the Pena Sierra and then to Jaca, and then higher, to come down in France, at Laruns. That's all. How the potbellied Moor would blow if his legs had walked as these have!"

"The brave men, as always."

"You would behave too, *Señora*, if . . . And Pablo . . ."

"He will take care of himself. He survived the Stukas. Why shouldn't he survive Franco? He survived Teruel and Guadalajara and the siege of Madrid. That's my Pablo, you can be sure of him. If he knew that I am here waiting, that for me thirteen years are . . . pah! That's what he told me when he marched out of San Feliu with the militia. You know where I'll be. I here, he there, it's all the same. Distance is not measured by seas."

"Pablo is dead, *Señora*. He wanted to protect us. The guards killed him. He saved our lives. He was a brave man."

The voice ripped around a stiff tall woman with plums for eyes and great long hands. Memories drummed requiem: good-bye, good-bye, fresh weeping, flight, hidden soldiers, walking and walking across snow, songs, faces of the tableland, faces of the coast, from Navarra and Valencia, from Castilla and Extremedura, boots and hempen sandals, wine and onions, the faces of the only story she knew that was honest and pure to its roots and of the only final test of manhood; her eyes were scraped by something. Her big hands pushed her up from the chair. She said, "I told you distance is not measured so. On your feet, man, on your feet. And sing with me as before. Sing to say farewell to Pablo."

The muted voice of a hatchet-faced Catalan woman, the gruff and broken voice of a florid man, in the small living room of a home on Nazas, singing, *With the fifth, fifth, fifth, with the fifth regiment, mother, I'm off to the front, to the firing line . . .*

THOUGH I MAY PRICK MY FINGER

All through the meal Robles reminisced. His words stopped only when he raised his wine glass. Then Norma would mechanically carry out her assignment and say to Ciefuegos, "And have you read 'Town Tattletale?' The Hindu ballet is coming to Bellas Artes soon . . . last Sunday, at the Jockey . . . in short, dignity and discretion ought to have . . . We ordered that tapestry from . . . and ate with His Highness and the Countess Aspacúccoli . . . I had the luck to find a very strong Orozco . . ." and when her

238

husband's rose-tinted glass touched the white cloth again, her mouth would close.

"I was telling you, Cienfuegos, that this drunken experiment of ours with oil has got to stop soon. We don't have the capacity to carry on permanent and large-scale exploration. Little by little the foreign companies will come back, undercover, but in reality to give us technical know-how and energy. Otherwise, we may industrialize only at a snail's pace, holding ourselves back in our pride to holler that the oil industry is the people's. But the real well-being of the nation, I tell you, has to be raised above such petty patriotism."

Cienfuegos watched the game silently and amused himself counting the number of minutes, always almost the same, that Robles developed his counterpoints. On the one hand, the banker's leaden figure, stiff and slow; on the other, the natural languidness of his wife. Robles abruptly lit a cigar and asked to be excused. "I have an extra-official meeting. But it is still early, Norma, entertain Señor Cienfuegos. Offer him a drink." With a quick nod, he disappeared.

"Cognac, *menthe,* anise?" Norma asked as she rubbed one wrist over the other, unconsciously repeating the gesture she used when perfuming.

"A cognac," said Ixca, watching her.

Silence lengthened. Norma made his drink. For several minutes Ixca simply warmed it.

"Don't feel that you must go," said Norma, although she was smothering a huge yawn. "To be quite frank, these situations are merely the way Federico shows his trust in me. He began them soon after our marriage."

"And have you found it possible to take advantage of them?"

Norma laughed. "Today a husband is betrayed mostly from a sense of duty. But I prefer to do only what is dangerous or pleasurable, *ja!*"

There was something uncomfortable and stiff about the blue-brocaded furniture. It matched neither the colonial architecture of the house nor the stained-glass windows, set with coats of arms, which marched up the stairs. A strange mixture of styles:

walls of imitation stone painted a yellowish-maroon, a second-floor balcony looking down on them, niches for various local virgins—Remedios, Zapopan—side by side with romantic busts and Chinese figures. Paintings by Félix Parra which had belonged to and been sold by Pimpinela. Cabinets of bric-a-brac, huge mirrors framed in gold of an artificial patina. Sofas of carved wood and blue brocade. Marble floor, dining-room chandeliers, the bars on the windows, everything was dissonant against Norma's blonde elegance, her jewels, her dress. Cienfuegos thought about this home born of the meeting between Robles and Norma, and named it: mestizo. His stare, fixed and intent, did not change, "You have been useful to your husband."

"I just told you that it is nothing I'm proud of. I enjoy doing things for——"

"No, that's not what I mean. I mean that in you, Robles got what he wanted of marriage. But . . . please tell me if I go too far . . . have you known how to make him useful to you?"

"Don't worry about going too far. We're people of the world. I don't lose anything by confessing that I married Federico because I was destitute. My family lost everything in the Revolution . . ."

"I met your brother in the north, Norma. He wasn't doing so well at the mine in those days. Perhaps, wetbacking, he is finding things a little better."

Norma felt that laughing and raising an eyebrow, as she did immediately, did not quite cover her sudden confusion. "Are you a professional joker, Señor Cienfuegos?"

"In a certain sense . . . I mean that you don't have to pretend with me. Accept me, or get rid of me."

"I told you . . . danger or pleasure."

"Then tell me what these names make you feel: Santa María del Oro, Rodrigo Pola, Pedro Caseaux, the hacienda of San Fermín, Natasha, Pimpinela de Ovando. Danger? Or pleasure?"

"If you care to call me new rich, or a social climber, or a prostitute, you make me laugh," said Norma, lighting a Parliament. "If you care to call me snob, you make me sad. But who isn't a snob, one way or another, these days?"

240

"And you, in which way?"

"I . . . Well, about names and money and feeling myself the finest Mexico has to offer. You know what it is to escape from ordinary middle-class life here? Do you know what it is to be chained by God knows what laws to modesty and mediocrity, bad clothes, shame, sadness, to be sad and chaste even when you lose your virginity? That's what I grew up in, and if I hadn't gotten myself out of it, I would be selling lotions in a shop today, and living with the dream of going to the movies Saturday. Call that snobbism if you want to, or call it talent, or will to live. But here I am and there down below are the rest of them."

"And what about *your* people?"

Norma stood. "I forbid you to mention them. I'll say it: my mother, my brother. They couldn't, they didn't have what it takes. And the things I have, *I* got, and they can't share with me. If that's snobbism, I'm proud of it. So, there you are."

"Maybe snobbism is something more serious than you think. Maybe it is even a kind of spiritual blindness: to consider everything in yourself, and nothing as it is in reality. The intelligent snob thinks only of intelligence. The social snob, like you, the snob of ignorance for whom to know nothing at all is the mark of superiority, the physical snob, all of them, what they don't like is evil, and what they prefer is good. Half the world they lose in indifference. But the world isn't by halves. To return to you, I call you Norma Larragoiti, the woman who has allowed Federico Robles to claim her before others and assert himself through her as he could not by himself, using her to overcome his past and his shame about it. His accomplice."

"You're graceful, I admit. Why don't you tell Federico about it? He's a self-made man and I . . . well, I've just followed my own destiny. I serve my husband only as this evening . . . talking about 'Town Tattletale' to people I don't know."

"Do you believe that? Or is it you just aren't aware? Think, Norma, for how could Federico have overcome, without you, your false style of friendship, your make-believe kind of marginal acquaintances, how could he have overcome so completely the obstacle of his birth? And I don't speak of it disparagingly, but

241

I'm talking about the down-drag, the pull toward the lowest level that exists in life in Mexico. Do you think money and success would have been enough to overcome those?"

Norma rubbed her cheek. "You've almost said what I said when I met him." Her eyes and lips caricatured ingenuousness. "Ah, one has to enjoy this wonderful cosmopolitan Mexico City, don't you agree? Enjoy it, yes, Señor Robles, because everyone has a right to pleasure after working hard all one's life, but a girl needs a real man with whom to enjoy it! A girl meets so many stuffed shirts without the least character, and so few real men, men she could help, why, in a thousand little ways, social life, clothes, taste, the true enjoyment of the true riches in life; don't you agree, Señor Robles?"

Norma and Ixca laughed together. With cheerful movements she served drinks. She stumbled against Ixca and both laughed again as they shook hands.

"Don't think you've made me angry, Cienfuegos. I begin to like you."

"Be careful! Remember what a terrible tale I could spread about the wetback!"

"*Touché*. But you knew about him all along. And besides, none of the nitwits around me have been able to find out, and they wouldn't believe you if you were to write it for them. My air, my money, ah! they say much more than words."

"So you see that there is less to separate than to join us."

"If I didn't suspect rather more about you than you suspect about yourself, I would say that you're becoming very close to being ordinary now."

"Straight to the bull's-eye. But let me insist: if a census-taker with imagination had to classify you, he would put you in a little new column under a small headline: Social Go-betweens."

Norma downed her cognac at one gulp. "*La Procuratrice des Hauts Lieux,* dat iz me."

"I imagine that Robles knew instinctively—and in Mexico, instinct corrects every weakness of intelligence—that neither money nor success was enough. On the other side there were those who, having more experience, were aware that nostalgia

for titles and past greatness puts no food on the table. *Ergo*:
Norma Larragoiti."

"*Ergo*: Norma Larragoiti! Social Climber Number One! *A la
bio, a la baa!*"

Ixca's eyes shone as they followed the curves of Norma's thin
body on the sofa. He tensed and relaxed his muscles and felt a
fluid force in every organ; beginning in his legs, it flowed
upward and gathered power in his sexual organs and belly, rose
through his chest and flowed outward through his eyes in a
charged current that moved to Norma and her sexuality, swept
around her legs as she stared at him and let her eyes become
opaque. With a laugh she caressed her wrist and broke the spell.
"You know, when Federico first told me you were coming to
dinner, I thought you were a woman. That name! Where did
you get that face, my handsome? Why don't you wear your hair
crew-cut? Sometimes you look like a gypsy, you need only earrings. And then you change into a savage . . ."

"Norma, listen . . ."

She threw her arms up and her hands came down on her
blonde hair. "Ay, be quiet. 'Instinctively those on the other side
changed themselves into baboons.'" She screwed her face up
and imitated his voice. But she realized that the usual tricks
would hardly be enough this time; Ixca Cienfuegos was not
Rodrigo Pola. She parted her lips and wet them and closed her
eyes. Cienfuegos threw his glass on the floor. The crash did not
change Norma's expression.

Why do I have to let him tell me what I want to say: why he
and not another? My world is finished and done. To get where
I am now wasn't easy, and all I want to do is enjoy it . . . and
this man wants to say words, words that make me want him
more and more until I crack apart, and I can't silence him with
words, but only with my body, and I have never felt my body
so dangerous and threatened with pleasure, never, neither the
one time with Pierre nor the one time also, repeated and monotonous, with Federico, and my body is going to ask without my
wanting it to, without my wanting anything because now I'm on
top where nobody can hurt or even touch me and now, now I

can't go any higher unless I'm destroyed, smashed, yes, smashed, yes, and . . .

Ixca threw Norma's glass down, too. Your love is like death, more than death, like an ocean able to take millions of bodies into the depth of itself and swallow them and never return them . . .

Love like death, but further from us than death is, love squeezed out of living to where we can't stain it, Ixca, carried to its own world, not touched by our dirtying hands . . .

One day it may happen, has this ever occurred to you, Norma, that you won't be here any more and there won't be anyone to tell people that this is Norma Larragoiti, whom you don't remember now, because you never even knew that Norma Larragoiti ever existed and lived among the highest.

Norma opened her eyes and looked at Cienfuegos's standing figure, fists closed, feet apart. She sought humility, gratitude in him, because those who wanted her always offered those.

"Is there a place we can't touch, where we are what we have the right to be?"

"There is a place."

"Why do you think so?"

"I was just there, with you."

She sat, soft, thin, a little abject. She felt loss of domination. Through all her body she was hearing what was not audible to Cienfuegos, a wounded cry, enjoying the wounded animal panting, the separate existence of every pore, every cell palpitating in her body, which never in its life had been truly surrendered and which now wanted to offer itself, a love neither she nor the man could touch, a love removed from those who would practice it.

"Tell me, 'I love you,'" she whispered.

"Why not live at the bottom of the sea . . . there is room enough . . ."

"Tell me 'I love you, I love you, I love you . . .'"

Norma knew she would never hear those words. Not from him. Never from him. She felt only the dark magnetic current which flowed from Cienfuegos to her and, standing, she squeezed

244

her body to his, her lips against his, their tongues met and she felt his back with her fingernails while Ixca's hands touched her breasts, warm beneath the wool dress, and his fingers turned her soft erect nipples.

"This is how I am," murmuring laughter, spoken between their lips, as her fingernails sank into his flesh, the voice in her throat low and soft. "And only you know."

The kiss prolonged like numbers counting. Cienfuegos chewed Norma's tongue and learned all the folds of her mouth. She disengaged herself. With a ferocious face she asked, "What does my husband have that I don't? Tell me."

"Power and the knowledge how to use it," Ixca said, smelling her lipstick.

"Come with me." She let herself lose all sense of motion and bumped against the stair rail and clung to his arm, caressing his skin. They went upstairs. She opened the door of the bedroom.

"Power! Power!" She laughed as she tore off her shoes and her dress. "Look! Nothing! And only you know it."

Her hands moved to her waist and then her arms stretched to Ixca. "I swear that I have slept only with my husband since my marriage."

Tense, fugitive, a flame in darkness, Ixca stood before her, shining because of the darkness he destroyed. "And you slept with him, afraid."

Norma covered her breasts with her hands and faced Ixca. "Yes, afraid. Look at me. My body, touch it, tell me if I wasn't right to be afraid I would carry another body like his inside me." She let herself fall on the bed.

"And do you want one like me inside you?"

"No. Come . . ."

Cienfuegos sat on the bed and put his hand to her throat. "Listen to me, unfortunate girl. Do you want my body or my words? For all I am willing to give you is words."

"You're hurting me."

"I shall hurt you until your tongue is paralyzed like a black avocado. Listen to me! You don't want my body, you want words, words to crush you and words to come back to you. You have no right to be satisfied with yourself, because you don't really want what you told me that you want . . . money, names, to be the best in Mexico . . . not for themselves alone, but only to use them. Now you have to be yourself, with all the consequences of the life you have, do you understand me? And isn't that what you want?"

An inarticulate groan, but her eyes showed, not fear, but an abjectness that was almost avid. Her body, naked, lost all will, seductiveness, lay inert.

"Then take power, for it belongs to you. You don't need anything else. And I shan't let you know my body until you swallow my words and they make you sick and confuse you, and you make my words your own."

He pressed his teeth against her lips until blood came. Norma groaned again, involuntarily, prolonged. With new strength she embraced him. Strength of her first surrender, her surrender without reason, ballasted by the insane and the unexpected, her fingernails in his flesh, her lips groaning, her eyes imploring. Her nails dug in deeper, and she put her lips to Ixca's as he breathed into her ear, "You'll do it, Norma, you'll do it?"

Not her voice, but all the echoes of a new world created in one moment, replied, "I'll do what you want, but you'll make me yours again and again."

Cienfuegos believed that she would: make, destroy herself. With open eyes he searched his tongue for hers, and in the accents of the passion in her armpits, and now he no longer felt her nails as they raked his flesh open. "Tell me 'I love you, I love you, I love you,'" Norma groaned.

Father, mother, grandmother, and five children arrived at the port of Acapulco in a 1940 Chevvy caked with mud and stinking of vomit and banana peels. For the first time they saw, the five children, the expanse of a sea, and they began to howl immediately. "Shut up, you damn brats!"

"Don't get mad at them, Pedro. It's only natural."

"If you had ever once in your life been a little considerate, a

246

little refined . . . Luisa, you remember that very handsome young man you were going with before you met this, this so considerate . . ."

"*Señora,* shut up! I may forget my manners!" the gray-haired man yelled from the steering wheel. "You forget, *Señora,* that I marched with Maytorena. If I could handle a drunken corporal, I can handle a fork-tongued mother-in-law!"

"Ahhhh, the hero! You never fought any more battles than I did, you loafer," cried the mother-in-law from the rear seat, where she was wrestling with the deluge of children.

"*Señora!* Even *my* patience has a limit!"

"Get on with you, lame-brain. When I think that Luisa could have . . ."

"Mother, mother, that's enough. Pedro, what kind of hotel are we going to? I hope it doesn't have a swimming pool; I'm so afraid one of the kids will fall in . . ."

"Sure, why not? That's all we need, after using up every cent of our savings on this crazy trip, to have a kid drown in the hotel swimming pool. Look, Luisa! We're turning around and going home. Now I see what . . ."

"Blockhead!"

". . . this vacation is going to be like, your crazy mother . . ."

"I'm no servant!"

". . . will be running around and you won't have a chance to do anything except watch the children . . ."

"And you, Pedro, won't have a chance to do any running around yourself, you mean."

"It isn't that. Add it up yourself; thirty pesos a day for room and meals, times eight, I'll be ruined, Luisa! And tips, and waiters, and boat rides, and good God there won't be no end to it . . ."

"So why did you promise us?"

"The big man! If Luisa had only married . . ."

The suffocating port was all around the ancient Chevvy, stink of gasoline and rotting fish. Shouting, the kids began to take their clothes off.

"This man wants to destroy me," thought Norma, stretched on the serrated sand of a private beach which lay, in a defile among great boulders, at the foot of a yellow house of blue awnings and flying terraces and bamboo screen-walls and coco trees and piney shade trees, stretched under all the light of the sky with her two golden nipple-points of light shining back. To destroy her, she thought now, as timid waves washed her feet, and she wondered whether she had thought it from the first moment she had known Cienfuegos. The sun was toasting her now, as it had another time of memories. She raised her head and looked at Ixca, far away in the sea, swimming rhythmically toward the beach. Faint sounds . . . distant sibilance from Icacos, the damp cries of swallows, repeating precisely, with a precision like the small prismatic head in the water. Was that what she had really wanted? she asked herself, that he should destroy her? She bit a finger. Why that word precisely, *destroy*? Wasn't she really talking about some other demand? What had she expected of the others? Ixca's body rose, glistening with spume and salt, and fell upon her; Norma could not speak, she looked at his tracks in the sand and loosened the knot of her consciousness and let herself be enclosed by his body, which claimed everything and took all her flesh, to annihilate it and drain it in a spasm like that of death; he wanted to exhaust what she was, to exhaust her completely and without offering words or counsel or the slightest promise of anything except the repetition of her destruction. And wasn't that what she wanted, just what he offered? Their bodies bound together on a wet beach, his spume and salt exciting her dry and sun, stopping time and the future, here, here and now was everything, the sun paralyzed, waves held forever in the instant before their breaking, and she thinking that her surrender was excessive and believing that she could see in the silence and in his complete demand an ironical smile and also pity, although disguised. She pushed his chest away. "Let me go now," she said in a throaty voice, and Ixca rolled across the sand, smiling, without saying a word, his body gleaming, satisfied and exultant, insulting her inanimation.

248

But there was something in his irony and his smile, Norma said to herself as she took her towel and lay it on the sand rumpled by Ixca, which was far from libertine and further from joking: a serious smile, a solemn irony, and that was what disconcerted her and made her move toward him, exhausted, squeezed empty, and fall on his body and feel again that he was demanding a mortal surrender of her only that he might know that she had come to the end of everything. But to know that, she realized as his lips bit hers, not like a gift, but a new demand which took away her defenses and made her the victim of a voluntary suffering, was like knowing that he had torn her open, the door to domination of her. And it was this incapacity to open herself and to make on him an equivalent demand that drained and maddened her; how was it possible—a larger wave finally crashed and sent water rushing swiftly around the two locked bodies—for him to have such force and feeling, when he in reality hung over a great emptiness and received nothing and allowed neither pity nor love nor even others' hatred to touch him? She had surrendered herself to Pierre Caseaux, that was true, but she had also received: he had ignited her womanhood. Rodrigo Pola had wanted only the momentary, the titillation of vice that was not vice. Federico had given a middle ground and made her his instrument, but only in a way that gave her a place in the frame of the world, a visible, external place which could satisfy her most urgent need. Only Cienfuegos demanded everything and offered nothing. She had to have a final explanation, Norma murmured, putting her mouth on his salty shoulder, an immediate, clear explanation . . . and why, it should not be necessary to explain. Cienfuegos smiled and stood and ran into the waves while she remained on the sand, strengthless, thinking that she could put on her bathing suit and make him understand that she was not always at his disposition, naked on a towel, waiting for him to come back, excited from combat with the waves and immersion in the great powerful liquid body, ready to empty his own vagabond body into her; but she could not, and she looked for Ixca's head in the sea and wanted that fatal contact again. For the first time she felt that she, slave to love, height. Little sounds surrounded her, the hissing waves and the sailing winds of swallows, and on the summit of great boulders Federico Robles's house stood out against the sky like an enormous yellow peach made of tinted plaster.

Dragged forward by a Great Dane with hard-boiled eyes, Natasha headed the little procession making its way along Caletilla beach to the Bar Bali. Her face was almost covered by a large coolie hat, a blue silk scarf knotted around her throat, and huge dark glasses; her body, however, had kept its sleekness, and she could show off her black slacks and cambric shirt to advantage. Charlotte, a little behind, waved a chubby arm at all the faces she knew emerging thick with oil and saliva from the sea, at other faces lying on mats the whole length of the little beach, which had once been clean, but was now the established dump for bottles and squashed coconuts and greasy humanity. Bobó and Gus followed; the former had lost his body forever, but still did not know it, and his bikini hung fortuitously like a dried leaf from a mountain of flour. Gus, in a striped beach robe, walked skipping to avoid lighted cigarette butts. On a motorboat offshore, Cuquis and Junior removed their aqualungs and the diving masks which made them look like a pair of sleek intrepid lizards, and waved their arms and shouted to the little caravan. "From Neptune to Bacchus!" Charlotte shouted back, wrinkling the too-solid foam eyelids which lay around her myoptic fish eyes, and pointed to the bar ahead. Natasha tied her Dane to one of the posts which supported the thatched-roof hut and looked for a table. At one in the afternoon the Bali had begun to fill with bathing suits and high Tom Collinses and planter's punches, everyone who wanted to be seen, waiting for their presence at the bar to be witnessed; later yacht aristocrats and the athletes now passing on skis behind motorboats, cutting near the buoyant heads of swimmers, would arrive. The eternal guitar trio. Charlotte, Gus, and Bobó elbowed their way to the table Natasha had taken and was holding. The ancient courtesan was snorting to find herself surrounded by sweaty teen-age boys with brushy curled back hair and rolled sleeves, Sacred Heart medals on their chests, who at the same time were encircling a straight-haired, dyed-haired, constantly smoking girl who did not understand their allusions and was begging for help.

"Did you see Cuquis with Junior?" Charlotte said, sitting. "Natasha, I swear you have to play your hand cool to grab that many millions. Just imagine, she was a clerk in a perfume warehouse. Now look at her, at all our parties with her nose in the air with Junior, who smells of money and is just as good-looking."

Gus and Bobó arrived. "Another excursion around these savage beaches and I hand in my resignation," Bobó said.

"Ugh," said Gus as he shook out his beach robe, " I agree that it's terrible. Ten years ago this was a paradise, no one knew you; at six in the morning you could run around naked if you wanted to; there weren't any tourists, everything was virgin, virgin . . ."

"And you, too, doll?" said Charlotte. "Oh, Gus, this may not be Cannes, and too bad, but thank God for what this stinking country does have to offer. At least you can see people you know and hobnob with the rich. What are you worrying about? It comes out in the papers that you were here, you were on Junior's yacht, you went to Roberto Régules's party. Everything is played down, but when you get back to Mexico City, the invitations arrive in showers. You make connections, you get rich, fatty, so stop beefing."

Gus licked salt off his swollen lips. "What materialism, Charlotte. There used to be a little spirituality in Mexico, the intellectuals were intellectuals and they didn't go meddling in snobbish snob's affairs. Now there's only goulash, the artist has to pretend he is a man of the world, and the good girls are know-alls, and no one understands anything. We aren't even human any more."

Cuquis and Junior came, dripping, up to the table. "Hi! Three Alka Seltzers and a rum-and-milk for the little girl. Be right back. Isn't the sea beautiful?" And they ran into the waves, holding hands.

Charlotte sighed. "After this revelation of natural truth, give me a double tequila. Didn't I tell you? 'Isn't the sea beautiful!' Oh, my God! *Comme elle est spirituelle, celle là.*"

"There's no other way," said Natasha, letting out a long

nostalgic breath. "How did Norma Larragoiti get started? Or Silvia Régules? *Tu le sais, chérie.* Both of them vulgar mediocre girls who caught their millionaires just by observing that the sea is beautiful and by looking blank. A Mexican man doesn't want any difficult problems with his wife. He prefers a nameless little nitwit who will feel safe and happy if he gives her money and will go to bed with him every now and then, like a cadaver, to be squirted full of male satisfaction . . ."

Bobó and Gus laughed. Charlotte waved her arm to Pimpinela de Ovando, who was walking along the beach, smoking, beneath a red parasol. Her pleated skirt was a rosebud among pyramids of tangled muscular teen-age kids. "Well," said Bobó, "Pimpinela's case is different. Look at the way she keeps her dignity among the sons of bitches she has to go around with. Just to get her beans."

Gus pulled his robe around his shoulders. "And tied to her virginity as if her aristocracy were defined by the preserved condition of her ass. Really, Bobó, that was all right when Mexico City was a village and everyone knew everyone. But now, with four million, frankly, no one gives a damn whether a girl has had it or not."

Pimpinela was received with forced smiles.

"Pimpi, darling."

"You're simply adorable."

"You've no right to make such a contrast with the poor trash who have taken over the beaches. That's throwing daisies to hogs."

Pimpinela sat. Her air was her habitual cold cordiality.

"What's the latest in Mexico City?" said Charlotte.

"Do you know what dirty business Señor Cienfuegos has gotten into now? We've been here a whole week, darling," said Bobó, "*sans* news and newspapers, dedicated wholly to a good time and mater nater . . ."

"*Brut,* nineteen hundred twenty-seven," Natasha interrupted.

"And now," he went on, "we're pooped. That party of yours was the end, Charlotte. I came out twice on the same society page, and you, too, along with that hairy-headed old man who

252

made the atomic bomb. So you see that nothing lasts and . . ."

Cuquis and Junior returned. "Hi Pimpinela," Junior said, laying a wet hand on her print. "Gee, this is really international. All we need now is Norma with her new great and good friend, as they say . . ."

Avid silence surrounded Junior's words, broken when Cuquis ran on headlong. "If you could see them all lovey-dovey on a secluded beach . . . how about going around that way again, Junior? We learn more little things than if we were private detectives." With one gulp Cuquis finished off Charlotte's drink.

Charlotte nervously moved her hands and feet. "Do you know him? Have you met him? I'm mean, it isn't that I'm nosy, but after all, if a married man is concerned, we'll have to warn his wife. It's all right for men to have their flings now and then. But only with second-raters, not . . ."

"You remember that jerk who was at your party, Bobó? The one who was so tight-lipped and just looked at us . . .?"

"Cienfuegos!" Bobó howled. "The smuggler!"

"I'm sure," said Pimpinela, after waiting, "that it's not money he wants."

"No," blurted Charlotte, "It must be for . . ."

Pimpinela hesitated a second or two, waited until everyone was hanging on her words, the four nerveless hot bodies and the two who, standing, were sun-peeling like roasted meat. "Federico Robles is ruined. Honestly. He's hanging on just to keep up appearances. It seems that he has taken all his bank's money for some crazy investment that didn't pan out; now he's trying to borrow to recover what he lost. Suppose I were to tell Aunt Lorenza that she's going to have to spend the rest of her days in an old folks' home? Remember, don't talk about it. I got it from a very special source and the same discretion that was asked of me, I must ask of you."

Six voices exploded around Pimpinela. "And Norma made me buy a thousand shares of I don't know what," Charlotte shouted furiously.

"Leave it alone," Bobó chirped. "She got God knows how much from Roberto Régules, and for good reason."

"And he discounts my father's bonds," Junior snapped indignantly.

Only Cuquis remained calm. She abruptly detatched herself from the general mayhem, and holding her highball high, walked, snaking, away. "Hi, Cuquis," a gay, drunken voice said. "Golden Girl, man's downfall."

"My darling eight columns!" Cuquis hugged the journalist, whose shirt was full of cheap Acapulco cigars. "You always show both the flowers and the briars, as they say." Cuquis let her eyelids droop and looked around the table at the journalist's friends, who acknowledged her *hello* with reticent smiles. "Isn't Acapulco divine? And what dirt to be swept up!"

The journalist, leaning over his glass, winked at his friends and said softly, "Well, tomorrow morning all Mexico City will know that you've hooked the greatest heir in the country!"

"Really, darling?" Cuquis planted her iodized lips on the newspaperman's bald spot. "And what will my family make of it? You know how hard it is for a girl to be independent in Mexico City. Right away, people start talking about you. They think you're on your way to whoredom." She raised her arms and scratched the newspaperman's head. "Junior's family wants to marry him off to that little bitch of a Régules girl. Now tell me, doesn't he need a girl with experience, who knows how to keep up with the crowd, and get along with men? Isn't that what he needs? Above all, don't write anything that will make me seem silly, darling." She sat down on his lap and crossed her legs. "Just like that Robles woman who has a lover crawling around her already . . . that poor old man, sunk . . ."

The journalist winked at his friends and put his ear near Cuquis's lips.

"What do you think about it?" she ran on. "When I think of all the poor people who have their little savings stashed away with him. It's enough to give you the whim-whams, isn't it? Swear you'll keep it off the record."

The journalist cleared his throat and squeezed Cuquis's waist. "Now, now, my adorable, my duty is to the public interest. You think I could sleep with a clear conscience after what you just told me? Myself, I don't bank with Robles. No, my dear, no, but you have done me a great service, believe me. You're going to prevent the ruin of so many humble, honest families . . ."

From the distance, Natasha watched. Skiers passed on the sea, rigid puppets, out of reach of the smells of sand stuck to bathing suits and the sweat of the three guitarists and the grease and oils that embalmed holiday bodies. And farther: stucco homes with straw-thatch, palm-thatch and mosaics, under the sun.

Cuquis slowly returned to the table. Her tight buttocks were squeezed into her bathing suit and pulled up by the straps that brushed her naked back and her shoulders.

"Since we can't write about politics, what would become of us, brothers," the journalist remarked, "if we didn't have these little scandals?"

Chino Taboada offered his squat body to the evening sun, lying on a beach mat with his arms spread and a cigar in one hand, a highball in the other. Now and then the hand with the cigar would descend to his ankles to scratch a bite. Two pads of cotton covered his eyes. The material of his bathing trunks, white stamped with facsimiles of famous autographs, contrasted with his tanned skin. Two rolled-up socks and a little red straw hat covered his extremities. Simon Evrahim stayed in the shade with a sun visor, a yellow scarf around his neck, wearing white linen plus fours. Seated tensely in a bamboo chair, Rodrigo Pola played with his drink and testily argued silent quarrels inside his mind.

"Well," he said at last, "it's box office, but maybe the censors will jump it."

"Give it to us," mumbled Taboada. The sea reached the foot of the terrace with a murmur. The afternoon had quietly turned into evening.

"Lesbians," Rodrigo went on.

"That's making a difference?" intervened Simon. "We'll adapt 'em, Mister. We'll nationalize them into good Mexicans . . ."

Rodrigo laughed with a queer sense of happiness. At last he

felt superior to ordinary men. Without knowing it, he was thinking about his Prepa days, the hours with Mediana and the group. He could have won the fame game a long time ago if anyone had told him that all he needed to know was its tricks. He knew now that there was no stopping him. He could have struck back years ago if anyone had just told him that all he needed to know was the trick, and that was to rise above all of them: bougeois intellectuals, brides awed by wealth, oppressive mothers. The game depended upon time and its players, and once in it, the solution was to make oneself indispensable.

"We'll change them to Mexicans, Señor Evrahim. And with that, everything takes care of itself. Universal theme, plus local color for the foreign market. Two goils, shall we say, reared in different ways of life. One is rich, the other don't have two cents."

"Great! Great enough for Cannes!" growled Taboada.

"Cannes and Venice, too, as sure as if you had the Lion of St. Mark on your shelf already," Rodrigo intervened with decision. "What happens to them? One has everything . . . the other . . ."

"Don't have nothing," sighed Taboada. "Born in the gutter, she takes care of her little brothers and sisters."

"An orphan, of course. You know, Chino, that's a bee-yoo-tee-full slum we can use. We'll make those scenes so true to life, they'll smell, and we won't spend for sets."

Taboada gargled with his whisky. "People want realism, Simon. Okay. We'll be more Italian than the Dagos. Just imagine it: location: clothes hung out to dry, gossip, a kid with a motorcycle belt, delinquents . . ."

"Remember, it's in Technicolor." Evrahim moved his leg impatiently and felt a singular moment of freedom, as if the sea breeze had whistled through a cemetery and ascended to his knee. "We got to shoot what will show in color."

"That's why we got the other broad growing up in a rich mansion, elegant clothes, a Cad convertible to run around in, with a chauffeur."

"Colossal!"

"Mad about mambo. Has wild orgies in her home when her

256

parents are out of town on business trips. Gets the monkey on her back."

"Stop!" Taboada sat up. "Stop, don't go on, I see it all! The other broad, the poor one, hunched, huddled, over a Singer sewing machine to send her runt family to school. At last, there's a big party, she shows herself that she can twist men around her finger. Then a theater impresario sees her . . ."

"Colossal! The role is made to order for Didi del Mar!"

"Meanwhile, the rich young bitch gets caught by her parents. The old man throws her out. She falls into the hands of a pimp . . ."

"Superb, Señor Taboada." Rodrigo's arm traced a wide circle. "The counterpoint idea is ingenious. Rich bitch, Christmas Eve, full of shame, she sneaks to her home. She sees her parents' meal laid out. She cries in the street, she can't go in . . ."

"Wearing mesh stockings and a sequin dress," interrupted Taboada as his eye cottons came unstuck.

"Too late! Too late, too late, she runs out on the street and is run over by a bus."

"While the other"—Taboada chewed his cigar furiously—"the humble broad, she marries the theater impresario . . ." He mopped his forehead with a towel. "Festival caliber. No doubt about it."

Rodrigo smiled again. Yes, he was part of the game now. And he would show them who he really was. Let them believe what they wanted to now, later they would be shown . . . he would write a really great screen-play . . . he would surprise them with his genius . . . Eisenstein, Pudovkin, Flaherty: Rodrigo laughed.

"Let's not go too fast." Evrahim moved his leg impatiently again. "We have a feminine public, too. We need heroes."

"Who sing," grunted Taboada. He stretched out again, satisfied. A waiter, suffocating in his striped jacket, passed to put ice cubes in their drinks.

"The rich bitch's father," Rodrigo sucked his drink with enthusiasm, "sings boleros in a top cabaret. The impresario, on the other hand, is only a country boy. In his leisure he dresses up like a *mariachi* and serenades the poor broad, while——"

257

"While she prays to the Virgin. We gotta have respect for religion, too," said Simon, with his hands on his hips.

Rodrigo's eyes passed along the esplanade of Taboada's country house. Tired corn mortars converted into ash trays stood on the low tables, pieces of an Indian kitchen, little clay figures. In the actual kitchen, Rodrigo reflected, they probably used pressure cookers and liquidizers. He wanted to ask Evrahim whether Hollywood homes had pots and pans on show in the living room, but he restrained himself when Taboada's voice began, "I got it. Listen, let Rodrigo stay here a week to write everything we've just worked out. You know what we want, kid, poetry, this has got to be quality. For example, the humble broad begins to go to pieces under the moral strain and the impresario brings her to Acapulco for a week end to recover and tells her, the waves are like her this and the sea is like her that, so her mouth is like and the palm trees are like—you get it? While I look for locations and you, Evrahim, work on the production. In a week we'll start the outside shots and in two more weeks we'll have the picture finished."

Simon wrinkled his nose and rubbed his bald head. "Rodrigo already has it visualized perfectly. He'll finish in four days."

"Ah, penny pinchers." Taboada stood and began to do Swiss gymnastic movements. His tits bounced and his hair, straight except where it curled around the nape of his neck, dripped vaseline. "Don't worry, *hombre*. . . . Hey, Simon, that little extra, that little pug-nosed girl who played the oppressed Indian in my last, is she free now?"

"Well, if she's not, we'll free her, Chino."

"Let them send her here to our friend Pola, so his work will go easy."

"It's going to be box office. What'll we call it?"

"Woczsyliczylszly is our expert on titles. He's in Cuernavaca thinking up one now. That's what we pay him for."

"Okay, okay."

"We'll give Rodrigo twelve thousand, because it's his first."

"Okay, okay."

Rodrigo rested his head on the back of the chair. He closed his eyes and hummed a bolero. He felt happy, a cold glass in his hands, his veins expanding under the sun, the slow, delicious heat of whisky in his stomach. The sun was setting a spectacular harmonious sky palette, as if to make him feel at home in the aesthetic intensity of Evrahim and Taboada. Conversation stopped so that silent homage might be rendered to nature. Rodrigo opened his eyes and felt like writing the words "The End" across the rose heavens.

"The water is too rough," Norma said from her black chaise longue in the middle of the broad sea-overlooking terrace.

"Okay, we take the sailboat," Ixca replied.

Norma did not want to move her bronzed body. Every pore reflected the sunset glow, and every pore, as she passed her hands over her shoulders, relived the past days, bathed in air and on white sand and through turquoise water, and the nights, the only nights of love, she told herself now, that she would always remember. With her eyes half closed, she watched imperceptible movements of Cienfuegos's olive body; he was gazing out to sea and slowly smoking, one foot on the terrace wall.

"Have you been happy?"

Cienfuegos did not answer. The dying sun flowed over his face and chest, tinted his skin, accented the olive with an ocher glaze.

"Punisher." Norma closed her eyes and puckered her lips. "Don't be angry, sweet. You know I'll do what you want me to, that I'm yours."

Ixca smiled, without turning. From the port, the noises of nickelodeons playing rock-and-roll began to rise. A quickening breeze wind-ruffled the sea.

"Come, Norma."

"This is a big blow coming. We're so comfortable here."

"Come."

They went down stone stairs to the wharf. Cienfuegos raised the sail while Norma dropped into the boat with crossed arms. Face down on the bow, she watched dark rocks pass beneath them as Ixca tacked the boat toward the open sea.

"What weather!"

The sea grew darker, its depth, blacker. Turbulent sky enveloped Norma in a placenta of opaque salt. She watched Ixca's back as he tacked, and she wanted to go and bite it. The insatiable desire to bite his back came on her, to do it even though she might never see him again, like a consummation of all the days and nights of love. She had the sudden feeling that she was never going to go back to the house. Those beds were permanently turned down, trespassed by Ixca's flesh, the body her teeth wanted to sink into now. She turned her face toward the shore, every wave carrying it farther away across darkness and rain.

"Do you love me, Norma?" Ixca shouted above the rattle of the sail.

"Yes, yes, more than myself." A hoarse roar drowned her words. "Ixca, let's start in!"

"Even more than yourself?" he shouted again. But Norma did not hear. Choppy breaking waves had begun to rise, to plunge the little boat deep between walls of water which now was bottomless and blind.

"Take the sail down, Ixca!"

"More than yourself?"

"We're going to capsize, take the sail down!"

On her knees, she glanced quickly to both sides. Two anonymous high arches, empty of light, darker than the sky they held up, raced past with open mouths, trying to find her. In this immediate danger she grabbed desperately at the life preserver and felt another hand, not desperate, jerk it from her coldly and lucidly: another hand which held her wrist and separated her from the preserver's hard circle. Norma felt another intangible circle sucking and pounding inside her head. The darkness was cut by silver beams. Then she felt wind in her mouth and Ixca's breath to her right, welded to the life preserver. "Give it to me, give it to me," she tried to scream. She did not want to trust that damp smile, like the smile of a shark shining in the cinder of darkness. A new crash burst. Again the silver world, this time as thick as saliva, and again the toenail stretching toward a far-away bottom and again air, and there he was, always, in the center of her eyes, a shining head, floating within the life preserver. Norma made three strokes, blood boiling, to the hard circle.

"Give it to me, give it to me!" she whined, scratching his face, digging her fingers into his neck, solid as earth itself, splashing and chopping water until she grabbed his head and pushed it down, down, and then she worked her arms into the life preserver.

The sea calmed. Clouds flew over, warm and swift, separating her from night. Tiny lights waited, and she paddled toward them. exhausted. Her own image shone before her eyes and her blood was hot with the thought of salvation, salvation of her body, her power.

Her chin rested upon sand. She loosened her muscles and closed her eyes. She felt the coming and going of soft wavelets past her lips. She could find no words for a prayer, only the word *Norma, Norma,* flowed from her mouth into the sea, strung together by a thread of spittle. Norma lay foamy and warm on the sand, unconscious.

Her head began to throb again. She opened her eyes. She ran along the beach, disoriented, until she came upon a stucco stair. She ran up. The road to Quebrada beach. She ran toward the door of a house, through a garden of shadow plants and bougainvillaea, through a living room open to the sea, until she reached her own room. She did not stop. Comb, towel, lipstick, mascara, her body and her face, a print dress, white shoes, a bag, money. She turned on the ignition key and raced to the highway. Through darkness she sped until at last the port's blue lights were around her. Traffic was slow, coming from the beaches to the hotels, convertibles with brown teen-agers whose shirts were open to the navel, bikinis and sandy towels and full-blast radios. The townspeople gathered at bayside docks, sinewy mulattoes, hotbellied Negresses, yellow children, little useless strings of fish, coconut vendors, all with their backs to the city, facing the sea, the ha-haw-haws of Americans in straw hats and bright skirts, with dark glasses, cigars, and cameras, the neons of bars and hotels, the smells of gasoline and rotting fish, incessant horns, cops whistling, juke boxes like accordions drowned in heat, buildings with bright impudent fronts which concealed straw roofs, a naked little girl with the tremble of malaria. Entwined bodies strolling the public beaches, wool bathing suits on obesity, permanents, beach robes, conquered sand castles, litter of cigarette butts and bottles, old tired hot dogs, the sea greasy, skies hung to dry, bobbing boats, gin and rum, bam-bah-*bam,* gin and rum, *bam,* bah-bam-bah-bam-*bahm,* gin and rum, it came and went from Playa Azul to Copacabana to the Bum-Bum, beat of tropical drums, writhing arms and legs, white vegetable fingernails encrusted on fingers of alcohol, cement, and dollars—all of it breathed into her face as her car raced. She stopped in front of a bar. The palm-frond roof trembled to the quadruple beat of feet and bongos and glasses and ice. She entered, threw off her shoes, and went onto the dance floor alone and with her legs apart and her arms moving, her lips and eyelids damp with sweat and make-up. A muscle man with curly hair and a small mustache and slanted eyes grabbed her by the waist. Norma wet her lips more and pushed her belly against his, wove her arms around his torso.

"Do you drink?"

"I drink. Let them line up a row of daiquiris *frappé* on the bar," Norma said, with her voice hoarse and happy.

Still dancing, she picked the glasses up one by one and chug-a-lugged them down, one after the other. The bongos' beat was her natural beat as she came and went, dancing from table to table and drink to drink. Other dancers abandoned the floor to her.

"This is what I like!" she cried in a whirl of skirts. "Let them know what's good! That's how I like it, let them leave me alone!"

"The boat's here."

"What boat, baby, what boat?"

"The gambling boat, don't play it dumb."

The little speedboat cut through the sea with them. Beyond the jurisdictional limit of the city, a white yacht with small phosphorescent flags rocked. Norma went dancing up the ladder. A red-faced fat old man barred her way.

"It's me . . . Macaracas," the curly-haired man called up.

"All right, boy, come on."

"You got dough?" Macaracas asked Norma.

She stopped cold. She saw his slanted eyes and burst out laughing and opened her purse and threw three one-thousand peso bills at his face. "Here, you son of a bitch, you'd better learn who's who." She fell upon the roulette tables. The yacht rocked. She ordered more daiquiris.

"There's snow," Macaracas said, coming up to her. "Don't you want to try it?"

Again Norma could not hold her laughter.

"I'm alive already, you know."

"No, man, I——"

"I don't need anybody, you understand me?"

"What a doll!"

"I can fuck them all, all of them, you know——"

"The way I like you, baby."

"Because I'm the best." She lifted her hands to his temple and then grabbed his neck, laughing continuously. "I'm the best there is . . ."

"A little later, baby, a little——"

"I've got them all between my fingers. Pimpinela, Rodrigo— even that dead bastard who drowned on me."

"Let's go, baby."

An unshaven gringo, skinny and nervous and wearing a skipper's cap, opened a door.

"I want, I want, I want my lemon ice . . ." Singing, she went inside, barefoot and hot, supported by Macaracas.

In the hall of the district courthouse, in the shadows of the interior patio with its bulletin boards of legal notices and its photos of unclaimed bodies, the judge's diminutive secretary jabbed his finger into his spread left palm and said, "I already know you gave me four thousand pesos, but there was too much evidence. Just no way to get around it."

The sweaty fat man he was addressing whistled between his teeth and said, "Who do you think you're making a fool of, eh?"

The other touched the fat man's lapels. "Take it easy, take it easy. I'll see what can be done."

Clean September air passes swiftly through the dark and moldy patio. Outside, a one-armed vendor sells red-backed Code Summaries, popular song-books, and copies of the *Official Daily*.

"I'll give him half and not a cent more. To the judge of the second court. Your business is going there next, so your battle is won."

The fat man smiles and wipes thick sweat drops from the inside band of his Stetson. "Christ. How much did the others give to win with the first judge?"

With a broken smile, the little secretary shows his yellow, spaced teeth. "Five thousand, my friend, no less. So you see that you are coming out ahead, eh? What can I do on the miserable salary they give me here? Tell me. And the cost of living going up every day. And now the war with Korea. I'm telling you, don't worry. I'm taking care of you. You're in."

A folder under his elbow, the secretary runs hastily across the patio, bows to a group of lawyers, and ascends the worn stone stairs with quick steps.

THE PARTING OF WATERS

Walking slowly around the golf links that morning, Roberto Régules did not stop thinking for one moment about what Pimpinela de Ovando had told him. A rich variety of tones of green, procreated by the rainy season with the help of an army of gardeners, surrounded the links. At the ninth hole he stopped and turned back, his gray eyes buried between his sun-browned cheekbones, his short hair blond and graying in the bright morning. The following foursome, men wearing Pacific Theater of Operations admirals' caps, cashmere sweaters, linen trousers, and spiked shoes, laughed, and he slowed and waited for them to come up.

"You've reached the stretch a little early today, *Licenciado*."

"Yes," Régules smiled. "I have to get to my office."

"At eleven, man?"

"Business, gentlemen, though you may not believe me."

They laughed and one of them said, "Business we all have."

"But this is really urgent. You will understand me, I think, Don Jenaro."

"I? I think so . . . ever since the trick Robles played selling out his shares ahead of time and without a by-your-leave to anyone, I've known what it means to sweat ink. . . ."

"I daresay"—Régules smiled, juggling a golf ball in his hand—"we must call that a lack of integrity. But there is no one to stop Robles, you know. I agree that we may work for our own interests, but only to the limit of still having respect for the interests of others. Too much ambition is dangerous, Don Jenaro." . . .

"You are telling me, sir? How would you feel to find yourself, between night and the next morning, an associate of that bandit Couto? That's what Robles did to us when he got out. Fifty-one per cent, and to a bastard, and there we were with forty-nine per cent, helpless."

"Ah! So it was Couto."

"The devil himself."

"My dear Don Jenaro, were the shares made out to bearer?"

"Unfortunately, yes, all to bearer."

"You are close, I believe, to Ibargüen, Velarde, and Capdevilla."

"There is no secret about that, *Licenciado.*"

"Don Jenaro, I invite you to a whisky, to celebrate our new partnership."

"Eh?" A light of understanding broke in Don Jenaro's wheezy eyes, and the two men walked away from the others to go to the clubhouse bar.

By afternoon, Régules was on the move. From his luxurious new office on Colón Circle he made one telephone call after another, a highball in his freckled hand, his body fresh and at ease after golf and massage. Each time his finger touched the dialing disk, it seemed to be twirling a circle of Pimpinela de Ovando's honey-colored eyes. In the brief waits between conversations he recalled the first time he had met her, back in the days when everyone went to Sanborn's for breakfast and he, recently admitted to the bar, had just arrived from Guadalajara, full of ambition: money and social position were his two categories, and both could be found at Sanborn's; and having the first already, he believed that Pimpinela de Ovando would give him the second. But looking back now, he congratulated himself that the de Ovando's closed pride had shut off his matrimonial pretensions. He had gained social standing himself; the categories were in reality only one, money, and his triumph was the more complete for his marrying his former secretary, Silvia, a girl of the middle class, by his receiving Pimpinela's requests for help in getting back the lost haciendas, by his being offered, now, her news about Robles's dangerous financial situation; his triumph was more complete than it would have been had he been inducted into the dusty clan of the de Ovandos.

"Silvia? No, that doesn't matter now, I'm calling on business. Ask your friend Caseaux to get in touch with me right away. What's the matter, have you lost your tongue? Cynical? Oh, no, Silvia, but if you are going to have separate maintenance from me, you can damn well do me an occasional favor in return. I'm *quite* serious, I want him to call me up within half an hour. Yes, I know it's Betina's birthday. But I'm going to be very busy. Give her a wrist watch, take her to the Versailles. All right. Good-by."

"Couto, my friend, what a surprise, you're never at home these days? Eh? Business? Well, we all have work. Listen. . . . Yes, I understand. . . . Listen: about those sulphur shares you gave me as security for the nine hundred thousand; something is about to break there. Oh, you knew already and didn't tell me? Well, Couto, we are friends, and working together, I think we can handle it. Yes, all we have to do is move fast enough. But why shouldn't I trust you, eh? To be brief, I want you to change the security from the sulphur to your holdings in Don Jenaro's chain. You'll come out a hundred thousand ahead, and you can unload your sulphur shares right away before the storm begins. Look, I'll tell you, if you don't do it today, I shall do it myself tomorrow. I need room. Oh, there are ways, there are ways, Couto, you know that as well as I do. Today you, or tomorrow I. All right. All right, friend Couto. . . . At your orders, always . . ."

"Don Jenaro? Tomorrow I'll have Couto's holdings as security for a loan I made him. Yes, I've talked with him, it's all arranged. Yes, a true buzzard, but all he can see is the quick profit, he has no vision. Now I shall exercise my rights as your associate, and by moving just a little, we'll . . . So Robles's concessions will be canceled today? Magnificent. And the suspension of credit? Of course, slowly, slowly, so there won't be any . . . Ah, Don Jenaro! are you interested in those lots next to your factory? You've used them already as an advance to Robles? Get along! Well, maybe I can take care of that, too. You tell me, eh? Clear violations of the labor laws? And you can start the labor men fighting about it? Good, good, give and take, give and take . . ."

"How are you, Caseaux? I'll go straight to the point: have you closed your sale of those lots to Federico Robles yet? Only the signatures lacking? Ah, he's paid you a big advance? That doesn't matter . . . he's writing *idiot* across your forehead, my little friend. Bah, one thing is business, another is nice talk; listen to me now, or go to hell. . . . Just what you heard me say. Those lots are worth at least two or three times what Robles is paying you. He's making an ass of you. I'll pay you twenty pesos a square meter myself. Just what you hear. You've a lot of debts, my friend, it isn't cheap to live on credit. . . . No, I'm not threatening you, but I admit it's only because of Silvia's begging that I have held onto your letters you . . . you understand me, eh? Ah, the advance! How much was it? Done, done, the money is here, at your service, to pay him back in the morning, and then you are out of it. Good-bye, my friend."

"Yes, *Señor*. Yes, this very morning I withdrew everything. Robles's situation is very bad indeed. He has invested in sulphur and of course you know what is building up there. Yes. I advise you because I know that you have an interest at stake. Bad policy, yes, to say the least. And the more depositors who know what's going on, the better. We have to guard the well-being of our financial family, eh? Your servant, sir, your servant. Yes, Silvia told me. When our wives can decide on a day, I'll be delighted. An honor. Until soon, then . . ."

"Licenciado Capdevilla? Régules. Ré-gu-les, with *R* . . . Yes, Don Jenaro's friend. Excuse me, I am aware of that, but I have some vital information about the industry. Yes, Robles's factory. I daresay that the competition he causes you is hardly loyal . . . yes, one might even call it underhanded, too. . . . Dumping? No, what I have, sir, is certain evidence that he has been violating the law. Yes. But of course, of course, at your service. Me, too, *Licenciado*. Your servant, sir."

Régules hung up and fingered his red silk tie and the corners of his handkerchief. He sat on a blue leather chair, and touched a button.

"Take a note, *Señorita*. Tomorrow, first thing, prepare a confidential memorandum for the Justice Department. Prepare a bill of sale for Señor Juan Felipe Couto, eight hundred thousand bearer shares, with cancellation of the previous agreement with Señor Couto. Bill of purchase, Señor Pedro Caseaux, ten thousand square meters at twenty pesos a meter; bill of sale, to Jenaro Arriaga, ten thousand meters at thirty-five pesos. Take care of these, and bring me, please, the personal file on Federico Robles."

He worked over Robles's file until quite late that evening, extracting figures and dates, everything that could help give a precise idea of the financier's life and fortune.

"You're burned black, my son, black as the nights I remember," said Widow Teódula as she let Ixca into her hut. It smelled as always: musty, damp, yet of dried flowers. "You look as though you had fought with the sun. What have you brought me?"

Cienfuegos let himself fall on the powdery floor mat. The hut was held motionless in a sphere of prayer, as careless about time as a prayer which asks that what already has happened be changed to not happened; as always, the same dust, the same stains from food and water, exactly as always on the same swept dirt floor below which lay the death cellar.

"What have you brought me?" Teódula Moctezuma asked again, with her eyes narrowed to two black nails hidden in her flesh, tense in their expectation of the rebirth of a lost world.

Ixca covered his face with his hands. His voice came hollow, violated, not from his body. "Our world is dead indeed, Teódula, forever dead, as if the ashes of your children and old Celedonio

268

had gone into the earth without a single tear or the slightest sense of feeding us."

"Son," said the old widow, chewing her gums as she bent over his shoulders like a scythe, "men don't make life, but the earth under their feet makes it, do you understand? Come who may or come what may, men who will take from us, time that will make us forgetful, yet always beneath the land in hidden places our feet can't stomp, there everything goes on the same, and the same voices can be heard as in the beginning. You know that."

Ixca, raising his head, kissed Teódula's hands. "No, I don't know it, I don't hear them. I've wanted to and for years I've waited with closed eyes, hoping to hear. But it is as if everything had been carried away in the wind of words. Today's sun isn't our sun, Teódula; it's a sun—how well I know now—to bake skin anointed with synthetic oil. . . ."

She stared fixedly at him, completely unable to understand. Anchored in her own day and year, she had no contact with the fleeting moment of his day and his year. Ixca felt her face flake away until there remained only a single shining and unset jewel dangling between sun and earth. The clink of her bracelets little by little drew his eyes and his memory together until he saw her again, her worn body, her time-gone dry face.

"Who knows where he comes from or where he goes? What you believe may not after all be true. Or it may be that new dresses and new rites that you and I do not know about may be the going on of our world. For the earth claims everything, this I know, son, I know with certainty, claims it back, swallows everyone, to return them to us as they ought to be, even if dead. There is no escaping the earth. That woman, Ixca, that woman you wanted to pull loose from the earth, up from the root . . ."

"Norma," he said tonelessly. "Remember her name."

"Norma. Maybe she can't understand as you and I do. Whatever happens, I tell you, she will end swallowed by the earth, you'll see. Where everything ends. There we will meet her. Not before, because what seems to be is not what is, men have no way to practice our rites today, nor to understand our surrender. But at the last, when they no longer speak nor think, then, my son . . . yes, then. Then we shall fall upon them and make them ours. There in our kingdom, afterward, then we'll be alive."

She squatted down on her heels near her cooking things and began to mumble. In silence Ixca tried to hear her, to thread her thoughts. He said, "But for our world really to exist, Teódula, is it enough for you and me to believe that it does and to try to make it live? Isn't that really all we can do? Should we ask any more? Do you understand me, Teódula?"

With sinuous strength the old woman shaped tortilla dough, "All I know is what I tell you. Our gods walk abroad, invisible but alive. You'll see, you'll see. They always win. They take our sacrificed blood, our killed heroes, our deaths fallen across a land of song and color. Here, my son, as in no other land; and you know better than I that their hands never drop from us, that from hour to hour they are always with us, as if to collect for all that has happened before, as if to say that everything ends as it begins, in them, their mystery, my son. There, here, in dreams when we do not call them. But we do call to them, my son, we go on calling upon them to give reason to our lives and we carry the last face, the only face which counts, always ready. You'll see, you'll see. If anyone escapes you, like your friend whose mother died, another will replace him. Before I die, I will see him, and I will give him my jewels and my last look, to know that someone knew. To him who will be the sacrifice, my son. We dry up, living, we are forgotten; they have fled from us and left us with the man who walks disguised by a metal face. But in death they do not forget us. Never, Ixca, my son."

She put the dough down, and with her knobbled old hands opened her eyes and stared at Cienfuegos's face, and in a voice he had never heard before, echo from a dead and forgotten age entombed in water and ashes and snails and drum skins, voice more of shaly scales than of words, she said, "We are coming near the parting of waters. They will die and we will be resurrected, fed by their deaths. We have to pay our debt to dreams. The city will pay it for us. Arch of turquoise, heart of stone, serpent wind, do not dream more."

And Cienfuegos saw, in words not spoken, in a tongue of

270

pronouncing fire, the sleeping city, the broken dolls' bodies of Federico and Norma caught in final slumber and rebirth.

"Look, *mano*, let's get away from here." A teen-age kid in skin-tight blue jeans, standing on the corner of Bucareli and Avenida Chapultepec, threw a bitter look at all the city's people and ways.

"But let's go home, to my house, Lalo . . ."

"Crap! At your house, just like at mine, they think you're in school. We'll take off when school lets out and we won't say good-bye to anybody." The other boy, shorter, wearing a fading yellow jacket, bit his fingers. "Okay, okay," went on the first. "I thought you said you would take off, too."

"But listen, *mano*, my mother will be all alone."

"In no time you'll be sending money back to her, won't you?"

"But the thing is, she wants me to finish school and have a career. You know how the poor woman works to keep me in school. If I don't go home, she'll be all upset."

"Only jerks work, *mano*. What do you and I have to wait for? Nobody in this goddamn city gives us nothing. But in Ciudad Juárez it'll be another story."

"And your cousin there, the one who'll make us rich, you still haven't talked with him?"

"No, *manito*, but he's okay, he's a buddy. He's got a night club there, I tell you, you'll be making dough there just by having a good time. What you got here? Figure it up yourself. Another year in high school and then two in college and then five or six at the U! Nine years without a nickel, *mano*, sweating homework for teachers who couldn't teach you to shit; no, *mano*, if that's what you were born for, stick with it, but me, I'm heading for Ciudad Juárez."

The shorter youth frowned and stared down; the other, skinny and nervous, combed his hair and rubbed the back of his neck and said, "This fuckin' city. You'll end up shining shoes. You've seen those kids with cars and money? You think you and I stand any chance against them? You think girls are going to pay us any attention, crawling around without wheels? The fact is, shit, you haven't ever even been with a woman."

The chubby kid looked at him with embarrassment.

"Okay, *manito*, get with it, get with it, up north everything will go smooth. Make up your mind."

Ixca Cienfuegos, walking toward Tonalá, crossed looks with the skinny nervous kid, and the kid stared back at him malignantly and bitterly. "That's how they all look at you here, Mimo. Full of goddamn pity! I'm getting out. We'll come back and show them some day." And with their hands in their pockets, the two boys crossed the street, dodging cars.

HORTENSIA CHACÓN

"He hasn't talked with you about me, has he? How did you find out about me?" He is too sweet, too modest. I don't reproach him because he keeps me secret. On the contrary, that's what I prefer. Except for the first time, when I met him, we've never seen each other except alone together here. As if our world could not be spread one centimeter wider. "Where you're sitting now, that's where he sits, too." And he lets me feel him far away from me at first. . . . "You're on the sofa, aren't you?" No, I don't reproach him and I'm not ashamed. Few things have precise limits, neither our love nor our hatred, and any other way I would be afraid, yes, afraid that we were dreams. I almost was a dream, and that's what pleases me in Federico, that his love and hatred have made me feel as I do, flesh and bone, today. "Ha, I'll bore you. Would you like some coffee? No, I know where everything is. Look there, where you're sitting, the brown sofa, the fireplace to the left. It isn't real, it doesn't work. And then a chair, and between them . . . but I bore you even more."

And my senses tell me that you have come to learn something, and I know you deserve to. How do I know? I come from far away, too, where people understand without words; my face would say it, if nothing else, for we grow up wordless, with only these looks, stares you can't save. We can't stand our true faces—how shall I say it?—there are faces that frighten us and carry us

272

to the limits of passions, good and evil, and we can't allow it, there are still so many laws and rules, we have to learn to measure things and not let ourselves be seen with horror and fear by others, those who would destroy us if we should show our true faces. And I feel that stare in you, and that you can see it in me, and so I can talk with you and you deserve to hear. I think we must be a little alike. Some people are. I mean, everyone is as he must be and that is not like anyone else, but at first I was the same, like standing water without waves. My mother was a servant and I was her illegitimate child, so that all through my childhood I was mute in a closed room where a single bed stood against walls lined with trunks and hand-down clothes. It wasn't too nice, you know. I was afraid of moving, of looking into the great rooms, afraid the children would say something to me, knowing my birthday was a secret Mother was afraid to let out to people she worked for, because that would have been like begging, until at last no one ever gave us anything, neither at Christmas, nor any other time. But that isn't important and . . . "I must be boring you."

No: what I want to say is that I learned then, in secret and without words, in the middle of my long childhood, I learned how to wait, and that is the same as saying, to be a woman (it isn't a woman to ask, to beg, to cause trouble, those aren't women, they never will be, they're bodies like rats with skins too soft that at the least flush of heat become scaly and stained; a woman has to wait, silent, without opening her lips, to wait for the moments of pain and the moments when she will be called, without asking to be called), and that I learned, not with words, I tell you, nor very clearly, but with certainty and deep in the silent places.

"My mother, a very humble woman, saved a little, Señor Cienfuegos. Peace had come. (I was born in nineteen hundred eighteen.) I was already too large, too backward, when I began to go to school. I learned to read and write, and then I learned to type. All of a sudden there were more opportunities for people like me."

But that separated mother and me even more. She was still

wearing *rebozos* and old skirts wrinkled from hanging on nails and her aprons, and her dry brown face never had make-up and her onion skin temples and her thick hairknot, and now I could wear stockings and use lipstick and go to movies and see how the stars dressed and talk with a different class of people. But that was later. Before there were only the stone kitchens with smells and braziers and spice-mortars and glazed tiles in the home I grew up in more than anywhere, Señora de Ovando's, I would spy on Señorita Pimpinela and later go out, trying to imitate her and to dress like her.

"Do you remember the furs they wore in those days? The linen skirts and the little hats like boxes or the ones with wide wings. And I wanted them, for who wouldn't have, and that was why I decided to go to school, and I started work as a waitress to pay for my studies."

No: my mother didn't understand. She believed that our place was fixed, that we had already done too much, fleeing from a village in Hidalgo to Mexico City without the least idea of what we would do here, she pregnant and I like a warm seed inside her, to look for work; she believed we were good enough as we were, that I ought to stay in my place and station and not go trying to sew myself clothes like those Pimpinela had, and far less I should go to work in a Chinese café surrounded by disrespectful men. And then, I, Hortensia Chacón, face Indian but very lovely, thin-featured but with thick lips, skinny but with good legs, met him.

"My husband, you know. One of those robust strong men who are not very tall, with curly hair and a thick mustache. There should be a photo of him there."

He wore a coat and necktie, and that was for me, his coat and tie, and he came into the café to drink a cup of coffee with milk when he finished work in the Treasury Department. How can I explain how he loved me? Yes: I went on, feeling new in spite of everything, and it was like finding a city, like finding this city, to notice where we were; forgetting everything to fly across rooftops and come down to rest a moment in a neighborhood movie, in Chapultepec Park, in a fair where you could have your fortune

274

told; and that was why I married him and had his children. We had three children. They must be grown now. I waited for him to take me to the movies and the fortuneteller again. What is it we wait for, *Señor?* I don't know. We wait only for something that can't happen again. Then why that memory? There are two or three: the moment before a kiss, the moment after giving birth; those moments I would have liked to make large so that the others, the endless moments which in point of fact form our lives, might be made little. But now life was different, I was a married woman who only waited (and that, as I told you, I had already learned to do), but needed to wait for something without losing it, and to know that they don't want what we have been waiting for and that waiting hasn't helped us and they don't even want us to wait: that was Donaciano, my husband. He never let me know that he knew I had been waiting, and maybe he could never have given me anything except to know that he knew, or saw, just saw, that I was waiting for what he could never give me; no, he was silence, fleshed silence (yes, even when his body felt itself vibrating inside me until he believed himself excited, but could accomplish only a sweaty and mechanical exercise), voice-silent, impatient to get back to his friends and drink himself half drunk without happiness or pity and without ever reaching himself through the liquor, reaching what ought to have been a drunkard of a man, horrible and glistening, and not dragging and ashamed as he was, or his love with another woman, who ought also to have been cold, but talkative. That is what he wanted of women, he went in search of talk more than sex, he looked for talk because talk could lift and carry him, and with it, he could impress his circle of friends, prestige and praise, but with sex alone he could have neither of these because it is consumed in a second, between two alone, and can never be recovered; it is too bitter to give prestige, too small and cruel to impress anyone; it comes back and yet it stays inside, to cure the deep wound it causes: there we know what we are. And I wanted to know what he was, waited for some truth from his touch. Or his shouts at a bullfight, hidden among thousands of heads far above the shining marionette who dominated him, dominated the

275

bull, the marionette who did not hear his dirty insults. Or his occasional fist fights just for the sake of fighting. And who were they, he and his friends; did they understand that their lives were poses, that that was how they showed that they existed? Maybe Donaciano when he would come home with his eyes shining believed that I was going to understand the new prestige he had gained by every shouted insult, every slap, every whore, every bar (but he had to suspect that I didn't, that I just waited for something very small and warm, a kiss, the fortunetellers at the fair, a movie, something that had nothing to do with the prestige he drained from his circle of friends); and that was how he violated me, he demanded everything of my body, he raped me with a force twisted out of its course to offer me the glory of his maleness through a mechanical and cold exercise . . . thinking, he, that the next day he would go back to a table and an archive where he would have to take orders and nobody would know about his stud prowess; that was what he must have been thinking every time he went to bed with me, because every time he was weaker, but just the same he never said anything to me, he didn't weep, he didn't want to face any truth, didn't want to confess himself a poor devil . . . which was what might have saved him, in spite of my disillusionment. He might have recovered something, two fingers of my love and two more of my respect; but a man like that never learns, he just goes on looking for dishonesty and false proofs, and so he never forgave me when I went to find him when my mother died, to his office, moldy and hidden, to ask money to bury her, and he just felt that not one of his pretexts was any good; there he was, only a minor employee who could not fornicate with the file cabinets nor get drunk with the water cooler nor punch his boss in the face; I saw him through his own eyes, in the desperate movements of his hands as he scribbled on bits of paper to hide his insignificance. Yes, I felt tender, but also disgusted; I couldn't, even if I had wanted to, tolerate his impudent puffed-up voice saying, This is no funeral parlor, get on out of here! That was the only way he knew how to make himself important, you see.

"I took everything from my husband, Señor Cienfuegos, but there came a moment when . . ."

"You never told . . ."

"No, not to his face. God forbid that I say it ever. Today I hate him and I would give anything if I could tell him the truth and call him liar. But I say it now as a dream of blasphemy in an empty temple. Don't make me ashamed, Señor."

That's how he was. Expenses went up and up and he didn't give me anything. There were five in the family now, remember; the oldest was growing up now and beginning to wear make-up; Chanito, who used to make up stories and tell them to me, dedicate them to me, who understood everything, and was my support in the last days; and the baby Severo, who died afterward: we were five, and that was why I told my husband that I would go to work, too. After all, I had studied typing. He was foolish again, looking for something that was neither in his life nor in what he was, something male to use in replying to me. "Just be quiet, you; don't you go out, it looks as if you don't have a husband and children, looks as if I don't work like a nigger, like I don't give you what I have. Looks like you are beginning to doubt I can support this home. Looks like you think I don't know the truth, that all you want to do is chain me down. Money don't mean anything to you! What you want is to keep me shut up here; you can't stand having a real man near you, you're dry, dry, dry, you can't come with me and I can come with you and with three bitches to boot." That's what he said to me . . .

"I went looking for work, Señor, and I found it. And when I got work, I took the kids and left, and he couldn't stand that."

Not because he loved us or because he needed us. Just because he needed an echo, because it was important to him for us to know about his drunks and his whoring, and that's how I explain what he did—he did it to have another echo, for someone to admire. That was the life my poor Donaciano had, and the last time I saw him was the first time I believe that he saw he could alienate me forever and realized that I, the silent woman who had waited, was stronger than he, could stand more than he (I who had stood violation and humiliation and disrepute and the tales of his uncleanness and whoring), that I was more man than he because I supported what was mine and his too, and only would not support his life as a half pariah, while he needed only to talk and his strength fled and not even in his dirty and drowsy coitus could he recover his life, but only new drunkenness, new fornications; he knew, and I saw it in his face the instant before he shouted and raised his hands to my eyes . . .

"A moment came, *Señor*, when I couldn't take any more. And because of that, he wanted revenge."

Hortensia slowly adjusted her dark glasses and almost smiled a little. Ixca Cienfuegos waited for her words, smelling the perfume of the flowers on the little bookcase.

In the hospital . . . all I thought about was what was the use of it all. Just that. My friends from the office paid for the doctors and took care of the children. Then my boss came. I didn't know him until then. I remember so clearly his soft voice wishing me well and assuring me that I would not need anything. He came back, I didn't know why, for I had left all that. He came back to ask me what had happened, and I told him, as I have tried to tell you. I began to wait for his voice, his presence, how shall I say it? like blessed bread, bitter bread, too, which obliged me to realize what had happened, not to forget, but to know the precise areas of my love and hatred. Before, with Donaciano, I had lived alone; never with Federico. Maybe it would be easier to stand solitude. Not to be alone is to die of shame, that's what Federico, without knowing it himself, because he lives alone, alone, what he has taught me. He has also told me his story, his childhood, his wife, and from what he told me I learned about myself, my life and my mimicking of Señorita Pimpinela and my longing for certain gone moments of love and my memory of my smelly girl-hood in kitchens and then the children, and everything, *Señor*, everything that I have wanted to tell you, but simpler and clearer. That I wanted to wait (this is what I have tried to say) for a man who would make me wait, that I didn't want to be everything for him, didn't expect that of him or of anyone, but only for him to be worthy of my waiting; a man who would know how to fight my battles for me instead of making me the narrow path of his defeats, you see (and not count over his minutes of vexation, but let me know them in silence, not make me the echo of his life among men, but that he would come home heavy and erect to my moment of accumulated longing and blind hope). Blind. They both wanted that, Donaciano, who blinded me, and Federico, who sought me blind. Who has made me long for the sight of his face and body, who has given me love while describing me to myself and telling me about the light that comes through the venetian blinds while we lie together, what appearance the light gives to my forehead and mouth, and I can only hear and touch and wait, waiting for something that with a penetrating erect strength, and without excuses, but respectful of me, tells me exactly what I am; and he has never raised me, nor buried me, but loved me as I am, just so, with my memories and my eyes more ashen than the center of the sun, and my hopes. To as much as I am he gives me his man's love. His love and also his hate. Yes, he has taken me away from my children. He pays for where they are, but that isn't the same. Maybe that's why I hate him, and I have told him. But he likes that . . . my love and my hate; the first alone would be only half my life; he taught me to hate Donaciano, to reconcile myself to the thought of his going to prison, to think about the revenge I have had. But Federico's brutality is sweet, you know. It's the brutality I deserve and want, and that's all it is, and I know that his true big brutality he confines to his doings with men, to the uses he makes of the people around him. The world which at last will be Federico's and mine is right here, believe me. Not yet, for Federico is not yet what in reality he is, but what life has made him. Like me. But behind, *Señor*, behind there is the true face. When Federico recognizes that I exist, *Señor*, that at least one person is alive outside him, outside what he has been, then he will become what he has to be, yes. That's the world I have wanted. He deserves no other, and I am full, full to offer it to him, to be everything he tells me that I am now: she who offers him something and not she to whom he offers. What is it that I give him? you wonder. I have never dared to ask him; it is part of what he looks for now that I don't ask nor try to enter his other

279

life. But I know, just the same, for my dry eyes sometimes flower again and create a mirror in which are born, more than reflections, troubled birds who circle behind my eyelids, wedded to the center of my viscera, and the city comes back to me, Mexico City which has gendered me and given me my life, has seen me run over its streets, drop my children on its floors, climb aboard its buses and question its nights without ever giving up the memory I ask of it, speaking to me always in sensations of warm and rotted things; I feel it so, *Señor*, and I turn to the air and the smell and touch which are left to me . . . to Federico, no, although he is air and smell and touch for me, and I ask them, What is it I give him? Is it darkness, the darkness where Federico Robles can find his light?

Hortensia coughed and moved her wheel chair forward. She decided, bitterly, to break the silence, and she said, "I'm sure he hasn't talked about me. How did you find out? What do you want of me? What are you doing here?"

TO CLIMB THE PRICKLY PEAR TREE

New dawn, new city. City with neither memory nor presentiment of headland, afloat on its tar river, nears the falls of its own decomposition. Atop dawn and the jointless timbers of the city's skeleton, Cienfuegos walked: from the red fortress of Vicaínas to the season of foundations and trinket shops on San Juan de Letran, tunnel where all the rags and hulls of the night before whirled to the brutal roar of what spoke nothing: bodies and papers, cabaret echoes and feet shuffling along sidewalks and parchment hands caressing fallen wombs, from Meave to Barba Azul to Bandida, opening three or four times during the night to make change for seventy or a hundred and fifty pesos, bruised juiceless fruit; to Madero, at this hour a museum of iron-shuttered windows, broken into by the deep fragrant hope of the marigolds of San Francisco and by the bolt-erect forgetfulness of the Palacio de Iturbe. Cienfuegos strolled as was his habit: hands in the pockets of his black raincoat, eyes focused upon distance and drawn nearer only when the inevitable architecture or a solitary human—street cleaner, cop, teen-aged kid, black-clad old woman—crossed the flat plane of his vision: Sanborn's, High Life, María Pavigani, Pastelandia, American Book, the Rex, Marzal, Kodak, RCA, Calpini, Kimberley, the Hotel Ritz. This was the city's hour. Under steel-gray light; only the essential, the profile, the pattern, alien alike to the terror and lie of other hours beneath sun or moon. Hour of the moment before resurrection. And Ixca was the notarized witness on these daybreak walks; from his curved fingers he could feel the spark flash which would put everything in movement, and today he asked of his fingers only that a final image be fixed. He believed that his blood knew the truth about Rodrigo, Norma, Robles. Norma and Rodrigo were now en route to their final masquerades. Robles was the inscrutable, the enemy, the master of the new world before which Norma and Rodrigo knelt; he who more than anything was slave to and rebel against himself: the Great (Decent) Bastard, the only one of them who had known or sensed worlds vaster in origin and in contrast to the world which today incinerated them all. And what was Robles's true beginning? Ixca, pausing at the corner of Madero and Palma to light a cigarette, knew that in some way it had to be something so simple that he, Ixca, would never understand it. The dark marginal life which Hortensia Chacón offered was a substitute, at most the faint reflection of the original. The use of power described by Librado Ibarra and also, in a different way, by Robles himself, was only a flight which presupposed a form, from that same obscure beginning. And at the end of that beginning, Ixca felt now, there the battle would be fought and one of them would win, either Robles, or Cienfeugos and Teódula. There, in the heart of thorns. Day collected authority. He looked about him and thought of the many open eyes, near his own. Thoughtful eyes precipitating morning and their concealed destinies. He walked on.

On Berlín Street in Colonia Juárez, in an apartment of velvet and varnish and veneered cabinets and perennials, Pimpinela de Ovando's eyes were touched by sunlight and opened. Norma

281

Robles had come back from Acapulco burned to a cinder, burned free of the trite family fantasy that had made her lick up to Pimpinela, feeling new strength in her limbs, a little wasted and skinny, but tense and vigorous as birth; had returned to tell Pimpinela that Benjamín had been fired from the bank and that she hoped that she, Pimpi, and the whole starving crew of them would die of hunger and get it over with; that was what she had said, and then she had arched an eyebrow: "And I know about your hacienda now, precious. If you think your rubbing up to Roberto Régules and pimping for his wife will help you, you're wrong. Federico fought in the Revolution for a reason, after all, and you won't be able to change him. I'm just letting you know. Better forget it, baby, because what Federico is going to let the newspapers say about you won't be nice."

Pimpinela had not been able to speak as she wanted to, with sarcasm, negligently, because Norma, skinny and brown and sprawled on the divan in a loose beach robe, gave no opportunity for the usual treatment, no opening for it to be used. Pimpinela did not understand the gratuitousness of Norma's new attitude. Contact between them had always been clear and well defined, upon the ground of their respective self-interests. Now everything was gratuitous, including Norma's quick following words. "Look, baby-girl. I'm not really from one of your snob old families. My father was a shopkeeper in the north and my mother was a vulgar old woman whom you saw once a long time ago, at the train station, do you remember? And you thought she was one of my servants. My brother dug rock in a mine all his life and now he's a wetback farmhand, and how does that make you feel? Because in spite of all your titles and your colonial ancestors, sweetheart, I'm more than you are. I'm on top now and you are on the bottom. And that fizzled-out old aunt of yours is no more than a servant herself, for all her deep blue blood, just as much a servant as my bedroom maid."

It seemed more unreal to Pimpinela, this uncomplicated truth, than the accepted fiction . . . lost haciendas, a great family in decay. Pimpinela felt that she would never again be able to say to Aunt Lorenza: Norma is a ragtail and her husband is a savage from god knows what jungle. Never again, for that was the truth, the confessed truth, with all its implications of poverty and penny-pinching for Pimpinela when Norma, with a fury Pimpi could not understand, rushed on, "Maybe you didn't know that my husband's parents were peons on your uncle's hacienda? Yes: and now you, all of you, are Federico's peons! *Ja!* What flip-flops, sweetheart. And so I tell you. But really peons, because your cretin nephew lost his job today and you'll just go on waiting to get your land back until mules grow wings."

Pimpinela, erect, felt all her never-spoken breathed-in precepts of good breeding, the sanctity and the mark of the de Ovandos, spin around inside her head, and she realized that they hadn't the least practical application, could not be appealed to, were forever used up and worn out; with no way to turn, she let her body slump and said, "But we need the land to live. Aunt Lorenza is very old, you know, and Joaquinito has never worked. How will they live? A thousand pesos means a lot to them. Think: they had everything, it's as if you were to lose everything tomorrow."

Norma's laughter, full, resonant, triumphant and enjoying it, boomed again in Pimpinela's head as she woke in sunlight on Berlín Street in Colonia Juárez.

"And what are you doing these days, darling?"

Norma had asked him to meet her in the Nicte-Ha. A maid had telephoned, and at first Rodrigo had decided not to go, to stand her up; he had sat at home the hour before their date, working on his second script—*Pasión Truncada* had now entered its last week of shooting—and savoring her waiting for him to appear, until at seven he had suddenly felt eagerness and a hope which did not leave him until he entered the bar and in the half shadow saw her unmistakable glow, her imperious demand for homage, her invariable condescension. "And what are you doing these days, darling?"

And he, instead of telling her, or perhaps it was really his peculiar way of telling her, had said what he had said the last time. "Oh, I don't know . . . I write a little . . ."

And again, as before, she had clapped her gloved hands behind a veil of smoke. "What are you drinking, darling?"

"A martini."

"Ah, and it always used to be orange crush!" And for the first time before her face, and without wanting to, Rodrigo's expression had shown distaste, while he narrowed his eyes and looked around the room at people concealed by shadows. "What, didn't I amuse you?"

"Oh, you have always amused me, Norma."

"I don't see how you can find anything very diverting, squatting in your eternal poverty. Aren't you ever going to do anything about it, don't you have any ambition at all, *ja?*"

"What am I offered?" Rodrigo felt that for the first time, his sonorous dialectic, so often polished and refined in solitude with only his hot plate and teakettle for audience, was about to be useful. To pretend to be a poor devil . . . then to astonish her by the sudden truth of what he really and gloriously now was. "Excuse me, Norma. I have no right to speak to you so. We have come—you understand me—to the last wall, where dignity vanishes. Where, to put it baldly, there is nothing to eat . . ."

"Darling, but that's why I wanted to see you today! A time comes when generosity is obligatory, don't you know, and the past is forgotten. Suddenly we remember that we have old friends like you to whom life hasn't been very kind, who deserve our compassion and help. I could talk to Federico, if you are interested, old man. I could suggest that he give you a good job. Of course, you aren't ambitious, so you'll be satisfied with almost anything, it doesn't have to pay much, just be secure. Suppose you knew that every fifteen days . . ." Norma's eyes were lost behind a swirl of smoke. One arm was on the table and her smile seemed frozen in the mask of the good Samaritan with *arrière-pensé.*

"Yes, Norma, that's true," Rodrigo replied, affecting an imitation of her eager manner. "With that I could be happy. And maybe some afternoon you would honor me by having a drink with me . . . you paying, of course."

Norma laughed. "Well, *tu,* I don't know. You know I have so many friendships, very demanding ones, of another type altogether . . ."

"Of course, I understand. Still, we could see each other alone, couldn't we? With the salary I would get from your husband, I could rent a better apartment and you could visit me there, we would be alone together just as when we were kids. And I would be very careful to do things just the way you like them. . . . I recognize in myself a certain mimetic talent, at least . . . and with your refinement, a table set for two, champagne, Cole Porter playing softly. *Life* advertisement style, you know. And after the meal you could take your clothes off slowly as the candles burned down, and I would squat and lick your ass, you bitch."

The waiter appeared. Unchanged both in voice and manner, Norma ordered Rodrigo's drink. She unhurriedly repinned her hair and sipped her sugar-rimmed drink.

"As I told you, very demanding friendships, of another type. To whom you don't even compare, *tu.*"

Rodrigo lowered his head. A pianist's fingers began to dance over a keyboard while a group of youths with their long hair in ringlets entered the bar and moved, hands in pockets and with swaying hips, their eyes cold, cigarettes dangling from the corners of their mouths, to barstools. Several middle-aged American women stared invitations at them and silently drank.

"Before," said Rodrigo, "before, do you remember, we never needed to hurt each other with words."

Norma wrinkled her nose. "Who's hurt? You think you ever hurt me? *Ja!* You still worry about an affair between a couple of adolescent monkeys."

But Rodrigo was talking again without hearing her reply. "How did it begin? Do you remember?"

"*Ja!* You tell me."

Rodrigo rubbed an eyelid. "Your uncle was a blond, very solemn Spaniard, the head of the linen department in the store where my mother worked. One day he called her in and asked her to invite me to a fiesta in your honor. Yes. I remember very clearly that at first I refused to go. I hadn't ever gone to such a party and I didn't know how to dance. But mother begged me, she said I must do it for her sake, to understand her position in the store."

"Gooses, both of you. And my uncle! He would have liked to see me stuck there forever, a pretty, vulgar little——"

"I took a long time dressing. Combed, and combed again, looked at myself in the mirror. Your home was in Colonia Juárez, near the corner with Reforma . . . what was the street?"

"*Ja!*"

"And I walked slowly, walked from Chopo, hesitating on corners, until the very last minute still undecided——"

"You don't change, darling."

"I was nineteen, Norma. You can't deny that I——"

"Oh, now you're even worse."

"Your little home was all lights. I heard a popular song . . ." Rodrigo smiled and hummed and then sang softly, "*Heaven . . . I'm in heaven* . . . So I tried to arch an eyebrow." He smiled again, as if Norma's mimicking arched eyebrow and pout were not in front of him. "I tried to assume a worldly man-about-town air, and then I went in. The boys were laughing together in a corner and sneaking looks at the girls, who were all in a line against the wall in those high straight-backed chairs and their rose and blue dresses, with their hands twisting their handkerchiefs——"

"They haven't changed either," Norma laughed.

"The victrola was playing, but no one dared to dance, and then your uncle told me that you were about to come down and that this was your birthday. I went on drinking punch with one eyebrow arched. Then you appeared. . . ."

"Little Lulu!" Norma swished her drink nervously.

"With your green eyes and your blonde hair, wearing a low-cut beige dress."

She put her drink down hard on the table. "Now be quiet. You think I'm the same? Look at my face and tell me? Is there anything left of that——"

"You smiled and said *hello* to us with a fresh smile. We were introduced, but you didn't speak, you just went on smiling as you drank your punch. Then you said that we ought to have met a long time ago, that you had heard a lot about me and my poetry."

"Brother of my soul! But how ordinary!"

"And I didn't know what to say. The whole world outside my classes and my writer friends was new to me, and what I finally said was that what you had just told me was like discovering that someone could hear me——"

"Don't remind me. What I had to do! Believe me, you were a blank."

". . . and could tell me things that made me happy. Then, more easily, I told you that my poetry didn't amount to much, and you said that I was so young and already famous, take a look at the kids standing there in the corner . . ."

"They aren't ambitious, eh?"

"Yes. Then you invited me to dance and I told you I didn't know how to and you placed my arms, always smiling, and put your hand on my neck, you squeezed me and led me. I just smelled your hair. I wanted to tell you that with you I could speak, bring out things, say what I was really thinking, and that if we didn't want to talk, it was enough just to be the way we were together, that in itself said everything."

"You ought to write advice to the lovelorn, lover."

"Then you invited me to walk in the garden, that little garden overstuffed with palms, and you lifted your arms and told me that the important thing was just one person, that it was good to have parties in order to meet someone with whom you could forget the others. Do you remember? And I told you I thought so, too, that——"

"Now tell me a pirate story."

"I took you around the waist and you leaned your head against my shoulder."

"You'll kill me laughing, baby-doll."

"I told you that one knew right away and it wasn't this or that idea that mattered, but a person, and you put your chin on my tie and asked me to come back to see you soon, and not to make any promises I wouldn't keep. I said 'Look at me, let me

287

see your eyes,' and you repeated my name. I just took your hands. I squeezed them, I moved your head against my cheek and lifted your face and felt as if my words were going into your mouth, and I begged you to let me be the first. You only repeated, 'I love you, I love you,' and you didn't let me say anything as you opened your lips and . . .'

All the noise of the bar, which Rodrigo had pushed aside, came back in a cataract of submerged words and clinking glasses and strident laughter. "Shut up!" Norma shouted. "You don't even know how to tell it! You've blown up an unhappy crush between teen-agers to I don't know——"

"I tell you just what I feel, that's all."

Norma looped her stole around sun-browned shoulders. "You didn't feel a damn thing. You made up what you felt the same way you make up everything, that you're a great writer, that you're going to save the world, God knows what next!"

He would have enjoyed a mirror. "And you?"

"I'm quick, boy, and you are lead-ass," said Norma, shoving her face at him with the same gratuitous ferocity she had shown before Pimpinela. "I knew that all you'd be good for was to feel me up a little. Now I know it better than ever. All you want to do is to think yourself so goody-good, the nice poor little boy who won't even hurt a fly."

"But your hands, your lips, everything——"

"Ah?" Norma curled her lips. "So you want it straight? Sure, I could have loved you, if you had let me. I can love anyone, it's a matter of will. If you had mastered me, or had let me master you; but you didn't want that, did you? You wanted to please yourself, yourself alone, to make your little nickels with me and then go and hide and feel very satisfied. But alone. You wanted the tickle, that's all. If you had had the guts to make me, I would have been very satisfied with you."

Rodrigo played with matches. "No, don't lie," he said. "It was all my poverty."

"In a pig's eye! Sure, I began to want money, but only later and only because I was never offered anything else. You didn't want to be mine . . . you wanted to be the savior of mankind,

288

with no real life of your own, and you wanted me to be only the sexless witness of your moral grandeur! Your great goodness! Your holy talent! You never told me, 'I'm going to master you or if not, you'll master me.' That's the difference between a pantywaist like you and a real man like Federico. He made me submit to him, he has always shown me, even by his indifference, that he has the money and the strength to subdue me. You, when?"

The author of *Lavender Verse* was aware of his pitiful figure, his false manner, everything that several weeks of success had not yet erased. "That's not true, Norma, I swear it isn't true. It was real. There's nothing more real than love, because it insists on the real presence of the person who is loved. That's what it demands. Only hatred can exist with unrealities, Norma, not love."

"There you are. You've said it yourself. You talk about the real presence, *ja!* When did you ever have my *real presence.* You went on making dreams."

"It's not so." Rodrigo wanted to overcome his sniveling tone. He was no different than at nineteen, when she had left word that for him she was not at home, and he had gone on telephoning just the same and had hung around the little house in Colonia Juárez and then the big one in the Lomas. "I kept finding you in other women, they were always you . . . your face, your body . . ."

The waiter drew near. Norma indicated with her fingers that she wanted their check. "Well, I didn't come here to offer you a shoulder to cry on, but a job, so you won't starve to death. Wise up, Rodrigo. This is a city of women who look out for number one, and every man who wants to can have his chance, but he's got to have dough. Men are making fortunes every day, and that fine green stuff is what you need. Throw your past in the trash, baby, and take aim all over. You'll see what happens when the women smell your money. And then all of a sudden you'll forget me, eh? Well, you want the job?"

Rodrigo let Norma pay the check. He walked behind her to the Juárez door. "My car's on Balderas," Norma said. "Can I drop you somewhere?"

The doorman of the Hotel del Prado was opening the door of a Jaguar convertible with leather upholstery and chrome handles. "No, here is mine, but thanks," said Rodrigo with a smile which was at least the smile of his richness and victory, the smile longed for all his life. Nothing else, he was thinking, this is all I want, *this* moment in front of *this* woman. Norma's face was a balm to cure him of all nostalgia, all soul-sickness. A newspaperboy ran between them, chanting, "Read all about the big bank-ruptcy! Famous banker has . . ." He lost her in the night on Avenida Juárez. He breathed deep, with his eyes he hugged the lights, the unsymmetrical walls, the avenue's canyon of prosperity. He got into the automobile which Evrahim, with unparalleled generosity, had given him as an advance on future movie scripts.

"No, they're not going to destroy me," said Federico Robles, in his shirt-sleeves, a swirl of secretaries and documents and lawyers all bent around his fat figure. "Once I said it to Norma, Cienfuegos, and today I say it to you: If I'm out in the street today, tomorrow I'll have my fortune again! You'll see!"

The imploring or authoritative voices of lawyers drowned him out. ". . . the declaration must apply to all departments . . ."

"Here's your sandwich, *Licenciado* . . ."

". . . if you want the union to . . ."

". . . I'll read it to you: Article four hundred thirty-seven . . ."

"Licenciado Régules called . . ."

"Ah!" cried Robles, waving a paper in the air. "Now he comes out of hiding, the vulture! Well, let him wise up, there's no welcome here except for his whore mother. If he thinks I'm going to fall over and . . ."

"Fiscal credits against current taxes . . . expenses of liquidation . . . general expenses . . ."

"Tell him that he's been a phony all his life, and if he thinks he . . . tell him that his mother can . . . !"

". . . privileged creditors, to whom . . ."

Robles whirled. His broken voice roared, "Out! Out of here, all of you! Go to the devil with you! Leave me alone!"

290

The door closed on the last lawyer and his rigidity trembled before eager peace and silence and loneliness. His body shrank. He fell on the sofa. Ixca, standing, observed him.

"A king forgets how to cook!" He stirred his body. An arm fell to the floor. "In Mexico you don't kill a man this way, Cienfuegos. Not this way, with newspaper lies and gossip, with the handiest slander. No, by God, not this way. Let them come at me face to face. Let them give me something to fight back against, like men. But not this."

From his stiff height Cienfuegos said, "Have you ever given your enemies that chance?"

Robles's head snapped up as if jerked by a spring. "What do you mean? I haven't done more or less than any other businessman. I never hurt anybody. Yes, I know what you're thinking. When you brought me the news that the Monterrey crowd were getting ready to sell out, I was pleased, Cienfuegos, I took you into my confidence, I trusted you with serious matters and I followed your advice to hit them first. Is that what you're throwing up to me now?" His head fell back again. "I've told you the story of my life. I come from a cornpatch, Cienfuegos, and I've come by hard work and ambition, with no help from anybody. So I have been industrious and the others drowsy? Sure, that's the whole story of the country in two words. That's all there is."

Cienfuegos smiled. Robles groaned and sat up on the leather sofa. His yellow skin was splotched like old marble. "The reporters will descend on me in a little while and this place will be hell. Look, there's a cheap restaurant nearby, on Aquiles Serdán. Wait for me there and we'll have a drink together and I'll quiet down. I'll be with you in just a few minutes."

Ixca walked along Avenida Juárez toward Bellas Artes. Manuel Zamacona came out of the sunken entrance to the palace, books under his arms. Alameda trees swayed. People were leaving offices and stores without aliveness, weighted with nameless indifference which did not even have the rebellion-flaming spark of injustice about it, shuffling, shuffling, shuffling along sidewalks. Newspaper stands were being folded up, long lines were waiting for buses: Lindavista, Mariscal Sucre, Lomas, Pensil. Manuel greeted Cienfuegos: "A round-table discussion of Mexican literature. It is necessary to mention the serapes of Saltillo, was Franz Kafka the tool of Wall Street, is social literature anything more than the eternal triangle between two Stajanovitches and a tractor, if we are not the more universal the more Mexican we are, and vice versa, should we write like Marxists or like Buddhists. Many prescriptions, zero books."

Cienfuegos took Manuel's arm. "Come along and have coffee."

"Sure."

Zamacona was shorter than Cienfuegos, and the books and the rolled raincoat under his arm made him seem round and little. Only his large, strong head with its fine profile set him apart from any other mestizos of medium height and strengthless body who might happen to be passing. "Look, Guardini, the Labyrinth of Solitude, Alfonso Reyes, Nerval," he said in front of the Banco Nacional de Mexico, touching the books. "And why? Our cultural life is a perpetual *status quo*, just like our political life. Only the *bourgeoisie* moves and moves again, works forward, takes the country over. In ten more years we'll be a country controlled by plutocrats, you'll see. And the intellectuals, who could be a moral counterpoint to this force that is overpowering us—well, they're deader than the fears of a raped virgin. There was a time when the Revolution was identified with intellectualism, just as it was also identified with the workers' movement. But when the Revolution stopped being a revolution, both intellectuals and workers discovered that they had become official, with . . . aw, the hell with it all! Fuck it all."

Manuel's laughter reverberated from the almost orange walls of the Post Office Department's Venetian palace. Ixca Cienfuegos smiled with him, for in Mexico it is in bad taste not to take your own shortcomings as a joke. Trolleys moved along Tacuba. Another palace, this one Mines; the echo of firecrackers where students were demanding vacation in advance. They entered the café. An aggressive smell of Flit ran along the gallery of booths faintly illuminated by the dying green light of neon tubes. Neither the showy *à la* United States hygiene nor the conventual stink, the sense of being in a convent given by the old

Mexican coffees, freed the place; it had no necessity at all, but simply was, and Zamacona associated it with the mongrel dog, bred of all strains, which ran among the tables, sniffing the holey linolcum floor.

"What will the intellectuals of Mexico do the day the debate begins?" Manuel smiled, letting his books and raincoat fall on the table in a heap. "For the day is coming, Ixca, when men are going to ask just that. No mass demonstrations, no bullets, nor even that the P.R.I. give way to the opposition. No, just that things can be said openly, that public figures can be discussed, and also social problems. P.R.I. candidates will continue to become presidents, as always. That's not the problem. What the public wants and will demand more every day is that the final candidate not be selected by a conclave of ex-presidents. They'll demand freedom to discuss men and our problems. Our sold-out press obviously doesn't help much. And the intellectuals are either the silliest Marxists in the world or men who believe it is more important to do serious work and thinking, even in exile, than to dirty one's hands with public affairs so stupid and automatic as ours."

A bovine waiter came near, scratching his balls, and Ixca ordered two cups of coffee. "There is always one more step that no one can avoid: violation," he said, with his mouth twisted a little. "Repeated lessons from the past aren't enough, we always have to take that one more step."

"And this is a country which has been violated too many times, is that what you mean?" said Zamacona, blinking as he lit a cigarette.

"No." Ixca's voice was a monotone, as if his true voice had become too faint. "Just once. Always once."

"When?"

"When it forgot that the first decision is the last one." Ixca's voice was too thick now, Zamacona was thinking, too conscious of some quality which Ixca had attributed to himself for no sound reason. "There is only the first decision. All the others are disguises."

Zamacona wanted to penetrate Ixca's obvious disguise. "What first decision?"

"The decision of the first Mexico, the Mexico tied to its own umbilicus, the Mexico which was actually an incarnation of ritual, which was actually created in an act of faith, which——"

"Which was actually under the heel of a bloody despotism concealed by a satanic theology," Manuel interrupted.

Ixca looked at him with a certain amused disdain. "And power today? In a few minutes Federico Robles is going to join us. Today he exercises . . . or at least he did exercise . . . power. You think his cheap market-place power which lacks all greatness is better than a power which at least had the imagination to ally itself with the great forces, permanent and inviolable, of the cosmos? With the sun itself? I tell you, I would rather be immolated on a sacrifice table than under the shit of cheating capitalists and lying newspapers."

The cups of coffee came, oily and steaming. Zamacona refused sugar. "Yes, I read the paper this morning. I'd like to know what a man like Robles loses. What he gives up——"

"Gives up?"

Manuel sipped the bitter coffee with displeasure. "Yes. I'd like to know whether his character really depends upon the power which has been snapped away from him today, or if there is something more, a real strength that won't let him fall no matter how he is shaken. That's what it matters to me to know, not the fact that Robles has gone under. For me," Zamacona said with a light smile, "Federico Robles happens to be a living man."

Cienfuegos's hand signaled that Robles was entering. The waiter bumped against the banker and called out, "Watch out there, look where you're walking there!" Robles smiled drily. He sat in front of Cienfuegos, beside Manuel. His aging, leathery, thick eye pouches contrasted with the brilliance of his barbed eyes. "Yes, the *Señor* and I have met. Now you see, eh, Cienfuegos." He dropped his hat at his side. "Neither clothing nor manner has changed, but even a waiter knows that I am no longer the great man. Watch out there, look where you're . . . not for many years has anyone spoken to me that way."

"It's a cheap joint for cheap customers," said Ixca.

"And I, too, am cheap again. It took me a long time to harden my shell. Well, I know Zamacona, so we can talk. You see how quickly a front collapses. To that waiter, I'm only a drowsy fat Indian who steps on his corns. It's hard to give a kingdom up, Cienfuegos."

"Is it harder for him who has everything to give up everything, or him who has nothing?" grunted Manuel, twisting to look first at Robles and then immediately at Cienfuegos.

"No, I'm not talking about physical things. Neither house nor car matters to me. What I'm giving up is power, do you understand that? Power which I created. Without me, without Robles's hands building and building these past thirty years, there wouldn't be anything, not even the possibility of renunciation. Without *us*, I mean, the little circle of the powerful, everything would have been lost in the country's traditional lethargy."

"The Revolution?" asked Zamacona.

"Yes, the Revolution. You both know how it began, and I lived it. Without a program or clear ideas, without purposes . . . no matter what my friend Zamacona may think. With leaders who were more picturesque than leaderly, who just happened to rise. Without true revolutionary tactics or thought. I agree that much was lost and betrayed. But something was saved, and we saved it."

"You, the efficient ones," said Ixca.

"Yes, *Señor*, those who were efficient. Carranza and Calles against men who would have led us to disaster: Zapata or Villa. Those who could build on top of apathy and laziness. Those of us who were willing to dirty our hands . . ."

Ixca found himself recalling, without wanting to, the scenes Robles had told him about: the battlefield of Celaya.

"Those of us who were willing to lick ass for those above us and to step on the necks of those beneath us. Who were willing to sacrifice a part of our dignity in order to save something more important. And am I going to give it all up now?"

Shining and sharp as the profile of a hatchet, Ixca's face pushed toward Robles. "Give up everything when you possess everything! That's easy. The terrible renunciation will come later, when you have to give up everything without having anything."

"Go to the devil," Robles grunted. "Not even God demands so much."

"God," murmured Zamacona.

"Of course." Robles swelled his chest. "If Jesus Christ impresses men, it is because he renounced saving himself as God in order to be sacrificed like a thief. Do you believe that the opposite solution would have been effective? To have been a thief in order to be sacrificed as a God? To me it . . ."

Zamacona's quick nervous voice interposed. "But Christ did not die like a thief, excluding the possibility of dying like God. He, indeed, precisely permitted every future thief to die like a God. His death assumed all deaths, all will to death, from failure to renunciation. For Christ didn't renounce merely his apparent and clear divinity, his being as God before onlookers, but he also renounced, by assuming them, the possibilities of being a man, a thief, a saint, an adulterer. Then all could die like God because a God had died for all. Everyone can be saved, everyone or no one. He who in anonymity and humility spins out his sacrifice life, and he who consciously stands against love and charity . . ." Manuel stopped a moment. In his voice there were accents which he had never heard before. He remembered his words of the month before at Bobó's party, and he felt surprised by the new movement of his thought. The surprise showed in his voice. "The greatest of criminals may say: I am going to commit my crime in full premeditation, I am going to inflict all indignities and injuries, including those which most wound the divine freedom of my brother victim; and just the same, the love which God feels for me, a bloody criminal, will be able to pardon and save me." Ixca stared at him with disdain and amusement. Robles looked fixedly at Zamacona's heap of books and raincoat. "The only one who can never be saved is he who is resurrected, because he can neither commit crime nor feel guilt. He has known death and come back from it."

"Lazarus?" said Cienfuegos.

"Lazarus. In the unconscious background of his spirit palpi-

296

tates the conviction that every time he dies, he will be brought back to life. He may be grasping and treacherous, he may commit all crimes with the certainty that on the day of death he will return to commit new crimes. No one may hold him to account. Lazarus cannot die on earth. But he is dead forever in heaven. The resurrected man may not save himself because he cannot renounce anything, because he isn't free, because he can't sin."

"But you demand that he renounce without having anything, don't you, that's your basic condition. Why? And speak slowly," said Robles.

"Because it is between the extremes of Lazarus and ourselves that the possibility of guilt is to be measured. He does not have it, we do. He cannot assume pain or guilt or suffering except his own, he has been hermetically sealed into life, nothing is important for him except the paralysis of knowledge, his own destiny." The waiter approached with a face of sleepy vigilance. Robles ordered a bottle of mineral water. "Therefore he cannot make his destiny to be like the destinies of his fellow men. Do you understand me, *Licenciado?* To renounce when you have everything is to gain very little, and the renunciation may be perverted by the sense of loss, the sadness and doubt. We lose our place among our equals. But when you give up everything and have nothing, nothing more is ended than the possibility of assuming the guilt and pain not, now, of your equals, but of all your fellow beings. That is the only richness which remains between renunciation and perdition. Naked of all that is ours, we may live only with others and for others. And you, *Licenciado,* are you going to give up everything simply to wail your renunciation, or to be done with renunciation and give up wailing, too, in order to tear away your skin of false individuality, and to cover yourself with the tears and naked blood of your fellow Mexicans? That is my question."

Robles went on staring at the stained tabletop. An unfathomable sensation of divination, strange to all his living logic, took hold of him, and he found his center of being in Manuel Zamacona's eyes. Manuel's words meant less than nothing to him; they were only the flux which permitted Robles to allow himself to be dragged to a place where two other eyes which had been forever forgotten were trying to capture the same image of him Zamacona saw. His skin was ashy. He almost did not hear Ixca's laughing words. "But my dear Manuel, your whole thesis is all right only if we cling to the idea of a personality able to receive, engender, and retain guilt and redemption and so on. But why should we have such an idea in a land where no person exists as an individual, but there is only air and blood and sun and tumult, one mass of twisted bones and thrones and rancor, and never a person?"

"Then this is a land held prisoner by Satan," replied Zamacona.

Cienfuegos narrowed his yellow eyes and laughed again. "The satanic! I am speaking seriously, not as a medieval weaver of myths."

Zamacona pounded the table with his fist and knocked over Robles's mineral water. Robles continued his fixed, trembling stare. "I'm talking about reality! About the dispersion and infinite rupture of human unity, about the dark union to which love cannot attain, nor can self-contemplation, because right down to the minimum oneness of his being, the individual is atomized. Without any reference to the vital tie that unites us with a loved one. Without the ability to admit that others are alive. Fictitious life which acknowledges only its own existence. That is the satanic."

Cienfuegos's paralyzed smile was denied by his dense and obscure eyes, narrowed in a gaze of hatred which threw itself upon both figures seated before him. His eyelashes fluttered. The waiter came closer, threw his arms in the air in malediction, then set about wiping up the spilled water.

"That's why I want to know," Zamacona was saying now, "what does this anonymous tumult you refer to really signify? Cienfuegos, what do you really feel? We gain nothing knowing only that there is confusion. What is the meaning of it, the nameless tumult, the twisted mass of blood and rancor which we call Mexico?"

"Upon that twisted mass depends salvation for all of us."

Cienfuegos thrust his face forward again, shining, pale. "Salvation for the whole world depends upon this anonymous people who are at the world's center, the very navel of the star. Mexico's people, the only people who are contemporaneous with the world itself, the only ones who live with their teeth biting into the aboriginal breast. The conglomeration of stink and chancer and scummy pulque and rotting bodies that putrefy in the mud, careless as to their origin. Everything else falls. Today is born of that very origin which, without knowing it, controls us, who have always lived within it."

Cienfuegos was asking Robles to reply, but the banker, sunk deep in his own body, was far away. All words came to him changed into memories which carried his eyes off, made his body rigid. He seemed a chunk of ashen earth seated on a wooden bench.

"Federico Robles would say," Cienfuegos went on, "that this is to ask that we hold ourselves back, that we not work, that we abandon industry, progress, well-being. That we destroy ourselves in order to wake and find ourselves in a desert no richer than our own skins and words. So that we may all begin at the true beginning, the body tatooed with wounds and scratches." And the world which flees and moans its complaining voices. Ixca did not know whether he had spoken or merely thought. You will know then that the pain of the lost, the true pain, is not yours. That there is another earth and other men who have lived in pain and failure on the equinox of suffering lined across Mexico, where all promises and all betrayal learned to walk. The sun is older and more wrinkled, and only here are its rays ancient and flickering, a sun which corrugates itself without ceasing, and there is always the night of the gods who fled terrified, nights of prayer, begging that that which was might not have been, nights before mirrors mimicking faces while fragments of those faces fall around our shoulders. And the faraway cry sweats from our palms. Nights loaded with bales and coffers of silver and gold, bayonet nights and stoning nights.

Cienfuegos knew that his words penetrated and ran like burning hares through Federico Robles's always older face, through

299

the unleashed impatience of his memories, his lost eyes and boneless flesh.

The savannahs of volcanic ash fly up to the constellations, Robles, Zamacona, in order to say that if Mexicans are not saved, no one will be saved. If here in this land animalized by alcohol and betrayed by resplendent lies, the gift is not possible, the gift that is asked for, grace and love, then it is not possible anywhere for anyone. Either Mexicans are saved, or not a single being in all creation is saved. But how to say it? Robles, Zamacona, if they had not lost their tongues, if all our speech is the color and sex and shape of muteness . . .

"And by this origin, Zamacona, it will be known that there has been no suffering, no upheaval, no treason, comparable to that which Mexicans have experienced. And it will be known that if Mexicans do not save themselves, not a single man in all creation will save himself."

"Yes," said Zamacona, moved by Ixca's words to shift his books, to play with a box of matches and to wet his cigarette butt in his coffee dregs. "But who will be named responsible for the pain and the betrayal? I insist, Cienfuegos, that it isn't enough to testify to the misery and torment, but responsibility must be placed. I say it seriously, for every Mexican who dies in vain, sacrificed, there is another Mexican who is guilty; and I return to my thesis: for this death not to have been in vain, someone must assume guilt for it. Guilt for every aborigine who was crushed and for every worker who is crushed, for every starving mother. Then, and only then, will the Mexican man be all humble Mexicans. But who will assume the guilt for Mexico, Ixca, who?"

Older minute by minute, his eyes flickering like lava flowing between petrified lakes, Robles heard and felt Manuel's words. "The frightening thing, Cienfuegos, is that sometimes one isn't sure whether this land, instead of demanding vengeance for every drop of blood that stained it, doesn't demand the blood itself. If I could be sure of that, then I would accept your ideas."

But that was not what Federico heard. Voices twined together like snakes spoke to him of a name forgotten long ago, wiped out by power and success, of the heat of a provincial capital, the boot-nailed words of a fat forgotten man, the noise of shots echoing across a field of dry dust and weeds. He covered his eyes with his fingers in a last effort to remember those names, trying to see in them, blindly, Zamacona's speech made physical. A man who died in vain, and a guilty man. Ixca and Manuel spoke on, and their words were lost in far away darkness and Federico was all alone, old and forgotten as the oldest drop of water in the oldest sea, his eyes closed, inviolate in the last buttress of his consciousnes, facing a memory which only today, the day of his downfall, could be summoned up. . . .

FELICIANO SÁNCHEZ

The holiday racket reached even to Feliciano's cell. Independence Day, and he locked up. . . . With a jerk of his blocky head he tried to make the explosions rhythmical, as if jubilation had become measured during his time in prison. Sound beat upon him, noises joined together formlessly: whence did they come? Not from men outside prison, slapping the hands of silence together; from somewhere else; from his memory, lights of fireworks, hiss of his blood. And then . . . how it heated Sánchez to remember those years . . . the great meeting, the trouble, and then locked doors. Sacrilege between walls. His fingers tapped to the beat of firecrackers. They really had him locked in this time, but it wasn't the first time: always he had been at the front, where trouble happened, exposing himself where no one else wanted to be. With the railroad workers, then the woodsmen, then the miners. If the whole business hadn't collapsed around him, he could have been taking his ease now, resting after his labor. They had stolen his voice from him again, and it would be the last time. He went to the door and shouted, "Hey, there! Hey, lead-ass!"

A Mauser-carrying greasy Indian came toward him. "You're looking for it, man, you're just looking for it."

"Cut the tough talk and answer me: Haven't the boys come?"

"Nobody has come. Nobody."

Always the same question and the same answer. Nobody had come from the union. Nobody had protested his imprisonment. They knew better.

"Listen, what kind of monkey business is this? For three days I been asking for a handkerchief. I got a terrible cold. I'm snot to my ears."

The soldier looked at him and began to laugh. The soldier walked away down the prison corridor, laughing, laughing. From a distant door he called back, "You're just made for snot, man."

Federico Robles has been selected to go, in his new salt-and-pepper suit, and make the situation clear. Just turned thirty-nine, Robles had a home in Cuernavaca at which other ambitious young lawyers gathered every week end, along with German diplomats and leaders of the Golden Shirts and conservative bankers, too. Soon his home in Colonia Hippodromo, rose-walled with allegorical friezes over the doors, would be finished. He had risen rapidly, and now this, his youth and the obscurity of his connections . . . made him the perfect choice to go to the provincial capital and disclose what dangers would accompany the visit of the labor leader Feliciano Sánchez.

"The man has become someone to be watched," Federico said. "Every day that passes, he grows stronger in Mexico City; but if he is cut down, no one will lift a finger. Those behind him are disposed to compromise, and in order to make sure of their positions, they will leave things in peace. Don't worry, no one will appear to revenge him. A pretext? There'll be one. Sánchez is a very brave man, he calls a spade a spade. He himself will give us our pretext. He's coming here to make speeches in the public plazas, to paste manifestoes on public walls, to subvert public order, my general. That is crime enough, don't you think? I tell you quite seriously: this man can ruin everything if he is not stopped in time. Both our leaders in the city and our foreign friends consider him a menace not only to the interests of our group but to the welfare of the nation. While there are men like Feliciano, no one can work in peace. Investors will be frightened and they won't give us one centavo."

"But if Sánchez is opposed also by the Government," the general's words clipped from his shadowed canvas chair, "wouldn't it be better to leave him to them?"

Robles tried to penetrate that shadow. They had seated him ten yards distant, off the terrace and in full sunlight. A large table stood between them. At the end of the terrace, several armed men stood watching. Others, slowly strolling, slowly smoking, came and went. "No, my general. What gives the bastard his strength now is his independence. But those who follow him will allow themselves to be ruled and fooled by the Government. The workers will lose faith in that sort of leadership, and it will not be hard to pull them into our fold."

The general's white teeth shone. "Very well, *Licenciado*. We will take care of him."

Face down on his cot, Feliciano lay coughing, his throat sore. A hand poked his shoulder. He grunted and turned his head.

"Get up."

"Oh, *Señor!*" Feliciano protested. "I don't feel good. It isn't even daylight yet."

"Your cold is what we're talking about. We're going to cure it for you."

He stood, buttoning his shirt, huddling his painful shoulders. He rubbed his eyes with his knuckles, rubbed his graying mustache. Without knowing what moved him, he followed the soldier out of the cell and suddenly felt chill September on his face. He climbed into a truck between two guards.

"Where are we going?"

"To celebrate Independence Day," said the soldier. "Take some tequila. It will get rid of your cold."

He tilted the bottle as the truck passed through the gates. A flickering rocket flashed high, proof that the celebration was going on. As if on a toboggan, Feliciano saw only the black stretch of highway illuminated by the headlights. But he could smell country all around, dry fields, could feel the basalt mountains, the grapples of moon and stone. The soldiers balanced their heads to the sway of the truck. And with every turn the wheels made, he breathed in the sterile countryside, heraldic powdery brown nature, the chill drawing near of dawn borne on wings of metal. The truck stopped. Wind whirled around his head.

"Right here," one soldier said to the other. The truck's spotlight fell on Feliciano, blinding him.

"Now, run!" The corporal shoved him off the highway onto a dusty footpath. Feliciano grabbed his belly; he wanted to disembowel himself. He fell to his knees on the hard earth. The corporal pulled him up and pushed him again. Dusting off his knees, Feliciano woke and ran and ran toward darkness escaping the spotlight.

"Shoot straight. Between the shoulders."

The serpent light caught him.

A soft hypnotic rain entered his back and Feliciano fell, open-mouthed, among the weeds.

Federico Robles was standing, watching the construction of his house. On the edge of the park, his face stiff, he watched the coming and going of workers, smelled paint and plaster and new bricks, imagined what the relief-work showing Ceres surrounded by grapes and cornucopias would look like. The man dressed in black waited beside him for an answer. Swift shadows from palm trees danced over Robles's brown and carefully shaven face, like a yellow pastry decorated with two brown buttons more brilliant and more penetrating than any eyes.

"No, my friend, no. I don't ask so much for my services. Thank the General for his offer. But a position in his next government would be too much for me. There are other men who have carried out duties far more important. Men with experience and talent in administration. I can be of more use if I don't appear publicly.

"Tell the General that I'll be quite satisfied with a few square meters of those lots which he has on the heights. There will be no expense and everything will stay, shall we say, in the family. Those no-good lots, you know, which won't be used for building, so far from the city, for a long time to come. Good-bye, then."

Federico reflected that some colored panes would be needed in the bathrooms, and he made a signal to his architect.

THE SKULL OF INDEPENDENCE

Dawn rose bright with sun, heavy with silence the morning after Robles, Zamacona, and Cienfuegos talked together in the café on Aquiles Serdán. It was September 15, Independence Day, and three hundred thousand inhabitants had left the city by unpunctual trains, by buses, in imported convertibles. Robles did not know how the discussion between Manuel and Ixca had ended. He left them and walked through streets, and his eyes did not begin to see again until he found himself again surrounded by the confusion of his office. Mechanically he attended to papers which spelled out his bankruptcy; forms, petitions, led his voice softly murmuring as in a slow dream. Dawn broke around him and he was in his shirt-sleeves on the leather divan. He did not see the first, most penetrating light; he could no longer tell the color of his own hands. He left the lights off and remained on the sofa.

There is someone who wants to look at me, he thought, someone who wants to see me from inside, who is not here beside me; he wants to see me in another way, leaving other eyes inside mine, like two eggs waiting for one shell to break.

That was all he could think about. He was alone. Nothing shone except his polished shoes and his eyes. In the half light growing out of dawn he squeezed his hands as if each held the handle of a whip until blood pounded through his veins. He thought of getting up and snapping on the light: what would he see? Files, a table arranged for orders and communication, an old safe, the portrait by Rivera, leather chairs, a window lightly blue-tinted: the seat of power. For the first time he felt that the place and the man had nothing to do with each other. He raised himself heavily and walked to the bathroom which adjoined the office, took off his shirt, exposing his brown hairless chest, the thick teats, the creased arms and belly. He wet his shaving brush and let hot water run. His razor moved and the dark face beneath the white mask of lather appeared.

"I'm off to Acapulco," Manuel said to Ixca. "This morning. Come along, we'll take my car, let's celebrate." They had drunk and argued together all night, Manuel adding contradiction to contradiction while Ixca had tried to speak more with his eyes than his words. The taxi left them at Reforma and Neva. "Here's my car, come on! Acapulco, Pearl of the Pacific! Enough talk, we're tired of it. Research now among the bikinis on the beaches, *manito*, the life we ought to have. You're coming, aren't you?" Manuel got into the car and looked out the open window. "I'm not brave enough to die for what I believe, and that's all. And if I don't have enough guts to do that, why go on jawing?" He drove away down Reforma. Ixca walked swiftly through thin morning fog.

At eleven that morning Natasha, Bobó, Charlotte, Paco Delquinto, and Gus left for Cuernavaca. Lally had promised them charcoal broiled steaks beside her swimming pool, plus two or three gossip columnists. They were deciding, as they drove through the stench from the Peña Pobre paper factory, what they would do to get even with Norma Larragoiti, who had fooled them all so flippantly and had treated Pimpi so disdainfully. They covered their delicate nostrils against the indelicate scent. Except Paco, who thrust his head out of the car and breathed in, deeply, pleasurably, dramatically.

At six in the afternoon the Zócalo began to fill. Feet filed silently into it from its four sides. An unorganized discipline kept everyone moving. At seven o'clock spotlights were uncovered and the cathedral and the palace and the city hall were thrown into brilliant light, while stone and dark heads, the milling *rebozos* and white shirts in the plaza, were illuminated, scaffolding erected for fireworks, silhouetted. The great black lagoon, the city's fangs, were crushed down between a heaven of dust and the old land of water.

Explosions burst silence, but were not needed to calm voices; space rounded and filled out with banging, without losing its echoes; clouds of ashy gunpowder smoke floated over the multitude. The scaffolding began to breathe light and to send paths of blue and scarlet and colorless sparks into the smoke of darkness. Between the blooms of light, a great fanfare of green, white, red trumpets, and the sky was filled with artificial fire, gunpowder smell and hot tortillas and fresh *jicama* and fried cracklings; ritual luminous in the air, bodies staked to dust, squeezed all together, a mass of dried viscera, eyes fixed upon the balcony.

"Death to the Spaniards!"

Ever since he could remember, Fifo had been coming to the celebration of the "Grito" to pick pockets and sell thick tortillas and later to shove up against women and shout, "Death to the Spaniards!" Now, elbowing his way through the milling crowd toward a better view of the great central palace balcony, the Bell of Dolores, and the band of artificial light, he lost himself, watching rockets. The crowd was chewing him up, he threw his head back and felt himself disappear into the multitude. While another multitude leaned out of palace windows and nested together like cups or pots: he wanted to know what was going on inside. The Bell of Dolores sounded hoarsely and the crowd groaned, threw their arms high, lit more firecrackers. Fifo tried to assume aloofness for his body and his name in the midst of all the heads over which flashes of rockets and spotlights flew.

"Fifo! Fifo!"

"Death to the Spaniards!"

"So early and you're drunk already?" said Tuno.

"What else is there to do?"

"Enough of this fresh air, Beto. Let's all haul ass over to the bar," said Gabriel.

They sailed off together, laughing, hurried down Moneda, whistling, Fifo cock-crowing, Gabriel scratching his black fuzzy chin.

"I know where we'll go. I want to fight somebody! Get the bottle out, Beto."

The bottle of mescal went around, and Beto shouted, "Ay, ay, ay, ay! Today death can scratch my balls for me! Fuck 'em all!"

"How about a blonde broad." Tuno sighed.

They threw arms around each other and rolled out along the alley leading to the Merced. The Cathedral and its buttery cupola were vibrating with lights between scaffolding and fireworks. They sang, whistled: *martyrdom begins in the cradle, and life gives . . .*

"Did you bring the coffin yet?"

"Yes, it's outside. May God will that you don't use it."

"What color is it?"

"Angel white. Solid oak. Don't you want the silk lining?"

Rosa Morales approached a room lighted by two wax tapers. From beneath her *rebozo* she took out a small yellow and purple Judas doll with a long black sharp-pointed nose. "I'll give it to him now. It's his favorite toy."

The undertaker took the doll by the nose and put it in the coffin on its side so there would be room.

"Will you do me another favor? No one will come until he is dead. Go and tell the pulque man that there will be a funeral today. I'll make the coffee myself."

Rosa went inside again. Jorge lay, blue-faced, with his tongue lolling out more and more. "Almost gone. You would have thought they would have told me what he's dying of. She lit a third taper, but could not keep her attention fixed on the image of the Virgin. Her eyes passed around the naked room: the clay totilla stove, the brazier, painted flowerpots, tortilla dough on the floor. She turned and looked at the child. He was dead. Rosa pulled the curtain which separated the room from the street and went out. Cheap bars, cheap groceries for Independence Day clients, a hovering curtain of smoke pushing down the whole neighborhood. Rosa felt that she was being punished, that God was poking fun at her. Tell me, Juan, what are we doing here? Why must it be one or the other if both are the same? She covered her face with her *rebozo* and picked up the small white coffin and carried it inside.

Manuel Zamacona couldn't find lodging in Acapulco and

decided to spend the night driving to Coyuca by way of Pie de la Cuesta. He had been on the beach until eleven, sweating in his flannel trousers, his sleeves rolled, the habitual mountain of books and his gabardine raincoat beside him. He drove away from the port. Wind beat books already cover-softened and wilted by heat. At Pie de la Cuesta the sea rumbled before a group of guitarists seated around a beach fire. The road wound down into a swampland and moved between thick tropical vegetation. Manuel noticed that the gas gauge read almost empty; the tank was leaking. Slowly he drove across dark and suffocating land where awakened *papagayos* were yodeling, until he saw lights ahead. Three or four thatched huts stood before a low whitewashed building from which clipped voices and a juke box sounded. Several yellow women were lolling about in hammocks and small naked children were playing along the edge of the highway, kept awake by the racket from the little bar. Manuel stopped his car a few steps from the bar and tried to breathe out all his tiredness. He lit a cigarette and leafed one of his books: *et c'est toujours la seule . . . ou c'est le seul moment . . .* He got out and opened the back of the car and took an aluminum can and walked toward the bar, repeating the Nerval. Slow dance music mumbled by the juke box contrasted with shrill voices from hoarse throats. Men dressed in white, their bodies almost motionless, shouted dirty words back and forth. Toothless mouths, swarthy faces livid.

"Excuse me. Could you sell me a couple of liters of gasoline?"

One of the men turned to Manuel Zamacona, his eyes red and flinty, and fired his pistol as swiftly as a bottle losing its cork; two, three, five times. Manuel dropped the aluminum can, gripped his stomach with his hands, and walked, open-mouthed, toward a road swirling with tropical smell, and fell dead.

All day Federico Robles had remained seated on the leather sofa in his office, stone immobile, dense and dark as memory, his eyes far away upon Alameda trees, upon the lost cupolas on Santa Veracruz and San Juan de Dios. Farther, a precise cloud of gunpowder and light began to rise from the great forgotten plaza, Santiago Tlaltelolco, and its flaking brown barracks walls, to the festive streets in Colonia Peravilla. But this was not what Robles saw: in front of his eyes, although only in his mind, eight red-ink newspaper columns announced the imminent fall of a great banking house, disclosed the audacious schemes in which its head had entangled not only the bank's capital but also its deposits; then an afternoon extra giving names, and the next morning edition showing an ocean of waving hands in front of the bank, a sticky invasion of people taking their money out, costly pressured transactions, and Roberto Régules's gray eyes and sharp face smiling at the palm of every hand reaching for its deposit. Régules had moved everywhere, swearing to the truth of Robles's mismanagement, blocking credit, opposing, obstructing, preparing the final collapse, buying mortgages at half their value, titles at a third, promising everyone a lucrative piece of Robles's ruin. And behind that image, in a wordless part of Robles's mind, the white face of Feliciano Sánchez glowed, and still further, in the last reach of memory, Froilán Reyero, speaking with his father beside the fire in a Michoacán hut. On the screening dust of the hut wall both faces shifted and mixed. Murdered faces, gunpowder and blood, both alike, both dead in vain without one voice to remember them or say, It was I, I am your murderer. Froilán Reyero, Feliciano Sánchez, two names that were a way of naming all the anonymous dead, enslaved, starving; and at this moment Robles felt the sadness and desolation of every Mexican life. Albano . . . old man of few words, and those few thrown away from the earth like hot stones at the center of the sun. Mercedes, woman mortared in darkness by Federico's youthful hands. Gunfire and sun, Celaya fields, seeds and manure, a violent horse, swift and taut in the fire of battle, the same horse as the other with . . . with . . . he wanted to remember that other name but could summon up only the faces and names of Froilán Reyero and Feliciano Sánchez; they surrounded his life and body like a placenta of fire, the world went away and there remained only a vast dark envelope, two wandering deaf stars and himself face down and unable to move, then rolling upon the earth without feeling:

". . . eh, Ibarra? An accident at work? . . ."

". . . it's better if the announcement comes from a private institution . . ."

". . . old man with earth mummied in his face, terrible eyes and terrible hands . . ."

". . . then the strike was on and everyone knew there would be no food . . . I was full of sorrow and fury and I still am . . ."

". . . he is a delicate, docile little Indian fellow who at an early age understood . . ."

". . . you should have seen them, their small porcelain faces . . ."

". . . and another daughter who would soon be sixteen . . ."

". . . twenty-five hundred shaved-head recruits were gathered in like sheep . . ."

". . . and now the time of the fat kine is coming . . ."

". . . Maycotte has dug in at Celaya! Villa has him surrounded! . . ."

". . . please may the wind always blow over me as it is blowing now, blowing now forever . . ."

". . . an old love, neither . . ."

". . . for the first time in Mexican history, a stable middle class exists, the . . ."

". . . and now we had indeed an international capital, ah, one had to enjoy this wonderful cosmopolitan Mexico City . . ."

". . . are we from the start what we are at the finish, or do we come to be? And you have no children, *Licenciado* . . ."

". . . I think now and then that this isn't really life, so complicated, so busy socially. I believe I do it only for you . . ."

". . . and we can't live and die blind. Do you understand me? . . ."

". . . do you feel good . . ."

". . . Hortensia . . ."

". . . and here it will be known that if Mexicans do not save themselves, not a single man in all creation will save himself . . ."

". . . who will take on the guilt for Mexico, Ixca . . ."

". . . Feliciano fell open-mouthed among the weeds . . ."

Brusquely Federico raised his hands to his eyes. Night had

311

fallen, and from all the city a sound at once concentrated and multiple and mute rose toward his office. The "Grito" was being celebrated, rockets and fireworks flew about overhead as he left at eleven and twisted his way to avoid groups of drunken Independence celebrants and children setting off firecrackers, and drove to the Lomas. The living room was dark. Federico called his wife and went upstairs to the lighted bedroom. Norma, on the bed in a negligee, turned. Both faces had become merely lines; Norma's red eyes, set expression, and relaxed body; Federico's old eyes and dry hands and bulk.

Norma started and did not finish an empty sigh, as her destiny of imitation stone walls and gold-framed glass and red rugs moved away from her forever. "The house will go, too?" she said softly.

Federico, planted like lead on the rug, looked around the room again. His body no longer belonged there. The color of the rug made him dizzy.

"Yes, the house, too."

Norma stretched her pillow. "And what are you going to do about it? Are we going to be beggars, or what? Tell me."

"This is only for the moment. I'll come back." Robles spoke automatically. He felt that yesterday, without his knowing it, silence and memories and lonely hours and voices had created a new desire in the guts of his being, a lust for a new showdown, and whether it might be destructive or cringing didn't matter. He stiffened his index finger. "Give me the jewels."

"*Ja!*" And what else? You want me to become a dance-hall girl so we can go on eating? Shall I take in sewing?"

"Stop screaming. The servants will hear you."

"I'll scream when I want to." She crossed her arms and stared at him from head to foot. "The cook went to her village for the holiday and one of Rosa's snotty kids is dying. You haven't come home or you would know." Her head fell. "I was dying of loneliness and there was nothing I could do."

For the first time Robles wanted to console her, take her in his arms with something more than the mechanical remoteness of the nights they had spent together when each had consciously

312

observed the other's movements. But this memory separated him from her complaining body. Nevertheless, for the first time Norma did not shine with the hygienic glitter of her toilette. Robles did not move a muscle.

"The jewels."

Norma moved to the end of the bed. "No. No! They're all that's still mine."

"You'll give me the jewels and you'll stick with me."

His immobility was horrible and unreal. "With you? But my big baby, you're ruined, aren't you? I spoke with Silvia Régules today and she told me what's really going on, what the newspapers haven't mentioned. . . . I'm married to my house and car and jewels, not to you!"

Robles stretched his hand toward her and Norma moved back into the pillows. "Get out, Federico. I don't want to see you today. I don't want to say things I shouldn't. . . . Leave me alone. We're not what we should be, neither of us. We both gambled. Okay. But now we are just what we are. Go away! Today I can't stand you."

He pushed toward her like an automaton, and she felt that he was moved by a monstrous and uncontrollable mechanism that was completely separated from the man himself.

"*Ja!* So it hurts you to hear the truth! Get out, Federico, get out. You're not going to touch me." But he reached her and crushed her to him, put his lips to her neck. Norma freed herself from his heavy metallic arm. "Get out! Get out!"

"The jewels," he whispered. "Give them to me now."

"I'm not going to give you anything." She ran to the door. "And tomorrow I'm taking them with me. I don't need you, do you understand? My world is complete, it's got nothing to do with a character like you. Get wise, get wise, I'm strong all alone, not because I'm married to you! What do you think I've been doing all this time that you have honored me with a once-a-week visit to my bed?" Her whole body shook with fury. "You knew our wedding night that I wasn't a virgin. What did you expect? How could you stand me? Was it because I gave you something that all your money couldn't give you? The feeling that you belonged, that you weren't just a barbarian and dirty Indian, that you could shake hands with society . . . *Ja!* And do you know . . ." Facing his stiff bulk, she began to laugh. His eyes had a faraway presentiment of having been made a fool of. "Do you know that I'm not strong because I'm yours? No one has to tell me how to live, and I can go to bed and do what I please not because I'm married to a pretentious fool, a peasant . . . . Have you ever taken a good look at yourself? Do you think you're in the movies, or what? *Ja!*"

She laughed, and felt that she was being dragged by the sea, the sea she had subjugated and ruled, until she touched land. She, she alone, standing before the man she had destroyed.

"Didn't you ever suspect the disgust I felt when I slept with you? How I had to control my feelings and the feeling in my body, too, and let you possess me as if you were anything except a man . . . a chameleon, maybe, but never a man. Did you believe . . ."

Robles's fury took hold of him. He overturned dressers and closets and tore down the drapes. Then his fury pushed him out of the room and into the halls and down the stairs, and Norma laughed on. When she heard his unsteady footfalls on the marble living-room floor, she shut her door and threw the key onto the confusion of the bed. She stretched out, her arms and legs spreading away from her body. As her laughter lost itself between her breasts, she sighed drily and furiously, a sigh not meant to impress anyone. She heard herself . . . and she trembled.

It was after midnight when Evrahim, Chino Taboada, and Rodrigo arrived at Lally's house in Cuernavaca. They had spent the day beside a swimming pool, discussing minor details of Rodrigo's new script. His original plot had been slightly changed from respect for the Catholic nature of the public: the nun who had abandoned her habit to conquer the world had become a B-girl who ended up in a nunnery. Lally's house was hidden behind a high rosy-brown wall. The doors had been framed in festive ribbons, and Paco Delquinto was dancing about the large terrace that overlooked the cliff with a bottle of champagne in his arms. "Lubitsch of Coatzacoalcos!" Bobó shouted when he noticed Chino's greasy figure approaching through the garden.

"Look, Bobó. This little house is great, it's ideal for the *Devil Crossed* picture we're thinking about," cried Evrahim.

"Rodrigo Pola, our new literary genius," Taboada introduced, waving his hands over the heads of Gus, Natasha, Charlotte, Pimpinela, Paco Delquinto, and the same newspaperman Cuquis had talked with in Acapulco.

Most of them remembered Rodrigo from Bobó's and Charlotte's parties, but Taboada's introduction persuaded them that they were seeing him for the first time. A collective "pleased to meet you." Only Natasha, hidden behind her permanent black sunglasses, laughed and smiled and held out her blue hands to him.

"He's good-looking, isn't he?" Charlotte said softly to Pimpinela.

"Yes. But more your style. A little dark." She turned to the columnist. "As I was telling you, to rise by one's own efforts is all right; what irritates people with breeding is not that, but the pretense, the lying. You know we accepted Norma only because we believed that she had suffered in the Revolution as we had . . ."

"*Chère,*" said Natasha, pushing her legs out of a canvas and leather terrace chair. "*Une révolution, ça ne se fait pas: ça se dit,*" and she stood up, smoothing the pleats of her velvet slacks. Rodrigo had awaited her, smiling. Natasha found his gold cigarette lighter waiting for her long Russian cigarette. "Mmmmm. Even to this, *mon petit.*" She took his arm to stroll the terrace. Rodrigo breathed deep of the valley's sweetness, avocado and *flamboyana.*

"I see that you decided. Now you have wings of one color. You sacrificed something, didn't you?" Rodrigo did not want to believe that these words were being spoken by Natasha. "*On n'a . . .* you have only one destiny. And why have a destiny opposed to the world's *mon vieux? Oh, la rébellion, les révoltés, on los a bien foutus, ceux-là! Mais toi!* I saw ambition in your forehead the first time I met you, you know. Only an ambitious man would have been so upset not to belong at the party given by *ma chère bête* Charlotte. Now you belong, *tachez, oui, tachez,* stick to them, stick to the way they are and you'll have everything. It isn't a question of doing anything, just *laissez faire.* The world belongs to the do-nothings, and the reformers are get-nothings. You'll see."

"Vautrin with skirts." Rodrigo laughed, pinching Natasha's cold arm.

"You've got *l'esprit, chérie* ... It seems that way, doesn't it? I belonged to another world, stable and dignified. It isn't very pleasant to be part of middle-class beginnings. It makes me laugh to be living in a culture Europe had its fill of more than a century ago. The dominant and monied class, its business connivances sanctioned by law. *Les révolutions ont toujours son Empire; les Robespierres devient Napoléons....* What can we do? That's the world for you. And the way the rules read, you play the game. You'll get there, Rodrigo. There are plenty of ways to make a fortune in Mexico. Nothing is respected except money in this bourgeois court. You have it, and you have everything in Mexico. Without it, you fall on your face into the thieving proletariat mob that is always one of the growing pains of a city. Yes, you're right. I'll make my little Rastignac, my Mexican Lucien de Rubempré."

Rodrigo echoed Charlotte's laughter while inside he felt ambition laughing, too. He observed that Pimpinela de Ovando kept watching him, his well-cut trousers, the fine-striped Bermuda shirt. This new Rodrigo was very different from the old one: olive-green gabardine suit with pegged trousers, shoulder padding, and wide lapels.

"Pimpinela is very nice," said Natasha when she saw their eyes meeting. "There is only one person who doesn't like her: Norma Robles. With all her money, she'll never have her style and breeding. That's why she's jealous, the little parvenu."

Natasha's words reassured him in his new attitude. Rodrigo's whole world, everything he had ever thought about and remembered, that dusty world of empty childhood, the long evenings beside Rosenda's rocker, his early efforts to achieve literary recognition—all this was wiped out forever. The disgusting words which had remained after Rosenda's life now joined her in her grave. Never again would they be thought of or repeated. The two threads of his life which were born of a gray morning and Belén's bullet-spattered wall and had ended in a ghostly conversation between his mother and Ixca Cienfuegos now separated and fled forever.

"Listen to those damn Indians!" Delquinto howled when a firecracker exploded in the ravine. "What the hell are they celebrating? That's what comes from having one viceroy with a wig and another with stripes and stars."

Rodrigo went to Pimpinela and sat where the columnist, who was now sambaing with Charlotte, had been. "Delquinto makes *us* laugh," said Rodrigo, underlining the pronoun. "Which is something in a society so unhappy as ours, where so few keep up social amenities as an example."

"It will come to that," said Pimpinela, her arm encircling Rodrigo's. "Ours is a new society. It has to be filed down. Fortunately, there are those of us who have salvaged some of the traditions. The Revolution was a horrible shock, but you'll see, not all was lost."

Rodrigo felt the invitation in Pimpinela's eyes. "You're right, Pimpinela. My mother, Zubarán's daughter, and he was Díaz's closest friend, always said the same thing. I could understand her; but we had to move from a palace in Colonia Roma to a poor little house on Chopo. This made us hold even tighter to real values."

"I like your sincerity."

They took each other's hands, and with his eyes he asked her to dance. A freshly perfumed braceleted hand stroked his neck.

"All of a sudden, Chino, you can see Rodrigo's good taste."

"She don't have much money, Evrahim, but for class . . ."

"He'll make the dough and she'll give him the connections. Two eggs for the price of one."

Lally, on her knees in front of the record player, chose a stack of straight blues songs and sighed over her champagne

317

goblet. She had to lose ten, oh Lord, kilos. *"I love you for senti-mental reasons.*

Gabriel was squeezed into the booth with one arm around Beto. Spilled glasses, cigarettes held to flames, the *mariachi* musicians singing. "Sing, let them sing! Today the world can scratch my balls! Ay, Beto! How damned sad I always get on Independence Day. You remember things you don't want to remember. It's like we always got to be looking for something. What makes us always be looking for something?"

The fat proprietor of the cheap restaurant got to his feet to make an announcement. "Tonight, ladies and gentlemen, in honor of our distinguished clientele and the national holiday, we offer a special banquet platter, prepared by the *Señora* to make eve-ry-body happy!" Cheers and whistles. The pores of the man's fat hands were visible. Steaming plates and platters went by, swarmed over with flies. Glasses of yellow sugar-topped pulque. Avid fingers, stuffed-full mouths smeared with sauces and dangling food shreds. Stained mustaches and shirts. Guitar fingers swaying bodies to the tension of a prolonged good-bye.

"Open up for me, I'm coming wounded!" Gabriel shouted from their booth. "Sing, sing as if this were our last day! Ay, ay, ayyyyyy!"

His cry floated over the seated and standing crowd, glassy eyes, dark flesh, damp lips. In the center strummed the *mariachis*, almond eyes, drooping mustaches, sombreros decorated with tarnished silver:

> *en las barrancas te aguardo, a orillas de los nopales*
> *como te hago una seña, como que te chiflo y sales*

Arms waved in erect and curved harmony, in challenge, with dry excitement. Throats filled with foam and the points of knives.

"Sure, Gabriel. The night of the fifteenth there ain't anything you don't remember. You need to talk with your buddies and get it off your chest." Beto tilted his glass and wagged his head. "Every goddamn blue thought you ever had. Every time you ever wanted to cry."

318

"Puro rimimbir moder," Tuno Englished, scratching an ear.

"You said it. I'm suffering, Beto, I'm suffering. If I couldn't talk with my buddies like you, who the hell could I talk with? We're one blood. I swear to God, Beto, you're my brother and I love you." Gabriel embraced the cabdriver and pounded his shoulders.

"I wanna fuck," Tuno observed, again in English, his face impassive and far away.

"If it wasn't for our buddies, Beto . . . Listen, I'll tell you. You knew that Yolanda, didn't you? The one they talked about being everybody's little mama, and then when you tried to get into her, you needed a chisel."

Fifo's fingers snapped to the music.

"That little girl with eyes like black plums, who wiggled like an ocean wave?"

"That's her. That's Yolanda. But you couldn't trust her, Beto. She's a tricky bitch, she treats a man's love as if it wasn't any more important than a hair on her ass."

"Them bitches who hurt a man, ayyyy! They're . . ."

qué se creían esos americanos
que combatir ere un baile de carquís

". . . Christ, Fifo, who wants to talk on a night like this?"

se regresaron corriendo a su país
se regresaron . . .

"To hell with the gringos! Uuuuuy, uuuuy, uuuuuuy! One Mexican is a better man that ten of them blond bastards! Sons of bad dreams!"

The *mariachis* made their guitars gallop. Women squeezed their men's necks. A faint odor of vomit began. Shouts and ancient howls. Shut eyes and clenched fists.

y sentir hervir la sangre por todito el cuerpo entero
y al gritar Viva Jalisco! con el alma y corazón

"George Negrete used to sing that. We'd hear his record in Texas, you remember?"

"Let the fuckin' gringos come!"

"There's Gabriel!" called a girl with a painted face and gold teeth.

The *mariachis* were served their drinks and began to play very slowly, caressing the nerve of each string. The little cabaret became subdued as Gabriel made his way toward the woman.

Xochimilco, Ixtapalapa, ay qué lindas florcitas mexicanas

A thin tall man wearing a felt hat and a gabardine suit entered, followed by his habitual open-mouthed companion. "Perfect, perfect," Gabriel said. He spread his elbows and stomped his feet and made his way forward, putting a hand on every shoulder, panting into every ear, his eyes opaque and wary. Steel glittered. Gabriel cried out.

"I told you you wouldn't catch me twice the same way, *manito*," the thin man with the bloody razor in his hand said. "Don't grab me that way. Let's go, Cupido."

Gabriel twisted on the cabaret floor among exploded fragments of firecrackers. The *mariachis* were silent. The man with the felt hat closed his razor and pushed toward the door. "Anybody who is looking for a dose of the same . . ." His companion opened his mouth wider and laughed and scratched his head.

Gabriel did not move. Beto reached the brown body with blood-dripped knees. The *mariachis* began to sing again.

se agacha se va de lado, querido amigo

"He's dead," the girl with the painted face said to Beto.

"Talk with the *Señora* for me, Doña Teódula," Rosa had said with her face hidden in her apron. "Señora Norma, I'll give you the telephone number. Tell her that he's dead and I have to stay with him." Hands on her lap, the old widow observed Jorgito's sharp cold face in an oak coffin beside a Judas doll. *Norma: remember her name.* Ixca had said that. The widow's deep, ancient eyes were taken by intuition, but did not change. "If the tall dark man comes to see me," she said to Rosa Morales, "tell him to wait for me, that I'll be back soon. Tell him to sit with Jorge."

"We are close now," she thought, seated on the wooden bench of a second-class bus which was carrying her to the Lomas. The driver looked uneasily at her in his mirror. Nobody rode to the

Lomas on a second-class bus that night. Servants and gardeners were at the Zócalo celebrating or had asked permission to go home to their villages. The widow's jewels clanked together as the bus hurried to reach its destination. Heavy gold worked in deep relief danced on her wrists; on her dry chest flopped a little gold mask with laughing slant eyes. "We are close now."

So when she left the bus, she was not surprised to see the sky alight with rising red smoke. A mansion of yellow stucco and stonework and elaborate windows and niches, of black gates and blue panes and tiles. Ablaze like resinous candlewood. Like a black clot, the burning door blazed at the end of a garden of roses trampled by firemen.

"Back, back!"

She narrowed her eyes across the heads of onlookers. Then, a serpent of gold, she moved through them to the gate. The streams of water stifled the fire back into its own haze for a moment. Immediately it flared up again.

"Stop that old woman!"

Shaking her bracelets and necklaces and earrings, she ran with the smoothness of a hare as far as the flaming door. Her ancient skin, her black eyes, all her life hidden from the world's eyes shown before the fire. She raised her arms, her jewels flashed in her hands.

"Thank you, my son!" she cried more with her body than her voice. And she threw the jewels into the smoke-suffocated living room.

Wet hot firemen's hands seized her by the shoulders. "What are you doing here? Don't you see it's dangerous?"

Teódula Moctezuma smiled with a smoky face. "My friend Rosa lives here, she's the cook, *Señor.*"

"There's nobody in the servants' quarters nor downstairs. If there is anybody, they're upstairs and it's too late. Get back, *Señora.*"

Teódula smiled again. With the heavy gold jewels gone, her neck and arms felt light. "This is what we both wanted, my son Ixca," she said as she walked away from Norma and Frederico's flaming mansion. "I told you . . . our gods walk hidden, but by and by they come out. To receive the sacrifice and our gifts."

With one hand pounding the door and the other over her face, Norma coughed. The nervous fingers of the first terror, when she had smelled dry smoke and then seen the great flames which were born at the foot of the window, had not been able to find the door key among the tangled sheets on the bed. Fire rose from below, up the outside wall, carried by dry creeper vines, and in one second was lapping the thin curtains. Norma ran to the door, screamed and beat it with her fists as red tongues came across the carpet, caressed the bed, at last touched her robe and the soles of her feet. "*Ja!*" she said when she felt fire's hand on her back. She fell to the bottom of her own eyes.

Outside a door illuminated by candle stumps Ixca Cienfuegos leaned against an adobe wall and listened to Rosa Morales's weeping over her child's coffin. Full divination shone in Ixca's eyes; all words and rites ran through his blood and knotted in his stomach. Four days to reach the fair, he said silently, between his teeth, to the dancing shadows projected from the doorway; four days, and then the flocks of headdresses will fly up to feed the sun, toward the east they will rise upon their legs, to the navel among the serpents of the sky. His inaudible voice chewed both shadows, swallowed Rosa's sobs. To the fair of sumptuous offering. Rosa, the final one, we will raise our gifts and our offerings high on feather arms among the mountains that want to destroy us.

He pressed his shoulder blades against the adobe. He wanted to be witness and did not know how to; he wanted to enter Rosa's tears and tenuous light and did not know how to. . . . Eight deserts, eight plains stand between us and the sanctuary. I shall see you as the first thing of night, I swear to you, because I know that we go to the fair together, where the souls of pilgrims sigh. The heart of mountains will open that we may reach the fair hidden. Oil among stones, blood on our hair, that we may arrive in dignity. The red dog will take us by the river. . . . Ixca bit his teeth, bent his shoulders in a prayer which he did not know how to voice. "Now we stand upon the regenerated earth, the same earth which dropped us, we are returned to birth.

We have not abandoned it, it is all a sepulcher. We have journeyed. We enter the new infernos, at the place from which we departed . . ."

Rosa's sobs, drowned out by his prayer, flowed in a drowsy stream. Sun hung in the dust. Teódula Moctezuma came, walking light inside her loose gown.

"I have completed the sacrifice," she hissed into Cienfuegos's ear. "Now we can return to being what we are, my son. Now we have no reason to pretend. You will come back to your own, here, with me. Norma has given suck to age now." The old women extended a finger, thin and yellow as a blade of corn, toward the dawning sun. "Look, there it rises again! Now we can go in. Another woman is waiting for you, my son, with her child, who now is with my babies and old Celedonio."

Ixca did not want to understand, only to repeat his prayer and her incomprehensible words. He was remembering Jorge alive, newspapers under arm in twilight before the Cathedral.

"Listen to her weeping, my son. The poor woman doesn't know. Just pray here, as we prayed to my children, and then we will go in and console her."

"A life is gone, Mother," said Ixca, against the wall.

"Go and sit up with him if you want to, my son. But now you are here, with us, with yours. Here you will live. Your other life is over. Each of us must be what he is, and you know it."

Teódula Moctezuma entered the room of candles and a coffin and the voice of Rosa Morales.

The city came apart. Last groups of weary *mariachis* went walking, yawning, tuning, strumming, singing among rose and green and gray walls, the new day's hymn:

> it was dawn when I began to love you
> one kiss at midnight, and the other at sunrise

MERCEDES ZAMACONA

Light almost extinguished her profile near the bright window. Beyond the glare was the plaza, where wind pushed against stone; damp-breathing tiles, small homes with window balconies and gardens shut away by winding walls, old remodeled stables, stagnant well pools. Mercedes Zamacona was slowly counting her rosary. Soon Coyocan parish vespers would be chiming. Other outside noises—bicycles, buses, voices—never reached her. This was the hour when she usually had her glass of milk with cookies, with sweets made by the nuns at San Gerónimo. The maid's steps moved over red volcanic stone, a broken window rattled as it was opened; then the steps again, dulled by carpeting, detouring around the pine sideboard:

"*Señora,* someone wants to see you."

"Manuel?" She turned away from the light. Wind blew graying hair pulled back in a tight knot.

"No. Señor Cienfuegos."

"What is he like?"

"Tall, *Señora,* very tall, and——"

"What else?"

"Dark, with very black eyes."

Mercedes repeated what the maid had only mumbled. "Dark, with very black eyes, very black eyes." She regained her composure. She noticed that she, who usually held herself ruler straight, had slumped in the presence of the servant; now she was ruler straight again. She adjusted her ruffled collar, the fine cameo. "You know the only person I see is Manuel. I'm not at home."

She looked around the room. Whitewashed walls as plain as the heels of the servant, now again part of the carpet, now again sharp on tile. She stiffened her back against the chair and turned her profile to the window. A dark man with dark eyes. Very black eyes. She picked up her rosary and opened her prayer book, but with a look of revulsion, closed it. Those were not living words: prose of sugar, wiped empty of solidity. Wind rose again and swirled leaves in the plaza. Then suddenly it was still. She looked out on the street. Words must come at the moment if they are to be strong with meaning . . . resonant with the terrible and obscure things spirit and religion are made of. Dark. She covered her eyes. Not wanting to remember anything, all these years all she had done was remember everything. Yet what else could she have done? Day after day, every detail. The least odor, the lightest breeze, fruit on the table, was enough to call it back and keep his image before her, his image and that moment. "No!" she said to herself, "not today!" and then aloud, the thoughts charging reinlessly.

"The spirit of truth shall be witness to me."

Yes. But only long afterward had she thought of those words from the Bible which her uncle, a priest, had made her memorize as a little girl when she was going to school in Morelia. A stiff schoolmistress who smelled of camphor had taught her to read and write, but it was her uncle who had taught her the words of the Lord, the words by which she had learned to distinguish truth and error, to hold to truth even in a world of temptation, where people talked about her, to know that truth will triumph in the end and give witness to itself and to her, as it gave witness to Christ. But this she thought, not then and perhaps not afterward, but remembered years later, only because her uncle the priest had made her repeat it over and over until she could never forget the spirit of truth:

"touch me not for I am not yet ascended to the father"

At thirteen a *señorita* knew all of reading and writing she needed and the rest could be better learned at home with her mother. But her mother is tied to a wheel chair and the older sister, unmarried and each day becoming thinner, like a sliver of metal filed down until only a shred remains, unchangeable and irreducible, and her brother an officer in the Federal army, executing rebels: four of them last Sunday, Mercedes, four rabble rousers who died together without fear of God, believing they could beg each other's forgiveness and give each other strength. She threw her yarn down and covered her eyes. Still not, still not: and she remembered what in reality had only just now been thought: not until we are called and judged, not before. He would believe she would be remembering his words; and listening to her brother's stories when he came home on leave with his tilted kepi and shining boots and the blond waxed mustache, *à la* Kaiser, home to their hacienda near Uruapan, and finding his sister a skinny cold line with black eyes, cornered in spinsterhood at thirty and already full of self-pity and making it her only pleasure; or to see her mother tied down to the wheel chair and deaf besides, as if she didn't have time to be simply wordless, silently reproaching God for her paralysis; and that was what had hurt, that soft unspoken anger between her mother and God, like chaff between two judgments, nourishing themselves and mixing without words and becoming a fine sifted sand where even talk is wordless; the brother judging with the saber, as silently as the coupling silence of their mother and sister, mute judgments balanced by all the blood and steel and all the dead who were judging the invalid mother and the virgin sister; and when Mercedes arrived from Morelia at the age of thirteen, her brown hair braided to her waist, a calico dress under which her nipples stretched and burned, with pains in her belly which no one explained to her because her mother had forgotten such things and her sister had buried them forever with her virgin shame under her mourning black: then in the evenings, seated silently in the thick-spined rocking chairs in the smell of freshly roasted coffee beans and the electric filing of crickets, the mountains outside beating down stealthily and the earth tropical and Mercedes's nose itched and she closed her eyes, perfumed stone and perfumed fruit moved down and down to her belly, moaning and crying, sweetness moving in through wide-open begging windows.

"But thou, when thou prayest, enter into thy closet, and when thou hast shut thy door, pray to thy Father which is in secret, and thy Father which seeth in secret shall reward thee openly."

I would have wanted, she thought she knew, to beat all those words out, rap and hammer what her mother and sister didn't hear, choir that she alone could have heard, and behind the closed door she would be able to pray, and thus there would be order directing the voices and her prayer and her life, joining them; but that was not the way: both life and prayer were too silent. In the mornings she would leave the house, ox carts were rolling thin dust and the sun was heavy, land and plants lay under it, corn, coffee, until her nostrils burned with pain. The

short road that became the corral and then only a path where
cocks were scratching their spurs, and beyond the newly har-
vested fields and the meadow that stretched to and was broken
by the river, and then, the mountain. She walked among the
harvesters and picked up black coffee grains, the valley heavy-
smelling, big men with big heads under straw hats, and when
she passed, their eyes raised, especially later, when she was
fourteen and her walk was different, measured yet light and
proud; there she was, fourteen and walking among the coffee
plants, comparing the looks the men gave her and still avoiding
them precisely because her walk was different, and she wanted
to hear the chorus of voices, the words she had never heard, but
which went calling through her body, through the marrow of
her spine, making a music which finally showed her how to
open and close the door, giving her faith, and to pray alone,
that she could be witness and then repent that black staring.
She believed she had thought that then: but she had fastened
herself to one of those looks and nothing had happened, because
she never saw him again, or if she did see the look, she had
forgotten the man, and she stumbled and stopped and glanced
back over her shoulder and heard a voice, her voice, saying,
Something will happen to me very soon, very soon something
will, and then quickly, but still not hurrying, with her legs weak
and her neck wet with coldness, she had returned to her home
and her corner room and closed the door and beat her breast
and cried silently in repentance for having provoked something
she did not even half understand. For there were things which
had not been given to her understanding, although the priest
her uncle had explained the Word to her and she ought to be
able to tell Him from the Devil; and God would reward her,
He who would see in darkness, would reward her even though
she had sinned in the moment she had believed herself to be
gaining pardon; but He would never reward her, she reflected
sagely, for not having lived and for having shut herself up in
silence and away from grace like the two other women in the
house. So she had to go on, to drop everything and follow everything, following in word and in spirit, but also in flesh.

". . . follow me and let the dead bury their dead . . ."

The ultimate limit and the innermost core of everything: buried-dead and dead-in-wheel-chairs and stiff rocking chairs in the stiff odor of starch and sedentary shut-in life of silence and unexpressed furies, suffocated by black garments, blessed by an uncle who smelled of dribbled urine; follow on to the execution wall where her brother's saber dropped at the sound of a nervous death command, and further she would follow because He had to be further, in each and all or none of the dark men who smelled of damp earth and coffee, and if not in any of them, then in the air sieved by hummingbirds or simply in that band of green which stretched from eye to eye; and sometimes she would climb the belfry tower, and with her head motionless, roll her eyes in their sockets, trying to absorb Him into her world and make it a place where the dead were not buried but a continuous movement of creation dropped from His fingers upon a green coast scattered with wicker rockers that could not rock, and He wanted to say something she could hardly hear in that silent rectangle formed by her corner room, her mother, her sister, her uncle, and herself.

"the spirit of truth . . ."

"I was ahungered, and ye gave me meat; I was thirsty . . ."

"the meek of spirit . . ."

"get thee behind me, Satan, do not tempt . . ."

Spoken by her uncle the priest. Far away was where she had to follow, and a rush of blood rose through her legs when she thought that far away was His world, not the prisoning house. Then her new way of walking and her awareness of her new breasts were not necessary, nor the consciousness of the inaccessible blade between her thighs, merely the simple existence of those shining new centers of being, like three moons singing among themselves, speaking of their sudden amazed birth; her other half, the round hidden moons, black before the sun, afloat in darkness: that was how she had felt. And all the secret looks among the rows of coffee plants were not enough to say it, to put her in sure touch with what only her imagination revealed to her in moments when she was alone on foot across the fields, on

328

her knees beside her baroque bronze bed draped with white net and aflutter with pale-green insects which flew, buzzing, or hung, out of reach of a sudden slap, whirling, imbecile, around the kerosene lamp, furious, drunk upon light which subjugated them, furious because they knew that wasn't night's natural light; revealed not like something solid and forever inside her flesh, but as an intermediary closeness preparing her for destiny. A deep phosphorescent drainage that bathed her so that she might truer discern the obligation in her prayers and her beating her breasts and begging for forgiveness. The three moons, and the blade, they dominated the green fertile world seen when she would climb the white belfry, world of cricket song and seed, Uruapan, flower patios, whitewashed flaking walls, waterfalls, and earth loamy with rich germination above the false sterility of volcanic ash, stiff men with skinny bones and heavy heads, tongueless women hunched over their bundles, food, wash, babies, the persistent forgotten sound from Tzaráracua drowning its roar in the moribund majestically colored vegetation which surrounded the fruitful horn of the Balsas, a warm scented air of procreation, aromatic slender fruits almost transitory between the original seed and the sweet liquor; and Mercedes thought, Something is going to happen to me very soon.

"Enter ye in at the strait gate: for wide is the gate, and broad is the way, that leadeth to destruction."

And afterward, when women would talk and remember, they would say that Mercedes, when she was fifteen, knew that her uncle would come from Morelia accompanied by a clean-cut youth without an ounce of extra flesh on him, taut like the landscape itself. It was his sexton, said the priest her uncle, a little Indian, humble, a hard worker who knew his place. He hammered those words as he had used to hammer the old Biblical phrases, while Mercedes saw, as he arrived and was sent immediately to eat in the kitchen and her uncle went on repeating, humble, a hard worker who knows his place; and she clung to the fugitive memory of dark eyes which had barely glanced at her and which had seemed still startled by a recent shock or discovery. Eyes that were like the eyes of the workers in the fields, but not many, as theirs were, but one pair united to and inseparable from the man. Then Mercedes knew that he was watching with his dark eyes through cracks in the mother-of-pearl panels which separated the dining room from the passage to the kitchen, and only she, seated at the facing end of the table, could know that they were there like two furious black insects lost in the darkness of the passage, finally going away with a tiny creak of the door. This happened in the mornings, when the three women breakfasted together, and again at the long afternoon meal presided over by her uncle the priest, and again at eight in the evening when smells of steaming coffee and melted butter came from the kitchen through the halls to the bedrooms grouped square on the second floor around the blue central patio. And every morning when she walked out to see the coffee plants, Mercedes told herself that today, yes, today those eyes would be shining for an instant among the brown leaves and all her body be astonished to discover him really present with her beneath the same sun. Days went by, hot and ridden with light. The eyes went on spying on her every meal. She went on looking for them on her morning walks. Then this time he was there, walking the same path in clothing of a city youth (but ill fitting: the priest had handed down from one sexton to the next), and they passed and Mercedes did not dare to seek his eyes. But she waited. She tied a shoelace and with the corner of her eyes followed him, and then she walked slowly on, stopping now and then to touch a plant, the nose of a mare, the boy walking ahead of her toward the corral at the end of the path. Then a heavy and heavier cloud of dust began to gallop toward them, a cloud full of snorts and whinnies, and Mercedes stopped and pressed against the fence and waited, paralyzed, for the avalanche of hooves to thunder past. She could see the stallion now, its flared foaming nostrils, its hooves raised to strike at the fence behind which she crouched as the stallion loomed over her and glared down at her breasts. Her hands covered her eyes. When she took them away, the boy was in front of the stallion, clubbing the animal with a nail-studded piece of wood, driving a black nail into the heaving back, reaching cautiously for the loose halter. The boy had his back to her. She could see only the tense muscles of his arm, the rumpled hair, the fist gripping the club. The stallion whinnyed, with the black nail buried in its back again, its whole body rose and fell with heavy snorts. Her eyes ran over the beast, fascinated, trying to discover in that brute exaltation the reason for her own body's rigidity. As the boy gained control of the halter and drew near the jerking head, the stallion's excitement increased, weeping eyes, damp snorts, flowering blood which dripped onto the dry earth, and between the powerful legs, the thick nervous sex blade like a seed of force, the vibrating origin of all the violence, insanity, and majesty of unchained fury. Mercedes could hardly breathe. Her eyes flashed from boy to beast. A river of power ran magnetically between man and animal, tied together now like a broken centaur. Tiring, the horse lowered its head, and then the boy's choler was loosed in turn, as if he had only been waiting the beast's subjugation to affirm his own human fury and power. Voiceless, his teeth clenched, with sweat dripping down his face, he beat the stallion with the club, opening more black blood clusters. Mercedes closed her eyes and thought of the animal's vibrating flesh, hidden now by the boy, man and beast identical in one irreducible grain. The tumult ceased. The path opened wide and spacious. Dust had settled to its invariable haze. Men were coming in from the fields to the place of combat.

No: she would never know how they had known, both of them, without even agreeing on a meeting place, the dark place where their hidden eyes went into their fingernails and fingertips; nor how they had understood, both virgin, both unseeing and unspeaking, what they had to do, to do as they did it without offense to either, by pure sensual inspiration, without voices, in the darkness of the sacristy room below the belfry, where light never came and their eyes dilated, trying to pierce the darkness and lance strokes of light not only from their eyes but from each new center of love offered completely to their dark and wise hands. Without having seen each other again, because he continued to spy on her only at meals, where she never managed to see him, but only his hidden eyes, and when she arrived at the room he was already there, and without speaking, she sought his hands and pulled his body against her no longer burning breasts, and both blindly moved for the other's lips, and laughed at the sound of candles falling with them onto the old church drapes, while outside they were accompanied by the bent sounds of afternoon, repose, siesta. She only wanted to feed his strength, only that; to give him part of her, so that with her he could conquer horses and with her open the way with the great club between his hands, while she would tell him that three stars lived and had, now, a reason for being and gave a whole world color and savor. Mercedes smelled coffee and wax candles and was sure that all her afternoons and mornings in the fields she had been preparing for this moment and that her thought then had been as clean as the event now, and that everything formed a natural part of her prayer and her journey, and for that reason the horror, the nightmare, the rupture of what she felt ordained by God, here in his certain and palpable incarnation, her God so confused with seed and sun and the fields at the foot of the hill, came in the mouths and hands of the two black beings and the voices and afternoon light which suddenly entered the ancient sacristy for the first time, permitting Mercedes for the first time to see their two bodies together, while the boy covered his eyes with his hands, not as if blinded, but as if trying to divide light from shadows, while her sister shouted and she hid her face beneath the black cloths and the priest roared and waved his arms like a buzzard.

. . . I told you, uncle, I saw those looks, and that uneasiness, and that new face in the girl. Girl! as if a broken glass could be put together again! To raise a vulture, Ernestina, I have raised a vulture and given him food when he hungered, and this is how he repays me, dishonoring a pure home, until this day inviolate, gossip and disgrace. And my example, uncle, my example of honor and chastity, my years sacrificed taking care of a sick mother so that this girl, this girl, look at them, like two dogs, look at them, the shame, the damnation and the sin; look at them! A vulture. That's what happens when you take an Indian among decent people. The two of them. The shame, shame, and decent people who will say, will say . . . My God, honor has ended, my God, devoured by sin and lust, pick up this girl, Ernestina, and hide her face from the face of honorable folk, and I will take care of this demon. You whore, whore, Ernestina! She is innocent, she was violated by this savage, she doesn't know, she doesn't understand what she has done, you will burn in flames eternal, Mercedes, you can't be saved, while I have grown old here, taking care of our mother. I'll teach you to tell a good girl from one of your misbegotten Indian sisters, like your mother, child of bad blood, and I here preserving the family honor. Tell me, uncle, tell me, uncle, and I and I and I and I, I, I . . . because Mercedes now had been forgotten . . . and I and I and I and I, I, I . . .

And she understood and felt the edge of a personal death, her own, her flesh and her fecund being, and she turned her furious face to the huddled boy while light and the familiar lost all symmetry and direction and she ran with abject pride, rumpled, to the house, before eyes raised from the sticky sleep of siesta. They would say that her pride had not been given to her, but that she had learned and formed it herself, though without wanting to, at this instant. And it was repeated to her over and over that she was a girl of good family and he a dirty Indian and her sister had sacrificed so much and her uncle possessed the word of God, and everything, the pride, the shame, the weeping, she held between her legs like a dry ripeness, like the broken strings of a broken Jacob's ladder of words and a half terror (after that day she had nothing completely, but everything by halves: pride and sin, love and shame) that pulsated as it rose to her abdomen and there, immediately chained like a charger held by its own fury, stopped by his own excess of strength, she knew that she was going to have a baby and she felt the unfathomable question, why, cross her breasts to the ringing of vesper bells, soft across the rich valley and the restless faces of men and women of Uruapan and those who came selling their labor from Reyes de Salgado and Paracho, from Tingambato and Parangaricutiro, from all the mournful humid earth which she carried now, with the warm eyes, between her hands, and Mercedes wanted to know it in all its seasons, seeding and harvest, drought and plenty, to squeeze and hurry all the seasons of the land across her breasts, and in this way, with all the heavy earth pushing down on her stomach, to hurry the time of her giving birth: that was how it was. Afterward people talked—to this day they talk—about that figure of satanic pride and innocent cloudy eyes who walked abroad at all hours with her swollen belly among the coffee rows, around the corral, even to the church, the house of God, shining in her dishonor, proud of her new shape, with the fetus shining in her like a last coal, by day and sometimes by night, too, padding over the dust with bare feet and asking peasants for a drink of water and staring angrily at the looks they gave her . . . as if they had never in their lives seen a pregnant woman, as if her body were not the same body it had been when she had used to walk among them and they had looked at her in a different way, as if it had not carried then, still sleeping, but the same, the same fruit as now . . . and then she was going to sleep to the dry sobs of her mother's and her sister's fists pounding on the bedroom door, pleading to be let in so they might pray together and not be condemned, Mercedes for her actions, Ernestina for her omissions, and Mercedes, swollen on the bronze bed, slept with her pride and her sin in her throat, condemning herself all over again every night, slept in the knowledge of sin and the hope of death, wrapped in the chaos of time and light into which her innocence and pleasure had been converted . . . and so the people talked. And so her mother and sister at last talked, too, speaking from their heavy chairs with their faces of iron, painted to look like flesh, talking about sin and the eternal perdition of souls, talking as if their eternal huddled silence had never existed, about virtue and honor, what that paradigm of a gentlemen, the deceased father, would have done, what the quick-tempered brother of firing squads and execution walls would do when he learned; talked about everything they had never in all their lives mentioned, and spoke from the charmed circle of their moral immunity, gained by gifts and plenary indulgences

334

and *rosarios* and Sunday canticles and all the dead they had visited; and they went on talking the very day Mercedes cried out and bit the sheets; they waited, talking and remembering their good works, for the fruit of sin to arrive and depart alone . . . evaporated from the earth by the heat of their good consciences; alone, Mercedes just had strength to reach the balcony of her bedroom window and open the window and cry words, not from her throat or her mind, words that gave voice to a woman alone giving birth, and she saw them pass, aflutter in their black garments, mother in the wheel chair and sister pushing it, both hurrying to the church while the baby made its way between her legs, living and smelling and restless as a river which flows only at night; dark, silent as the moment of conception, palpable in his darkness and his silence. And she had strength now only to take the scissors from the table and fall on the bed again and twist and bite her nails and then, with sleepy eyes and her mind carried back to some other, any other, day and hour except this day and these hours, double over her exhausted flesh and use the scissors and then hold him by the feet and slap him, while someone was singing a song of some other day, a song which only when she heard it sung again would she realize that she had heard it before and then forgotten, and forgot the baby, too, and woke, and did not find him, while her breasts burned like two stones cast up by an earthquake in her flesh, and she looked for him to offer her painful breasts with the milk fretting to come out, and the baby was not there. Only then did she remember and look for the missing part, the father, and in her hazy dream curse and condemn him to darkness, that of the child's conception and birth, to live blind and imprisoned; condemned him to the condemnation of his misused power, the power she remembered in the taming of the stallion and the flux of their copulation, condemned him to a useless trajectory, and thus in her delirium was assured that the true fruits of his power would never be any except those of hers, too; condemned him without thought and without voice while she felt for the missing son of the missing father, to recover his strength in the darkness. And only then she remembered the name of the father of her son, remembered the word she had never said and had heard the priest her uncle pronounce only once or twice; now, without power to remember it again in her whole life, gushing from the center of her sleep and her pale prostrate body, she cried, "Federico!"

Here, forever, in that moment of meeting between memory and name, Mercedes's memory stopped. There was darkness. Nothing shone except the brooch on the twisted skin of her neck. She closed her eyes and afterward remained several unmarked and unmeasured hours with her eyes larger and larger on the pillow, looking through the walls of her bedroom and seeing the last face, the unseen face of her son and the scarcely remembered face of the father, and from the living room came the murmur of agonized prayer, soft and clear in the warm evening, as the priest put his pasty face and eyes, two red raisins encrusted on the flour mask, near her mother's eyes, which were not there now and which possessed another mask, wolflike, but not by reason of her sickness and fatigue and pain, but because she was not there, because she had gone and hidden, imprisoned by the terror of so many never-said words in the last refuge of her flesh and future; his pasty head very near, saying, Your daughter has cursed herself, Ana María, she has sinned against the flesh and also against the spirit and never again will I enter her bedroom to hear her confession and repeat with her the words which might give her the consolation of our Holy Mother Church and thus salvation; and you, Ana María, you also have to condemn her and stand beside God and the Church so long as she does not humble her head and accept the ashes of repentance; and he was thinking, Save me, my God, save me from Thy Hell and upon this earth from Thy afflictions and make me a just man and permit me, in Thy Name, to distribute justice in this world, pardon and punishment, and do not let me open my heart to those who offended Thee with their concupiscence and their sin: condemn this girl and save me from executing Thy terrible will and Thy condemnation, my God, though I am ready to be Thy executioner and prove my faith. And he said again, putting his lips near the ear of the mother who was not there now: Be strong, Ana María, and condemn her with me in the name of your husband whom God has in glory, in the names of all those dead in the bosom of the Church, condemn her forever, for I believe that grace will never again descend upon this unhappy girl and that her repentance will be no more than a trick of the satanic pride which dominates her. And he was thinking, without knowing that an echo of his thought, which she would understand without knowing it, could reach to Mercedes's bedroom: Well, now she has suffered and she knows that every poor human being is capable of tolerating all pain for himself alone and without more aid than may be found within himself, and so she will find the just word and the straight road to spiritual peace on the other side of her pain, without needing me, and will touch Thy fingers and feel Thy breath close to her pain, and without need either of my words or of my right decision in Thy Name, nor of the pardon which I may offer her, like Thyself, in Thy Name, and she will become in truth a woman of God, without me, without me . . . And Mercedes heard the murmur of her uncle's thought and was already pronouncing the words of life and death which she had learned in two instants of flesh open and flesh fecund, and in them she was finding peace and decision. Therefore she was able to leave the house, walking stiff and erect, as she would always be afterward, erect, and with the new feeling of aggressive resignation which would never leave her—things don't happen, things have to be done—erect, with a blue-silk sunshade and two grips and an Indian servant girl, to look among the orphanages of Michoacán and all the Bajío, with her purse full of heavy gold pieces which the mother who was no longer there had given her wordlessly, frightened by the priest's litany, terrified by so many never-said words, one moment before losing herself forever in the perdition of her flesh. Mercedes could travel the Bajío in an old hacienda buggy with the servant girl and a driver dressed in white, and the blue-silk sunshade, near new thunder uttered by machine guns, among banner staffs, looking along the eyes of the soldiers for the dark eyes of he who had given her the child, sure that somewhere his obscure sexuality was stiffening itself in domination of a powerful horse, that his power required such contact and conflict, until she finally gave him up for dead the day, a few days before the battle between Obregón and Villa, when she found the rosy face and delicate profile which had been left in Celaya along with her sister's signature. With the baby she had traveled to Mexico City. She bought a house in Coyocan and had the child baptized Manuel and reared him in the love of truth; and so the years passed simply by passing, held motionless in two or three moments which summarized all her time and all life: Father of my son, you will not have more strength than you have gained with me, and you will have to come back to my image and to that of your son to find truth and the origin of your strength, and everything else will be discipation, pride without fruit and the most horrible of crimes, the crime which is not known as crime. . . .

The sky had darkened. A cavalry troop returning from the Sixteenth of September parade clattered across the plaza with weary hooves. Mercedes stood and closed the window. Once again the servant's steps approached by their habitual path, coming to announce dinner. Mercedes walked through darkness. Her erect shoulders carried only her moments of revelation and love and pride and redemption. Nothing had happened afterward. Manuel Zamacona had not died an absurd death in a bar in Guerrero last night. Federico Robles had not unchained his power before returning to find the truth offered by Mercedes in the first seed. She sat at the table and emptied the pitcher of perfumed chocolate into a brown clay cup.

THE EAGLE FALLEN

Dawn light condensed around Federico Robles. Silent old man, wrinkled suit, hands hidden in his pockets; in his opacity he seemed the origin of the very light that bathed him. Without direction or sense of direction he had walked through neighborhoods which were unknown to him, which had risen beyond the limits of his awareness during those years when he had dedicated himself to the strict small urban circle where his life and

338

power had flowered. Not looking for anything, foreseeing nothing, he walked a cold blind route, guided only by his old eyes, which scarcely touched the city's gray thickening skeleton, through the residue of Independence celebration. Women stood in lines before morning milk-stores of the neighborhood, with their children wrapped in their *rebozos;* women hurried around him; he knew that no one observed him very long, that his dark figure seemed out of place to no one, that his sudden age did not seem strange, nor anything about him: his was now the common being accepted by all. He stopped a moment, crossing a street, and the roar of a truck came nearer than the roar of fire which stopped up his hearing. His body moved again with furious weight through the halls of the Lomas mansion, with a never desired, never conscious intuition of destruction; jars crashed on the marble floors, lamps were pulled out of their connections, a tablecloth was swept clean of its silver and china and the cold meal which would never be eaten, down fell the candelabra which illuminated the dining room; the sound of Norma's sobbing laughter as she beat her door while he left the light of silver and burning candles on the marble floor, left the house and got into his automobile and shot off downhill through the Lomas, all his memories superimposed and dancing, light and laughter, burned flesh and destruction. When he opened his eyes with a sudden shock and hit the brakes, he was breathing the air of dawn in a part of the city he did not know. He felt himself at the end of a long journey. Unpainted walls closed him in. Light and telephone posts formed an impenetrable forest of wire. In his suit wrinkled by three days' life, he got out of the car and looked at the street sign: Fray J. Torquemada. A straight street where the toneless pavement color was also the color of walls and sky. Robles walked. He had no goal, he was lost in a secret urge. Smells came together in a nested haze, waning before the oncoming day. The smells of steam and trolley wheels, escaping gas, flowers being carried to market, damp urine against walls, wrapped in a transparent weightless air. Streets had neither name nor face. They rolled and twisted beneath his steps like a gray serpent. A murmur of litany and sobbing came

339

less from voices than from the high haze which circled an adobe hut.

"Morning star."

"Ark of the alliance."

At an open window he narrowed his eyes to see through candlelight. A white wooden coffin surrounded by flowers and kneeling dark bodies.

"Ark of David."

"Lamb of God."

"Be calm, be calm, Doña Madalena."

"He had to find those who would kill him."

"Poor Gabriel," said the old man with sleepless eyes and the baseball cap between dried-bread hands.

"He came home so full of dreams, with his presents for everyone. Who could have foreseen!"

"He was my buddy," Beto sniveled. "Drink your coffee, Don Pioquinto, there's nothing to do now."

"We'll find that skinny son of a bitch, we'll——"

"Respect, brother," said Tuno, with his head down.

Smells of wax candles and gardenias filled the room as Federico Robles moved into it.

"Come in, *Señor*. Were you his friend, too?"

Beto took Federico's will-less elbow and put a glass of yellow pulque in his hands. "Gabriel has left us, *Señor!* He didn't look for it, I swear. It just came to him. That's luck."

"Luck," Federico repeated in open-eyed dream.

"Who knows why anyone dies? Whatever we try, we end with God." Beto raised his glass in gesture of *salud* to Robles. "But Garbiel, *Señor*, so young. To die that way, for no reason at all, and so quick, without a chance to see the face of his killer, without a chance to defend himself. That's to die for no reason at all, *Señor*."

Robles's old eyes passed over Gabriel's rigid corpse, the wet stain on his abdomen, the chain of women who surrounded the body. Eyes and flesh and death of the people. This is my cousin Froilán the morning he was executed in Belén, said Robles's still aging eyes, although his tongue could not pronounce the names, nor his memory recall who they were. This is Feliciano Sánchez, shot in the back as he ran across a field of weeds.

The brown-skinned obese aging man looked at the door, at the clearing sky of close, ferocious stars driven earthward by the trembling sunrise. He wanted to fly toward those stars, to fly because he felt himself pasted to earth and imprisoned among murdered dead. You don't have to do anything to die, the divining voice said, no will is needed to die in vain. He looked again at Gabriel's body. Who will explain his death? the almost enraged voice boomed; who is his assassin, who is the assassin of all our dead? With a dry sob no one heard, Robles fell on his knees in the dust. Beto touched his shoulder.

"He was one of us," said Beto. "As if we were not all different from each other, but all the same. Do you understand me? As if Gabriel were me and I were him. That's how we were."

Federico's knees buried themselves in the earth: surface-dry earth of forever-hidden subterranean lagoon, lagoon at the ancient, damp, froglike core, the place of meeting between men. He felt understanding through his body. Far from his bone and blood, in other lives which in this moment of defeat and rendered flesh were his own life, the mute lives which had fed him, he felt the true meaning. Those mute lives whose names he could not remember multiplied in mortal pantomime until they covered all Mexico with all failures and downfalls and assassinations and battles. Then they came back again and spoke to him, recognized him, their own body.

On his knees, Robles raised an arm, passed his hand across Gabriel's frozen forehead.

Every step was a memory now. Four floors; on each, two apartments. Stairway of broken, chipped, cracked mosaic winding beside a wall dirtied by hands. Only gray fell through the skylight. Memories at one time confused and without settings, inexplicable to the light of everyday reason, the haste-woven noose-thread of everyday understanding; but no longer confused: now they fell in their true order and their original ambiguous meanings. Albano Robles and the damp sun-baked earth. Froilán

341

Reyero, his long mustaches wetted by the pitcher, Froilán, in the tumult of carbines and hunger and bullet-spattered walls, for whom not to be alone was like dying with shame. Mercedes Zamacona, warm and dark in siesta-time, convoking a wordless and sightless meeting within her flesh where all seeds germinated soundlessly between love's hands, in whom the house of life stretched as one single deep plowed line of unconscious power. Celaya: fields open to rivers of flesh, cannister and bayonet and diana bugle call and horseshoes burned from gallop, fields where all of one world appeared and all of another world was born, created by those planted in those fields with blood and gunpowder. Librado Ibarra: nights of youth and ambition, nights deformed by the city, nights spent learning fraud, nights when roads opened easily and were bounded only by deception and the tacit justification. Feliciano Sánchez: last blood act, last death decision before arrival at the place of established channels where no one can hurt us, where no one lives and everything lasts, in a sphere of complacency and simplicity and long perpetuity . . . the sphere of Norma Larragoiti. And the last step of the cracked stairs and the last memory, where the foot could lose balance and life topple, too: Hortensia Chacón.

And as if the sound of a bat had accompanied Federico in his ascent, the eyeless woman was waiting behind her open door, seated in her wheel chair. Neither he nor she spoke; they took each other's hands and Federico moved the wheel chair through the little living room to the bedroom. There, always holding her warm hand, he looked at her. Hortensia's delicate Indian features smiled faintly. Dark lenses hid her eyes. Blood pulsed in the pads of her fingers, lightly resting on Federico's. They sat with life between their fingers and without speaking, man and woman, both brown skinned, part of the blood slave from a life which forever had forgotten life, both dressed in the clothing of Western civilization, with only their fingers to tell them that they were the same. A common sweetness anticipated a recognition. They still did not speak.

Federico was feeling that today the sun would reach its highest flight over a desert of color . . . sumptuous, wounded. And that here, between her fingers, he would know it. He caressed her hair.

"You've come," Hortensia said at last.

"Yes."

"I've waited so long for you."

"You waited for me."

"So long."

With her eyes in her fingers, Hortensia found the edge of the bed and sat beside him. Then she lay down. Robles put his cheek to her breasts. Desire drew near. Blind, in the darkness of the room, both sought it with tact and direct breathing and without words. It was not as if they were alone, nor as if they were one; nor was it as if they were two. They were two, yes; but each was the other. It was this wordless wisdom which communicated desire to Hortensia and will to Federico, and the other wisdom was distracted by the moment of flesh, the wisdom of the other being living now in the warmth between them both, the being which now recognized them and claimed its own life in the contact between them, man and woman. There was no need to say it. Their entwined bodies, their trembling intercourse was the first caress given to that child already alive, the child who at this instant was obliging them to join their sexuality.

Federico slept and Hortensia watched over him. In his sleep he saw the face with mustaches wet in the jar of clay, heard it telling him that loneliness is not terrible, the pain is to be with others. Hortensia watched over his sleep with her open blind eyes, so that when his eyes opened, the first thing he would see would be her . . . and in her he would see the world.

With suffocated steps, night descended upon the sixteenth of September, 1951.

343

PART THREE

BETINA RÉGULES

Jaime Ceballos had always distinguished himself by his ambition and ability. When fifteen, he began to publish poems in brief-lived provincial reviews, and as a law student he was several times called upon to make public addresses, once at the dedication of a dam, before the Governor, and once on Independence Day before the President himself. As a student he was in all ways brilliant, and his model deportment, his mature dress and behavior, earned him the kindly notice of good society in Guanajuato. Consequently, when Betina Régules—one of the most popular young belles in the national capital, she whom society columnists had named "the golden girl," daughter of the famous lawyer and man of affairs, Don Roberto Régules—when Betina came to Guanajuato for the spring season of 1954, a host of matrons set to maneuvering a meeting.

At first Betina spoke with almost no one. She was always correct and smiling, but she always maintained the barrier which stands between casual acquaintanceship and the merest intimacy. Perhaps she was somewhat chilled by the provincial atmosphere. The first times she saw Jaime, she treated him exactly as she did all other local gallants. But gradually, as she became accustomed to the social climate, she granted him her open favor. He felt the barrier drop away in an action so trivial as her smile when she powdered her nose. Jaime escorted her to a ball; their cheeks slowly approached each other, presently he dared to squeeze that nineteen-year-old waist, and at last their heads were joined

347

in a single profile and swayed to a rhythm far from that of the orchestra. Matrons seated in file along the walls were full of contentment.

"A most adorable girl, Betina. Who would have suspected that such a belle, after such triumphs in the capital, would fall for one of our young eligibles?"

"Home calls the wandering heart, Doña Asunción. Her father is, after all, also from Guanajuato; it was from here that he set forth to conquer the world."

"What a lovely young couple!"

"And Don Roberto so wealthy! What a match for Jaime! Now he can go to Mexico City to a post in Don Roberto's empire! Ah, they have both, both won the great lottery."

No night seemed long enough. First, hand in hand, they walked along the Presa; then, arms about waists, along the golden streets; finally their eyes shone in the darkness of Betina's car and their lips repeated the same words, each time as if the first time, and then there was silence.

"Are you happy, my love?"

"Yes, Jaime . . ."

"My cigarette doesn't bother you?"

"No, really, I'm just fine."

"Really?"

Until they felt their lips and tongues joined and Betina's breasts squeezed against his shirt.

Nights of young love, winged nights. The animal warmth, bittersweet flesh, attempting to preserve timeless, fleeting moments.

"Forever, Betina?"

"Forever, Jaime, my love, my love!"

"My life! I would like to fill your hair with stars . . ."

"Don't talk, Jaime, hold me . . ."

And Betina's hair filled with stars and the two bodies fell together, embracing, her trembling hands on his neck, his fingers buried in the small of her back and with feather pads caressing her waist, her arms, the visible parting of her breasts. Provincial nights, as languid as they wished them, and as silent . . . or the

348

murmur of their favorite record played over and over in a deserted bar

and our love is here to stay

while their feet slid slowly from side to side and Betina felt Jaime's passionate breathing in her ear.

Only on Sundays did Betina change character. Then when she would appear for five o'clock teas in the hotel, quite different from the girl she seemed when with Jaime, and would show off her provocative and severely cut dresses among the unvaried tulles of the local belles. Then Betina would arch an eyebrow and affirm her superiority and her elegance, and the word "ordinary" would flash from her lips and from her eyes at every moment; and then she took pleasure in dancing lively and complicated steps while the provincial couples were stumbling about on either side of her.

"In Paris we stay at the Crillon," she would say in a louder voice than she usually used with Jaime: "Papá says that all French history has happened there. Imagine, the guillotine was set up in the same plaza."

Jaime felt her different, but he rather enjoyed and applauded her leading him into an attitude of independence before the provincial: for he, too, had to adopt it.

The first of June, Betina went back to Mexico City. When Jaime graduated, he would follow her and they would see what lay ahead.

His thesis was not so brilliant as all had expected. He repeated, with inner satisfaction, his excuses: the long nights, the long hours writing the daily letter, the continuous warmth in the pit of his stomach.

The singing, ash-blonde languid girl met him at the Buenavista station. She waved her hand, but all Jaime could see was the little grimace of distaste about her mouth. He got down, dressed in his black Sunday suit, his vest, a carnation in his lapel, and ran to hug her.

"No, Jaime, not now, they're watching us."

They hurried, in her yellow MG, with its top down, to the pensión which had been recommended to Jaime, a house on Milán.

"Think about what we're going to do, Jaime. Which do you like? Golf, or tennis, or riding?"

"You know I'm no athlete, Betina. My studies——"

"But we're going to take care of that. Choose right away. I'll pick you up at nine this evening. Ah! don't you have something to wear that isn't so solemn, more British, eh? You know, elegant but comfortable. And listen, don't use flowers in your lapel."

"I don't know . . . I'll have to buy something . . . see if you can't go with me."

"Okay. Here we are. *Cia*, my love. Until nine!"

Betina pulled away, shining under the sun and raising a cloud of dust and smoke.

Bobó's drawing room was the same as always. Betina and Jaime were received by a cordial host, who had grown fatter and sillier over the years, wearing a vest that had once closed on the foppish bulk within, and balancing a gold cigarette holder between his yellow teeth. Bobó cried to them, "Darlings! Enter and apprehend Eternal Verity! Yonder strolls a beggar with tray and victuals! *Voici, O Rimbaud . . .*"

And he trotted away into the haze of tobacco and gin. Jaime felt himself ill at ease in his black suit, wrinkled by his trip, and even the thick school ring on his finger seemed out of place. He constantly fingered the points of his handkerchief and surreptitiously polished his shoes against his trousers cuffs.

"Gus, darling!" Betina said as she embraced a fat little man with plucked eyebrows.

"Loveliness! Such a long time! Since the Ides of March!"

Both of them roared in honor of their little private joke, and Gus, with his arm around her waist, stared at Jaime and said, "Betina, introduce me to your casket salesman."

But Jaime had turned his back and was going toward the bar. Betina followed him with clenched teeth. "At least you could show a *little* breeding, my dear . . ."

Both moved into the swirl of the party, Betina with full knowledge of her ground, Jaime, trailing behind her, singing the same words over: very pleased to, very pleased, I arrived today, yes, Betina told me . . . He looked around the room, the sharply and differently colored walls, the paintings, the statuettes. From high on the stairs, Pichi, her eyes heavy with mascara, was sighing, "My royal romance! Now my royal romance is coming!"

Bobó approached Betina and Jaime. "Now we're in the time of dead leaves for sure. Just a little while ago your mother and father were the youthful part of my parties, and now, you're the princess of the salon. How much water has gone under the bridge! What deceptions, and what suffering! Mexico City will never be the same after the horrible death of Norma . . ."

"Well, she was a little common, the poor girl, but after all," interrupted a Charlotte who had become dry and hard, as if losing the oils of life, but who still brandished the same old lorgnette . . . though now it seemed to hold together as if with adhesive tape. "What a way to die, burned to a crisp in the middle of the Lomas! I tell you, old Huichilobos is still among us. Say . . . and have you heard anything about the famous banker?"

"Nothing," said Bobó, chewing his cigarette holder. "Well, that he married a nobody, something of that sort. And what news is there of the imposter Vampa?"

Charlotte raised a hand to her heart. "Ay! Don't remind me of that fatal blow. I didn't know how to breathe afterward. Just think how he fooled us!"

Bobó's face wrinkled in pain. "His only title was to a pizza show in 'Frisco. He was cook there."

"And we treated him as blue blood! Don't remind me, Bobó, I die of anger . . . and imagine, Pierre Caseaux gave him a job in his kitchen. Every time I eat there, I have the feeling the macaroni knows all my secrets."

"Ay, but how unfortunate!" Betina laughed, fingering her diamond collar. Charlotte's myoptic eyes passed over Jaime. "No, my dear, but there have also been a few happy events. I'm enchanted, Bobó, to see what a lovely couple Pimpinela and Rodrigo have turned out."

"Don't you remember I told you the first time he came to a

351

party here," Bobó said with enthusiasm; "I remarked precisely: That boy has talent! Eh?"

"Yes. And how they receive. That house in the Pedregal is simply beautiful. Everything in such fine taste. Suddenly you see who is who in this miserable cactus patch."

Countess Aspacúccoli approached, chewing a mouthful of salad. "I've lost my keys, darlings. Who will invite me to sleep tonight?" Her avid eyes passed around the group and lit upon Jaime. "You, unknown youth?" she decided with an imperial gesture. Everyone laughed, and Jamie could not help blushing; and when Betina saw this, her laughter stopped in mid-air and she stalked off to the powder room. There she found Natasha, now reduced to a womanhood that was merely skin and bones beneath, and a puffy Cuquis with wrinkles around the mouth.

"*Salud,* Betina," Natasha muttered as she applied her perfumed lipstick. "We've observed your future. That's he, isn't it?"

"A true puff of nothing," said Cuquis emphatically. "And that's why you broke up with César? Well, frankly, my dear . . . and to think this little saintly hypocrite is going to catch so many millions! Bah! What a waste, my love."

Her face in her hands, Betina cried.

"To know destiny is not to possess it," Rodrigo Pola was pronouncing to his attentive servants. "In the movies, success is a perpetual adventure and risk. He who dominates, triumphs, he who knows how to make his talent the servant of the masses. It is clear that in Mexico we have an enormous public which demands works which it can understand, easy to be at ease with, yet with class. All of us, stars, writers, producers, owe our being to that public, our public!"

"Your success has been marvelous, Rodrigo," Charlotte insisted. "You don't intervene in the selection of new stars?"

"Well, that isn't really my field, but my suggestions carry *weight,* you understand." A gray three-button Italian suit, a silk tie. His agile face radiated complete self-possession.

Junior went up to Jaime. "So you're Betina's new chap, eh? You know, my mother is fantastic. She went to the Basílica to

352

beg the Virgin not to let you and Betina get married! My God, eh?"

The tropical orchestra entered at a moment of general indifference and began its rhythms and repetitions *vacilón, qué rico vacilón, cha cha cha, qué rico cha cha cha*

Looking at herself in the mirror, Cuquis said to Betina, "Don't forget to remind your father about my business. Those lots in the Barrilaco, you remember?"

But Betina was not listening. "It isn't that he is poor," she thought with her compact in her hand; "it's that he doesn't know how to do things, it's that he is sad, yes, and commonplace. He doesn't feel at ease with wealth and elegance." But the memory of his kisses and caresses came back, striking against that thought, and then she remembered him, too, badly dressed, clumsy in conversation, unable to shine with the unequivocal luster of what she owned or her elegance, and she saw his nervous hands and felt his kisses, his kisses, his kisses.

ricachá, ricachá, ricacha, así llaman en Marte al-cha cha cha

"Nothing is new, but only novelty is successful," Rodrigo was going on to his circle of admirers, who were throned on happiness just to hear his voice. "That's the secret of the good screenwriter. You saw the success *Naked Souls* had. The eternal Romeo and Juliet story, but changed to a humble setting, a wide-belted Romeo, an impoverished Juliet who happens also to be the daughter of an old blind bullfighter. Then, cha cha cha, which is the latest, and Doris Leal in a role directly opposite to her usual ones. The old tried formula, dressed up to seem new. Bull's-eye."

pican, no pican los tamálitos de Olga, Olga

"Here's my royal romance," Pichi sighed each time someone else came in.

"Who's your silly romance, Pichi, if you know yourself?" Gus said softly into the girl's ear. Pichi's face flushed, and she just repeated, "He's come now, Gus, he just came in, my royal cavalier . . ."

tome chocolate, pague lo que deba

Pierre Caseaux entered with a shining new girl with gazelle

eyes. "There's Señor Pola," the girl whispered, with her lips full. "Are we going to arrange my screen test?"

pimpollo, pimpooooollo, pim-pim-pimpollo

Jaime was left alone with his arms crossed before the window. Betina drew near him and took his arm. She wanted to make light conversation, and with a singing voice she said to him, "What do you think of the crowd, Jaime?" She put her hand on his arm. "Tomorrow we're going to see Papá. He agrees with everything and he wants you to go to work right away. He told me that he's going to give us a house in Colonia Anzures."

They were silent. Jaime slowly rubbed her hand.

no quieeeero codazos, ni tampoco cabezaaaazos

RODRIGO POLA

Rodrigo left the party at one in the morning and descended to Avenida Insurgentes. His car was parked at the corner of Nápoles: he unlocked it and was about to get in when he saw a dark figure seated inside. He jumped back a step and slammed the door. For a moment he trembled with fear, trying to make out the bulky shape through the window. A bitter smile answered his stare, and Rodrigo opened the door again.

"I've changed so much?" the voice of the brown face said.

"Ixca! But after three years . . ."

"Get in. Let's take a ride."

Rodrigo continued along Insurgentes. The Cienfuegos beside him was a different man, changed not only in the collapse of his physical appearance, his shirt without tie, the soft and flabby face. Ixca's fingers rubbed the leather upholstery. "This is not like your room on Rosales," he said at last, as the Jaguar reached the intersection of Insurgentes, Chapultepec, and Oaxaca, where a smiling face blew smoke rings from a Raleigh advertisement.

"Where can I drop you?" Rodrigo asked while he waited, pulling on his gloves, for the red light to change. This was December, and a light but biting wind crossed the starry night.

"Where are you going?"

"To my home . . . in the Pedregal of San Angel. But I can drop you anywhere you want."

"It doesn't matter where."

Observing Rodrigo's new face, tanned by sun, reddened by whisky, Ixca smiled. His heavy camel's-hair coat. His yellow gloves.

"What have you done with your life?" Rodrigo asked.

"That's not important. What have you done with yours? Give me a smoke."

Rodrigo took a cigarette case from his warm overcoat pocket and pushed in the dashboard lighter. Ixca's eyes squinted through smoke. "Now you're where you wanted to be, aren't you? I'm happy for you."

"For what?"

"Your success, your money, your wife. It's not like the old days on Rosales, that morning when I found you in your little room with the windows shut and the gas on."

Rodrigo laughed hard. What had happened to that confession written on browning pages taken from a novel by Pio Baroja. He would have liked to read them to Ixca now. But his first decision when he left that house on Rosales had been to take nothing with him, neither his clothes nor the brass bed, nor the teapot and cups, nor the Pio Baroja, nor his writings, but to leave everything with the janitor to do with as he saw fit. Because he did not have those yellow pages now, a comfortable little demon began to buzz inside his elegant new clothes, and to insist that somehow the words be recovered for Ixca.

"Gas! Success! My wife! Money . . . !" Rodrigo laughed as he stopped for the light on Obregón. "Obviously, who's complaining . . . but wasn't that life mine, Ixca? Do you think that because I'm here now, I'm no longer there? Do you believe that a new life destroys and cancels out the old one?"

"Your new life has to wipe out the old one."

"Ideas, ideas." He pulled away with a jerk. "Only ideas, Ixca, that's all you know to answer a man with, always prescriptions and recipes. Has this prescription grown boring? So, try this other one! Shit, how easy. And you, with your mystery, your unknown past, your what? You park yourself on the side and watch the parade go by. Blow your nose, piss on the skull of wormwood destiny, eh?"

"*In vino veritas.*"

"Go to hell! You must be . . . I don't know, a pimp of some sort, that's the only way to understand why you play with people the——"

"Play?"

"Yes, play. That's the only way to explain it . . . your hiding my mother's death from me, your . . ."

"Would it have made any difference to you?"

"Difference to me?" Rodrigo thought about Rosenda, the only really important witness his prosperity and success could have. Norma? No, not Norma: Norma had once served as witness, that evening when they came out of the Nicte-Ha together. And then Norma had ended for him, he thought, not without a certain shame that he would have liked to confess. But Rosenda had never been witness. And now it was hard to reconstruct his mother's face, harder than to recall her dust-changed body, her concentrated scent. An endless chain of advertisements and colored electric lights—Christmas was near—tied Insurgentes together in one long glitter. "No, I don't know, not her, not the way she was, with the same name and face she always had, maybe not. What would have made a difference to me would have been to let her know, because she never knew what I wanted to be, but only what I was; not what I became, but what I was then; that I wanted to do well, really, not to end everything and not to destroy myself, or just to find excuses for failures. Shit . . . now I'm looking for excuses again. You set me back, just as always, Ixca."

But between the spoken words, thought words were doubting his honesty. Why did he have to please Cienfuegos? His new life demanded a certain conduct of him, a conduct which above all had no need to explain or justify itself. And just the same . . .

"Listen, Ixca, it would have been very easy in those days to destroy everything, and yet I had something which no one could destroy. And today I have things which beg for destruction,

356

which demand to be blown away by the wind, and I save and preserve them. I sent love to hell, self-respect, my vocation, everything. And my mother knew I was going to do that, that was why she demanded those bourgeois defenses of me, the ones she gave me when she gave birth to me. My mother understood me . . . why not? But she always understood me just as the event was happening, she didn't understand . . . how can I say it? the long series, the whole life, but only each occurring moment she understood, and without saying anything, Ixca, she watched me looking for excuses for a life that was far from what I wanted to be and do. We were like a game, two players who never meet, each one playing like crazy, believing that the other is in the game, too."

"And today you're doing the same thing yourself, aren't you? You can't really see yourself no matter how hard you try. I know you want to be sincere now, Rodrigo. Yet all you're really doing is asking for my pity and trying to make me accept your new hypocrisies. You're a——"

"Shut up, you son of a bitch! You, who can't understand anything, who lives like a shadow, stirring up trouble, eating life you never live yourself. The merely human! The purely man! The son of the great whore. It would be well for *you* to give yourself a reason for living just once and just once feel yourself a poor bastard who . . ."

"I've done that. There's no reason for you to tell me to."

Rodrigo jabbed in the lighter. "The merely purely human man! The strong man who can carry his tragedy all inside! Coward! You've never given anything to anyone, nothing except your words and prescriptions, the evil solutions of the just-purely-merely-human, but oh the just man. You've never loved, you've never . . . bah! You can't fool me any more."

Ixca smoked slowly, in the corner of the seat. "What I did with Norma hurts you."

Rodrigo jammed the brakes on, slamming Ixca forward against the windshield. "Don't you say that again, you bastard, or I'll . . ." He shook his fist in front of Ixca's face. "What the hell do you know about it? You, who fucked her once to find out what I

357

never knew . . . but who the hell knows why you do anything . . .
not because you loved her; you never loved her, nobody has
ever loved her more than I did, you hear me! Nor am I going
to suppose you did it to prove to me that you could get so easily
all that I could never have. But you never fucked her every time
you had to go to a whorehouse, *mano,* you never had to give
every whore her face and body so you could know a little love,
you never had to tell whores the words you would have told
Norma, that you thought and felt only for Norma. You never
had to make dozens of bodies and faces without names take the
place of Norma, you bastard!" In his corner, Ixca smiled. "Sure,
mano, sure, laugh. What difference does it make?"

The car slowly moved forward again. Rodrigo's gloved hands
listlessly shifted gears. Just this once, he was promising himself,
this once, and never again. He was thinking that so many
explanations were possible, and that none would ever take him
back to what pained him, and that he had no reason to go back.
Pain had no place in his new life.

"Excuse me, old man." Wasn't that the better way, he reflected.
"I know that you're my friend, that everything you did was . . .
that from your point of view everything you did was . . . Two
and two are four, and all that. Curtain. No, that isn't it. But when
you have talent and don't cultivate it . . . when you know you
can love, but you don't love . . . when you know truth, but fill
yourself with lies . . ."

"And now, now that you have everything?"

For the last time, he promised himself. "What? Pimpinela?
She gives to me. Her name, her elegance, her social relations . . .
just as Norma, without knowing it, gave, too. And I go on giving
to no one. That was why I married her. So she could give to
me . . . even her virginity. And she had to believe that I give
her something too. Aunt Lorenza can rebuild her goddamn
house on Hamburgo and amuse herself throwing out the Jews
and Spaniards and once again receive her beloved mummies at
tea. Joaquinito can die in peace, sucking a bottle of Hennessy.
Benjamín's feeble-mindedness doesn't matter any more. But I've
given her nothing that is mine, Ixca. On the other hand, she

has helped me. She leads me to the right people, she introduces me to the Pedregal mummies. But she doesn't know who I am, and she'll never know."

"That's better, eh!"

"Don't laugh. She won't know what a shit I am. She sincerely believes that I'm a great man, that with ten box-office hits I built a white house with high white walls and a stone garden and a swimming pool and Henry Moore sculptures and a Jaguar at the door and a wife with a distinguished name. I'm sure that's what she thinks and that she feels very satisfied. But what I am and will go on being, like earth changed into an island, what I think over and over when I'm alone . . . because these are thoughts I can't talk over with anyone, no one would let me . . . or what I have been and have done . . . Look." He raised his hands from the steering wheel and held them in front of Ixca's face. "They're no different from any hands."

"Behave yourself. Don't play games."

"A hand that makes a fist to fuck and a hand that writes and moves and feels a woman and plays and works. Look at it. With that hand all I've been able to do is wipe away snot, Ixca. This hand—you know it yourself, I'm not asking for your pity!—could have written great poetry, could have loved Norma Larragoiti. Look at it: could have, could have, could have! My mother thought this hand could take away her poverty and her death cult. Could have. And it didn't even close her dead eyelids. No, I was very busy wiping away snot. Could have!"

In the corner, locked inside himself, Ixca said, "Be quiet now. You upset me. You have what you deserve."

"Deserve! What did my mother deserve—that my father be resurrected from the execution ground? What did Norma deserve —that a gutless nobody named Rodrigo Pola should love her? So what we are is what we deserve to be. My mother and her memories, Norma and death, and I and snot."

They passed Nuevo León. Cars moved faster. Lights became farther apart, gardens, larger.

"You won't give away my confidences." Rodrigo smiled.

"I'm only your spectator."

"Sure, that's much more convenient. It's like being The Only Free Man." Rodrigo smiled broadly. "Let's see now. The first time was in Prepa, with Tomás Mediana's group. You were seventeen then, but your face was hard. Then again during the strikes at the university. Then not until nineteen hundred fifty-one when you reappeared as the pseudo-confidante of Federico Robles. And now. What are you doing now?"

"I don't live in Mexico City. I did everything I had to do here."

"Just what? Take the juice out of Federico and Norma and then take off? A brave life for the man of justice!"

Ixca remained shut up in his corner of the car. Tieless, wearing a wrinkled black jacket and old gray pants, nothing set him apart from any man in the city. "Everyone finds his destiny. Even I."

"Destiny! Ah, you used to talk a lot about that. And sacrifice."

"Sacrifice," Ixca's voice murmured. "And that was how Norma died, though she didn't know it."

"Yes? Tell me about it. What did you have to do with it?"

"I? Nothing. They told me what happened."

"The one who lost everything was Robles. Do you know what happened to him? I heard that he married again." Rodrigo was driving smoothly and confidently. He wanted this to be the last impression Ixca would carry away. They passed a number of one-storey restaurants, shops for roast chicken.

"Yes, he married. He lives in the north. I believe he owns some land and raises cotton. In Coahuila, I think. He has a son."

"The fire was never explained?"

"No. Robles went to the police and said that it was his fault, that he was guilty of Norma's death. He was terribly upset and they didn't believe him, especially as they knew everything else that had happened."

"Who could have made up that crazy story? Poor bastard, after all. They say it was all the doing of my distinguished colleague at school, Roberto Régules. Well: and you?"

Cienfuegos felt the old brilliance come back into his eyes. "And I?"

"Yes, and you. Sometimes I ask myself whether you really eat and sleep." Rodrigo laughed.

360

Ixca put his foot on top of Rodrigo's right foot, which was lightly touching the accelerator.

"Careful . . ."

He pushed Rodrigo's foot down as the car gained speed. "And I? What do you want? My memories, my life? Do you think I wouldn't give something to know, too?"

"Ixca, take your foot off . . ." Rodrigo touched the horn, which began to sound above the screaming of the tires.

"You think that I remember my own face? My life begins again every new day . . ." He was shouting. ". . . every new day, and I never remember what happened before, never, you see, it was all a terrible game, that's all, a game of forgotten rites and signs and dead words; she'll be satisfied now, yes, she'll be satisfied . . . she believed that Norma's death was the necessary sacrifice, and that once the sacrifice was given, we could return and bury ourselves in lives of poverty, mumble hysterical words over our debts, play with humility!"

"Ixca, take your foot off the accelerator! I'm going to lose con——"

"She forced me to live with that servant girl and her children, again in darkness! You don't know my mother, Rodrigo . . . my mother is stone, serpents, she doesn't have . . ." He shouted and laughed and pushed his foot down harder and harder. Headlights of cars and buses whirled by like streaks of lightning. At last, without stopping laughing, but without the least sound of laughter, he raised his foot. The car stopped abruptly with a shaking of oil and the smell of burned brakes. They were in front of the Convent of Carmen. Ixca turned up the collar of his coat and bent his laughing head to Rodrigo and got out. The car pulled off toward the Pedregal, and Cienfuegos stood against the wall of the old convent and laughed and felt cold come into his bones. A light fog hung over the garden, a haze which moved around him, filed his edges, penetrated him and changed him into fog, too, less transparent and less real than the vapor which at every breath swept up from the ground. December's cold wind pulled him along the avenue, across the city, and his eyes, living and light, absorbed homes and sidewalks and men and rose to the center of night until he became, in his stone-eagle, air-serpent eyes, the city itself, its voices, sounds, memories, presentiments, the vast and anonymous city with its arms crossed from Copilco to Indios Verdes, with its legs open from Peñon de los Baños to Cuatro Caminos, with its brown twisted belly button at the Zócalo; he became the tubs and the roof tops and the dark pots, the glass skyscrapers and the mosaic domes and the stone walls and the mansard roofs and the huts of tin and adobe and residences of concrete and red tile and iron gates, names and smells and all bodies sprinkled the buried length of the great heavy unbalanced valley, all tombstones, and above all, all voices, voices: Gervasio Pola, who, like his son, wanted to save himself alone; Froilán Reyero and Pedro Ríos and Sindulfo Mazotl, who died with their *Viva Madero!* in their throats; Mercedes Zamacona, with her intimate memory of a dark love and the first rise of power; Norma Larragoiti, covered by a grave of mink-skins and jewels; the stiff Catalan woman who with tears in her eyes sang songs of the War in Spain; Federico Robles, carried back to the beginning of the beginning to discover others, and so himself; Hortensia Chacón, waiting with blind eyes for a voice to speak faith in her existence; and all the secure and thoughtless gigglers, Charlotte and Bobó, the Countess Aspacúc-coli, Gus, Pedro Caseaux, Cuquis, Betina Régules, Jaime Ceballos; and a leatherworker from the north who arrived in his City of Palaces full of dreams; a clown who didn't have money enough to buy paints for his face; Rosenda at the bottom of her grave, at last united with the dust which was her first hallucination of words and love and fecundity; Librado Ibarra, who merely lived his life; an old man with yellow mustaches who remembered the old palaces; Gladys García, with her unconscious prayer for a minimum of happiness; and Beto, Fifo, and Tuno, and Doña Serena, and the gratuitous cadavers and crazy deaths of Manuel Zamacona and Gabriel; and a family who spend all their savings for a vacation at Acapulco, and Feliciano Sánchez, dead on a field of weeds, and Pimpinela de Ovando, and at last his own voice, the voice of Ixca Cienfuegos, saying:

362

WHERE THE AIR IS CLEAR

Lords of night, because we dream in it; Lords of life because we know that our lives are only endless failure preparing for the last failure; heart of opening blooms: only you do not need to speak, and only our voices do not speak. You have no memory, because life is all at once; your births are as unaging as the sun, as brief as the membranes of fruit; you have learned to be born every day, to be aware of your nocturnal death: how could you understand one without the other? how could you understand a living hero? The jade knife is long and night gave it to you with a toothless and bleeding mouth; how can you reject night's supplications, the mirror demands of your own image? Long is the blade, near are our hearts, the sacrifice is swift, offered without compassion, without anger, swift and black, for you ask it of yourself, because you want to be that wounded breast, that lifted, flaunted, held-high heart murdered in the spring of resurrection, the eternal spring where gray hairs, caresses, transitory joinings, permanent separation, and all forebodings may not be enumerated nor even known; kill him, you kill yourself: kill him before he can speak, because the day you hear your own voice, you will not be able to resist him, but will feel hatred and shame and will want to surrender to him what you cannot surrender— life—to him who is not you and who has no name, as you have none; kill him and believe in him, kill him and have your hero; ask him to pull the coals near his feet that his flesh may rise as high as dust and your own dust float over the valley clouded as precisely as meridian names, thick heavy names, names which may be clotted with blood and gold, rounded names, pointed names, lights of stars, ink-mummied names, names dripping like drops of your unique mascara, that of your anonymity, face flesh hiding fleshed faces, the thousand faces, one mask Acamapichtli, Cortés, Sor Juana, Itzcóatl, Juárez, Tezozómoc, Gante, Ilhuicamina, Madero, Felipe Angeles, Morones, Cárdenas, Calles, Obregón, Comonfort, Alzate, Santa Anna, Motolinia, Alemán, Limatour, Chimalpopoca, Velasco, Hidalgo, Iturrigaray, Alvarado, Gutiérrez Nájera, Pánfilo de Narváez, Gutierre de Cetina,

Tetlepanquetzal, Porfirio Díaz, Santos Degollado, Leona Vicario, Morelos, Calleja del Rey, Lerdo de Tejada, Moctezuma, Justo Sierra, Amado Nervo, Zumárraga, Xicoténcatl, Bazaine, Axayácatl, Malinche, Zapata, O'Donojú, Genovevo de la O, Winfield Scott, Allende, Abasolo, Aldama, Revillagigedo, Ruiz de Alarcón, Vasconcelos, Carlota, Fernández de Lizardi, Escobedo, Riva Palacio, Sóstenes Rocha, Zachary Taylor, Gómez Farías, Linati, Posada, Forey, Huitzilíhuitl, Vanegas Arroyo, Tolsá, Sahagún, Pancho Villa, Antonio de Mendoza, Sigüenza y Góngora, Fernández de Eslava, Echave, Díaz Mirón, Bernardo de Balbuena, Servando Teresa de Mier, Nezahuapilli, Mina, Antonio Caso, Juan Escutia, Lupe Vélez, Cervantes de Salazar, Carranza, Vasco de Quiroga, Xavier Villaurrutia, Avila Camacho, González Ortega, Nezahualcóyotl, Cantínflas, Labastida, Maximiliano de Habsburgo, Quintana Roo, Iturbide, Emilio Rabasa, Eulalio Gutiérrez, Anaya, Miramón, Ignacio Vallarta, Roberto Soto, José Clemente Orozco, Bernal Díaz del Castillo, Juan Alvarez, Guadalupe Victoria, Victoriano Huerta, Bustamante, Andrés de Tapia, Ignacio Ramírez, Nuño de Guzmán, Juan Diego, Cuauhtémoc, Altamirano, Pino Suárez, Abad y Queipo, Manuel Acuña, Otilio Montaño, Nicolás Bravo, Tizoc, and you without your name, you marked with the red wound, you who buried your child's umbilicus with red arrows, who were well loved of the midnight mirror, you who scratched the dry land with your fingernails and squeezed out maguey juice, you who wept at the altar of the twilight monsters, you who were judge and high priest, proclaimed you were flower of turquoise, cornflower, you who fingered labial women monkey-handed, as one anointing wedlock, you who danced strangled by flutes, who journeyed the trail of the spotted death dog, you, you yourself who watched the agony of a resurrected sun, who showed the way, who fell riddled in the lagoon, who wept your orphaned downfall, you who gave birth to a new son with two navels, who painted the crimson angel and sculpted the spiny god, who planted sugar cane, who forgot your symbols, you who prayed among tapers, who lost your tongue, who bore the burden, who plowed in hunger, you who lifted staffs and hurled stones, you, nameless in your decapitation, you of the pillory, you, and you who had no ammunition, who were born without memories, who spitted yourself upon bayonets, you who fell shaped by lead, you who walked barefoot with a rusty musket, who sang the names, who adorned yourself with tissue paper and colored cardboard, who lit the rockets, you who sell lottery tickets and fruit juices and hawk newspapers and sleep on the ground, you who wear charms around your forehead and you who bandage your head against the weight of your load, you who vend fish and vegetables, you who shuffle your feet in dance dives and run along streets with your mouth open to see if a word falls into it, you who run fast to cross the lead-hailed river and gather nearby oranges, you, you, pack-back who did not even know when you were lashed, you who feel your children come into the world hollow-cheeked and black, you who scratch for food, who sleep in doorways, who cluster like flies upon buses, who cannot speak your pain, who merely hold on, who squat on your heels and hold on, want bitterly and cannot have, you who are left alone in your slum and must defend yourself, you who are shoeless, you greasy-mouthed and drunken, you come and gone with neither greeting nor farewell, you who count over all you do not have and have not lived, who sit to weave chair bottoms, who strum the guitar for pennies, are blind and whistle as you cross a street, who gaudy yourself of a Sunday and buy a purple *rebozo*, you who bring a handful of herbs to market, who fall upon your cot and wait for your man to come, you who dig through garbage and salvage cigarette butts, you who will always fail and yet always tell them to kiss your ass, go fuck their mothers, you who pitch coins, who die of measles, who blew up a Judas doll while you, you stayed praying to the Virgin, you who stepped in front of a trolley, you who had a fist fight on the corner, you who died last night, kicked the bucket, took your table to be hocked, you who set off firecrackers on the day of the Holy Cross, who pilgrimage on your knees to the Basílica of Guadalupe, who finger-spread your lips and whistle at a boxing match, who drive cabs, come home and find a child dead, who eat cracklings and pasty chili tortillas, tamarind and bruised maguey, twice-fried beans, cheese and califlower and maguey worms, barbecue and *pozole*, spiked punch and Manila mangoes, rotting watermelon, chocolate sauce and burned sugar, sour pulque and *chilaquiles, chirimoya, guanábana,* glass candy and striped candy, you who wear blue overalls and a straw hat, a striped T-shirt and mesh stockings and denim pants and a print shawl and a silver-buckled belt and rings with sun-stone and rose aquamarine and a zippered jacket and you who don't give up and you who suck my prick

and in the hollow center of everything, my heart spins

and on the other side of the bank you, ladies and gentlemen, you who wait for wealth and fame; I, we, you, ladies and gentlemen, never you *tu,* always you *usted,* you *ustedes* who have violated fate to escape *tu*-ness, you who, one day changed, one birth, might have been the same carriers of burdens, the same beggars as they; but you who are the singled-out, the elect of the cactus kingdom; you who travel and go and come and have names and clear destinies and you who zoom up and dive down, who build highways and blast furnaces and corporations and combines and sit on boards along with Mister Here-is-my-capital and Mister Whole-hog-or-nothing, you who club at the Jockey or the Versailles or the Ambassadeurs or the Focolare or the Yacht, at the penthouse of Don Lick-my-ass, at the hacienda of Don Stuff-it-up, you who enamel your faces and fuck cosmetically, who show your knockers and your pompom and your poodles, and you who buy your tweed by the bolt and you who jump into your shiny Italian convertibles with chrome trim and seats smelling of sacrificed cattle, and you who have the first row on first night and are friends of the Sugar Czar and Beebop Queen, and you who are treated unctuously, who keep your distance, you who are wide as the world is round, and you with a bidet and lotions and you who name names, bloop, woop, and you ancestors, wheeee! Cortés did not quite wipe out the Indian! Don-At-your orders, Doña This-is-your-home-too, Mister Kiss-your-feet and Miss Let-me-wipe-your-ass, most respectfully, yours sincerely, after you always, effective as of this date, no re-election, RSVP.

366

And we dreamed the dream and the words remained on the point of a blade, in the laugh of a rocket: he said my nose shines a long way, like the moon, my throne is silver and the face of the earth brightens when I stand in front of my throne, and they answered him from the house atop the pyramid, the mansions of fish: the yellow cornhusks, the white husks, are here, but at night when the neon lights go out and human bodies are squeezed against the dogs and one looks for a niche to sleep, covered with sacks and newspapers, again he tells us to look at us, hear us, don't leave us alone, don't abandon us, give us our children, ancient secret, ancient refuge, grandmother of dawn; and his double replies: Your words, your trees, your stones will be slaves! and then they had mouths in every joint of their bones and bit with all of them, and then the baby was born, the mother died, and the child had the happiness to be reared by serpents and the four hundred hares carried off the sacred bones of the mother: thus the voices spoke and their words circled in air and their words became an eagle-feathered shield, turquoise dart-words; and we know that the mother has a masked face and the children may go out under her aegis to wave flowers in smoky places and all the voices singing at once may be heard across the mountains and in the wings of hummingbirds, in the claws of tigers, in the sculptured stone; a file of boats on the lake sing like emeralds, stone stairs sing and oily hair: we have not come to live, we have come to sleep, we have come to dream; all voices sang, but an eagle eats their tongues and the stone is fire-blackened, cries and whistles, alarums sound, the headdresses and golden scepters are raised over the city one last time, city dead with a stiff phallus, death of mute scream; and then the time of plague and pestilence began, gold was seized from sepulchers, flight to the mountains, search for forest, descent with iron-ringed mouths into mines; while others wore cassocks and tunics and cowls and others went barefoot and in poverty, speaking humbly; then the other side of the medal: overseers and slave drivers, clerics and advocates, festoons and friezes of streaked gold, the emporium of Cambray and Scita, Macón and Java, and the emporium of chronicles and petitions, pilgrimages and sermons, feasts, gallantry, silver harness, gold and silver embroidery, attorneys for the crown, scriveners, aediles, chancellors, go-betweens, the fatherland peasant who becomes the colonial prince; and the black hood: devil-possessed, lapsed in heresy, dogmatist and Inquisition-hounded . . . and then, the eternally memorable effort:

because old Hidalgo wants only liberty for the enslaved

because Morelos, beseiged by eagles, wants better rule, general happiness

both their heads are stuck on pikestaffs and marched about to howling laughter; blood-streaked silver hair, Morelos's leather head still wearing the white scarf which had been his banner since the first skirmish

because a caste system has been infamously maintained by law and the Indians are tributaries plunged constantly into deeper degradation and distress in spite of all laws to the contrary; the king's land must be parceled out among them (these are not my words but the hunger of my heart)

fatherland comes first, but victory does not go to the lance-high heads but to Iturbide, laurel-crowned, selected by imperial courts, and with him the first men of the Empire because of their rank and wealth and the backing of the Church and its ecclesiastical ten per cent of all revenues, its one thousand five hundred and ninety three nunnery farms, its city properties purchased with donations and pious legacies, its state annuities received by orders of both sexes, its twelve hundred and four parishes whose parishioners give over the first part of their produce, its altars at the Basílica of Guadalupe, including *retablos,* paintings, bells, ornaments, statuary, candelabra, candlesticks, crosses, censers, and jewels and gold and silver

because now it is the night of May, 1882, and Doña Nicolasita has become a princess and the others, ushers and chamberlains

because Hidalgo wanted only liberty for the enslaved and the crown lands for Indian villages (these are not my words but my heart's hunger)

because Santa Anna the cockfighter proclaims his absolute adherence to progress, federalism, liberty, to all the abstract concepts

which the morality of the century imposes, and he is Mexico's
Supreme Redeemer: religion and prerequisites, one eight hundred pesos for Monsieur Remontel's cakes, another for the parish
priest who buried the Redeemer's amputated leg; don't deny
me the one title I want to leave my children . . . a good Mexican;
and Mr. Poinsett, the Scotch Rite and the York Rite, *El Sol* and
El Correo de la Federación, the extremists and the moderates,
Barradas and Gómez Farías and the morbid cholera
Old Zack's at Monterrey Bring on your Santa Anna For every
time we lift a gun Down goes a Mexicaner brown ravines of
Buenavista scrubby plains which belt Cerro Gordo mute bells
of Puebla and at last the Ayuntamiento of Mexico City protests
in the name of its members and in the most solemn form, before
the world, before the commander-in-chief of the North American
Army, that although the fortunes of war have placed the city in
the power of the United States, its spirit will never be volun-
tarily subject to any person, commander or authority, except
such as may be designated by the Federal Constitution and
sanctioned by the Government of the Republic of Mexico, no
matter how long foreign occupation may be prolonged . . .
Captain Roberts of the Rifles, who had commanded the assault
upon Chapultepec Castle, was designated by me to raise the
Star Spangled Banner upon the National Palace, the first foreign
flag to fly over this building since Cortés: which was observed
by all my troops with great enthusiasm. The Palace, which had
filled with beggars and thieves, was placed under the guard of
Lieutenant Colonel Watson and his battalion of Marines.
because Mr. Lane is now in Arizona and Raousset de Bourbon
the French privateer has taken Guaymas, and His Serene Highness Santa Anna decrees upon which occasions Councilors of
State may use batons, while a regulation establishes that only
members of the cabinet may dress their lackeys in yellow the
national treasury is expended buying decorations in Europe
governorships and army commands are bought and sold while
the polka is still danced there are those who pleasantly lend
to the Church, using church lands as surety and in this manner
become great landlords

and so again the dark faces and the stained flags the mute words the shining eyes of revolution in Ayutla the curtain falls on the carnival but its glitter must be paid for in Tacubaya, liberal leaders Ocampo and Santos Degollado are assassinated by General Márquez while their words drown in the waiting dry earth of brown ribs: "All Church holdings must be handed over to the Nation . . . A congress must be convened to draw up a liberal constitution . . ." While other words bow down before Maximilian's throne: "The Imperial Crown of Mexico (*non te fidare*) is offered His Royal Imperial Highness (*torna al castello*) Prince Ferdinand Maximilian (*tronto putrido di Montezuma*) for himself and his descendants (*nappo galico pieno d'espuma*) . . ." And Juárez, the Indian from Guelatao, with his black cape and his stove-pipe hat, travels in his black carriage across a land leveled by drought and gunpowder, green spine deserts, closed-fist mountains, while at Chapultepec it is decided that while in chapel the chief almsgiver must never address the Emperor or Empress directly, and that the Director of Chamber Music must present his programs for advance approval, and it is decided that for meals there shall be a Great or State Setting, an Intimate Setting, and another Field or Outing or Picnic Setting, and it is further decided that women of the court may show their breasts at the capping of cardinals, said breasts to wear the order of San Carlos and the Insignia of the Empress; and further it is decided that the anonymous river shall continue washing blood upon execution walls the length of the tropic flatland and the width of the high plateau, that bodies shall go on falling before the shells of Bazaine and Dupin, that the great Mexican blood lake shall not dry, shall never dry, the only eternal river, the only dampness flowering beneath the furious sun; but it is also decided that in the depth of the national heart national mourning shall never be worn except for the deaths of the Emperors of Mexico *adios mamá Carlota* and during such periods *adios my tender love* court officials shall seal all communications with black wax Carlota now knows that "I shouldn't have dishonored the blood of the Bourbons, humiliating myself before a Bonaparte adventurer!" and Maximilian thinks that he knows that "I will continue at the helm until the last drop of my blood is shed in defense of the nation!" Brave General Márquez, gallant General Miramón, intrepid General Mejía, patriotic General Vidaurri, and facing them, twenty-five thousand nameless men who march along the banks of the San Juan and close the circle around Querétaro *you abandoned those enviable lands where you lived with your Carlota you challenged Juárez although he had not offended your nation* it is seven-five in the morning, July 19, 1857 *such was the end of a son of Europe who wrote the last page of his bloody drama, which history will never erase, on the memorable Great Hill of Bells* his valet ran to extinguish flames caused by the *coup de grâce your noble wife in vain went to Paris, only to receive Napoleon's slight; in vain she went to the Vatican, only to go mad* his cadaver was embalmed, eyes taken from a church virgin replaced the once living ones, hairless body now after immersion in tanks of arsenic, black body now after injections of zinc chlorohydrate, and so aboard the good ship *Novara* And Juárez's impassive face speaks again Mexicans! Today the national government returns to establish its seat in Mexico City. Mexicans! Now all our efforts are combined to obtain and consolidate the benefits of peace. Peace was indeed the nation's true desire from one end of the Republic to the other But Peace was after Porfirio Díaz came to power Peace was Mr. Hearst and Mr. Pearson Peace was shoot them while they're hot Peace was no politics at all and an excess of order Peace was Indian farms gathered in by great landholders Peace was rural armies Peace was enforced peace, the conscriptor and the petty political boss Peace was Belén and the Valle Nacional, a great slave camp Peace was strikes at Cananea and Río Blanco Peace was a satiric newspaper with skull caricatures And Madero says: "General Díaz wishes to do the best he can for his native land, insofar as this is compatible with his indefinite continuance in power. We are ready for democracy." Then the Liberals: "The Mexican people must no longer entrust destiny to the hands of General Díaz, but must return to the role which by right is theirs. In the coming elections, choose! If what you want is shackles, misery, national humiliation before foreign powers, gray downtrodden

371

life, then uphold the dictatorship which provides these! If you prefer liberty, economic improvement, dignity as citizens of Mexico, active life as your own rulers, then come to the Liberal Party, brother to all men of virility and dignity . . ."
and Díaz's medaled chest and great white mustaches which hide the linear lips and the powder-bleached Indian skin and the wide nostrils, quivered as a flight of doves circled Chapultepec Castle: "I should observe with pleasure the formation of a Mexican Opposition Party."
and all men and songs and speeches and orders and battles and rites are only the memory of tomorrow, the memory we did not wish to find today: when pregnant *comet if you had only known* time gives birth to all its children and all bones rise from the mourning land and speak their words and fall *comet if you had only known what you were foretelling, you would never have appeared* tombs and faces are stippled with fire and blood and memory *lighting the sky* is at last everyone's, everyone here today, all living and divining one another like drops of water spraying over the ruins, recognizing each other over the earth line-ruled in blood *on the twenty-second of February, day of black foreboding* and in the storm of smoke, over swift horses and hearts which let themselves drink by night, and the cannon which clear dust from their throats Ciudad Juárez la Ciudadela "lands, hills and waters which have been usurped by the Díaz landgrabbers shall be returned to the people" Villa united with Urbina and with Don Maclovia Herrera and Pereyra and the Arrietas and boss Contreras "for the organization of an army charged with furthering our purposes we name Venustiano Carranza first commander" *good-bye all my friends I sadly say farewell don't be so hopeful about this world of traitors* the name . . . is the name of all of those and of those who came before them, the river of earth which runs from a river of voices strung from a footprint the size of a man, from a tomb the size of a man, from a song the size of a man only the land speaks: Bets down, bets down! Memories down! And here is the face of everyone fixed for one second, open like a prayer, balcony beneath the sky, the only face, the face of all, the only voice from

the armpit of Puerto Isabel to the toepoint of Catoche, from the thigh of Cabo Corrientes to the teat of the Panuco, from Mexico City's navel to the ribs at Tarahumara

and afterward the smoke drops, the hooves sleep weary on fields, guitars quiver the last strumming melody *Yes, sir, that's my baby I wonder who's kissing her When the m-moon shines over the cow* and the swollen city, the center, without memory, plaster sap squatting on its ass on the dry earth   dust and the forgotten lake   wine of neon gas   face of concrete and asphalt where sex is a drowsy hunter   where the slaughterhouses of prostitution work day and night near the jugulars of garbage; the city which milks the moon and loses its tracks, the city which is Candelaria Pantitlán Damián Carmona Balbuena Democracias Allende Algarín Mártires de Río Blanco Bondojito Tablas Estanzuela Potrero del Llano Letrán Norte Artes Gráficas San Andrés Tetepilco Progreso del Sur Coapa Portales Atlántida Altavista Polanco Guadalupe Inn Florida Nochebuena Américas Unidas Letrán Valle Vértic Navarte Eugenia San Pedro de los Pinos Hidalgo San Miguel Virreyes Jardines del Pedregal Neuva Anzures Roma Pino Suárez Santa María Barrilaco Popotla Elías Calles Atlampa San José Insurgentes Peravillo Nacozari Magdalena de las Salinas Héroes de Churubusco Buenos Aires Juárez San Rafael Lindavista Tepeyac Ignacio Zaragoza Deportivo Pensil Cuauhtémoc Marte Retorno Sifón Coyoacán Tlacopac Oxtopulco San Jerónimo Alfonso XIII Molino de Rosas Boturini Primero de Mayo Guerrero Veinte de Noviembre Jóvenes Revolucionarios Aztecas Lomas de Sotelo México Nuevo and its four million; city which is Gabriel scratched by sewers, vapor Bobó, Rosenda witness to all we forget, Gladys García of carnivorous walls, Hortensia Chacón's motionless pain, Librado Ibarra's immense brevity, Teódula Moctezuma of the fixed sun and the slow fire, Tuno of merry lethargy, I of the three navels, Beto of welded laughter, Roberto Régules of the twisted stink, Gervasio Pola, rigid between air and worms, Norma Larragoiti of varnish and cut stone, Fifo of entrails and tendons, Federico Robles of the violated outrage, Rodrigo Pola to his neck in water, Rosa Morales of slow ash, the faces and voices dispersed again, broken again,

373

memory returned to ash, the wetback who flees north for work and the banker who subdivides, he who saves himself alone and he who saves himself with others; city which is the slave and the overseer, which is I myself before a mirror mimicking truth, he who accepts the world as inevitable, he who recognizes someone besides himself, he who loads himself with the sins of the earth, dream of hatred, you who are of love, the first decision and the last, which is also to do your will and to do mine, city which is also solitude hurried before the last question, which is he who died in vain, the step too far, eagle or sun, unity and dispersion, heraldic emblems, forgotten rite, imposed way, beheaded eagle, dust serpent . . . dust which flees in constellations over all the city's profiles, over broken dreams and conquests, over old summits of headfeathers and blood, over domes of cross and iron, palaces of waltz and polka, over the high walls which cover the view of mansions with swimming pool and three automobiles and bodies hidden among mink and diamonds; swift dust which folds all spoken and unspoken words:

"one of us at least must save his skin; for us to die together is not so important as that one of us not die . . ."

"we know all secrets. What the country needs, what its problems are . . ."

"God help me not to lose my pride, it's all I have, all I can really feel is my own . . ."

"nothing is indispensable in Mexico, Rodrigo . . ."

"your father had no destiny; he had death, from the moment of birth, death for himself and his own . . ."

"as when you raise a hand in class because you're the only one who knows the answer, or as when you're waiting, on the street, for people to watch as you give money to a beggar . . ."

"my friend, don't believe that you don't need someone to grow old with. Everything that can be shared is never lost; it's like having it twice, eh . . ."

"all of a sudden the bastard begins to pity you . . ."

"Christ, what wouldn't you give to be able to work and make a living here in Mexico City . . ."

"then we knew that the sun had hunger, too, and that it was

374

feeding us so that we could return its swollen hot fruit to it . . ."
"all I want is for you to come back and warm our bed once
more before I forget your face and body . . ."
"and in this way birth and death both would unite us, birth
and death forever . . ."
"I do want to belong, I do want to get out of this mud-hole of
failures that I have inherited from them . . ."
"live and die blind, do you understand me, live and die trying
to forget everything, to be reborn with each new day, knowing
that no matter how we try to forget, everything is still present and
living and presses against . . ."
"you got dough . . ."
"we have to guard the well-being of the financial family, eh . . ."
"as if to collect for all that has happened before, as if to say
that everything ends as it begins, in them, in their mystery, my
son . . ."
"we wait only for something that can't happen again, there are
two or three; the moment before a kiss, the moment after giving
birth; yes, or death . . ."
"think: they had everything, it's as if you were to lose everything tomorrow . . ."
"if Mexicans do not save themselves, not a single man in all
creation will save himself . . ."
"for every Mexican who dies in vain, sacrificed, there is another Mexican who is guilty . . ."
"tell me, Juan, what are we doing here . . ."
"if it wasn't for our buddies, Beto . . . Listen, I'll tell you . . ."
"and each of us must be what he is, and you know it . . ."
"condemn this girl and save me from executing Thy terrible
will and Thy condemnation, my God . . ."
"father of my son, you will not have more strength than you
have gained with me . . ."
"he was one of us . . ."
"I've waited so long for you . . ."
and Gladys García stopped on the Nonoalco bridge, swift inside
dust, and lit the night's last cigarette and let the match drop on
tin roofs and breathed in the city's dawn, the steam of locomo-

tives, somnolence of flesh, wisps of gasoline and alcohol and the voice of Ixca Cienfuegos which passed, with the tumultous silence of all memories, through the city dust and wished to touch Gladys García's fingers and say to her, only say to her: Here we bide. What are we going to do about it. Where the air is clear.